FIGHTERS OF THE CODE

CB ARCHER

Cover Illustration and Design Copyright © 2016 by CB Archer
Book Design and Production by CB Archer

ISBN-13: 978-0994773715

First Edition: 2016

Wish to learn more? Visit Annals of Gentalia at the following locations.
Website: www.annalsofgentalia.wordpress.com
Facebook: www.facebook.com/annalsofgentalia
Twitter: @CB_Archer
Goodreads: CB Archer

Dedicated to Going Alone
(Seriously, it can be dangerous! You should probably take this with you!)

◈ Chapter 1 ◈
RECREATION COMPLETE

Zing! Just a single round after being given the chance to recreate himself Anders was in the brand new Island of Islana Expansion for the massively multiplayer online role-playing game Annals of Gentalia. He liked himself just as he had been originally created, his dashing elvish good looks, his *#6* light blond *Hairstyle*, his sexually broken bigger than average elvish booty of holding, and especially his Night Ranger (Ranged Style) lifestyle. When the opportunity was presented to Anders for recreating his avatar he simply skipped it.

The first thing Anders noticed was the vastly improved graphics in the Island of Islana Expansion. The Developers had really pulled out their A game and the polygon count was way up. Anders was impressed with his new realistically sculpted muscles, excited when he noticed that he was now blinking his eyes in a new random pattern, and overjoyed when he felt that his fingers could now bend without grabbing a weapon. Overall, Anders felt more important and knew that he was still the protagonist.

The cave he found himself in was a waiting room. Ignoring the boring brown stone walls, Anders turned his attention to the thousands of floating balls of light. They were small and probably unimportant, so instead of worrying about them, Anders took advantage of the private rounds before anyone else bothered to show up to give himself a really good going over.

Anders equipment was in order. An endless supply of arrows hung in his quiver, ready to be shot out of his *Slimey Bow+*. A *Slimey Sword+* was hanging in the air beside his *Super Duper Snazzy Belt*. If Anders ever felt like taking a direct approach, his sword was sharp and ready.

Both weapons had been a gift for sexually helping out The Titan. The weapons were constantly improving their stats and could even change appearance as Anders got better equipment. His *Slime Armour* set with the *Frost Gigas* (ass pounding) *Boots* were still as normal as they could be. Although he still had no *Standard Issue Undergarments* on, he still had the cute little *Pink Slime Jockstrap* equipped.

No *Standard Issue Undergarments* probably meant that Anders still had his special sex abilities. While he could have just checked his Status Page, he took a more direct approach. Placing a hand sheepishly into his *Slime Pants (s)* he placed a finger between his cheeks. A telltale drip of goop leaked out when Anders gingerly touched his button. He still had his *Stretch* power, that was a strange relief. Partially to be absolutely certain and partially to try out his now bendable fingers, Anders stuck a finger inside. He definitely still had his powers, he definitely had wonderfully bendable fingers, and most importantly he definitely still had a broken TorTech-Headset that let him personally feel every wonderful pleasure note that his onscreen avatar experienced. Anders pulled down his *Slime Pants (s)* for better access and lost himself for a few blissful rounds. After the magical sexy pleasure tingles started to hit his finger he executed a *Smile Animation*.

One of the little balls of light that had been floating around in the scenery, ignored until this moment, flew up and looked Anders in the face. The bright light faded slightly and it changed into a small glowing humanoid shape with butterfly wings. The soft glow made it impossible to determine if it was wearing clothes or even if it was a particular gender. It looked over Anders with a discerning eye, only lingering for a short moment at Anders' half pulled down *Slime Pants (s)*. The elf was embarrassed and tensed up. The sudden tightening up on his finger caused the magical elf butt to emit some intense tingles. The pleasure caused Anders to moan as well as change to *Blush Shade #1*.

Anders removed his bendable finger (which caused a squish noise that only further embarrassed the elf), pulled up his *Slime Pants (s)*, and tried to hide his erection with his hands. The Quest Fairy had used the awkward pause to decide on a course of action and change its swappable palette to green.

> Green Quest Fairy's Text Box: Welcome to the Expansion, the Island of Islana! I am your personal guide and keeper of all things Quests. You can always depend on me! The first available Quests are nearby. You may call me Quest Fairy—

> Anders' Interruption Text Box: Don't you Quest Fairies ever knock?

> Green Quest Fairy's Text Box: The Knock Quest can be obtained in—

> Anders' Interruption Text Box: Never mind.

The wonderfully bendable moment was over, so Anders decided to take a more thorough look through his other bottomless container, his *Ultra-Pack*. Its deep and broken unstoppable storage still did not reveal his supposed *Ultimate Prize* from the final boss, Narbenock and the six Dragons that Anders had accidently created. The encounter had left him with nothing but a refilled mana reserve (shot into his magical absorbing bottom) and some heavy experience points. The twelve new Levels were really exciting and would definitely shoot him up to second or third highest Level in the group, but they really didn't seem like an ultimate prize. Perhaps a sternly worded email complaint was in order.

Before he was able to press send on his complaint, another avatar began to sparkle into the waiting area and Anders promptly forgot about the whole idea.

Zing! The glimmering was big and beefy and it left little doubt in Anders' mind who it could possibly be. Barely fitting into his *Diamond Plate*, a familiar muscular avatar was standing in front of Anders. Mr. Max almost did his patented *Flex Animation* when he saw an audience, but he had obvious second thoughts on the matter. Flexing would mean a full body flex for Mr. Max's giant dick after all.

> Orange Quest Fairy's Text Box: Welcome to the Expansion, the Island of Islana! I am your personal guide and keeper of all things Quests. You can always depend on me! The first available Quests are nearby. You —

> Mr. Max's Interruption Text Box: There are available Quests nearby? Where are they Quest Fairy? Take me to them!

Mr. Max was ignoring the surrounding area completely, and was following the floating orange Quest Fairy blindly. So blindly in fact that he walked right into Anders.

> Mr. Max's Text Box: Oh The Dragon Cultist? That is strange, I didn't know that NPCs could come into the Expansion.

> Anders' Text Box: I am not the Dragon Cultist Max.

Max still had no idea who Anders was. He was still so oblivious that he wouldn't even notice Anders' gender.

> Mr. Max's Text Box: I thought I would be all alone with my bros! You are a Night Ranger (Ranged) I see adventurette. A good choice, they are certainly the best at long ranged attacks even with the new classes they introduced.

> Anders' Text Box: There were new classes?

> Mr. Max's Text Box: Of course, more than double the original classes. I myself almost switched. You see, having a secondary weapon decreases your primary weapon power, which is why I picked Warrior originally. The new class without secondary weapons had a multi-attacking type

> primary weapon of Fists. My calculations indicate that a single weapon is slightly better in almost all regards so I didn't change.

> Anders' Text Box: There were new classes?

> Mr. Max's Text Box: Yes, I just said that. Double the original number, since there were 2 of each type added. Melee, Ranged, Attack Magic, and Healing Magic, there are now 14 classes total! Well, there is one more than double, but nobody in their right mind would ever pick that new multi-class Mystic.

> Anders' Text Box: There were new classes?

> Mr. Max's Text Box: Yes, and a bunch of new races as well.

> Anders' Text Box: I didn't know there were new things! I didn't even look.

Anders could tell Mr. Max was confused just by the look on his face, confused was a pretty standard state for Mr. Max.

> Mr. Max's Text Box: Shouldn't a Dragon Cultist know everything about the Expansion? I mean NPCs would know stuff like that.

> Anders' Text Box: I am not the Dragon Cultist, Max!

> Mr. Max's Text Box: Really? I was pretty sure that it was NPC Quivillis the Queen anyway. Maybe it was her after all.

> Anders' Text Box: No, the Dragon Cultist was NPC Narbenock!

> Mr. Max's Text Box: Impossible, he was the one that sent me on all of those quests. That doesn't make any sense.

> Anders' Text Box: That was the plot twist!

Zing! A glimmering avatar was coming into the area, and whoever it was had absolutely perfect posture. Anders recognized the light elf from Breaker's party with the impossible to remember and even more impossible to attempt to pronounce name. She was almost unchanged, from the pre-expansion Calea, although she had altered her face slightly. She was now wearing a smart pair of *Pince-nez Glasses*, something released for character creation in the Expansion no. Anders initially thought that she looked more intelligent, but changed his mind and decided she looked even more like a know-it-all.

> White Quest Fairy's Text Box: Welcome to the Expansion, the Island of Islana! I am your personal guide and keeper of all things Quests.

> You can always depend on me! The fir—

> Caëlahenãilenẁhei's Interruption Text Box: I can obviously depend on you being exceptionally long winded little Quest Fairy.

> Anders' Text Box: Hello Caela.

The light elf, that may as well have been a boy in a dress due to her jiggleless frame, looked down at her keyboard and closed her in game eyes while she typed in her very long winded reply.

> Caëlahenãilenẁhei's Text Box: I didn't suspect that I would be the first one into the expansion, however I also didn't anticipate that I would have materialized before so many others. Now that I think about it with a greater attention to detail though I suppose that it does make sense that others may want to change more aspects of themselves than some simple appearance modifications like myself. The new-fangled occupations might have been interesting to try out, but that would completely destroy the fact that I employed a Code to change the name of my class to Rocket Sorcer—

> Caëlahenãilenẁhei's Text Box: ess.

Caela was still too long winded to fit in a single Text Box.

> Mr. Max's Text Box: Rocket Sorcerers are a good class, but hardly anyone ever picked one. There are only two avatars with that class. You, and an light elf with an impossible to pronounce name that was working with Breaker right before we left for the expansion. You however are far more attractive than that stuffy other one.

Both elves were taken by shock.

> Caëlahenãilenẁhei's Text Box: Stuffy?!

> Anders' Text Box: Attractive?!

> Mr. Max's Text Box: Yes, you seem far less stuffy and far more attractive than that other light elf Rocket Sorcerer.

> Caëlahenãilenẁhei's Text Box: I am that Rocket Sorcerer! A female Sorcerer is called a Sorceress thank you very much.

> Mr. Max's Text Box: No sorry. That isn't an old class, and it wasn't added or I would have heard about it.

> Caëlahenãilenẁhei's Text Box: You are tiring.

> Mr. Max's Text Box: Not really, I just had a nap.

Zing! Thankfully another avatar was sparkling into the area. Anders was happy that there would be someone to break the obvious tension that was quickly developing here. Anders recognized the tall gray coloured avatar's outdated equipment, but not the name. He still looked like he was from one of those old school black & white games. The only hint of colour was on the avatar's very outdated and faded belt, but it was so old that it was almost gray as well. This was warrier. Well, warrier with a changed name. That might be bad, he had been Breaker's number one stooge after all even if he did eventually have a change of heart and stab the big jerk.

> Gray Quest Fairy's Text Box: Welcome to the Expansion, the Island of Islana! I am your personal guide and keeper of all things Quests. You can al—

> samuri's Interruption Text Box: …

samuri used the *Friendly Wave Animation*.

The wave was friendly, and the newly named samuri wasn't chopping anyone in half, it was a good start. Anders was pleasantly surprised. Despite the lack of useful information the renamed avatar was offering, it did stop Mr. Max and Whats-her-elf from arguing. At least about what they were arguing about before he showed up.

> Mr. Max's Text Box: Who is that? I don't remember her at all.

> Caëlahenãilenŵhei's Text Box: It is clearly warrier, he has renamed himself samuri. Interesting he both spelled it incorrectly and forgot to use a capital letter yet again.

> Mr. Max's Text Box: warrier? Where is that punk? He is Breaker's damn stooge from before! Where is he? I'll tear him up!

> samuri's Text Box: …

samuri used the *Confused Blink Animation*.

> Caëlahenãilenŵhei's Text Box: Obviously, samuri is warrier. He looks exactly the same, he just changed his name.

> Mr. Max's Text Box: No, that is just some random unimportant lady. Why is she even here? warrier is Breaker's number one evil henchman, but then he had either a change of heart or just was fed up with Breaker and slashed him in front of The Plague of Shadow's Summoning Pillar.

> samuri's Text Box: …

samuri used the *Shrug Animation*.

> Caëlahenãilenŵhei's Text Box: God you're thick.

> Anders' Text Box: You have no idea.

Zing! Another shimmering avatar was coming into the area, Anders could tell by just looking at the light that it was friendly, yet bossy. Lissa's uniquely won purple hair was the first thing that materialized in. She was the same Mendicator class and looked identical except for her new ears. They were far more pointed now to accentuate the fact that she was indeed a half-elf and not a human as originally thought. Anders was thrilled, he #LikedLissa.

> Purple Quest Fairy's Text Box: Welcome to the Expansion, the Island of Islana! I am your personal guide and keeper of all things —

> Lissa's Interruption Text Box: #Perfection! Something to hold all my extra junk. Come here you!

> Mr. Max's Text Box: Another avatar I have never seen before. We didn't have a regular elf with us. Where are all these new avatars coming from? This new expansion is supposed to be locked for 200 cycles!

> Lissa's Text Box: I'm not a regular elf! I am still a half-elf! I look exactly the same! I only changed my ears. You already remembered my name before!

> Anders' Text Box: I am a regular elf, and in your party.

> Mr. Max's Text Box: Who are you both now?

> Caëlahenãilenŵhei's Text Box: Seriously, bonehead? She is the Healing Class from your own party, and he is the one that killed the Dragon Cultist.

> Lissa's Text Box: No Caela. We all call him meathead.

> Mr. Max's Text Box: Who is meathead now? Not another avatar! This expansion is supposed to be locked!

> Caëlahenãilenŵhei's Text Box: Either one works really.

> Anders' Text Box: This is only going to get better isn't it?

Zing! The next avatar to sparkle in was exceptionally tall. Given the unique look and the fact that the sparkling never stopped Anders knew it must be the soft spoken female troll Yallundy that he had accidently fell in love with for an entire split round due to her unwavering beauty and colour changing teal accents.

Constantly-Colour-Changing Quest Fairy's Text Box: Welcome to the Expansion, the Island of Islana! I am your per—

Mr. Max's Interruption Text Box: Hello Yallundy, I see that you have changed from Soother (Healer Style) to Soother (Effect Style). A pretty good decision given the larger amount of avatars you would likely be working with now. Sure, you gain the Status Effect removal spells later, but who cares about Status Effects honestly? So... there are going to be what... count my bros... you... so like six or something?

Yallundy's Text Box: Yes Max, that is why I changed Styles.

Lissa's Text Box: Seriously? You can remember her name? You've never even Text Boxed to her before! Flaming Pit, she only Text Boxed 12 times total in the first Book! #JawDropping. I forgot she was even in it!

Mr. Max's Text Box: Of course I can remember her, look at how unique Yallundy is! A female Troll, there are only a few hundred of those.

Lissa's Text Box: Seriously meathead? I am the only avatar with a non standard hair colour. It is bright purple! I am more unique than that.

Lissa used the *Repetitive Single Foot Stomp in Rage Animation.*

Caëlahenâilenẁhei's Text Box: There is currently only one Rocket Sorcerer avatar in the entire game! Technically, I am the most unique avatar there is!

Anders' Text Box: I'm the protagonist!

Mr. Max's Text Box: Oh. Are you friends with Fair Maiden? I remember she had unique hair, wasn't it orange? I thought the purple hair looked sort of familiar. Sure, it is no orange, but it is different. Why did you pick regular elf as a race when humans have all the Skill Bonuses? Humans are the best, mathematically speaking. At least regular elves have something better than those half-elves. They only have that useless Mysterious ability. Oh and I just met you light elf, but I thought you told me you were a Rocket Sorceress?

Lissa's Text Box: I am a half-elf. Honestly it hurts to talk to you.

Caëlahenâilenẁhei's Text Box: Insufferable.

samuri's Text Box: ...

samuri used the *Shrug Animation*.

> Anders' Text Box: I agree.

Zing! Hopefully the new avatar sparkling in could help resolve this problem. The avatar was made of shorter sparkles and was sprouting a gnomehawk. It had to be Gliint, the gome with horrible lag issues. The Armour and weapons the little gnome were holding did not look familiar at all to Anders. The brown accented gnome had changed his class from Backstabber to something else.

> Brown Quest Fairy's Text Box: Welcome to the Expansion, the Island of Islana! I a—

> Lissa's Interruption Text Box: We are not done yet, meathead, you will pay for your forgetfulness!

> Mr. Max's Text Box: How much does that cost? I spent so many Gold Coins last cycle to defeat Breaker. I doubt I could afford it.

> Lissa's Text Box: #SurroundedByIdiots.

> Yallundy's Text Box: Hello Gliint! You changed your class.

After several rounds without a reply it was evident that the gnome's lag problem had not been resolved by coming into the Expansion.

> Mr. Max's Text Box: Look, a lady gnome Chemist! Their long ranged Gun attacks and short ranged Bomb attacks can be a deadly combination. Who is she?

> Yallundy's Text Box: That is Gliint. He's your biggest fan. All he ever talks about is you. You just signed his ass a few rounds ago in Breakers of the Code.

Zing! Yet another avatar was shimmering into the starting area. Anders was again hopeful that whoever it was could help stop the situation from escalating further. When he saw who it was he again lost hope. A freaky single *#36 style eye* was staring at him from an otherwise completely hidden face. The only visible change Anders could see was a longer white tuft of hair that was likely bangs hanging down from under the *Sapphire Cowl (s)*. It was the multi-gendered night elf, Roodg Scenerbane, destroyer of scenery, killer of spellcheck, and owner of both sets of switchable genitalia.

> Red Quest Fairy's Text Box: Welcome to the Expansion, the Island of Is—

> Roodg's Interruption Text Box: hI THERE Red Quest Fairy! i'M Roodg!

Red Quest Fairy's Text Box: Hi!

Anders wasn't exactly sure why he kept getting his hopes up when new avatars were showing up. It didn't seem to be getting any better.

Gliint's Lag Text Box: *Blush* Hello Yallundy! I changed to Chemist because the Bombs go off after a few rounds. So my lag wouldn't matter anymore!

Caëlahenâilenẁhei's Text Box: Hi.

Roodg's Text Box: hI.

Red Quest Fairy's Text Box: Hi!

Lissa's Text Box: Are they still doing that 'hI Hi' thing from the last book? They are stuck in a loop of some kind and now they have even gotten that framing device involved.

Mr. Max's Text Box: Oh hello again i'M Roodg. Why did you change your name from dUH Roodg?

Roodg's Text Box: cAUSE I AM ALL DIFFERENT! LOOK!

Anders' Text Box: Your hair tuft is bigger?

Roodg's Text Box: yEAH! i CHANGED MY FACE ALL UP 2!

Lissa's Text Box: Well obviously.

Zing! Twinkling told Anders that another avatar was on the way. Anders thought while it was materializing. Since the pompous Kray had been turned into a black husk and Breaker should be banned for life, there was a pretty good chance it would be Palcath or Fournimer. Either would be welcomed by Anders, Fournimer because he was really handsome and Palcath because he could stop the madness. It however was neither as the twinkling formed into the female shape of an NPC.

The NPC Zal Finn had a brand new class as well as a new Roman Numeral. Her appearance had not changed at all. She was still as generic as a background NPC, but now she was wrapped in interesting brightly coloured clothing and wielding some sort of carpet as a weapon. The clash of the interesting and the generic was hard for Anders to comprehend.

Pink Quest Fairy's Text Box: Welcome to the Expansion, —

Zal Finn III's Interruption Text Box: Thanks Quest Fairy!

> Gliint's Lag Text Box: *Wave* Hello Roodg.

> Mr. Max's Text Box: Zal Finn, why did you change from a Warrior (Skill Style) avatar? Warrior (Skill Style) is the best class in the game. That is why everyone picks it!

> Caëlahenâilenŵhei's Text Box: Why would you possibly know her name bonehead? You don't make a lick of sense.

> Lissa's Text Box: You get used to it.

> Zal Finn III's Text Box: I was tired of being just like everyone else's avatar, so I picked the Dancing Ninja Assassin Class (Left Foot Style).

> Anders' Text Box: If you wanted to be different than everyone else, why would you make yourself look like that?

> Zal Finn III's Text Box: Look like what? You mean super sweet looking right?

While Anders did think that a Dancing Ninja Assassin (Left Foot Style) was pretty unique and would stop Zal Finn III from being just like everyone else, he wondered if Zal Finn III had thought about changing her appearance a bit to stop looking just like everyone else. Anders was sure that she hadn't changed any of her default appearance settings.

> Zal Finn III's Text Box: Hello Lissa. Sweet! I like your new ears!

> Lissa's Text Box: Thanks Zal.

> Zal Finn III's Text Box: Caela, you look so much smarter!

> Caëlahenâilenŵhei's Text Box: Thank you Zal Finn, I enjoy your new Roman Numeral III.

> Zal Finn III's Text Box: Yallundy, you changed styles!

> Yallundy's Text Box: Thank you for noticing Zal Finn.

Zing! This time the new sparkles coming in were short and stocky. Anders was hopeful that they were a rational but overacting dwarf lad. When Palcath, the self-appointed party leader, came into existence with his close cropped *#5 Facial Hairstyle* Anders was relieved.

> Yellow Quest Fairy's Text Box: Welcome to—

> Palcath's Interruption Text Box: I am not interested in another

annoying mascot flying behind me for an entire game, so just be quiet little flying quest lad.

Yellow Quest Fairy's Text Box: Humph.

Gliint's Lag Text Box: *Wave* Hello Zal Finn!

Palcath's Text Box: Hello lads, lasses, and Roodgs.

Anders' Text Box: Thank the Maker. Palcath!

Palcath's Text Box: You sound concerned. What's wrong, lad?

Anders' Text Box: Everyone is fighting with each other.

Palcath's Text Box: So? Everyone is always fighting with each other, lad. Haven't you been paying attention so far?

Anders' Text Box: Well… uh can you make them stop or something?

Palcath used the *Close Cropped Beard Scratching Animation* as he thought.

Palcath's Text Box: I probably could, lad.

Lissa's Text Box: What took you so long, lad? We were worried you were changing your race into something that would require an even more obnoxious character trait! Like having to say 'lord and lady', 'pals and gals' or 'gruggrugg and gruegrue' in every Text Box.

Mr. Max's Text Box: Palcath is a Defender. There is no one here named lad!

Lissa gave Mr. Max a *laser guided bunny missile* glance.

Palcath's Text Box: No, I was just interested in what was new Fair Maiden. I guess I took longer than I thought, lass. I knew I didn't need to rush though.

Lissa's Text Box: Why not?

Gliint's Lag Text Box: Zal Finn… I changed my entire class. Why didn't you notice that? *Frown*

Zal Finn III's Text Box: Oh yeah? What were you before?

samuri's Text Box: …

samuri used the *Head Shaking Animation*.

Zal Finn III's Text Box: warrier is still exactly the same though, right?

Palcath's Text Box: Lass, Fournimer is in our party. If he was given a chance to remake his avatar he would spend hundreds of rounds doing that. I didn't feel the need to hurry.

Lissa's Text Box: I guess that makes sense, you are just lucky I'm not getting called a gruegrue right now.

Mr. Max's Text Box: Where is Fourni anyways gruegrue? He should be here. I remember he was with Palcath, Duh Roodg, Yallundy, warrier, Fair Maiden, and Zal Finn at the final battle.

Gliint's Lag Text Box: *Wave* Hello Palcath!

Caëlahenãilenŵhei used the *Explain Plot Animation* directed at Mr. Max.

Caëlahenãilenŵhei's Text Box: You didn't even fight in the last battle. Anders and Breaker did.

Mr. Max's Text Box: I know who Breaker is, but who is Anders?

Lissa's Text Box: That is Anders! Right there!

Mr. Max's Text Box: What? Where?

Lissa's Text Box: The green accented elf you stalked to find Slime Cave? He is the reason you couldn't complete the Insta-Wiki contest! He has special abilities that compliment yours precisely? He has been travelling with you since Book One - Chapter 18 when we all met you! You slashed his face and broke your avatar giving him that badass scar! The possible love triangle in the series involves both of you. All the Books are named after him and he is the main protagonist! If you should know anyone's name at all it should be his! That is beyond #SoFuckedUp!

Mr. Max's Text Box: No, that sexy elf lady is the Dragon Cultist! I remember fighting with her and filling her up right before we went after Breaker. I remember winning that encounter.

Anders couldn't help but change to *Blush Shade #2*.

Caëlahenãilenŵhei's Text Box: What is wrong with your party? How did you even manage to get this far?

Lissa's Text Box: #FullDefensiveAction. There is nothing WRONG

> with us!

> Roodg's Text Box: yEAH! wE ARE sAWESOME!

> Caëlahenãilenŵhei's Text Box: Sawesome? That's not even a word!

> Roodg's Text Box: hI!

Caëlahenãilenŵhei changed to *Blush Shade #1*. With her porcelain white skin it was blatantly obvious.

> Caëlahenãilenŵhei's Text Box: Hi.

> Anders' Text Box: Palcath, make them stop!

> Palcath's Text Box: Why? It is just getting good, lad!

> Anders' Text Box: Please? There are way too many characters here to follow, I'm getting confused.

> Roodg's Text Book: yEAH! wE NEED TO SPLIT UP. sOMEONE FIND US A BOAT!

> Palcath's Text Box: Fine, lad.

The stout dwarf performed the *Shh Animation*.

> Palcath's Text Box: Everylad, shut up!

The most impressive thing to Anders about this unassuming statement was that is actually worked. Everyone else did shut up.

> Palcath's Text Box: It is almost night everylad, Fournimer will probably be finished his face refinement by morning and then we can head towards that big city in the distance. Now, we should all eat something and then get some rest in a *Portie Tent*. Since *Portie Tents* can fit six avatars I assume that someone in your party has one.

> Caëlahenãilenŵhei's Text Box: That would be me; I am the one who is prepared amongst my adventuring party.

> Lissa's Text Box: Saw that one coming.

Everyone nodded and sat down on one of the supplied chairs in front of the *Portie Tents* and took out something to eat. Mr. Max took out something that would certainly taste like a pre-heated waffle iron since all the food in the game tasted like appliances except the *Bacon*. Everyone else took out one of the kinds of *Bacon*. Anders took a bite but spit it right back out.

Anders' Text Box: Why did they change the Bacon? It was the only thing worth eating! It tastes awful now.

Palcath's Text Box: This *Bacon* still tastes great, you must be crazy lad.

Roodg's Text Box: sEE Caëlahenãilenŵhei CHANGED ALL THE pORTIE tENT CHAIR COLOURS 4 HER AVATARS!

Caëlahenãilenŵhei's Text Box: Hi.

Roodg's Text Box: hI!

Red Quest Fairy's Text Box: Hi!

Lissa's Text Box: Not going to happen, Leaders only. Stop asking.

Roodg's Text Box: bUT! Palcath JUST CHANGED Anders' CHAIR TO GREEN!

Palcath's Text Box: Anders defeated The Plague of Shadow solo and unlocked the Expansion for us. That lad is a hero.

Lissa's Text Box: Yep. Leaders and Anderses only!

Caëlahenãilenŵhei's Text Box: Anderses? Where do you avatars even come up with these words?

Palcath's Text Box: Caela, lass, *Portie Tents* only sleep 6 avatars; there were 7 in your party. How did that work?

Caëlahenãilenŵhei's Text Box: Breaker made Gliint sleep on the floor.

Gliint's Lag Text Box: *Thumbs up!* This Bacon tastes even better in the expansion!

Caëlahenãilenŵhei's Text Box: Okay, it is definitely the time to regenerate for the night time section of the cycle. Alright, my *Portie Tent* variety is a *Portie Tent Ultra+* and yours is just a *Portie Tent Ultra*. Therefore, my *Portie Tent* is far more luxurious. Since we seem to have agreed that we are merging parties, at least for now, I have decided something important. It is about the sleeping arrangements and how they will be assigned differently than anticipated. This *Portie Tent Ultra+* is now the girls *Portie Tent*. Your regular store-bought *Portie Tent Ultra* is now for—

Caëlahenâilenŵhei's Text Box: the boys.

Palcath's Text Box: Why does that matter? We should just stay in our *Portie Tent* and you in yours, lass.

Zal Finn III's Text Box: Nope! I have to agree with that 100%. There just needs to be a girl's tent now. We need to gossip, have pillow fights in our bras and panties, practice kissing each other, and other slumber party stuff like that.

Yallundy's Text Box: Our *Standard Issue Undergarments* have all exploded though Zal Finn.

Zal Finn III's Text Box: Even better!

Palcath's Text Box: Girls… kissing each other? Naked ones?

Palcath's eyes glazed over for he was lost in thought. He had completely forgotten to call the girls lasses, but he didn't even notice. It took quite some time for him to snap back to reality.

Palcath's Text Box: It doesn't work out though Caela, lass. Once Fournimer gets here there will be seven guys and five girls.

Caëlahenâilenŵhei's Text Box: Your math is wrong again dwarf. There will only be eleven of us in total, and your math adds to twelve.

Palcath's Text Box: My math is not wrong this time, lass. With this party that still adds up to twelve avatars.

Gliint's Lag Text Box: *Giggle* Panties!

Palcath's Text Box: Regardless, it is time for this lad to turn in.

The girls retired into the fancier white *Portie Tent Ultra+*, while the boys retired into the not as fancy yellow *Portie Tent Ultra*. Only Gliint and Roodg stayed outside. Gliint for lag reasons, but Roodg claimed to need to stay up for a bit to update their Player Pager first (much to the dismay of a few confused avatars who wanted to see where Roodg would go sleep).

Gliint's Lag Text Box: But wait, *Panic* all of my stuff is in there!

♦ Chapter 2 ♦
THE PRETTY BOYS

The rooster had cawed, the *Portie Tents* had been put away, and *Bacon* had been consumed all long before Fournimer was even close to showing up. Anders had plenty of time to complain about the mysterious change in the *Bacon's* taste that only he seemed to notice. He also had enough rounds to be told to shut up about it, and to stop whining about the missing *Ultimate Prize*.

Finally around Mr. Max's third sandwich break an avatar began to materialize into the area.

> Lissa's Text Box: It is about time. Scarfy has been making us wait for him for almost an entire cycle. #SoFuckedUp!

> Palcath's Text Box: Agreed, but with that lad it was expected. Why is he coming in so skinny?

> Mr. Max's Text Box: Yes, he is supposed to be muscular, not some string bean. He's really short as well.

Zing! What materialized was not Fournimer. It reminded Anders of a sundried prune. Rough black skin was stretched across a skeletal frame. Every bone could be seen showing through the sickly flesh. The haphazard assortment of equipment it was wearing clashed so badly in colour that it actually hurt his eyes to look at it. Two eyes set into deep non blinking sockets looked out at the avatars.

> No-Colour Quest Fairy's Text Box: Welcom—

> Zal Finn III's Interruption Text Box: Holy fucking shitballs, what is that?

> Caëlahenãilenŵhei's Text Box: Clearly it is a monster! Everyone ready your weapons!

> Mr. Max's Text Box: I didn't read about a new monster type that looked like that.

Holding out his *Katana,* samuri made a *Stop Animation* gesture that meant that everyone else should stay well back. Everyone was more than happy to allow samuri to be the initial target, so they followed his instructions and backed down.

> samuri's Text Box: …

samuri used the *Wave Animation.*

> Kray's Text Box: Oh hi warrier. Or samuri. Kay, I guess you changed your name or whatever.

The monster was Kray. The skinny jerk that Breaker had been absorbed to death (He got better). He was no longer a regulation elf, he was a flakey husk of an elf, a custom made fright elf.

> Caëlahenãilenŵhei's Text Box: Kray? Why are you here, Breaker killed you.

> Yallundy's Text Box: No, he was listed as one of the avatars that was accepted into the expansion alon—

> Palcath's Interruption Text Box: Are you sure he isn't dead, lass? The lad looks pretty dead.

> Roodg's Text Box: nEAT!

Kray adopted his typical *better than everyone else stance,* which he would now keep active until the end of recorded gaming time.

> Kray's Text Box: No, I'm okay, kay. warrier saved me from Breaker at the last round. Look at me now though!

> Anders' Text Box: Yes. Look at you. Now you are a horr—

> Kray's Interruption Text Box: I know. Kay, I am so skinny! I'm so hot now.

Anders' Text Box: What? No I mean look at your skin it is s—

Kray's Interruption Text Box: I know, kay! I am so thin now.

Anders' Text Box: But you were allowed to change your appearance! Why wouldn't you put your flesh back on an—

Kray's Interruption Text Box: I did change my appearance! I went from Body Type #1 (average) to (skinny), kay. Now I am extra super thin and hot.

Anders' Text Box: But you are a horrible flesh husk of a monste—

Kray's Interruption Text Box: Shut up already! You're just jealous because you made yourself even chubbier, kay. Why would you do that? You had a perfect opportunity to make yourself a proper weight for a gay elf and you made yourself even fatter.

Anders was forced to used the *Confused Blink Animation* out of pure shock.

Anders' Text Box: I didn't change anything! I'm not chubbier! It is just the polygons!

Kray's Text Box: Yes you are, kay. Like, you are now blocking my camera view. It's pretty bad.

Anders' Text Box: I am? Really?

Roodg's Text Box: kAY, U R A LITTLE BIT i THINK. bUT IT'S CUTE. i LIKE YOUR BUTT OF HOLDING. dON'T CHANGE!

Lissa's Text Box: Maybe you are slightly, kay? Just more elf for the pushin'.

Palcath's Text Box: Kay, I wasn't going to say anything lad, but he might be right.

Gliint's Lag Text Box: *Gasp* Kray is alive?

Kray's Text Box: See, kay? You are way too chubby.

Anders' Under Breath Text Box: You are still way too short.

Kray's Text Box: Thanks for saving me samuri! I appreciate it, kay!

samuri's Text Box: …

samuri used the *Nod Animation*.

Kray changed to *Blush Shade #4*, on the black burned skin it resembled blood stains.

> samuri's Text Box: …

samuri did not change his *Blush Settings*.

The telltale zing of another avatar materializing into the area could be heard and everyone but Gliint looked in that direction.

> Lissa's Text Box: Finally it is Fournimer! That Scarfy guy, I tell you!

> Palcath's Text Box: No… I don't think so, lass.

> Mr. Max's Text Box: Of course it is. There are Fourni's wings coming in now. Look, here are his horns and tail! Finally his black scales and emo *#8 Hornstyle*.

Zing! The now half-dragon Breaker burst into the area with an impressive gust of *Serpent Speed*. Within a single round he was flying high in the sky with his black scaly half dragon wings. He was overly dramatic while doing so, almost as if he was putting on a show. Because he was. The world breaking, map shattering, douchebag had arrived., not nearly as defeated as originally thought.

> Black Quest Fairy's Text Box: Wel—

> Breaker's Interruption Text Box: Shut up and die you annoying little shit!

With a Stretching Out of His Wings and a Dramatic Movement of his Claws Animation Breaker grabbed the Black Quest Fairy in his claws and folded the floating thing neatly in half with a sickening snap. The other Quest Fairies gasped in alarm as it fell to the ground, dead.

> Breaker's Text Box: Now for more important matters. You should all have left here by now to make my later reveal more exciting, but whatever. You will all pay for what you did to me! Just sooner than I planned.

> Mr. Max's Text Box: What did we do to you? When did you become a dragon?

> Zal Finn III's Text Box: What are you yammering about? The teams both tied.

> Roodg's Text Box: yEAH! wE ALL WON! rEMEMBER?

> Caëlahenâilenŵhei's Text Box: We are in the Expansion right now.

> That is exactly what you wanted.

> Anders' Text Box: You're a badaction half-dragon with final boss powers now! What's there to be mad about?

> Yallundy's Text Box: You really should have been banned, but you're not. You should be excited.

> Lissa's Text Box: Seriously? You are mad, after everything you did? #SoFuckedUp!

> Kray's Text Box: Kay, thanks for making me look so good! I have no problem with you!

> samuri's Text Box: …

> Palcath's Text Box: Lad, you are obviously crazy. You have everything you ever wanted and more.

> Breaker's Text Box: Quiet fools! My fury knows no end! I will crush you with my… wait… what do I have? Oh! That is just so awesome! With my new ability that lets me summon a dragon army! Bwahahahahaha!

With a Stretching Out of His Wings and a Dramatic Movement of his Claws Animation Breaker summoned forth six brightly coloured dragons. They were slightly different than the dragons Anders had created with Narbenock before losing track of his *Ultimate Prize*. As if they lacked all the passion that they once had.

> Gliint's Lag Text Box: *Shrug* But Breaker you are so cool now!

> Anders' Text Box: Hey! Those are my dragons! I made them, with love and arrows.

> Breaker's Text Box: Get over yourself. It was coded to happen, you just modified it. They are The Plague of Shadow's dragons, not yours. You are just some nameless arrow donor. Get real. Besides, I stole them fair and square! Now dragons… kill!

The Dragons took no rounds to think about what to do, and just started to attack the avatars randomly. Thankfully, the avatars were a pretty well balanced mix and had a very over-leveled beefy Mr. Max on their side. Anders shot an arrow at Breaker in an attempt to finish him off, but the Purple Dark Dragon teleported in and took the hit.

Within a few high-intensity rounds the Blue Ice Dragon had fallen and had turned into a glowing ball of light. Gliint had set up a *Blast Bomb* that finished the dragon off, but since he lagged out after setting it, the Bomb had almost finished him off as well.

It exploded almost instantly due to the gnome's *Increased Speed Code.* After Yallundy had scraped Gliint off the wall and healed him, the ball of blue light had returned to Breaker and absorbed back into him.

The Orange Light Dragon fell to a barrage of spells from the light and night elf magic users, and the Yellow Wind Dragon was cut in half by Mr. Max. The Green Earth Dragon was taken down by Zal Finn III's flashy dance move combo, her *Nicely Patterned Carpet,* and one of her new *Throwing Stars.* Lissa cracked the skull of the Purple Dark Dragon, and swore at it for using purple without permission. Finally, Anders fired an arrow that Palcath had timed perfectly with his coded *Expanded Battle Log* eyes and took out the Red Fire Dragon in a single exact hit.

The balls of different coloured light all returned to a not worried Breaker.

> Breaker's Text Box: That is just peachy really. Great job with the dragons. But... I can't be hurt as long as they are active, and I can just summon them all again! Thank you gayboy for these wonderful things! You jerks will run out of resources eventually! I will not!

With a Stretching Out of His Wings and a Dramatic Movement of his Claws Animation Breaker summoned absolutely nothing.

> Breaker's Text Box: What? Once per encounter. Crap. Stupid rules, now I am all out of resources!

With a Stretching Out of His Wings and a Dramatic Movement of his Claws Animation Breaker began to fly away with his tail between his legs. A few stray ranged attacks hit him before he was out of range but they were nothing life threatening.

> Breaker's Yelling Text Box: You haven't heard the last of me!

> Lissa's Yelling Text Box: Yeah, we figured. #BackgroundAntagonist.

Once Breaker was gone there was nothing left to do but wait for Fournimer and complain about how Breaker's multicoloured dragon brigade had earned them absolutely no experience. When everyone was good and upset with Fournimer, about 200 rounds later, the final avatar finally materialized into the area.

Zing!

> Blue Quest Fairy's Text Box: W—

> Green Quest Fairy's Text Box: Don't bother, they clearly don't care.

> Pink Quest Fairy's Text Box: Yeah, don't say anything or they might fold you in half like they did to sweet Tyreese!

> Blue Quest Fairy's Text Box: they killed Tyreese? those monsters!

> Gray Quest Fairy's Text Box: I loved him, I never got to tell him that

and now he is gone forever.

Red Quest Fairy's Text Box: I don't think these ones are as evil as that Breaker guy.

No-Colour Quest Fairy's Text Box: Yeah well, don't count on it, like at least two are PVP broken or something.

Orange Quest Fairy's Text Box: I'll do my best to keep this avatarette under control. I can do this!

Gray Quest Fairy's Text Box: I will avenge you, Tyreese!

Yellow Quest Fairy's Text Box: No. We all will, gal.

Everyone was more than ready to give Fournimer an earful when he finally materialized in fully.

Caëlahenãilenŵhei's Text Box: It is about time you primping pretty boy, we have... oh my.

Lissa's Text Box: Seriously Scarfy! That took way too long to... #TooFunnyForWords!

Zal Finn III's Text Box: Let's hurry up already and get going! I want to see what... hehehe, sweet!

Roodg's Text Box: hI Fournimer! ... nEAT!

Kray's Text Box: Let's go already, kay! This is getting pretty stu... Ha! Classic.

Anders' Text Box: It is about time Fourni, we have been sitting here... *blush*

Yallundy's Text Box: I am just glad you are here, I was worried that... oh sweet Maker.

Palcath's Text Box: What took you so long, lad. I mean that was way more time than it took you to shave when... whoa!

samuri's Text Box: ... ...

Mr. Max's Text Box: Hello Fourni Bro, let's get moving! ... You changed your class, huh?

Chapter 3
FINALLY FOURNI

Gliint's Lag Text Box: How much lag do you have if I beat you through character recreation, because... *Giggle* Look at him!

Fournimer's Text Box: what? it's cool! right?

Lissa's Text Box: Scarfy... Jive... I am getting rid of both of those and thinking up a brand new nickname for you now.

Palcath's Text Box: Well I mean, well lad. It's just not what I expected.

Roodg's Text Box: u R sAWESOME! tHAT IS NEAT!

Anders' Text Box: But your... butt.

Mr. Max's Text Box: What is the big deal? He went from a ranged class Night Ranger to a melee class Champion. That is a little different, but certainly not that map shattering. I mean Champions even have a close ranged javelin attack.

Palcath's Text Box: We are not Text Boxing about his class, lad. We are Text Boxing about that.

> Mr. Max's Text Box: The *Fancy Scarf (s)*? Yeah, it should have changed to melee class style Armour with the class change, but it was a broken item so it makes sense.

> Lissa's Text Box: Not the scarf you meathead! That!

> Mr. Max's Text Box: The weapons then? Yes, he has a Spear and Javelins now, but he changed his class remember, it is to be expected.

> Anders' Text Box: Not that Max. That!

Anders used the *Point Animation* directed at Fournimer's lower section.

> Mr. Max's Text Box: What do you mean? He was always a Centaur! Wasn't he?

> Roodg's Text Box: LoL. nOPE!

> Fournimer's Text Box: I think I look super!

The brand new centaur did think he looked really super now, it had taken a lot of turns to get himself perfect, but it was worth it. Looks were not the real reason why he had changed into a centaur though, it was for function. Fournimer had decided that the increased size of the horse section could potentially solve his incompatibility issues with either Mr. Max or Anders, depending of course on how the love triangle worked out. He was a much more reasonable size to deal with either now. After seeing Anders though he realized that he had forgotten to change out his *Hairstyle #6* to something else. It did look much better on the elf.

> Mr. Max's Text Box: More like Studly!

> Roodg's Text Box: mORE LIKE sAWESOME!

> Lissa's Text Box: More like... uh... yeah. I don't have the new nickname yet. Anyone have a good idea for his new name? I'm taking suggestions. Take a few rounds to think and then type it in. #VoteForYourFavourites!

Everyone took a few rounds as per Lissa's advice and thought. Fournimer was not impressed and added one of his own. Caela supplied three, to prove she was both intelligent and clever.

> Caëlahenãilenẅhei's Text Box: Fourny? Fourse? Centimer?

> Zal Finn III's Text Box: Horseymer?

> Palcath's Text Box: Fourincanter?

samuri's Text Box: …

Roodg's Text Box: Fournitaur?

Anders' Text Box: Fournihunk?

Kray's Text Box: Big Old Horse Butt?

Mr. Max's Text Box: Bhrose?

Fournimer's Text Box: Fournimer!

Yallundy's Text Box: Fournimount?

Gliint's Text Box: Foquine?

Lissa's Text Box: Great job everyone but Fournimer. Those were all good, I am going to write them down and use them all at some point. Imagine, me using a spreadsheet, I never thought I would see the day. I think that you are all winners, but I am giving special mention to Yallundy. I like hers the best, but I am a bit surprised she actually participated.

The silver skinned Troll was a little embarrassed and she used the *Shuffle Feet In Place Animation*.

Yallundy's Text Box: Everyone else was doing it.

Fournimer's Text Box: enough already Lissa! can't we just drop this and head out already?

Lissa's Text Box: Nope! This is too much fun! Also, how many times do I have to remind you again to call me Fair Maiden?

Fournimer's Text Box: wait. nicknames are my thing. why are we even discussing this Chick?

Lissa's Text Box: CHICK?!

Roodg's Text Box: hEHEHE.

Fournimer's Text Box: yes, Chick. if you are going to have a contest to give me a stupid nickname I am going to use Chick again like I originally intended!

Lissa's Text Box: Come on Jive Scarfy, that isn't even a good nickname!

Fournimer's Text Box: too bad Chick. let's see, what about everyone else? I need to review!

Blue Quest Fairy's Text Box: The Review Quest can be found i—

Lissa's Interruption Text Box: Come on, anything but Chick!

Fournimer's Text Box: Anders is Dude, Palcath is Man. Max is Bro. Roodg was Guy, but I might need to change that.

Roodg stepped forward, as Roodg was prepared for this exact moment.

Roodg's Text Box: cALL ME THE SHADOW NOW!

Fournimer's Text Box: I called Breaker Buddy and warrier Jive Turkey.

samuri's Text Box: …

Fournimer's Text Box: then we have The Finnster.

Zal Finn III's Text Box: Sweet! I still love it!

Fournimer's Text Box: what about everyone else? let's see, I guess I need to make up some more… we have Sparkle, Rocket, and Gnome.

Caëlahenãilenẁhei's Text Box: Rocket isn't horrible, I kind of like it. I accept that nickname.

Yallundy's Text Box: I really like Sparkle.

Anders' Text Box: Palcath, make them stop! This sort of feels like filler to me.

Green Quest Fairy's Text Box: The Filler Quest can be started by talking to—

Palcath's Interruption Text Box: Yeah lad, you're right, this has filler written all over it. Okay everyone let's stop this and rest before we head towards that city over there.

Yellow Quest Fairy's Text Box: There are 23 Quests, 19 Quest NPCs and 5 Hidden Quests in—

Fournimer's Interruption Text Box: hey! this is important character stuff for me!

This might have been important character stuff for Fournimer, but Lissa would have nothing of it.

> Lissa's Text Box: You made us wait for two whole cycles for you to show up! Now just listen to the dwarf, Fournimount and mush!

> Caëlahenãilenŵhei's Text Box: Mush is for sled dogs Lissa, you must be thinking of giddy-up.

> Gliint's Lag Text Box: But, Gnome? *Shrug* That's just my race.

> Brown Quest Fairy's Text Box: The Race Quest is found on Spire —

> Mr. Max's Interruption Text Box: Yeah, listen to the Dwarf Man. Let's rest and get to Onn next Cycle. It is supposed to have much better equipment than the Level 50 stuff!

> Zal Finn III's Text Box: Onn?

> Mr. Max's Text Box: Yes, Onn. That city in the distance. It is named Onn.

> Orange Text Fairy's Text Box: The City In The Distance Quest can be started by talking to NPC—

> Caëlahenãilenŵhei's Interruption Text Box: So they had some impossible to remember, sixteen syllable, random c starting word full of strange unknown accents, dashes, and apostrophes for a starting city in the old map, and then they name the one here Onn? Just one little syllable. Nothing at all complicated or confusing? Not a swirl or an accent? Just Onn? A name that nobody could possibly forget. It is so impossible to forget that I can't even forget it on principle. That is the seriously foolish logic of a serious fool. What kind of top rate idiot made that kind of decision? I just do—

> Caëlahenãilenŵhei's Text Box: not believe it.

> Mr. Max's Text Box: The last one was pretty hard to remember, but once you remember that the stupid name was Caelahenailenwhei you are good to go.

Caëlahenãilenŵhei's eyes flashed with the intensity of a *Lightning Blast*, a move she was seriously considering casting upon Max.

> Yallundy's Text Box: It is time to rest. For certain!

> Caëlahenãilenŵhei's Text Box: Yes, enough foolishness, everyone to

their respective gender designated *Portie Tents* to get some regeneration.

Palcath's Text Box: Okay, now that that lad Kray isn't dead we have eight boys and five girls. We simply can't have gender specific tents.

Caëlahenãilenŵhei's Text Box: Where are you getting this math from? There are only—

Roodg's Interruption Text Box: hI!

Caëlahenãilenŵhei's Text Box: Hi!

Red Quest Fairy's Text Box: Hi!

Lissa's Text Box: Not this 'hI Hi' crap again. Okay we are not arguing this anymore. We actually already decided. #ElectionOver. Roodg and Anders get into the girl's tent already.

Roodg stepped forward, Roodg was ready for this as well.

Roodg's Text Box: cOOL.

Anders' Text Box: Wait, what?

Caëlahenãilenŵhei's Text Box: We never Text Boxed about... Roodg?

Roodg's Text Box: hI!

Caëlahenãilenŵhei's Text Box: 'Hi!

Kray's Text Box: No way, Anders is way too chubby to fit into the girl's tent! It should be me in there. At least I have a decent number of Ranks in Hair Braiding, kay!

No-Colour Quest Fairy's Text Box: The Hair Braidin—

Caëlahenãilenŵhei's Interruption Text Box: You are covered in soot and your skin is constantly flaking off in big black chunks of refuse! There is no way in The Flaming Pit that are you ever stepping foot back into my pristine white *Portie Tent Ultra+* again!

Fournimer's Text Box: why don't you have the *Ultra+* Man? it sounds so much +er.

Palcath's Text Box: Simply because I have never even heard of it, lad!

Caela stuck up her finger to call everyone's attention to her. She was getting ready for yet another long winded explanation.

> Caëlahenãilenŵhei's Text Box: I won it in an Insta-Wiki Contest by being the very first in a long line of avatars to open a Golden Chest. No other avatar has one because this is simply the only one. It is the premium model, everyone inside gets their own custom room with decorations of their choice, a triple sized bed with cotton sheets, Armour set model mannequins, a full service weapon rack, a half service weapon rack, automatic display shelves, and a storage chest. Everything can be customized in a colour of your choice. That is why you are not going inside to smudge it —

> Caëlahenãilenŵhei's Text Box: Kray, kay!

> Anders' Text Box: Let's go inside! Right now!

> Roodg's Text Box: yEP!

> Palcath's Text Box: Come on Fourni, maybe I can change your bed into a stable.

> Fournimer's Text Box: I never even thought about something like that Man!

> Lissa's Text Box: Besides Kray, we need to Text Box to Anders and Roodg, in private, kay.

> Kray's Text Box: But my hair-dryer is in there! Hello, kay?

~ ~ ~

The group settled into their respective tents but Anders could not shake the feeling that Kray was getting soot all over his green bed in Palcath's Tent. At least he had a new hair-dryer to make him feel better. Caela's *Portie Tent* was pretty *Ultra+*; it even had a den with comfy chairs. Anders melted into a comfortable chair (that had its very own drink holder) and relaxed. The colour even changed to green automatically. The whole place had wonderful art, statues, a mini-game arcade, and even smelled refreshingly like vanilla. It was no wonder that Caela didn't want it to get smudged.

Even though it was time to eat, Anders was on his best and cleanest behavior. While looking through his *Ultra-Pack* Anders saw *Mountain Bacon, Desert Bacon,* and the not mentioned yet (but highly coveted) *Jungle Bacon.* The smell of all the *Bacon* made his stomach do a *Double Jump.* A shiny purple *Gribblet Pickle* stuffed in the back corner of his pack caught his eye when it glinted. Anders knew they tasted like an old timey gramophone but he couldn't keep from staring at it. Anders started to talk to take his mind off of the luster of the pickle.

Anders' Text Box: What did you need to speak to us about?

Lissa's Text Box: Nothing. We just voted for who we wanted in our tent and you got the most votes Anders.

Anders' Text Box: Really?

Roodg's Text Box: yEAH!

Lissa's Text Box: Yep. We just like you better. We all had two votes. Scarfy got disqualified by Caela for turning himself into a horse though. But, even before that, you got five votes Anders. #ElfBestie!

Anders' Text Box: Five votes?

Roodg's Text Box: i VOTED 4 U 2 Anders! yOU ARE sAWESOME!

Anders' Text Box: Well thank you girls and Roodg! That makes me feel pretty good.

Lissa's Text Box: Don't spread it around that we are nice. Okay Loverboy?

Lissa used the *Wink Animation*.

Anders' Text Box: Deal!

Anders used the *Wink Animation* right back.

Caëlahenãilenŵhei's Text Box: Yes, but I don't understand why is... uh... Roodg is...

Roodg's Text Box: hI!

Caëlahenãilenŵhei's Text Box: Hi!

Zal Finn III's Text Box: What Caela is trying to say is this. Why is Roodg here when... uh... they didn't get any votes? Besides, why did Roodg get to vote?

Yallundy's Text Box: Of course Roodg should be here and voting beca—

Roodg's Interruption Text Box: i'M sAWESOME 2!

Lissa's Text Box: You mean besides the obvious 'hI Hi' reason? Well Roodg makes sense, trust me on this.

Zal Finn III' Text Box: Okay Lissa! I trust you! I sort of wanted Horseymer in here to Text Box to though, because that guy is so rad! He makes me want to use my new sweet *Double Dance* ability.

Pink Quest Fairy's Text Box: The Double Dance Renovation Quest can be found on Spi—

Lissa's Interruption Text Box: Thank you Zal.

Yallundy's Text Box: Of course you trust her Zal Finn III. It is more than obvious tha—

Caëlahenäilenŵhei's Interruption Text Box: There are not going to be horses in here! Not on my carpet!

Lissa's Text Box: Speaking of clean elf carpets, maybe you should calm down with those *Gribblet Pickles* there Loverboy before you drop one of those pickle cores on the floor. Purple juice would never come out of a white carpet.

Anders' Text Box: I haven't been eating anything though…

There they were. In his lap when he looked down. The pickle cores of eight shiny *Gribblet Pickle*s (why did pickles even have cores?). In his hand was another with a single bite taken out of it. He ran out of the tent embarrassed and disposed of the strange fruit evidence discretely. After coming back inside Anders couldn't get the taste of old timey gramophones out of his mouth, and sealed his *Ultra-Pack* to prevent the oddly delicious smell from getting to him again.

Zal Finn III's Text Box: Why would you be eating so many of those? They taste like an old timey gramophone!

Anders' Text Box: I didn't even notice I was eating them. I guess I was distracted. I am never going to get rid of that taste now.

Anders didn't know why, but he suddenly didn't mind if the taste never left. Old timey gramophones were the new *Bacon* as far as he was concerned!

Yallundy stepped forward.

Yallundy's Text Box: That is why I voted for Anders though. He needs us right no—

Lissa's Interruption Text Box: We should get some sleep everyone.

> Next cycle will be a big one!

Everyone but Yallundy agreed and they went to their separate rooms for the night. Quite a few rounds later she was still huddled in her chair, that was constantly changing colours due to her broken trait. She was pretending to sip on *Hot Cocoa* while looking into the fire. She could hear sounds from behind closed doors. Lissa was a snorer, so thankfully there was good sound proofing in here. Caela was talking loudly in her sleep again, but as usual Yallundy couldn't make out any actual words. Zal Finn would be just sleeping normally and generically. Scuffs of furniture being moved around could be heard from Anders' new room. Obscure sounds were coming from Roodg's room; Yallundy couldn't picture what the multi-gendered avatar could possibly be doing in there.

Yallundy used the *Sigh Animation*.

> Yallundy's Text Box: I wish Gliint got voted in. He never interrupts me when I a—

> Zal Finn III's Interruption Text Box: Please go to bed Yallundy, we are trying to get some sleep.

Yallundy used the *Sigh Animation* again.

> Caëlahenȧilenẇhei's Sleep Box Text: Stop sighing so loudly in there!

~ ~ ~

> Kray's Text Box: I can't believe that they chose him, kay! I have a much higher Sympathetic Ear Score than him!

> Palcath's Text Box: It has been hundreds of rounds of this same sob story, lad! Now go to sleep before I cut off your Sympathetic Ear, kay!

> Kray's Text Box: Kay, but he better not be moving any of the stuff I use to increase my Morning Routine Score!

> Fournimer's Text Box: just go to sleep… uh… I forgot to give you a nickname, kay. if you don't shut up you will never need to worry about your Morning Routine again!

> Kray's Text Box: Kay, if chunky butt so much as touches my *Angelic Hair-Dryer of Cloudy Comforts* he is so dead! It gave me a bonus to my Hair Braiding Score!

> Mr. Max's Text Box: Whoever you are, if you don't stop Text Boxing I

am going to use my much higher Hair Braiding Score on your eyelashes! I have a 75 in it.

Kray's Text Box: Well I am glad I am in his old bed then! I am going to *Double Shot* so much of my flake in here, kay!

Gliint's Text Box: *Facepalm* I am the one sleeping in Anders' bed! His bed is green! That is the red one, kay. Now if you don't shut up I am going to delete myself, recreate as a Night Ranger, get the Breaker Code for PVP, and then come back here and *Double Shot* you in the face!

Kray's Text Box: Kay, I will just have to prove that I am much better than he is. A better Night Ranger, a better hair braider, and a better gay elf!

samuri's Text Box: …

Kray's Text Box: He didn't even pick a reasonable gay face! He looks like an old lumpy dwarf or something, kay!

Palcath's Text Box: Hey, lad, kay!

Kray's Text Box: I don't know who he thinks he is fooling with that big chunky butt of his. He may as well be a big fat centaur, kay!

Fournimer's Text Box: hey, kay!

Kray's Text Box: I bet he tries to pretend to be gay by using the same stupid Animation over and over again, kay! Something lame like the *Perplex Animation*!

Mr. Max's Text Box: Hey, kay!

Kray's Text Box: He is so tall, that doesn't work for gay elf boys, kay. Everyone knows that all gay bottom boys are short! The shorter a guy is here the more of a gay bottom boy he is!

Gliint's Text Box: Hey Kray, kay!

Kray's Text Box: I bet he isn't even a total bottom. Kay, what kind of gay elf isn't a total bottom? It is like a rule or something you know?

samuri's Text Box: …

samuri got up out of bed and walked over to Kray. The silent gray avatar used his PVP ability on the red bed and chopped the legs off from the floor. He solemnly picked it up. Kray was still Text Boxing and didn't even notice. samuri started to walk towards the door with both the red bed and the self proclaimed better hair braider in tow.

> Kray's Text Box: Well no matter. I am much better than him, kay. I am so glad that you all agree with me. Starting next cycle I will be the best gay elf. Kay, I can get like a whole 12 Length Units of cock up there. I would like to see him do anything close to that with that fat butt of his. I will be the best! I can easily use my *Elf Mask* to outdo him! I am sure I can, kay. I will be the best gay elf ever. I am better than the best. Kay.

samuri came back inside and nestled back into the purple bed.

> samuri's Text Box: …

> Palcath's Text Box: Dear Maker, thank you, lad! I was at the very end of my patience.

> Fournimer's Text Box: thank you so much. I am releasing you from the Jive Turkey nickname. you can have something cool, like Maverick.

> Mr. Max's Text Box: I know you only got into this world early by mistake fellow adventurette, but I owe you one!

> Gliint's Text Box: *Smile* He was getting really close to getting a *Blast Bomb* dropped beside him, thanks for shutting him up.

samuri used the *Smile Animation*.

◈ Chapter 4 ◈
PICKLED KISSES

Pal-loosh! This pebble didn't fare any better. It didn't even skip once and Fournimer let out a *Sigh Animation*. He used to be better at skipping stones before his new centaur angle of trajectory had messed up his perfected method. Fournimer looked down at the pile of rocks at his hooves and shook his head. He walked back to the higher ground of the embankment, and picked one up without needing to bend over. He had not anticipated how much harder picking things up off the ground would be as a centaur, and rather than risk falling into the water again while trying to crouch down so close to shore.

A scenic owl hooted in the background somewhere; it didn't signify anything, but it was just there to remind Fournimer that it was still late at night. The only other sounds were the faded background music that was probably a harpsichord but was too far away to hear, and the murmuring of a far off Kray still shamelessly promoting himself outside. It was just quiet enough for the centaur to reflect on things. His main thoughts were of how he couldn't sleep. It may have been that he wasn't used to sleeping in a stall, or while standing up, but it felt like something more than that. It was if his mind was telling him that he had important decisions to make, but he couldn't for the life of himself figure out what they were.

He stumbled and cursed at his hooves as he reached for another pebble to toss. This time he tried his old underhand throw from when he used to throw pebbles in the pond when he was younger. The centaur used the *Smile Animation* as he saw the pebble skip a good seven times before disappearing in the water with a 'Th-Urghuh Blerg' noise.

Fournimer was worried that whatever made the sound effect was some pond dwelling tentacle rape monstrosity that he had just pegged in the head, but follow up Th-Urghuh Blergs and sobbing noises could be heard from the shore. It probably wasn't a monster, so the centaur tried to use *Stealth* to investigate. He didn't have *Stealth* anymore though due to his class change, and instead stumbled into the clearing that the noises were coming from.

The noise turned out to be Anders, getting up off the ground and wiping his mouth. He looked uneasy, so Fournimer reached out to steady him. Fournimer fumbled his centaur movement controls and needed to be steadied in return.

> Fournimer's Text Box: sorry. still getting used to the new movement controls Dude.

> Anders' Text Box: That is okay Fourni. It was still a nice gesture.

Both avatars stood motionless for a few rounds, at a loss for words. After neither could think of what to say they both changed their *Blush Settings* to *#1*. It was the centaur who finally broke the silence.

> Fournimer's Text Box: I couldn't really sleep either.

> Anders' Text Box: Oh, I was sleeping fine, but then my stomach decided that snacking on fourteen and a half pickles over the course of the evening wasn't a great plan and decided to revolt.

This time it was Anders who toppled a bit, but his fall into Fournimer was instead graceful. The elf tried to move, but his legs were too shaky to support his own weight.

> Fournimer's Text Box: are you alright Anders? we should get you back into bed right away!

Using his newfound melee class strength, Fournimer hoisted Anders onto his back. Anders slumped forward and wrapped his arms around Fournimer's human waist which made Fournimer feel surprisingly happy. He started to trot towards the *Portie Tents* but Anders' squeezed his humanoid midsection.

> Anders' Text Box: Actually, this is kind of nice Fourni. The wind up here is really cool. Can we maybe just go for a walk or something instead? I don't feel like sleeping anymore.

> Fournimer's Text Box: sure. I'd like that. a lot. but I'm not terribly good at controlling myself yet.

Anders squeezed harder and pushed playfully into Fournimer's back.

> Anders' Text Box: That's okay, we can practice together.

They slowly made their way around the little rock throwing pond. Anytime

Fournimer would stumble Anders would offer words of encouragement, and anytime that Fournimer used his controls properly Anders would cuddle and squeeze the centaur's human waist. Although there was more words of encouragements than squeezings, they made it to the other side of the pond and stopped to watch the moon setting over the horizon. The morning portion of the cycle would be coming soon, but neither could deny how beautiful the new moon of the Expansion was.

After a long silent moment, Fournimer let out a *Sigh Animation*, and Anders followed with a *Concerned While Riding a Centaur Animation*.

> Anders' Text Box: What's wrong?

Fournimer looked back at Anders. He had been ready to make up an excuse for the sigh, but when he looked into Anders' deep protagonist green eyes instead he shocked himself when he blurted out the truth.

> Fournimer's Text Box: my *Wonder Kisses* power sucks!

Anders was surprised by the outburst, but could only *Laugh Animation*. Anders kissed Fournimer on the neck and sweeping romantic music played accompanied by the little bursting green and orange firework hearts that slightly improved Anders' experience and gold coin totals.

> Anders' Text Box: I still think they are cute.

> Fournimer's Text Box: but they don't really even do anything! I feel silly compared to everyone else with their cool powers.

> Anders' Text Box: Well, what do your other levels for it do?

> Fournimer's Text Box: other levels? you can get other levels?

> Anders' Text Box: Yeah, mine only started as *Stretch* until I unlocked the other parts. Maybe yours is like that as well?

A sudden vigour filled the centaur. He had no idea that there were other levels for abilities or why no one had told him about them until now.

> Fournimer's Text Box: no way! that would be so amazing! what do I do?

> Anders' Text Box: I accidently said their names. You should try saying different kinds of kisses and see if anything happens!

> Fournimer's Text Box: okay. uh… Eskimo kisses? butterfly kisses? French kisses? body kisses? that kiss that is all upside down when you are hanging from a web kisses?

> Anders' Text Box: They are *Wonder Kisses*, try using wonderful words?

> Fournimer's Text Box: right. so amazing kisses? delightful kisses? awesome kisses? **Happy Kisses**?

> Anders' Text Box: Stop! **Happy Kisses** is in bold and capital letters! What did you just learn?

> Fournimer's Text Box: nothing... nothing happened.

> Anders' Text Box: Odd. Mine happened when I was using my power. Maybe you need to be kissing when it happens?

It did not take much convincing, but Fournimer was disappointed that whatever *Happy Kisses* was, it didn't unlock during his make out session with Anders. Despite the fact that Anders tasted like old timey gramophones, neither Fournimer nor Anders wanted to stop trying to make it activate. They kissed until the Rooster cawed, signalling morning had arrived.

> Fournimer's Text Box: it was really fun trying, thank you for the help. we should get back.

> Anders' Text Box: No wait. Roodg always sleeps in anyways. I have another idea.

> Fournimer's Text Box: what?

Anders changed to *Blush Shade #4*, he had been on *#3* for some rounds now, but he was going to be bold about this. He reached over to Fournimer's ear and whispered inside, making sure that his hot breath teased the centaur's neck.

> Anders' Whisper Text Box: My powers only activated during sexual situations. We should try and see if that works.

This time it was Fournimer's turn to change *Blush Shades*, going all the way up to *#7*. Anders kissed the Centaur on the cheek, earned a few more coins, and deftly jumped down and vanished under the centaur's horse section. Everything was out of view for Fournimer.

> Anders' Text Box: Holy Maker, Fourni!

> Fournimer's Text Box: what?! is something wrong?

> Anders' Text Box: I dunno. I've never really seen a real horse down there... but I'm pretty sure that hung like a horse isn't sufficient. What animals do horses brag about being as hung as? Cause it is that. You are fudging huge!

Anders demonstrated by pumping the huge centaur shaft in his hands. Fournimer was surprised by how much he could feel Anders' touch. It sent shivers up his elongated spine. Judging by how much distance the elf had to cover, and by how he needed to use both hands, Fournimer concluded that he was indeed hung like whatever animals horses bragged about being hung like.

> Anders' Text Box: You're balls are pretty big as well. They sort of look swollen.

Anders reached forward and touched the centaur's balls and Fournimer cried out in alarm. He hadn't noticed, but now that he was being stimulated it felt as if he hadn't came in cycles over cycles. He bucked his hooves and started to whinny, and he didn't even have time to warn Anders. Just a few rounds of touch had done Fournimer in, and he started to shoot.

> Anders' Text Box: Gah! *Spurt* Quick! say **Happy Kisses**!

Fournimer released one more big shot of pent up centaur spunk and yelled out a guttural scream of *Happy Kisses*. He nearly fell down, but remembered that Anders was under him and steadied himself with a nearby scenic fence post. Anders had been right, the phrase needed to be said in a sexual situation to unlock and Fournimer had now unlocked it. Anders sprung up from under Fournimer, his upper body completely covered in horse spunk. Fournimer was embarrassed.

> Fournimer's Text Box: sorry! still getting used to the new body. I didn't know I was so close.

> Anders' Text Box: That's okay. Just some warning would have been nice.

Anders jumped up and delivered a friendly cum covered kiss to Fournimer. This time little blue and red hearts joined the exploding green and orange ones.

> Fournimer's Text Box: what did they do?

> Anders' Text Box: Uh… It looks like I gained a couple of Mana Points. So the blue ones restore a few MP, the red ones were probably Health.

Fournimer used another *Sigh Animation*.

> Fournimer's Text Box: that sucks. you recovered like five of each? we have thousands. these still suck!

> Anders' Text Box: They are cuter now… otherwise yes. Still, they did improve.

> Fournimer's Text Box: the other three levels better be more useful!

Anders' Text Box: Maybe, maybe not. But we are going to have fun finding out.

Anders used a *Wink Animation* and then jumped into the pond to get cleaned off before returning to camp. Fournimer stood shocked on the shore for a few rounds and decided to join the fun. It was after jumping in that he realized that he didn't know the controls for horse swimming. Fournimer sank like his own pebbles with a pal-loosh.

◈ Chapter 5 ◈
ONWARDS TO ONN

The now refreshed party finally left the starting cave only two and a half cycles after getting access to the Expansion. Anders didn't ask why the red bed was now stationed outside the boy's *Portie Tent*. Honestly, he didn't think you could even move the beds. All of his own attempts to secretly move his bed closer to any potential love interests hadn't done anything useful except give him a good workout.

They were headed towards the large impressive city in the distance. From the starting cave entrance near the pond they could see the entire island that was the expansion. The Island of Islana was as impressive to take in as a Gigas cock. It really was more of a continent, despite that it was called an island. It was not as large as the original map, but it had a lot of new areas.

Four huge spires stood tall and were located on the extreme corners of the island, nestled on top of different mountains, making them even more ludicrously tall. They each had a unique look.

The spire located on the south was on top of a volcano. Fire was even spurting out of the sides of the mountain. The surrounding areas were red with an obvious fire element motif. There was a burning forest and a field of pure thick reddish smoke. To help sell the look, the mountain that held this up was marked with a giant letter A.

The western mountain was completely encased in thick ice. The spire itself was made of a clear ice like substance that was most likely ice. The entire area was blue and was surrounded by a huge snowfield and a frozen forest. On the mountain that supported this spire was a large engraved letter B.

The northern area was green and lush and it had rock crags covering the tower, so it was likely the earth area. There was another forest, this one looked very lively and there was also an area full of large pillars that probably involved jumping puzzles. This mountain had been labeled with a giant letter C.

The final eastern spire was metallic and had rods sticking out of it at odd angles that lightning was constantly striking. It was yellow and wind all mixed into one. The forest here was full of lightning, and due to the heavy clouds probably rain as well. All of the trees were charred but were the sort that were also breakable. There was also a big wide open area that looked ominous. A nicely painted big D was on this mountain, but a stencil had been used.

A huge suspension bridge from the absolute top of each spire connected them to a centre spire that was high above where they all currently were located. This centre spire even had multiple spires. There were two lower spires that had suspension bridges that linked to the uppermost spire.

The lower spire on the right was covered in shadow and seeing it fully was hard. A dead twisted forest surrounded the spire as well as an area that could only be described as being sharp. This side must be the dark themed area. The mountain here was stamped with the letter E repeatedly.

The left spire was hard to even look at due to the intense brightness. This was a light area and a glowing forest was beside the spire. An area that looked pointy completed the side's bright and light look. This mountain had a big embossed F across it.

The final uppermost spire was hidden in the clouds except for the very bottom where the bridges entered into a misty forest. This spire exuded penultimate final area and was probably dangerous, but all that could be seen was that the mountain holding the whole thing up had multiple floating Gs around it.

Before them was a small path towards what was the starting city of Onn. The city resembled the island itself, with spires in each corner and one in the middle that was a castle. The path to the city was clear, but right after Onn they could see a forest path that lead to a small spire structure past the city on top of a mountain. The mountain was labeled with something as well, but from here it wasn't visible. Anders guessed it was either the letter H, or something completely unrelated just to mess with him.

> Roodg's Text Box: i THINK THEY NEED MORE SPIRES! tHERE ISN'T ENOUGH!

> Caëlahenãilenẇhei's Text Box: A few more forests would be appreciated as well.

> Lissa's Text Box: Extra mountains could help to really set the whole look off.

> Fournimer's Text Box: some more giant out of place letters would

> complete this place for me.

> Blue Quest Fairy's Text Box: The Complete Collection Quest can be found on Spir-

> Palcath's Interruption Text Box: Let's just go.

The background music was one of the licensed songs in this game. *Onnwards to Onn* by *Caution Step*. That was easy for a unlocking a licensed song and Anders was thrilled; it would be available all the time now in the Sound Test menu to enjoy.

Onn was not difficult to reach. There were absolutely no random monsters, puzzles, or anything else annoying in the way. If you could walk in a straight line you could make it to Onn. So naturally only laggy Gliint and the newly horsed Fournimer had any trouble doing so. Gliint got over his problem by having Yallundy carry him. Fournimer got over this problem by pretending to know what he was doing and running into everything. Within only a few rounds Onn was reached and it was even more impressive than the low polygon distance model had made it look.

> Mr. Max's Text Box: Quick! Let's go inside! I can almost feel all the waiting Quest Icons! Just floating there quivering and all alone. They are waiting for me to caress them and press accept. Don't worry little icons, daddy Max is here! He will collect all of your wonderful experience points!

> Orange Quest Fairy's Text Box: Inside Onn there are multiple quests to complete… hey wait up!

Mr. Max had vanished inside and everyone else had begun to follow. Gliint was currently frozen but was still tucked gently under Yallundy's arm. Anders stepped towards the gate but felt a hand on his arm holding him back and turned to look. The hand belonged to a dwarf who also was keeping back Lissa and Fournimer. While Palcath was not holding back Roodg, the night elf had noticed what was going on and stayed back.

> Palcath's Text Box: Okay lads, lass, and Roodgs. What are we doing?

> Fournimer's Text Box: it is the Island of Islana Expansion, Man. we are going to Onn. I know you didn't get much sleep last night but wow.

> Blue Quest Fairy's Text Box: the Island of Islana has a grand total of—

> Palcath's Interruption Text Box: I'm well aware of that lad, that isn't what I'm Text Boxing about. What are we doing?

> Lissa's Text Box: I agree. What are we doing?

Fournimer's Text Box: we are going to Onn!

Lissa's Text Box: One more outburst like that and you're out of the discussion Pallyboy! #Disqualified!

Fournimer's Text Box: okay, I'm confused then. what's going on?

Anders' Text Box: Something is going on that is deeper than the surface, I can feel it as well. Something is strange.

Lissa's Text Box: Things have been off, like since way before now. I can't place it though.

Palcath's Text Box: I know, I have felt unsettled for awhile, but I don't even know where to start, lass.

Roodg's Text Box: iT IS OBVIOUS. sOMETHING IS WRONG WITH THE GAME ITSELF. Breaker SHOULD HAVE BEEN BANNED BUT HASN'T. tHE OLD MAP SHOULD HAVE BEEN RESET ALMOST INSTANTLY AFTER IT WAS DESTROYED BUT IT WASN'T. nOBODY OFFICIAL ANSWERS ANYTHING ON THE wORLDfORUMS ABOUT BROKEN AVATARS OR SEX POWERS. iT IS COMPLETELY STRANGE THAT AVATARS CAN EVEN BE BROKEN AT ALL AS THE GAME'S RATING DOESN'T MENTION NUDITY OR SEXUAL SITUATIONS.

Roodg did the *Thinking Animation*, while everyone else did the *Jawdrop Animation*.

Roodg's Text Box: bROKEN AVATARS ARE NOT SUPPOSED TO HAPPEN. tHESE BROKEN PERVERT MONSTERS ARE CRAZY AS WELL, THEY GLITCH OUT AND ARE FUNCTIONING OUT OF THEIR NORMAL RANGE. iT IS STILL IN THEIR CODING SOMEWHERE FOR SOME REASON. tHIS COMBINED WITH OTHER FACTORS LEAD ME 2 BELIEVE THAT THE GAME IS FAR MORE BROKEN THAN WE THINK.

Roodg's Text Box: iF THEY COULD FIX IT THEY WOULD HAVE. iF THEY COULD REPAIR AVATARS THEY WOULD. nOT DOING SO IS REALLY BAD PUBLIC RELATIONS. iF THEY HAD ANY POWER AT ALL THEN NOTHING Breaker DID WOULD HAVE WORKED & HE CERTAINLY WOULDN'T HAVE BEEN ALLOWED 2 COME IN WITH US! sOMETHING FISHY IS GOING ON HERE!

Red Quest Fairy's Text Box: The Something Fishing Quest is located on Spire D.

Roodg's Text Box: cORRECT?

Palcath's Text Box: …

Fournimer's Text Box: …

Lissa's Text Box: …

Anders' Text Box: …

Roodg's Text Box: wHAT? LoLZ YOU ARE ALL LOOKING AT ME FUNNY!

Palcath's Text Box: Sorry, it's just that I didn't expect you to say that. However Roodg, you are right on the gold coins.

Palcath found his almost forgotten "Is Roodg Smart or Not" file and gave yes a checkmark.

Roodg's Text Box: i KNOW RIGHT?

Lissa's Text Box: You know what, Roodg is right. I complained on the WorldForums and all my posts were pushed to the bottom. I kept tabs on other complaints and most disappeared even though they were getting bumped. Someone was pushing them off or keeping them under wraps.

Anders' Text Box: Now that I think about it all the monsters are using normal combat moves but just twisting their intent. The Pink Slime had to spend rounds and rounds to get ready because it didn't have the right equipment.

Palcath's Text Box: Why would the Developer lads even put that in their game and then not be prepared for it?

Fournimer's Text Box: yeah! all the complaints I submitted to the Admins about glitter were completely ignored!

Lissa's Text Box: They better get their act together soon though and get their mind out of the gutter. The class action lawsuit against this game is probably going to destroy their company if they don't. #GameOver.

Anders' Text Box: They are getting sued?

Palcath's Text Box: Yes. Didn't you hear, lad? Some politician heard from concerned parents that strange things were happening and are trying to sue *Tornado Tech* and get this game banned. I saw the footage on the news; thankfully they didn't have anything nearly as graphic as the things we have seen. Just some troll lad with nipple pasties.

Lissa's Text Box: #SoFuckedUp. Hopefully some bigot with useful connections doesn't get bent over a chest and get gayed up the ass before we can do something. I like this game and I am not going to give up my purple hair so easily.

Fournimer's Text Box: if they are going to get shutdown, why don't they just stop it?

Lissa's Text Box: Especially since a shutdown would mean a permanent deletion of all avatars! That would kill kill everyone, everything, and even everywhere.

It was a sobering thought that Roodg summed up best.

Roodg's Text Box: eEP!

Palcath's Text Box: Wait a round! I think I got it. Do you think those lads are broken as well?

Lissa's Text Box: Which lads?

Palcath's Text Box: The Admin and Developer lads! I think they must be. Why else would they just stand by and let their income get destroyed. It is the only thing that makes sense. They must be broken.

Anders' Text Box: Why would they break themselves though, that doesn't make sense?

Palcath's Text Box: I doubt they did that lad. There is something else afoot here.

Roodg's Text Box: sO THE ONLY LOGICAL CONCLUSION IS THAT THE aDMINS & dEVELOPERS ARE BROKEN AS WELL. bUT THEN THE QUESTION IS: iF THEY WOULDN'T BREAK THEMSELVES, WHO DID? wAS IT THAT BLOATED IDIOT Breaker IN AN EFFORT TO STOP THEM FROM ENDING HIS REIGN OF TERROR, OR WAS IT SOMEONE ELSE ENTIRELY THAT WE HAVEN'T EVEN MET YET?

Palcath's Text Box: Stop sounding smart Roodg, you are freaking me out.

Fournimer's Text Box: so what if they are? there is nothing we could possibly do!

Palcath's Text Box: No, probably not, lad. We can however test the theory out at least.

Fournimer's Text Box: how could we do that? also why would we do that? we should be spending our time here wisely. especially if this whole place could be shutdown at a moment's notice.

Lissa's Text Box: Says the avatar that wasted two full cycles turning himself into a show pony. #MyLittleShownie.

Palcath's Text Box: We can call for an Admin, lass. It would test out if they are broken or not.

Lissa used a quick *Facepalm Animation*.

Lissa's Text Box: I completely forgot about In-Game Customer Support! I wish I thought of that way back when I was locked in the tower.

Anders' Text Box: Do we want to call one then? It could solve some issues.

Palcath's Text Box: Or cause even more issues, given our luck. I'm not so sure we should anymore. What do you lads, lasses, and Roodgs think?

Yellow Quest Fairy's Text Box: Hey pal, to start the Our Luck Quest, look in Onn for the hidden cat wal—

Lissa's Interruption Text Box: It probably couldn't hurt. We are broken though, they might notice and ban us or something.

Fournimer's Text Box: I think we should think about it some more first. we don't need to do it right away, but we should keep the option there.

Anders' Text Box: True, we haven't even done anything important yet in the expansion. Let's just take some time to think.

Palcath's Text Box: Maybe we should sleep on it.

It was agreed upon and almost all of them nodded in agreement.

Roodg's Text Box: oKAY. I SUMMONED ONE!

Lissa's Text Box: Why would you do that? We just agreed to wait!

Fournimer's Text Box: yeah The Shadow? you know what, The Shadow nickname doesn't work at all. I'll just go back to Guy!

Roodg's Text Box: sORRY. WASN'T PAYING ATTENTION! wAS LOOKING FOR HOW TO SUMMON AN aDMIN. tHEN i FOUND IT. sO i DID! wE GOT TO GET THIS STORY GOING ALREADY SO WE CAN GET TO SOME SEX SCENES!

Palcath's Text Box: That's the Roodg I know! You had me worried for a bit there.

Roodg's Text Box: iT SAYS IT CAN TAKE UP TO 2 CYCLES FOR 1 TO SHOW UP ANYWAYS! lOTS OF TIME TO THINK.

Lissa's Text Box: I guess two cycles is enough time to think up what to ask.

Purple Quest Fairy's Text Box: The Quest Two Cycles is #SoScrewedUp. First it must be started by talking to—

Administrator Owen's Interruption Text Box: It probably would be enough time to think. However, it takes much less time than 2 cycles for an Admin to show up when there are only thirteen avatars in the Expansion. It also doesn't hurt that the Admins have been waiting for you to summon them for who knows how long now.

◈ Chapter 6 ◈
ADMINISTRATIVE SUPPORT

The glowing ball of light that was Administrator Owen could not move independently. He was heavy, for a floating orb, but with some sweat-inducing rounds of shoving they managed to support the weight of the Administrator enough to push him inside Onn. Afterwards they realized that they could have probably just summoned the floating ball of mass again after they were inside and avoided all of the work.

The entire party had been gathered and stood in a circle around the glowing ball of light. Everyone except Mr. Max, as it had been impossible to track the avatar down. He could be heard running around Onn completing Fetch Quests with extreme glee. A frazzled Orange Quest Fairy was following him around frantically unable to keep up with his intense quest speed. They had decided to not try to get his attention for a few reasons.

1. He would probably never understand what was really going on here.
2. He had thrown Gliint crashing into a building. All just to get to one of the little Red Exclamation Points that marked Quests. Max was dangerous when Questing.
3. He was getting them all credit for many completed Fetch Quests, which were the most boring kinds of Quests. (Anders guessed this fact as he had only thus far completed part of one Quest.)
4. He was earning them Quest Rewards, while they were doing more important things.

The party followed the instructions given and soon a total of five Administrators were present, even though they had tried to summon six. The Admins spent a round and gained solid form by unfolding themselves, each was wearing a mystical robe with a cowl. A different mystical symbol marked each Admin on their chest and was glowing brightly. Each Admin shone with their own light, but all were a shade off the normal colours. They were Administrators after all; they were allowed special colour schemes. They didn't have any concept of standing in rainbow order, which annoyed Anders slightly.

Owen was the leader of this group, even if he was now glowing magenta. On his robe was a glowing symbol of a nearly full circle. Only the top was open and inside was a line that reached the middle of the circle. The symbol radiated pure power.

> Administrator Owen's Text Box: Wait, where is Administrator Yvonne?

> Administrator Ivy's Text Box: She only sometimes shows up, why?

The cyan Administrator Ivy was more feminine in shape than the other Administrators, this was likely caused by the fact that she was a woman. There was even long hair coming from under her cowl. Her symbol was an arrow coming horizontally out of a circle with two strange branch things, one coming from the top, and one from the bottom. It was an U.nidentifiable S.oftwood B.ranch of some kind.

> Administrator Ethelred's Text Box: It isn't important. She is probably just getting a sandwich, I was smart enough to get one before I was summoned. Wait, where did I put that sandwich? I can't find it anywhere. Did someone take it? Which one of you guys took my stuff? I know someone did! Oh, never mind I found it, it was on the plate, sorry. False alarm. Sorry.

Anders was dissapointed with Ethelred; he was not even close to being red. This Administrator was yellow, but not good old Palcath yellow. This was the softer lighter yellow that was also used as the accent colour in Palcath's *Portie Tent*. His symbol was a horizontal line, branching outwards. There were three squares, one on the top and two on the bottom. It involved an alternate term for *Mana Potions* that Anders had only heard once before from the role-player Palcath, an Ether.

> Administrator Allen's Text Box: Good point Ethelred. Finally, someone important has summoned us! We have awaited this for some time now. It was right in front of us this entire time but we just couldn't find it! We can finally rejoice.

Administrator Allen was glowing orange. It wasn't a Mr. Max kind of orange, but was a soft gentle Flaming Pit Hound aura orange. He had a dot with quarter circle pulses coming out of it as a symbol. Anders wasn't quite sure what a WhyFhy was. Perhaps it was some kind of monster.

Administrator Umple's Text Box: Rounds are Gold Coins, let's just skip the crap and get to the point already.

Umple was a nice shade of lilac. His symbol was a sideways horn. It had circular lines coming outwards that indicated intensity or even Volume. Anders guessed that the non present Yvonne would probably have a green motif and another computer related symbol he would try to describe obscurely.

Administrator Owen's Text Box: Fine you grumpy old buzz-kill, (don't ever change, and see you tonight for beers). I'll get to the point. Okay, Breaker! We have been looking all over for you!

Lissa's Text Box: What do you mean Breaker? Breaker isn't here.

Administrator Ethelred's Text Box: What? Where did you put him? He is supposed to be in this party!

Palcath's Text Box: No sorry Administrative lads, he isn't.

Administrator Allen's Text Box: Why not? That is foolish! I am confused! Puzzled is what I am right now.

Caëlahenâilenŵhei's Text Box: Simply because he is a megalomaniac Backstabber idiot.

Administrator Allen's Text Box: Well then, where did he go? He can't be far. Did you lose him?

Administrator Ethelred's Text Box: Did you try looking on your plate? That's where my sandwich was.

Zal Finn III's Text Box: We don't know where he went after he flew off! He just up and zinged away.

Gliint's Lag Text Box: I get it! Sometimes Y! They are all vowels.

Administrator Ivy's Text Box: He... flew off? What do you mean flew off? Explain yourself. Well, I'm waiting.

Fournimer's Text Box: Buddy is a crazy half dragon with stolen Ultimate Boss Powers.

The statement took the Admins by complete surprise. Sparks of sudden understanding flashed in their eyes (that were hidden under cowls).

Administrator Owen's Text Box: Buddy is a crazy half dragon with stolen Ultimate Boss Powers?

Kray's Text Box: Yeah, kay. He used his *Breaker's Belt of Awesomeness* to absorb all sorts of things, avatars and monsters mostly. He almost absorbed me as well, but instead he just made me really thin and hot. I'd wear one of those belts for the stat boosts, even though it looked sort of shabby, kay. Sometimes sacrifices must be made.

Administrator Ethelred's Text Box: He made a custom item that gave him absorbing powers, kay? Everything is finally starting to make sense. Everyone listen to this guy, the hot and thin one. Hey, look it's my stapler! I thought I had lost it. I'm going to staple the crap out of some things after this.

Anders' Text Box: What?

Administrator Allen's Text Box: A stapler? No, the Belt, you must mean the Belt. Why would he need a custom belt though? For what purpose? What are his goals? Did he have a plan?

Roodg's Text Box: yES, TO DESTROY ALMOST THE ENTIRE MAP & KILL ALL THE npcS!

The sparks of sudden understanding flashed even louder in the Admin's eyes. The flashes were so intense that they made an audible ting noise.

All Administrators' Simultaneous Text Boxes: That was him?

Anders' Text Box: Okay, stop! You are the absolute least informed 'Secret Council Group Full of Mystical All-Knowing and Mysterious Members' that has existed in the entire history of 'Secret Council Groups Full of Mystical All-Knowing and Mysterious Members'!

Lissa's Text Box: Yeah! That is #SoFuckedUp! How do you not know any of this?

The Secret Council Group of Mystical All-Knowing and Mysterious Members huddled up and started to whisper amongst themselves. After what was at least seventeen rounds they turned back towards the avatars and straightened out their robes.

Administrator Owen's Text Box: Okay, we are going to level with you here.

Roodg's Text Box: sWEET! lEVELS!!!

Administrator Ivy's Text Box: Not Level with you, level with you! We are not going to get into that joke!

Administrator Owen's Text Box: Some of our Administrative Powers were sealed the exact moment that... the first avatar got broken? It was built into the programming?

Administrator's Umple's Text Box: Yeah! Good idea! If only that stupid elf hadn't gotten himself shtooped by that Pink Slime, so much of this might not have happened!

Quite a few eyes were on Anders, who executed the *Mortified Expression Animation*.

Administrator Owen's Text Box: Now Umple, you crotchety old man (I'll buy the first round okay?) it would have probably happened eventually given what we know. You need to stop always blaming the gays for your problems!

Regardless, many of our abilities have been compromised. Not everything mind you, but mostly our movement and interacting abilities. We can no longer appear into an area unless we have been summoned by an avatar.

To make things worse we can no longer access the WorldForums or any Player Pagers. We can only monitor the WorldForums with Ivy's secret dummy Account. All our other private Accounts were deleted once we tried to help anyone, so Ivy doesn't dare post in there anymore.

We have become prisoners in the very game we are supposed to protect!

If what you say about Breaker is true we definitely need to find him now!

Caëlahenäilenŵhei's Text Box: Oh my Maker! Your Text Box is huge! It even has multiple paragraphs! How do I get one of those?

Palcath's Text Box: Why don't you Adminilads just find him then? Can't you just look him up? Why do you need to even tell us all these things?

Administrator Ethelred's Text Box: We can't find Breaker and we haven't been able to see him since we scolded him for publishing those simple Cheat Codes. I have the incident tracker here... somewhere.

Caëlahenäilenŵhei's Text Box: Zal Finn III, can you use your eyes to find him?

Zal Finn III's Text Box: I have never been able to see Breaker with them. I assumed it was because it was his Code!

Administrator Ivy's Text Box: No, you wouldn't be able to. Those are the same eyes that Administrators can use to find things. We believe that Breaker has rooted himself through a dummy account to become untraceable.

Administrator Owen's Text Box: If Breaker has advanced from simple Codes that can unlock either simple Admin Abilities, or unreleased content, to actual item manipulation then we must find him!

Caëlahenãilenŵhei's Text Box: Well it is obvious where the blighter is. More than obvious actually. Since he can take to the air and he fancies himself as a Maker, he is obviously in the very pinnacle of the spires of that giant conglomeration of spires over there. It is simply where a self important half-dragon who now has Ultimate Boss powers would be. So just take your Secret Council Group of Mystical All-Knowing and Mysterious Members and go over there with haste! Even if you can't talk to him at least you can do something about him right? Now hurry over there and deal—

Caëlahenãilenŵhei's Text Box: with him!

Administrator Umple used the *Slow Clap Animation*.

Administrator Umple's Text Box: Unfortunately no. We can only go into areas where avatars are currently located. Thanks for the pep talk though, I appreciate it, really. Even if he is there, the game would claim that he isn't, so we couldn't go. It is a completely stupid thing that was broken even before the game broke. I told them it was a stupid idea but they didn't listen to me! They never do, darn kids. Since Breaker is hidden we can't just pop over to where he obviously is and find him!

Fournimer's Text Box: that is stupid Secret Coun... yeah, I am not typing that all out. that is so stupid S.C.G.O.M.A.K.A.M.M.!

Administrator Allen's Text Box: He accidently found out our greatest weakness, a loophole that can surpass our once mighty abilities, the way through all of our clever tricks!

Palcath's Text Box: Let me guess, now we need to go and find Breaker for you lads and lasses. Then once we find the half-lad we have to summon you all so that you can deal with him?

Administrator Ivy's Text Box: Could you please?

> Roodg's Text Box: hEY! wE GOT 2 THE REAL PLOT BY cHAPTER 6! iT IS A NEW RECORD! nOW TO FIND SEX!

Roodg was ready to run out of here and look for some steamy action, but even more plot got in the way.

> Administrator Owen's Text Box: Normally, if you travel through the Onn Forest through that exit there you will get to The Airship. That can take you to Spires A through D. You would need to unlock the Final Gates in A and B to get to Spire E. Similarly, you would need to open the Final Gates C and D to get through to Spire F. Once the Final Gates of E and F are open you could progress to Spire G and reach the top.

> Lissa's Text Box: Is that it? That is hardly anything!

> Administrator Ethelred's Text Box: It would be normally a lot of work, but we just Control A'd the Airship for you. Now you can just skip all that crap and go right to Spire G!

> Roodg's Text Box: nEAT!

> Administrator Allen's Text Box: Now go! Hurry hurry! Get up there! Fast as Ni Hao Bunny©!

> Roodg's Text Box: wHY?

> Administrator Ivy's Text Box: What do you mean why? Because we told you to, that's why.

> Roodg's Text Box: wHY SHOULD WE GO AFTER HIM 4 U? wHAT WILL U DO 4 US? sEXY THINGS?

> Administrator Ivy's Text Box: What can we do for you? I didn't think about that.

> Administrator Allen's Text Box: I guess we could… Waive Monthly Fees? Give Free Downloads? Find other Fabulous Prizes?

> Roodg's Text Box: k. wE WILL DO IT FOR THAT! tHEY BETTER BE REALLY FABULOUS! r WE STILL BROKED?

> Administrator Owen's Text Box: Uh… Broked?

> Roodg's Text Box: yEAH. bROKED. fILE CORRUPTED!

Administrator Ethelred's Text Box: Oh, that... I just found my... my Administrator Diagnostic Apparatus™ under this microwave? It says that you are still broken characters, but it says your Save Files have been fixed. Yeah, sure.

Roodg's Text Box: nEAT! lET'S GO! sEX!

Administrator Owen's Text Box: Yes neat indeed. Thank you for that Ethelred (I'll buy you a beer as well). The monsters here are pretty high Level though. I'd suggest getting some new equipment first!

Administrator Ethelred's Text Box: No problem, I should buy you one back for all the crap you spouted about... staplers?

Administrator Ivy's Text Box: Nice save! I mean, see you all up there in just a bit!

With a flash of light the S.C.G.O.M.A.K.A.M.M. were gone.

Roodg's Text Box: fINALLY! tHEY ARE GONE! aLL OF THIS PLOT AND YAMMERING IS GETTING IN THE WAY OF WHAT IS REALLY IMPORTANT. wE NEED TO REMEMBER THAT THIS IS A SEXY BOOK AND GET TO SOME GOOD STUFF ALREADY! i AM so BORED.

Anders' Text Box: Wait!

Palcath's Text Box: It's too late lad, they are gone. Why did you need them to wait?

Lissa's Text Box: Well for starters, we didn't ask them most of what we wanted to ask them! They got all the info they wanted out of us and then just split! We did learn that they are broken, but we didn't ask why or how it happened! That was sort of a vital piece of information. We probably knew more than they did! #ExpositionFail.

Palcath's Text Box: Son of a bitch! You are right, lass. That didn't answer much.

Lissa's Text Box: Well, we did learn that we aren't broken anymore.

Zal Finn III's Text Box: And that if we find Breaker we will win fabulous prizes! Sweet!

Mr. Max's Text Box: We have a purpose now fellow adventurers!

Follow your leader and we shall finally bring justice to Breaker! Then win some fabulous prizes!

Caëlahenāilenŵhei's Text Box: You were paying attention to that you bonehead?

Mr. Max's Text Box: Yes, once I ran out of Fetch Quests.

Zal Finn III's Text Box: Sweet, we should buy new equipment first then. If they suggested that, it is probably a good idea.

Mr. Max's Text Box: I checked the Onn store already! This stuff is beyond awesome! All their Equipment has a Level 65 or higher requirement. Only I am above 65.

samuri's Text Box: ...

samuri used the *Shake Head Animation.*

Mr. Max's Text Box: Oh, wait. That nice girl from last night is Level 68. the Dragon Cultist is Level 62 I notice, so almost there.

Palcath's Text Box: It will take forever to get that high of a Level, lad! There really isn't time, we need to hurry! Let's just get it and put it on later.

Mr. Max's Text Box: We have a bigger problem than that Palcath Dwarfman, son of dwarf. The cheapest thing were the kinds of gloves, and a pair of them cost 64,000 Gold Coins.

Roodg's Text Box: tHAT IS A WHOLE BUNCH OF HORSE KISSES! cAN WE START WITH THE KISSES NOW PLEASE?

Lissa's Text Box: What? But we spent all of our Gold Coins buying *Mana Potions* to kill Breaker in the last book! We can't afford that, that is #SoFuckedUp.

Mr. Max's Text Box: I would have had enough Gold Coins to buy everything, except for one avatar a set of boots, but I spent all of my 89,758,900 Gold Coins on *Mana Potions* for some reason!

Gliint's Lag Text Box: See you soon Admins! *wave*

Fournimer's Text Box: can we maybe borrow some gold coins guys?

Zal Finn III's Text Box: We have a problem as well. It's not sweet.

Caëlahenãilenẇhei's Text Box: Yes, Breaker charged us all of our gold coins to join his expansion bound party. We are completely broke as well.

Roodg's Text Box: wELL SNAP!

Yallundy's Text Box: We could sell some of the excess items that we have jus—

Palcath's Interruption Text Box: Crap! I just realized that we didn't even find out if there was a puzzle or anything in Onn Forest lads, lasses, and Roodgs!

Yellow Quest Fairy's Text Box: Pal, besides monsters the only thing in there is a hidden golden chest that you will miss if you don't loo—

Lissa's Interruption Text Box: We have no way of finding out unless we go inside.

Purple Quest Fairy's Text Box: #AnnoyedGrunt.

Yallundy's Text Box: That doesn't really matter because we can find out before we go inside. The ability that I have is called *Emp*—

Fournimer's Interruption Text Box: crap! I didn't remember to complain about the glitter!

Yallundy's Text Box: That glitter is really slowing down Glii—

Anders' Interruption Text Box: Crackers! I didn't ask where my *Ultimate Dragon Cultist Prize* is!

Yallundy's Text Box: Isn't it obvious? Your *Ultimate Dragon Cultist Prize* is curr—

Zal Finn III's Interruption Text Box: Let's just see what we are dealing within that Onn Forest place.

Yallundy used the *Sigh Animation*. samuri used the *Pat on the Shoulder Dual Animation*.

◈ Chapter 7 ◈
SO BORED!

> Roodg's Text Box: fINALLY! tHE STUPID PLOT STUFF IS OVER. tHERE HAS BEEN WAY TOO MUCH TALKING! nOW WE CAN GET TO SOME SEX!

> Palcath's Text Box: Not a chance Roodg. We need to use the rest of the cycle to plan our strategy for going into Onn Forest while under leveled and under equipped.

Roodg used a *Foot Stamping Animation* which was quickly countered by Palcath with a *Having None Of It Animation*. Roodg relented and stood in the boring semi-circle with everyone else and prepared to talk about boring things.

> Palcath's Text Box: Okay lads, lass—

> Roodg's Interruption Text Box: tHE MAGES STAY BACK AND BLAST STUFF RIGHT?

> Palcath's Text Box: Well yes, but th—

> Roodg's Interruption Text Box: yES, CHECK THE ELEMENTAL WEAKNESS, i'VE HEARD YOUR PLANS BEFORE. gOOD ENOUGH? sEE YOU TOMORROW!

Roodg left the boring semi-circle and left earshot before Palcath could protest.

How many near identical strategies could that dwarf think up anyway? Roodg was sure it was a lot.

There were more important things to do than plan right now, there was sex to find! It was already Chapter 7 for Maker's sake. All of Onn was here to explore, and Roodg was determined to spice something up.

Dancing through the city, Roodg checked every nook and cranny for something sexy. Roodg checked the entire spire castle, behind the cat statue in the fountain in the town square, the empty moat around the castle, the guard towers shaped like spires, the merchant district, the secondary meowing merchant district, the castle again to double check, the path that they all had taken to get to Onn, and finally the castle again to be extra sure that there was nothing hidden in the kitten room. Exploring Onn lead Roodg to a startling conclusion.

> Roodg's Text Box: omm! tHIS PLACE IS SO BORING!

No orgies were in the streets, no closed doors were hiding a quickie, no NPCs were secretly hookers, not even following the cat that walked under the newly painted fence paid off in any love-stuck skunk action.

> Roodg's Text Box: tHIS PLACE IS ALSO FULL OF CATS.

A wolf howled in the distance. Night had fallen upon Onn and its plethora of cats. Roodg sat down on the bridge to the castle over the empty moat, defeated. The *Portie Tents* were getting set up in the town square. Roodg kicked absent mindedly and let out a *Heavy Sigh Animation*. Stupid Onn was stupid boring and it was time to go back. Roodg stood up with an audible "plink". Roodg looked around. Standing up had never caused a "plink" noise, pondering about "plinks" had never caused a random succession of "dings", and raising an eyebrow had never caused a "tilt error warning".

There was a faint light coming from the moat, right under the bridge. It was only visible now that it was night. Roodg jumped down and noticed that there were in fact two lights, directly opposite each other.

One light was coming from a small crack behind a large wall with a cat face motif. The wall itself looked as if it could move, perhaps even talk. The lights coming from within were flashing random colours. The mysterious noises heard on the bridge came from behind this cat wall.

The other light was more subtle. In a small crack of a repetitive solid brick wall was a single slightly askew brick. A faint glow was coming from this small gap. It exuded a faint hint of humidity and the murmurs of faint whispers.

The choice was obvious to Roodg.

> Roodg's Text Box: i CHOOSE NOT CATS!

> Cat Wall's Text Box: Congratulations on finding the sec—

> Roodg's Interruption Text Box: nOPE!

> Cat Wall's Text Box: But what about the tilt error warning you heard beyond me? You must be curious about that!

> Roodg's Text Box: aLREADY PICKED THE NOT CATS WALL. sORRY. tILT ERROR WARNINGS WILL BE RESOLVED IN BOOK 3 BY SOMEONE ELSE!

> Cat Wall's Text Box: Fair enough.

A solid brick wall with a single crack. The solution was obvious to Roodg. Wrap a scenic pebble with a slice of *Bacon*, place the scenic pebble against the wall, use a *Nuclear Fire Grenade* to shift the scenic pebble under the wall as the *Bacon* crisps up, hit the scenic pebble with a *Shovel*, and bingo! The slightly higher wall would give just enough room to wedge a *Sweet Peaches* pit into the wall crack and then force it to slide open. (Roodg had a lot of experience with scenery destruction.)

The wall slid away to reveal a small corridor which lead to a curtain. The curtain was as solid as a sheet of iron, dripping wet, immovable, and locked. This curtain lead to something important enough to keep well lit, steamy, and locked.

> Roodg's Text Box: wHO LOCKS CURTAINS?

> Red Quest Fairy's Text Box: This curtain was locked by NPC Zecxie. You need to be a Melee Class to even find out about this place.

> Roodg's Text Box: oH HI! i FORGOT YOU WERE FOLLOWING ME.

> Red Quest Fairy's Text Box: Hi! Don't worry, happens all the time.

> Roodg's Text Box: wHERE IS NPC Zecxie?

> Red Quest Fairy's Text Box: She will not be here until the Coliseum unlocking NPCs arrive on Cycle 30.

> Roodg's Text Box: aWE! bUT THERE NEEDS TO BE SEX HAPPENING RIGHT NOW! i AM so BORED!

> Red Quest Fairy's Text Box: There is sex happening right now! Well soon I bet, they are all kissing and giving backrubs now, but there are bulges in loincloths that are just straining to escape. I can see it behind the curtain from up here.

Frantically jumping up and down provided no hint to Roodg of what was actually happening behind the curtain. The crack in the curtain was just too high and near the roof to see beyond. There were straining loincloths so close to Roodg, but they may as well have been spires away.

> Roodg's Text Box: i CAN'T SEE THE BULGES!

> Red Quest Fairy's Text Box: You just discovered a completely secret area on a whim by using a pebble wrapped in *Bacon* to move a door. Are you really going to let not being tall enough stop you from seeing straining bulges?

The Quest Fairy was right. Roodg wasn't going to let a minor setback get into the way of a sex scene. With a *Grim Determination Animation* Roodg was in full scenery destruction mode. The combination of a *Lightning Blast* spell, liberal doses of *Furniture Polish+*, a fully absorbed *Absorbing Cloth*, three scenic vines, a *Fall to Your Knees in Defeat Animation* to get into the right position, and the stairs that let characters out of the moat were all that it took to solve the problem.

> Red Quest Fairy's Text Box: That was inspiring work.

> Roodg's Text Box: sTRAINING BULGES ARE AMAZING INSPIRATION!

> Red Quest Fairy's Text Box: How will avatars that don't know about your Vine Rope get out of the moat if they fall in?

> Roodg's Text Box: sHHHH! bULGES NOW.

Roodg danced up the stairs in victory. The first lewd glance over the curtain did not disappoint. A straining loincloth had just lost in a strenuous game of contain the large throbbing cock when the previously mentioned large throbbing cock sprung free from its forced confinement and started to bob up and down in a mesmerizing fashion. A bulbous jade green head stood proudly at the end of a forest green shaft that was accented with dark green veins. Drips of slightly green tinged cum were gathering at the slit of the member and refused to make the final desperately anticipated step of dripping off.

The big green member stared at Roodg, but due to being behind a locked curtain all Roodg could do was watch and hope that someone else would take the marvelous green member into their hands. It didn't take long for a large yellow hand to grab the green dick and start to lovingly stroke the member up and down. Just as the desperately hanging on drip of cum was about to fall and cause Roodg to grin in happy content a hearty yellow tongue greedily licked the drop up. The yellow tongue brought the tantalizing drop to a mouth that did a great job of swallowing it even with two jutting out lower tusks that should have prevented easy swallowing procedures. The mouth flicked its flat tongue along the green shaft causing the member to not only swell to a larger size and cause more drips to begin accumulating at the tip.

It took until the yellow fanged mouth fully swallowed the pulsing green member for Roodg to remember to zoom out the camera and see what was going on in the scene.

> Roodg's Text Box: oH LOOK. tWO ORCS ARE GOING AT IT!

> Red Quest Fairy's Text Box: Two orcs? I count six.

Roodg was pleasantly surprised to zoom out further and witness the entire scene. There were six orcs in the melee coliseum entry room that had been turned into a sauna with some burning coal sconces and buckets filled with a liquid that might have been water. The hot steam was filling the room with a heated haze of sticky sex, or that could have been the assortment of large sweaty orcs.

The orc with the impressive green member was as green as his cock, but his nipples and lips matched his brighter cockhead. His husky frame was heavy with muscle and a full coating of furry dark green hair. He had the biggest tusks of the bunch and they were pierced with a total of three silver rings. No hair adorned the top of his head but he did have a full beard complete with sideburns. Much of his leather armour was already tossed aside, excluding of course all of the sexy straps.

Still swallowing a green cock, the yellow orc was shorter and stockier than the others. Muscles adorned his frame but he had some extra weight units as well. His bigger belly and ample rump were jiggling as he was getting happily spanked by his green friend. Body hair covered only certain areas of his body, mostly on his jiggly bits. He had a nice mop of long dark yellow hair that was gripped tightly in a clawed green hand. His plate armour didn't even need to be removed for this, just selective pieces needed to be pushed aside.

There was a blue orc surveying the entire scene while slowly jerking off his hefty uncut dick. His impressive helmet blocked his face from view, but the helmet was the only clothing this orc with the pierced, indigo nipples (complete with a connecting silver chain) was wearing. Taller and thinner than the other orcs by a wide margin, he was also the furriest.

Tied back in a topknot with a receding hairline, the purplish hair of the purplish orc was as stoic as the orc himself. This orc was the most muscular of the bunch. It stood with crossed arms and absolutely no emotion in his face besides that of boredom. He was more oiled than the other orcs but that might have just been due to his overall lack of body hair. This orc, who regularly waxed, was getting his burly cock with the pinkish head licked greedily by the two remaining orcs. None of the chain armour he was wearing obscured any of the important places.

The two remaining orcs were brown and thankfully twins to help speed up the orc descriptions. They had beefy frames with muscular stomachs that had abs despite being of a plumper size. Roodg could see their big hairy balls hanging down between their legs as they were on their knees making out with each other as their purplish friend fucked their kissing mouths. To differentiate the twin orcs one had a short ponytail and goatee and the other a faux hawk with a five o'clock shadow. Their fur armour was identical but for the type of animal pelt used.

> Roodg's Text Box: oH NICE! bEAR ORCS! hOT.

Reaching down to make use of the bear orcs so nicely licking each other Roodg took a round to think. Six sweaty and manly orcs were enjoying a private man orgy in a sauna. This was as burly of an encounter as they came and Roodg decided to follow suit as only Roodg could. Armour was quickly pushed aside and gender swapping powers were activated to make the most of the manly display.

> Roodg's Text Box: dOUBLE PUSSY FINGERING TIME!

> Red Quest Fairy's Text Box: Well, that's something. You have both sets of parts and can switch them?

> Roodg's Text Box: yES, NOW SHHH! iT IS ABOUT TO GET GOOD AND I AM FAPPING.

The orcs were ready to take this to the next level. They gathered around a big wooden bench and the green orc and purplish orc sat on opposite sides of the table. The two growled at each other, eyes fierce, and just as the yellow orc finished making a chart on a nearby whiteboard the orcs began going at each other, in arm wrestling. The green orc lost after a heated and strained battle to the much more muscular purplish orc.

Roodg stopped fapping and watched on in confusion as the orcs took turns arm wrestling each other in a round robin style tournament. The purplish orc won every challenge without much effort, but it was the battle for second place that was most exciting (if you could call an arm wrestling contest exciting after just witnessing orc blowjobs). The final contest for second place was pretty one sided, the yellow orc was sure to win but slipped in oil and lost the match to a surprised green orc.

> Red Quest Fairy's Text Box: This is confusing.

> Roodg's Text Box: mEH. sTILL GUNNA FAP TO IT.

The two finalists met in an impromptu battle ring, stripped completely naked, rubbed themselves in copious amounts of *Orc Oil*, screamed battle-cries in orcish, charged at each other at full speed, and began a full on orc wrestling match.

> Red Quest Fairy's Text Box: Getting better.

> Roodg's Text Box: iNCREASING SPEED.

Blurs of oily orc flesh writhed against each other in a mass of purplish arms, green legs, and excited throbbing orc cocks. The bigger muscular purplish orc was winning thanks to his straining rippling muscles taking better to massive amounts of *Orc Oil*. The green orc was no match and everything he owned was getting manhandled by the bigger competitor. The purplish orc had the green orc in a submission hold that was so close to the ring's edge that a big straining orc dick was bouncing free completely out of the ring.

> Red Quest Fairy's Text Box: Wow, look at that thing bounce.

> Roodg's Text Box: zOOMING IN!

For the second time in the competition *Orc Oil* played a role in a surprise victory. The purplish orc's body took to *Orc Oil* better, everywhere, and the purplish orc's foot took far too well to the *Orc Oil* and when he tried to throw the green orc out of the ring he instead slid on the greased up floor and flew out of the ring himself. The green orc had won at *Orc Oil* wrestling and all of the other orcs congratulated him by rubbing every part of his body with their clawed hands.

> Red Quest Fairy's Text Box: I can't even keep track of all the hands!

> Roodg's Text Box: dEPLOYING SECONDARY HAND!

Shuffling over to rejoin the others, the purplish orc stopped briefly to collect the spare tub of *Orc Oil*. With a look of disappointment the purplish orc opened the tub by biting it with his big tusk and took a big dollop of *Orc Oil* in his hand. It was time for the victor to claim his prize and the purplish orc spread the cheeks of the green orc wide, greased up the puckering green hole, and deftly stuck his purplish cock all the way in with one fell swoop. The green orc cried out with exquisite bliss.

> Red Quest Fairy's Text Box: They were fighting to see who got to be the bottom?

> Roodg's Text Box: sAWESOME! cLAIM YOUR PRIZE!

Multiple colours of orc cocks where getting fiercely shoved towards the green orc all while his body was getting slapped, spanked, and twisted in pleasurable pain. His green clawed hands were busily jerking off meaty brown cocks, the blue orc cock was stuffed into the occupied hole to join the purplish cock, and the yellow cock was stuffed into the greedy green mouth. The green orc's tusks created a cradle for the heavy yellow cock, increasing the stimulation on the member and decreasing the effort needed for the mouth.

> Red Quest Fairy's Text Box: So that is why orcs have tusks. I finally understand.

> Roodg's Text Box: oRC CULTURE IS AMAZING!

Green orc flesh was quivering with need as it rocked itself back and forth on the wonderfully full cocks. As the battle progressed every colour of cock was placed deep within every different green hole. The brown twins were the first to cum out sepia toned orc spunk deep into the green orc's used hole at the same time as they were sharing the experience. The blue orc screamed out while getting an expert tusk job and shot out enough jizz to fill the green orc's mouth twice. The yellow cock couldn't find a hole in time and instead showered its load all over the writhing green body. The purplish cock held out the longest due to its impressive muscles and it continued to fuck the green orc hard well into the night.

After a mighty bellow the purplish orc came deep into the green orc ass. So much purplish cum was getting shot into the green hole that it was spilling out of the filled hole well before the purplish orc had even come close to finishing. As purplish cum was oozing out in thick streams the green orc could no longer contain himself. The joy of being pounded full of thick hot *Orc Oil* caused a gigantic explosion of the faintly green cum to shoot forth from the green orc as he grunted out in victory. The huge globs shot well across the room, coating many orcs in the process. A single strand even shot with just the right trajectory to fly right over the locked curtain and hit one of the voyeurs right in the face.

> Red Quest Fairy's Text Box: Hey! Right in my eye!

> Roodg's Text Box: lUCKY!

The orcs had already fallen asleep in a big rainbow of beef. The secret show was over.

> Red Quest Fairy's Text Box: Even with the facial, that was exciting. Should we go back?

> Roodg's Text Box: oNE ROUND. sOME OF US DIDN'T GET A FACIAL. jUST ONE MORE ROUND. oKAY. gOOD. wE CAN GO BACK TO THE PLOT NOW.

> Green Orc's Sleepy Text Box: Come back soon okay?

The Red Quest Fairy changed to *Blush Shade #Fairy*, but Roodg simply used the *Grin Animation* as they returned to the plot.

◈ Chapter 8 ◈
THE REIGN OF THE GOLDEN GRIBBLET

Researcher's Note: According to our team, progress through Onn Forest to reach the Airship was slower than the party had anticipated. Despite our researchers repeated attempts to discover the true story about this troubling time, all of the avatars within this book continually declined our requests for interviews. Here is a fragmented list of events, pieced together as best as possible from a tattered journal later found by our recovery department.

This journal somehow shifts colours by itself, our current theory is through something called magic. It is covered in blood, sweat, tears, mud, water, icing, and seven other fluids we decided not to identify. This journal has Ni Hao Bunny© on the cover; she is smiling while pulling a palm tree out of her purse.

Please note that the events in this journal are the express opinions of only one avatar and do not reflect the views of Tornado Tech Games®, their game Annals of Gentalia™, the expansion Island of Islana™ or any of their subsidiaries.

Cycle One: Our first trip into Onn Forest was a total slaughter. The enemy, a Golden Gribblet, was faster, stronger, and had higher defense than we thought possible. Just one caused a total party wipe. We can reload though, our saves have been repaired! It was not a big deal, we could now simply just try again. Nothing could keep us down and I was informed of such.

Cycle Two: I used the *Wave Animation* this morning at Gliint, he *waved* back in a

Text Box. He never uses the real animations anymore, which is sad. I miss that Gliint, but I understand his reasons.

Cycle Three: The Administrators were summoned before we went into Onn Forest in an attempt to give us some much needed Gold Coins. They did not show up.

Cycle Four: It is official. There is nowhere else we can go. We looked everywhere. Everything in this map except Onn, Onn Forest, and the port in area require Airship travel to get to from here. We are stuck here.

Cycle Five: No Administrators coming yet have put some on edge. We have simply put the *Portie Tents* up in the town square and left them there. It no longer mattered to take them down, the NPCs avoided them anyways.

Cycle Six: An official plan is formed by Palcath, Mr. Max, Lissa, and Caela. With the eye hacked stats of our Golden Gribblet tormentors it is determined how many must die before we can afford to buy new equipment thanks to their Gold Coin drop rate. We only need to kill three for the first step to be completed! Anders kills one of the foul things in a single shot! We celebrate, but the magical shot is a one-time deal. Only two more golden Gribblets to go!

Cycle Seven: Kray has demanded to be let back inside the good *Portie Tent*. It has affected the other's sleep, you can see it in their faces.

Cycle Eight: Yes, we know it is only one monster. Yes, we know it is the very first monster. Yes we are trying our best. Just shut up and actually help Kray, kay!

Cycle Nine: samuri, of all avatars, told us something. I still have no idea how. In the Expansion we have three Accessory Slots instead of two! We tried everything but only Anders was able to equip anything, and only because it was already there when he looked. I can't see *Pink Slime Jockstrap* being a standard Accessory though.

Cycle Ten: Many have given up hope in Onn Forest. We still try every chance we get but our spirits are breaking. Gliint claims to be able to hear the horrible Golden Gribblet Giggly Grunt audio clip sound even from here.

Cycle Eleven: Caela was talking in her sleep again, this time it was so loud she kept everyone up except Lissa who battled her with map shattering snores.

Cycle Twelve: This was the last cycle that we sung our friendly campfire songs. I am afraid to even take out my *String-Harper* anymore. I was informed that if it shows up out of battle again that it will be burned. It is too bad the only chest we found in Onn had a weapon for me, I can't even attack with it.

Cycle Thirteen: I found an interesting broken looking book in the castle library about the new races. Centaurs apparently are very virile and replenish their fluid levels at an alarming rate. They need to find release almost every cycle or risk blue balls. That might explain all of the experience points Anders has been gaining, the random screams at night about obscure kiss types, and how Fournimer hasn't shown signs of problems yet.

Cycle Fourteen: A particularly nasty incident with a hair-dryer occurred, I already want to forget it but just cannot.

Cycle Fifteen: Zal Finn was talking to a pair of random NPCs and for the longest time I had no idea which one she was. She talks to them almost more than she talks to us. They do like her though.

Cycle Sixteen: Lissa is getting sick of healing others all day long. Our attempts to slay more of the mighty beasts have still proven useless. Morale is at an all time low.

Cycle Seventeen: Somehow Roodg has made a sign, the ink was red. Th— ** *Tattered journal section* ** —zz it said. Some of us were concerned as the duo-sexed avatar marched back and forth in protest.

Cycle Eighteen: The boys have taken to changing out whom sleeps in the red bed. The bed is now permanently outside and the boys are slowly looking better. Apparently they switched Kray from the red bed to the green one and Kray has not noticed yet.

*** The page for Cycle Nineteen has been ripped out. ***

Cycle Twenty: We started the bartering system. There were no Gold Coins to be found anywhere, as all had been wasted on *Potions* by this point. A new official currency had developed amongst us, the all-mighty *Bacon Strip*. Mr. Max was eating like a Maker at this point, trading his *Bacon* reserves for nearly anything else he could.

Cycle Twenty-One: The constant helpful reminders from the Quest Fairies are starting to wear very thin. While they are much more comfortable around us now I am amazed they are all still even alive. Except Tyreese I guess.

Cycle Twenty-Two: Our second success! Even if it was an accidental string of critical hits, we celebrate with extra *Bacon* rations! Only one more win and we can afford the first item on our list. It is only one item, but it will help immensely I think.

Cycle Twenty-Three: The Administrators are pronounced dead by Mr. Max. Nobody really knows where they are, but I know that they are not dead. Nobody listens to me though, of course. Mr. Max *Combi-Fusioned* them a grave out of a *Headstone* (which made sense) and a *Pinch of Sexy Dangerous Pixie Dust* (which didn't).

Cycle Twenty-Four: I accidently walked in on Kray at the 'end' of a 'solo-session' looking at a Player Pager. He shot his seed just as I came in and got it in my hair. By the time the haze cleared the little jerk was gone. He never apologized.

Cycle Twenty-Five: They came from the air without warning! Breaker's Dragons. Had Palcath not been sleeping outside we would have been massacred. Spirits soar but Breaker is nowhere to be found.

Cycle Twenty-Six: I noticed something strange, samuri is never around at meals, and he must eat in private. It makes sense really, all things considered. I think I will try and talk to him about it sometime. He has nothing to be ashamed of, everyone here has something.

Cycle Twenty-Seven: Roodg might be delusional, claiming a desperate need to find Zecxie to join in on the orc train. Anders might be delusional; he claims he saw a hooded NPC figure with a cloak watching us from near the bakery.

*** Cycle Twenty-Eight only has doodles of hearts, the letter G, kitties, and bombs. ***

Cycle Twenty-Nine: Mr. Max no longer has *Bacon* for trade. Our crippled economy almost crashed without new incoming funds.

*** Cycles Thirty and Thirty-One have been made illegible due to a footprint. ***

Cycle Thirty-Two: Anders stopped fooling himself. Everyone knew that besides Mr. Max he had the biggest supply of *Bacon*. He was always pretending to eat it but sneaking appliance food. I kept trying to tell him that it was bec— *** large burn mark *** —e traded his prized *Bacon* reserves for any appliance food he could get his little elfy mitts on.

Cycle Thirty-Three: Fournimer has learned *Restful Kisses*. Not sure how he thought of saying that, but now he can replenish Stamina Points with yellow hearts. The most useless ability yet, as you can recover those by sitting down. He was not impressed.

Cycle Thirty-Four: I am getting more worried. Gliint, Zal Finn, and Kray have all claimed to have seen the hooded bakery NPC watching us. I wonder why just them?

Cycle Thirty-Five: There have become two opposing factions, those with *Bacon,* and those without.

***Cycle Thirty-Six this Page has been torn out, with teeth. ***

Cycle Thirty-Seven: After the problems we had last cycle, a new and powerful faction lead by Lissa surfaced. She rose up against the corrupt *Bacon* oppressor and took down the regime. The once *Bacon* starved feasted like royalty.

Cycle Thirty-Eight: Caela was arguing with herself in her sleep again. I caught either Zal Finn or a random NPC listening at the door but I used the *Scowl Animation* and they left.

Cycle Thirty-Nine: Additional food sources have begun to dwindle. Alarm sets in as we discover that the only foods in Onn were extremely expensive due to having strange and useless benefits. They were all themed to the bakery next to our camp and smelled so great. The smell however was deceiving and they all tasted even worse than normal appliances. Plus they had an aftertaste that wou— ** *Tears mark the page* ** —thout any income to speak of once cherished possessions had slowly been sold off just so we can afford some of the ill tasting treats. Starving to death would be marginally better than eating another one of those pastries.

Cycle Forty: Zal Finn has stopped showing up for battle, she is listless. We cannot find her during the days despite looking everywhere. Every NPC in this town looks just like her, which makes it impossible. We are tired of hearing "Welcome to *Onn*!" while talking to NPCs looking for her and decide to just let her hav— ** *Mud obscures the rest* **

Cycle Forty-One: I found where samuri eats his meals. He noticed me come up and got startled, trying to hide his *Double Danish*. I gave him an *Understanding Hug Animation* and he gave me a *Smile Animation* in return.

Cycle Forty-Two: Anders and Gliint both have claimed to have seen the hooded Bakery NPC with an actual Quest Bubble above it. Their afternoon 'smell-the-baked-goods-while-drooling sessions' now are over.

Cycle Forty-Three: Caela threw Kray out of her *Portie Tent Ultra+* in the middle of the night. Apparently, he had been sneaking in for awhile now. That does explain all the extra soot near the fire I have been vacuuming up lately. Caela was yelling at the sooty elf at double volume. I didn't know that Caela slept in her old *Initiate's Jacket* and nothing else. It makes sense, it is all cute and fluffy, even if it barely cov— ** *big soot stain* ** —gina.

Cycle Forty-Four: It was inevitable. Tensions mounted. Anders shot Kray in the back after being called chubby for the eight hundred and seventy-sixth time that I had counted. You could see the fire burning in Anders' eyes since he used the *Fire Burning in Eyes Animation*. Nothing fatal happened as neither was broken for PVP. Kray had his back turned and felt something, but didn't notice what had stung him. Anders looked a little happier and now Kray has an arrow sticking out of his back, likely permanently as Kray never sleeps.

Cycle Forty-Five: The Dragons are becoming relentless. They prowl the skies and attack us on sight. They provide no experience and only further dwindle our resources. Whenever one dies it simply turns into a ball of light and drifts away.

Cycle Forty-Six: This cycle will always be remembered as The Cycle The *Bacon* Ran

Out. We all ate our last pieces bravely together. There was more team spirit than had been seen for a very long time. Anders got sick on his *Bacon*, I tried to tell him that it w— ** **large blood smeared section** ** —ry called him super fatty, kay.

Cycle Fifty-Seven: Gliint is arguing with Fournimer for some reason I don't really know why, the only word I heard was 'woman'.

Cycle Fifty-Eight: A vicious day for Dragon attacks, all but the Blue Dragon attacked us. Fournimer saved either Zal Finn or a random NPC woman from a deadly tail attack.

** *Cycle Fifty-Nine until Cycle Sixty-Three have all been ripped out.* **

Cycle Sixty Four: I noticed that Anders, Lissa, Caela, Kray, samuri, and Gliint were all talking. They were all in good spirits for once and were taking wagers on something related to Mr. Max. I don't know what.

Cycle Sixty-Five: Mr. Max has taken to attacking walls in an attempt to let off steam or gain experience. Nobody is really sure which.

Cycle Sixty-Six: samuri has started to help Mr. Max attack the walls.

Cycle Sixty-Seven: Gliint woke up during his turn in the red bed with the hooded Bakery NPC staring him right in the face, Quest Marker clearly visible. Poor Gliint used an Animati— ** ***Conveniently smeared section to protect interesting plot developments later*** ** — all wet. Only Kray, Anders, Zal Finn, and I believe the poor gnome. I am just glad he was alright. We step up the night watch, someone is now always awake.

Cycle Sixty-Eight: There was a WorldForums post about the old map. Things have gotten really bad there. I think we need to appreciate what we have here, but I doubt anyone agrees.

Cycle Sixty-Nine: Mr. Max has finally cut down a building. A small tower near the castle has fallen to his might. We did not gain any experience, but it falling did accidently destroy a small family home and we found enough Gold Coins inside to split a *Double Danish*.

Cycle Seventy: Mr. Max had a breakthrough. He can now suddenly remember Kray's name. For some reason, that I will never understand, the only avatar that gets upset about this is Kray. Lissa, Caela, Gliint, Anders, and samuri are overjoyed at this turn of events. After all the arguments previously with Mr. Max about forgetting names, now they are all happy about it?

Cycle Seventy-One: Yes, he remembers your name Kray, we get it, kay. It is a good thing. Why are you so pissed off? Drop it already.

Cycle Seventy-Two: Shut up Kray! Nobody likes you!

Cycle Seventy-Three: Kray finally calmed down and stopped arguing with Mr. Max about remembering his name. Mr. Max sparked a four Cycle long argument with the fright elf husk and didn't even know why. There is a very good chance that both of them are indeed a meatboneheads as claimed.

Cycle Seventy-Four: The Quest Fairies are plotting against us, at least according to Palcath. The dwarf may have gone off the deep end, but he is telling all of us to watch out for them.

Cycle Seventy-Five: Palcath and Lissa went off to — ** *Rest of page is water soaked* ** **

Cycle Seventy-Six: I see a verbal fight break out but am not close enough to hear. Palcath and Fournimer were arguing about something. When Lissa, Roodg, Mr. Max, and Anders showed up it turned into a more logical debate. They laughed a bit and to me it looked as if they all felt very foolish. The fight ends with some Animations; Anders used the *Embarrassed Animation*, Mr. Max used the *Flex Animation*, and Fournimer used the *Scowl Animation*.

Cycle Seventy-Seven: It is a miracle! Anders had enough magic power to kill three of the stupid things in one run! It makes sense now that I think about it. I wonder who is filling him up and why they kept interrupting me when I asked about this. Everyone was in grand spirits. Even Zal Finn showed up from the NPC woodwork. When the Yellow Dragon showed up it was quick— ** *Black smudge* ** —sson it will not soon forget.

Cycle Seventy-Eight: The first item was purchased. It was a pair of gloves for Anders. Many were confused and Kray complained a lot about the purchase. When Anders' Bow and Sword auto-upgraded it shut up Kray. Possibly for the first time ever. Roodg claims to have discovered the Healer's Gate, when others come to look and discoved it is just a brick wall Roodg is ignored for several cycles.

Cycle Seventy-Nine: These little bastards sure can drop the Gold Coins and Experience. Now that we have gold coins and Anders could shoot again nearly everyone was in good spirits. Fournimer still hadn't talked to anyone for cycles. We feasted on ill tasting pastry and the little bastard's dropped *Golden Gribblet Pickles*. Appliances have never tasted so good.

Cycle Eighty: Nobody could find Fournimer this morning. His spear was a vital part of the attack plan. I had seen the Centaur leave towards the long abandoned port in area the night before and knew where to look. I found him and he was upset. We had a talk and a hug. It has been awhile since I've been to the port in area but I swear this place smells different and there are less Quest fairy lights.

Cycle Eighty-One: Roodg was outside the castle randomly casting magic on a streetlamp for several rounds. Eventually the streetlamp melted and Roodg dragged it away to use as a bridge to get to a closer look at the Healing Court of the Unseelie Queen, whatever that was.

Cycle Eighty-Two: Progress is finally being made. We have nearly completed Weapon Acquisition. Unfortunately, step two is Armour, this will take some time.

*** Cycle Eighty-Three until Cycle Ninety-Six are all blank ***

Cycle Ninety-Seven: Finally, things are getting more back to normal. Spirits and outfits are at an all time high. The *Golden Gribblet Pickles* drops are sweet like appliance flavoured candy compared to the bakery items. Even the creepy hooded bakery NPC does not stop anyone's good time anymore! I wonder why can only the Ranged Classes can see him? Even I can't get a read on him. Fournimer and my chats are continuing in our secret place, he is a sweetheart.

Cycle Ninety-Eight: In an attempt to help save the excitement in the original map the Developers announced an idea. There would be a new Insta-Wiki Contest. A winning team could be allowed entrance to the Expansion early. If we allow this the Expansion will be locked for everyone else for an additional 100 cycles, for a total of 300. There is much debate but we are given a secret ballot. It passes 7 For, 6 Against. Breaker also voted given the numbers, but I can't determine who voted which way. I voted yes in the hopes that they have money we can borrow.

Cycle Ninety-Nine: I knew this would happen eventually. Fourni and Anders had a big fight. I talked to both afterwards. I really don't know what the main issue is, but since it stems from the charged magic arrows Anders shoots, it must be related to how Anders is getting mana.

Cycle One Hundred: Have we really been stuck in Onn for 100 cycles already? That is more insane that Roodg's glee for claiming to need all of the *Fence Posts* in town to help reach the Den of the Magic Mushgrooms thanks to there not being a Higgins to talk to.

Cycle One Hundred-One: I spotted Gliint and Fourni fighting again. Gliint got really mad at Four— *** clear smears dot much of this page *** —elped Fourni clean up afterwards. I am pretty sure Fourni had no idea what happened, he had been pent up for awhile and had passed out at the release.

Cycle One Hundred Two: I really need to work on not destroying important parts of my journal. Every time something comes up that is secretly plot related something happens to the page. It is probably just my *Emp*— *** plot smear *** —alking.

Cycle One Hundred Three: We finally went past the first stupid monster in the *Onn*

Forest!

Cycle One Hundred Four: This *Onn* Forest is so darn confusing, warps are everywhere. Nobody is impressed. Now that we can kill things here we have no idea where to go.

Cycle One Hundred Five: Note on *Onn* Forest directions: Up, Down, Up, Down, Left, Right, Left, Right… then where do we go?

Cycle One Hundred Six: Well it isn't up, left, down, or right next. There must be another way to go or something we missed.

Cycle One Hundred Seven: Caela was arguing with herself about the directions in *Onn* Forest. Part of Caela thinks that the next direction is up. The other part thinks it is down. Personally I think I agree with the down part.

Cycle One Hundred Eight: Anders, Fourni, and I went to our spot and talked. Really talked. They t— ** *It looks like tears had hit and smudged the writing* ** — and when they came back Anders had gained a Level! That sly horse.

Cycle One Hundred Nine: samuri has really opened up lately during our meals together. Despite all my efforts though I still haven't gotten him to Text Box even a single word. He does use animations though.

Cycle One Hundred Ten: I wonder how many more times I will catch Zal Finn up after hours hanging around Lissa's room? I think that the first time I caught her snooping she was only accidently eavesdropping on Caela on her way to eavesdrop on Lissa. Just tell her already Zal.

Cycle One Hundred Eleven: Where is Roodg going every night? Come to think of it I haven't seen hir after dinner since ever. It must have something to do with all the missing fences.

Cycle One Hundred Twelve: While Zal Finn was snooping around all night she accidently caught Kray snooping around in our tent again. Caela's fury was intense. She used her entire mana bar on the little soot stain, almost even using one of her tightly guarded *Mana Potions*.

Cycle One Hundred Thirteen: NPC Shopkeeper Franklin's Wife Mandy was accidently hit off her walking path by the green dragon today and fell onto a scenic woodcutting axe, chopping her in two. She had no quests and was technically useless here, but still, sad.

Cycle One Hundred Fourteen: We found an obscure post in the WorldForums by someone named Yvi. It speaks in riddles but after many rounds Caela claimed to have figured it out. She believes that it is from the missing Administrator Ivy. Roughly translated it comes out to: Stop asking for help you idiots! We know where you are. We have a lot of stuff on our plates. What in The Flaming Pit is taking you all so long! Hurry the fuck up and get to the Makerdamn Airship already!

Cycle One Hundred Fifteen: Roodg keeps vanishing at night so I talked to samuri and he agreed to help with a *Nod Animation*. We simply could not find Roodg after dinner. We had an idea, next cycle we are going to follow hir.

Cycle One Hundred Sixteen: samuri and I followed Roodg into an alleyway after dinner, when we turned a corner however there was nothing. It was as if the avatar had vanished into exceptionally thin air.

Cycle One Hundred Seventeen: There was a winner to the secondary Insta-Wiki Contest. The new avatars are showing up on Cycle 125. We have vowed to be out of here before then for some reason. We are close to breaking the Onn Forest. They kept interrupting me when I said I already knew the way out due to my *Empathy*. Let them find it themselves then if they can't listen to me. Interrupt all you want when I am talking, find the way yourselves.

Cycle One Hundred Eighteen: samuri, Caela, and I followed Roodg, closer this time. The same alleyway lead to the same results. A vanished Roodg. After much exploration and Caela arguing with herself about it, samuri accidently found a secret door by using the *Lean Animation* against the wall. Roodg was deep underground in a very long hallway that ended at a strange doorframe that was missing the actual door portion. Roodg claimed to have found this final ranged room while attacking a window some time ago. Much noise could be heard from the other side of the door, but it wouldn't open. Despite staying up far too late none of us could manage to figure out what this was for, all we knew is that Roodg claimed that whatever was behind here had to be sAWESOME.

Cycle One Hundred Nineteen: We are ready to leave at a moment's notice. We have every new Weapon and Armour. The Armour is not rated (s). It is all so boring to look at that it isn't even worth describing. It does have high stats, but not as high as the Gigas Gear some have. Onn would have been so exciting if we had gold coins when we got here. We do look pretty modest now, and none of us have the right items to throw in with the *Portable Anvil* to spice them up. It is strange, but not being (s) is disappointing. We even now have a stash of *Potions* and appliance pastry for backup.

Cycle One Hundred Twenty: Searching through this annoying puzzle of a location has earned us so much experience. Even if they just had to keep going left, it took them far too long to figure that out. Mr. Max has reached Level 98.97 (and he is beyond excited and will not shut up about it), samuri is 78 and Anders just got to 74. Everyone else averages out at Level 69.

Cycle One Hundred Twenty-One: Anders and Fourni asked me to meet them at the special place tomorrow night. They need to Text Box to me about something important. About my Gliint problem, whatever that means. I am nervous but will still go, and I certainly do not have a problem with Gliint. He is the only one who doesn't interrupt me.

Cycle One Hundred Twenty-Two: They have found the way out! There was a glade to one side and to the other was the Airship! We were going to leave this accursed *Onn* next cycle, and can get going on our mission before those other avatars show up. When we got back to camp Anders and Kray were missing, nobody had seen what happened to them. We tried to go back to look but everything had respawned! We needed to rest. We would have to look next cycle. Nobody was in good spirits anymore. I couldn't sleep, I was too worried. Fourni came and asked if we could go for a walk.

*** The Ni Hao Bunny© Journal ends here ***

◊ Chapter 9 ◊
THE ELF OFF

> Kray's Text Box: You're just jealous, kay!

> Anders' Text Box: Kay, for the last time, I am NOT jealous!

> Kray's Text Box: Of course you are, kay. You have been jealous of me since we first met!

> Anders' Text Box: I am not jealous. I am worried, kay!

> Kray's Text Box: Nope. Jealous. Kay.

> Anders' Text Box: Don't you remember what the Spiderboy said after he tied us up here?

> Green Quest Fairy's Text Box: The Spiderboy is not relevant to any quests.

Kray hung upside down and was immobile. He was completely wrapped up in webs. His arms were stuck crossed had given him a permanent look of smugness. Anders thought it was appropriate, as the avatar nearly always had them crossed like this anyways. His black sooty skin and sunken in features under the *Webbed Status* looked very realistic given the circumstances. It was as if the avatar had already been eaten by a spider.

> Kray's Text Box: Of course I do, kay! The Spiderboy said that when he got back here he was going to have sex with the cute one, and then eat the ugly one!

> No-Colour Quest Fairy's Text Box: Yeah well, the Spiderboy is not relevant to any quests.

Anders, who was tangled in webs, had his arms stuck behind his back. Struggling had proven useless. He could only really move his arms, but his hands were completely covered in the web. For some reason webs were not considered a trap, so Anders' still neglected *Auto-Trap Release* item did not activate.

> Anders' Text Box: Yes, that is what the Spiderboy said exactly, kay. What is concerning me is that after that he said that he was going to get his friend.

> Green Quest Fairy's Text Box: The Spiderboy is not relevant to any quests.

> Kray's Text Box: Big deal, kay! You are just scared to find out that I am the cute one and that you are going to be dinner.

> Anders' Text Box: No, I am scared because the Spiderboy said that he was going to let his friend have sex with the ugly one, and then eat the pretty one, kay!

> Green Quest Fairy's Text Box: The Spiderboy is not relevant to any quests.

> Kray's Text Box: It will be worth it to know that I am the pretty one, kay!

> Anders' Text Box: Either way we will both end up dead! Maybe even dead dead, kay! We haven't died to a boss yet or gotten eaten. Now can you please try to bite through the webs that are on my wrists already? You could probably reach them if you just tried!

> Kray's Text Box: No way, kay. We are not going anywhere until we find out who the Spiderboy thinks is the pretty one!

> No-Colour Quest Fairy's Text Box: Yeah well, the Spiderboy is not relevant to any quests.

Anders didn't understand this lunatic, or how he thought. How could being called prettier possibly be worth sacrificing yourself? Also, saying kay in every darn Text Box was not only annoying, it was infectious! Anders made a mental note to try and stop doing it.

> Anders' Text Box: Kay, fine. You win already! You are the pretty one. Now shut up and bite my cuffs!

Anders' Text Box was accented by a loud grumble from his stomach. They hadn't eaten anything all cycle.

> Kray's Text Box: Not good enough chunky butt, kay. We are waiting until the Spiderboy gets back and that is final! Why don't you eat some more while we wait?

> No-Colour Quest Fairy's Text Box: Yeah well, the Spiderboy is not relevant to any quests.

The constant fat jokes had started to become more than hurtful. Anders looked at his naked self hanging from the webs and then used the *Sigh Animation*. He really did feel fatter, and he was positive that he even looked fatter now. Every morning he would look at himself in the mirror (that was in Kray's old room) and feel a little bit worse about himself. Anders wasn't exactly sure if avatars could get eating disorders, but he was pretty sure that he was developing one.

Anders decided to use the intense feelings he was having on this round and use them to lash out at Kray, instead of continuing to feel bad about himself.

> Anders' Text Box: I am only stuck here because I tried to save you from the web glade, the least you could do is get us out of here you skinny little fright elf jerk! Thank you for reminding me that bosses are perverts that want to rape us, I had nearly forgotten all about the rape!

> Kray's Text Box: Kay, you are so welcome! Also, I am a skinny little elf, aren't I! Jealous much?

Before Anders could press Enter and send his Text Box reply that told the skinny little elf where to go and what bakery item to ride to get there, the web began to tremble. Anders looked up and saw that the Spiderboy had returned. He was a light purple skinned elf from the waist up. His ears were bigger than a normal elf's and he had delicate, ethereal features. He had long flowing white hair that sparkled like the web. If not for the fact that he had eight eyes he could even be mistaken for an elf. He was even wearing a little vest, snug that hugged his lean physique.

His lower body however looked nothing like an elf. His torso was attached to a large spider body and it came out from where the head the spider would be. The body was shiny and slick, with large stripes of red covering the otherwise black body. He reminded

Anders of a black widow (which did exist here, but where the size of helicopters).

The Spiderboy's friend appeared next. It was just a lazy palette swap of the Spiderboy. He looked exactly the same except that it had slightly lighter skin, a blue vest and green stripes on its body instead of red.

Anders still thought bugs were neat. However he was not impressed that one of these things was going to eat him sometime later. Even if he probably would just respawn, having your insides melt into goo to get sucked up by a pervert would be unpleasant.

The two Spiderboys grinned, revealing their fanged mouths, and went over to their respective targets. Anders had a giant boost of confidence when the Spiderboy with the red stripes came over and started to kiss him. He was the pretty one! One of the Spiderboy's fangs pierced the elf's tongue and delivered a little bit of venom. It made the entire area feel a little bit numb but warm. Despite the horror of what would occur later Anders was still the pretty one and couldn't help but use the *Smile From Ear to Ear Animation*!

> Kray's Text Box: See kay! I *kiss* told you so. I am the *kiss* pretty one! The original Spiderboy *kiss* came after *kiss kiss* … *kiss* me!

> No-Colour Quest Fairy's Text Box: Yeah well, the Spiderboy is not relevant to any quests.

What was wrong with Kray? The original Spiderboy was the red one. It was clearly the green one fingering his hole. That took some serious ignorance of the actual facts. Maybe there was more wrong with this elf than just being a skinny little dried up jerk husk. Anders couldn't think too much on it though, the ORIGINAL Spiderboy's kisses were filled with little bites. Each bite felt warm and made Anders feel strange. It took him a few rounds until he could place it. The bites were intoxicating; each little bite was getting him more and more drunk. Now that this game had alcohol use as well, the rating would surely go up!

> (Green) Spiderboy's Text Box: You were right dude, he is totally my type. I'm so into this! A bit tight and dry though.

> (Red) Spiderboy's Text Box: Mine feels open and really wet.

Anders had relaxed quickly to the probing fingers of the Red Spiderboy and moaned. Despite the horror of what would happen after this, the alcoholic bites had done an excellent job of lowering his inhibitions. The Spiderboys were climbing all over the webs and biting the elves everywhere. After a few well placed bites, Anders was ready for what was going to happen next.

The Spiderboys lined themselves up for the next phase of this encounter. Despite themselves, both elves were giggling and having a very good time of it.

> (Green) Spiderboy's Text Box: I've near run out of spit, I don't think that I am going to get into this elf.

> Kray's Text Box: Sure you can, kay, just squeeze my nuts a little!

The green striped Spiderboy complied with a none too gentle squeeze. Kray yelled out in either pleasure or pain, Anders wasn't certain. Two squirts of the elf's cum shot out. One landed directly where Kray had aimed it, on his own face, while the other landed in Anders' *#6 Hairstyle*. Anders was certain that Kray had done that on purpose, but before he could complain he got a whiff of the seed.

For a few rounds Anders vision clouded over, as if his entire body had relaxed. It was not mistakable for anything else. Kray had just shot out his own flavour of super entrance relaxing *Minotaur Musk*. The lovely stuff had relaxed Kray as well, as the green Spiderboy was already buried deep inside.

> (Green) Spiderboy's Text Box: Wow, this thing is as tight as fuck!

> Kray's Text Box: Jealous chunky? Urgh! I can take all 12 Length Units with hardly a problem! Good luck doing that with that chunky butt of yours! All yours can do is store fat, kay!

12 Length Units was really nothing compared to the challenges that Anders had faced before with his butt of holding. The look on Kray's face made it obvious that was very close to his maximum, if not just past it.

With barely any trouble the Red Spiderboy had bottomed out in Anders. The strange spider penis was rippled and the constant expanding and contracting delivered many sensations to Anders and the elf was tingling out pleasure notes like a pro.

> (Red) Spiderboy's Text Box: Crap! This one tingles. It is like full of magic jelly or something. Damn it feels good.

> Kray's Text Box: Kay, so Anders is full of jelly? That is what makes him so special? Everyone likes him so much because of jelly? That's just stupid.

Suddenly, Anders had a plan. He was pretty drunk at this point, but he was also pretty sure that he was still lucid enough for this to work. There was only one problem with this plan however. It turned his stomach, but for this to work he needed to be nice. While he was nice almost all the time, the problem was for this to work he was going to have to be nice to Kray. He swallowed his pride (plus two Spiderboy fingers) and put it into motion.

Doing his best to create as many tingles as possible Anders moved back and forth on the hard chitin covered member. Once the red Spiderboy was really enjoying himself Anders bit his own lip, hard. The intense pain stopped the tingles abruptly and the Spiderboy was upset. Anders Text Boxed while still tasting the blood.

> Anders' Text Box: It is all out of tingles for now. It will start up again if you change positions. Put me on my back and then enter me again.

The Spiderboy was not thinking right, and wanted to feel the intense tingles again. Anders was released from the webs and soon was on the ground. The Spiderboy was getting ready to enter again when Anders interrupted.

> Anders' Text Box: No wait, I just need to move a bit this way, and then turn a bit. Just give me a round here.

> (Red) Spiderboy's Text Box: Why do you need to—

> Anders' Interruption Text Box: Okay big Spiderboy! Go for it!

> Green Quest Fairy's Text Box: The Spiderboy is not relevant to any quests.

That was close, the Spiderboy had almost snapped out of his sexual frenzy. Once the elf gave him the go ahead though the Spiderboy was again lost in the moment. Anders was penetrated and he did his best to move on the Spiderboy's rippled cock. While the feeling of it was nice he wanted to make sure of a few things. One, that the tingles would happen again and two, that the rock he had positioned himself over would cut through his bindings during the heavy thrusting.

The red Spiderboy was happily plowing into Anders, both cutting the bindings slowly and pleasuring both sides. With a particularly nice thrust Anders felt his bindings give way. The Spiderboy enjoyed himself so much he was completely oblivious to the fact that he was now lined up exactly were Anders wanted him to be, with his spider face right next to Kray's crotch. He let forth a mass of tingles and quickly grabbed his nearby (and newly changed) *Fangbow+* while the Spiderboy was distracted. With the *Fangbow+* charging secretly behind his back the hardest part of this plan would have to begin. He was going to have to be nice to the skinny little jerk hanging above.

> Anders' Text Box: Kray, you were right. I am… I am jealous of you!

Kray perked up upon hearing this.

> Kray's Text Box: Really, kay?

> Anders' Text Box: Yes. I'm sorry that I denied it this long. It is just that I was so jealous! You are so thin and hot that I just couldn't stand it.

> Kray's Text Box: I knew it, kay!

This was having the exact effect that Anders had hoped for. With each compliment Kray's equipment would twinge happily. Anders started to lay it on thick.

> Anders' Text Box: You are so much better at the Hair Braiding Skill

> than me!

> Kray's Text Box: Kay, Ahhh!

> Anders' Text Box: You deserved to sleep in the girls' *Portie Tent* and I didn't!

> Kray's Text Box: Kay, Ahhhhh!

> Anders' Text Box: I am sorry about the incident with your hair-dryer! You were right!

> Kray's Text Box: Kay, Ahhhhhhhhh!

> Anders' Text Box: I am really chunky, compared to you I am like a Bluegra Whale!

> Kray's Text Box: Kay, Ahhhhhhhhhhhh!

> Anders' Text Box: You are a much better gay elf than me!

> Kray's Text Box: YES!!!! … Kay!

That last one did it. Kray had been complimented to orgasm and began to shoot his musky elf spunk into the face of the red Spiderboy. Overcome with the relaxing vapours the Spiderboy stopped his actions.

Anders had just enough time before the musk cleared to reveal his *Fangbow+*, shoot and *Sneak Attack* kill the green Spiderboy with his charged up shot, collect their equipment, open the red chest in the glade, and use his sword to dramatically slash Kray free from his bindings. An Anders dressed in only a cute pink jockstrap carrying a naked Kray flashed out of view for the stunned red Spiderboy. The Spiderboy came to and shot his web seed onto the ground but was too stunned to react or give chase.

> Anders' Text Box: See you later Spiderboy!

> Green Quest Fairy's Text Box: The Spiderboy is not relev—

> Anders' Interruption Text Box: Then why is he on the Book Cover?!

Anders was pleased with how that worked. Kray was so pleased with the compliment induced orgasm that he had passed out in a self righteous coma. Now that Anders was safe he could complete the Insta-Wiki for the Spiderboy.

> **Creature Name:** Spiderboy
> **Class:** Taur
> **Level:** 68

Special Attacks: Webshot, Ensnare, Ensnare More, Spiderbite, Widow-maker, Drain

Drops: Tough Web

First Player Encounter Notes: The Spiderboy is not relevant to any quests. – Anders

There was nothing Anders could do now but wait. It was nearly nightfall and he was still feeling pretty drunk on venom. He was camped right near the Airship and everyone would be here next cycle.

Anders wasn't sure why he did what he did next. Perhaps it was just all the pent up sexual energy, or the Spiderboy venom still coursing through his veins. It might have been the cycles and cycles of constant torment from Kray, or maybe even just the events of the past few rounds. It might have been how Kray had been willing to sacrifice them both to prove a point, or it might have been the incident with the hair-dryer. Whatever the real reason, to Anders if felt like the right thing to do and he did not regret it.

Pulling down his Slime Jockstrap Anders began to masturbate furiously. Smiling as he stuck a now bendable finger into his still relaxed entrance, he began to thrust in and out to increase the pleasure. Within just a few rounds of intense sensation Anders began to cum. Aiming carefully he managed to get every single drop of it onto the unconscious Kray's burnt red *#3 Flippy Hairstyle*.

Anders' Text Box: Jerk.

◈ Chapter 10 ◈
A DRAMATIC ENTRANCE

Y allundy's Text Box: Thank you for taking me here Fourni.

Fournimer's Text Box: no problem Sparkle, I really couldn't sleep either.

Yallundy's Text Box: I know you are worried about him, you shouldn't be though I can just feel him around. I don't know why, I just can.

Fournimer's Text Box: thank you. that helps. it is getting late though. I think we should probably get back.

Yallundy rested her hand on Fournimer's horse's back and gave it a pat and a good scratch. It was hard to not treat the horse section of Fournimer like a real horse.

Yallundy's Text Box: I agree, let's get back to ever—

Gliint's Interruption Text Box: So this is where you are always sneaking off to! *angry face* How could you Yallundy? With a horse no less!

A shocked Yallundy tried to reply, but just couldn't. For the first time ever Gliint had interrupted her. Her heart sunk a frame.

> Fournimer's Text Box: wow Gnome, calm down!

> Gliint's Text Box: Enough lies! I will not let you take my woman! *fist shake* Also, the nickname Gnome is lame and you should be ashamed!

> Fournimer's Text Box: your woman? you have it all wrong here. Sparkle and I are just friends! also, that nickname is way better than the one I gave Kray!

> Gliint's Text Box: Prepare to eat my Chemist *Blast Bomb* Pallyboy!

> Brown Quest Fairy's Text Box: The Prepare To Bomb Quest requires a minimum of four avatars to complete fully. *Thumbs up!*

Fournimer stomped his hooves in the dirt. It should have intimidated the small Gliint, but the gnome did not back down.

> Fournimer's Text Box: good luck little gnome, I can run circles around you now that I've practiced running in circles!

The gnome would not be intimidated. Gliint sparked up one of his *Blast Bombs* and lit the fuse.

> Gliint's Text Box: Die you woman steal—

> Yallundy's Very First Interruption Text Box: STOP THIS RIGHT NOW! BOTH OF YOU!

Gliint and Fournimer stopped in their tracks. Gliint absent mindedly dropped his Bomb, which rolled just a Move Unit away and exploded almost harmlessly. This was the first time Gliint couldn't move for a reason other than lag.

> Yallundy's Text Box: Fourni and I are just friends, Gliint!

> Gliint's Text Box: Is this true?

The little gnome stared down (stared up) the much larger Centaur. Fournimer held his ground, but got exceptionally aroused while doing so. Fournimer still couldn't remember what had happened after the little gnome had stomped his feet at the centaur so many cycles ago, but he didn't want a reminder. He needed to calm down the gnome quickly, and before Gliint used a real animation.

> Fournimer's Text Box: yes! Dude and I were going to talk to her tonight about you. then Anders went missing so we couldn't.

> Gliint's Text Box: *Eyebrow raise* About… me?

> Fournimer's Text Box: yes about you, and you just proved our point

> Gnome!

> Gliint's Text Box: *Another eyebrow raise* I did?

> Fournimer's Text Box: you both obviously have feelings for each other but are way too shy to say anything! just stop pretending already and kiss each other! I can't handle the drama anymore.

His own words struck Fournimer pretty hard. He was pretty sure that described his own situation exactly (with multiple avatars).

> Gliint's Text Box: Is that true Yallu—

Yallundy interrupted a Text Box yet again, but this time by picking up the little gnome in her big troll arms and kissing him deeply. Fournimer thought it was a little bit odd, since she was easily three times his size. The kiss went on for many rounds, and Gliint only lagged out once during the experience, a new personal best.

> Yallundy's Text Box: Yes!

The moment ended with the sound of a *Zing*.

> Fournimer's Text Box: what was that?

> Gliint's Text Box: *Smile* You wouldn't know, but that is the sound of a new avatar coming into the expansion.

The Zing noise continued to get louder, soon it was too painful to hear and the avatars were covering their ears.

> Fournimer's Text Box: then what is that?

> Gliint's Text Box: *Wince* Something is wrong!

Some vague shapes were beginning to materialize in the nearby cave. The Zing had started to vibrate the rocks, the ground, and even the air. Energy began to gather into the area, large circles of black met in the centre of the cave. The entire thing felt broken and wrong. Something clicked with the mechanics of what was happening and Gliint understood, he jumped in the way of the cave and used his body as a shield.

> Gliint's Text Box: GET BACK YALLUNDY! IT'S A BOMB!

The bomb detonated with intense force.

> Yallundy's Text Box: GLIINT NO!

~ ~ ~

Breaker used the *Smirk Animation*. Trying to let in new avatars into this world, not on his watch. He had voted no for a reason. The Codexplosion had gone off exactly as planned and scattered the remains of that new party all over the map. There would be no new avatars here ever again to interfere with his plans of revenge. Only he could travel back and forth to the main game now. The fact that three of the regulation old idiots were standing right beside the cave was only icing on the *Grand Fullcake*.

This Bomb, which he had named *Breaker's Bomb of Awesomeness*, was the second step of his plan. It was really step eight, but these idiots had spent so long in *Onn* that this had gotten pushed up. Now that the *Breaker's Bomb of Awesomeness* went off it would break not only the portal to this world, but the entire world. He had to push this part of the plan up as well thanks to the early arrival of new avatars. Now however, there would never be a new avatar coming in here to interrupt his plans and nobody here could ever go back!

Best of all those idiots were now forever broken! Hacking the very world itself, it was genius! Breaker laughed with the *Laugh Animation*. Hopefully, one of those three idiots over there just tested permanent death for him. He would need to monitor them to find out.

Rigging the portal to explode was far easier than changing the Code on his own abilities. That Codexplosion to destroy the world was nothing compared to attempting to just tweak his dragons. Coding on things or items was so much easier than avatar Code, it was impossible to alter his appearance so he couldn't have wicked demon horns, but he was finally starting to get the hang of ability altering. Testing the effects was by far the longest part of the process, taking at least a cycle after each change.

It was well worth it though, now he could send the Dragons wherever he wanted. Multiple times in one battle even. Currently they were out patrolling the world, attacking any avatar on sight. The Dragons had managed to kill a few, but at least now if one succeeded it would be permanent. It was annoying to wait for the next part of his plan to happen, but at least these morons have given him more than enough time to prepare.

He finished watching the debris fall from the Codexplosion. He was greeted by a huge Purple Dragon nuzzling his neck. This meant that there were avatars near the Airship site now, it was time to get ready for step one of his plan, that was now step three. Finally the pace was picking up.

With a Stretching Out of His Wings and a Dramatic Movement of his Claws Animation Breaker flew off into the night.

~ ~ ~

Palcath's Text Box: This is just great. First those lads Anders and Kray go missing. Then Fourni and Lundy disappear. Now that little lad Glint is gone!

Caëlahenâilenŵhei's Text Box: Do you suspect that these incidents are related?

White Quest Fairy's Text Box: Returning The Related is a quest that involves several stages of fetching. To get this quest go to Spi—

Palcath's Interruption Text Box: It is strange that they are all happening right before we leave here, but I don't think so lass.

Roodg's Text Box: wE NEED TO FIND THEM! i WANT TO LEAVE oNN soooooo BAD!

Zal Finn III's Text Box: Well, we think we know where the gayboys are, so we should spend our time looking for the rest!

Lissa's Text Box: Let's hurry. We only have a few more cycles to get out of here before those other avatars show up.

Palcath's Text Box: No we don't lass.

Mr. Max's Text Box: Yes we do dwarf Man! The new avatars are coming on cycle 125. We have only been here at The Siege of the Golden Gribblet for 122 cycles.

Palcath's Text Box: No, they will be here this cycle.

Caëlahenâilenŵhei's Text Box: Your math is incorrect again dwarf.

Palcath's Text Box: I keep telling you lass, except for that one time when it was wrong, my math is never wrong!

Lissa's Text Box: Crap. He's right. I forgot we waited for 2 whole cycles for Fournicanter to show up. #SlowShowPony. Plus we took that cycle to plan. It would be on this cycle.

Caëlahenâilenŵhei's Text Box: I completely forgot about that as well. I feel foolish now. Lundy, Gliint, and Centimer are probably just waiting for the new avatars at that little port in cave down the road.

Palcath's Text Box: Correct lasses. My math indicates that they should be here right about—

Palcath's Text Box was interrupted by an exceedingly large explosion from the direction of that little port in cave down the road. It felt like a Codexplosion of great magnitude.

Zal Finn III's Text Box: What in The Flaming Pit was that?

> Roodg's Text Box: aN 8.0 MAGNITUDE cODEXPLOSION!

> Zal Finn III's Text Box: Unsweet, what the heck is a Codexplosion?

> Roodg's Text Box: nO IDEA! bUT GO!

~ ~ ~

Anders and Kray slept through the Codexplosion. They were too drunk to notice.

~ ~ ~

The smoke finally cleared. It had been thick, dark, and had geometry unlike anything anyone could describe. It had magic draconic energy and little black pixels that sent shivers down the spine. It felt like, and even smelled like, Breaker.

> Caëlahenãilenŵhei's Text Box: There I can see something coming through the smoke for a dramatic reveal!

> Zal Finn III's text Box: I can hear it walking, it's a horse!

> Pink Quest Fairy's Text Box: If you enjoy sweet horses and sweeter racing then Spire—

> Mr. Max's Interruption Text Box: Fourni Bro!

Through the smoke strode a very solemn Centaur. Two huddled avatars were riding on his back.

> Lissa's Text Box: What happened?

> Fournimer's Text Box: there was a Bomb. it felt like Breaker for sure. new avatars coming into the map set if off. we were too close to run. then Gliint jumped forward to protect Lundy and me.

> Caëlahenãilenŵhei's Text Box: Oh my Maker! Is everyone okay? Where is Gliint?

Gliint slumped off of the Centaur's back.

> samuri's Text Box: …

samuri used the *Look Relieved Animation*, as did everyone else.

> Gliint's Text Box: *Wave* I am alright. I am right here.

> Caëlahenãilenŵhei's Text Box: Well thank goodness everyone is alright

then!

Gliint's Text Box: I lagged out... *Tears* just after jumping in front of everyone...

Fournimer's Text Box: then a huge rock exploded out of the cave and came right at Gliint. Lundy jumped in... and pushed him out of the way.

Gliint's Text Box: If I hadn't lagged out... if I had just... maybe if...

Everyone's eyes looked over at the slumped over avatar still on Fournimer's back.

Caëlahenâilenŵhei's Text Box: Wait, what happened next? Yallundy? What happened? Say something!

Gliint's Text Box: She can't. She's... dead.

◈ Chapter 11 ◈
CONTINUING ONN

Yallundy was not at the respawn point in town that had been set. Nobody Text Boxed a single word for the rest of the night. Gliint stayed up all night and held Yallundy's lifeless hand. When Breaker's Blue Dragon landed the night Gliint killed it solo before anyone could even react to help. The little gnome was full of rage and had the *Blast Bombs* to back it up.

As more and more rounds passed avatars came by to try to comfort the little gnome but he turned everyone away without a word. He was content to just sit there, head hung down, in silence.

The rooster finally cawed and it was the beginning of a new cycle. One by one it had sunk into the avatars during the night. Their files had been broken again, or at least one had. Yallundy couldn't reload her Save File. Her avatar was stuck here and wouldn't disappear. Yallundy wasn't coming back. She was dead dead.

Caela, Fourni, Lissa, and Zal Finn prepared a memorial shrine near the destroyed house by scrubbing the graffiti off of the Administrator's Grave. samuri, Palcath, and Mr. Max made the last preparations and got everything ready to leave.

They propped up Yallundy and covered her in the little dropped flowers that were used to Combi-Fusion *Potions*. They put her equipment and other favourite things next to her, including her destroyed Ni Hao Bunny© journal that was the basis for Chapter 8. They held a ceremony for Yallundy and finally about midday got ready to leave. Both Gliint and Yallundy's Constantly-Colour-Changing Quest Fairy refused to leave her side.

> Caëlahenãilenẁhei's Text Box: Please Gliint, we need to go. You will do nothing for her here. At least if you come with us we can help bring the one responsible for her death to justice. She will be able to rest in peace if we do.

> Gliint's Text Box: I know you're right. Please just give me a moment alone. I'll meet you in Onn Forest. I just... I just want to say goodbye. *sigh*

> Caëlahenãilenẁhei's Text Box: Of course.

The party went into Onn Forest and waited for many rounds. Just when nearly everyone was about to suggest that maybe the gnome had lagged out, he came into the area. The gnome was upset, as if he had lost all the spring in his step. He wasn't even walking at full speed anymore. A terrible weight was now on his shoulders.

> Gliint's Text Box: *Sigh* Let's go.

The party followed the insidious path to get through the horrible teleport maze that was Onn Forest. Everyone knew the way by heart, (just going left) and nobody Text Boxed a word the entire trip. When they got to the Airship they found Kray and Anders. Anders was sickened, almost as if he was hung over and Kray's hair was standing up at all sorts of weird angles. The silence was finally broken by the avatar that could never leave the silence alone.

> Kray's Text Box: Geeze, kay! What took you guys so long? We've been waiting here for like ever!

> Zal Finn III's Text Box: We were... delayed.

> Kray's Text Box: Kay, you all look worse than barfy over there! What the hell happened? Who died?

That earned laser guided bunny missile eyes from everyone. Gliint had his *Gratling Gun* out and it was pointed square at Kray's face.

> Gliint's Text Box: Yallundy died asshole!

> Anders' Text Box: What?!

The gnome lowered his weapon, and walked towards the Airship. After a Text Box he was gone from the area.

> Gliint's Text Box: Shut up! *Done* We are going now! Get on the Makerdamn Airship!

Tears welled up in Anders' eyes. Kray just shut up and walked towards the Makerdamn Airship.

> Anders' Text Box: What happened?

> Palcath's Text Box: We'll tell you about it on the Airship lad, we shouldn't keep him waiting.

~ ~ ~

The Airship was impressively beautiful, but the entire majesty of the situation was lost on the party. Epic scenery, grandiose music by *Ainsely's Arrow*, and well animated cut scenes did nothing to lift their spirits. Nobody really cared except Roodg, who was busy taking screenshots. Anders had been told of what had happened, and he and Fourni had gone inside the small private room Gliint had gone into. It was a fruitless attempt to talk to the gnome.

On the deck of the Airship was a table that had unreadable maps, little figures, flags, and other fanciful objects that served no purpose. It really looked like a strategy table, even if nothing was useable. Everyone who was not inside the private room had gathered around the table to talk strategy, except Roodg who was still taking screenshots.

> Palcath's Text Box: We have a problem now. Our original idea for a two party sweep will no longer work, because the lass is… Without two healer types we are going to have to try something else.

> Caëlahenäilenŵhei's Text Box: As much as it pains me to say this, that is completely true. We need a new plan.

> Roodg's Text Box: hUH?

> Lissa's Text Box: I can handle healing everyone, but we will need to stick together.

> Purple Quest Fairy's Text Box: The quest Stick Together #SoScrewedUp. Be sure to take a lot of *Ultra Glue* if you pla—

> Mr. Max's Interruption Text Box: That may be the best idea then. Let me take the lead fellow adventurers!

> Roodg's Text Box: wHAT IS THAT?

> Zal Finn III's Text Box: No, we should keep our Golden Gribblet formation! Defenders in front, then Melee, then Magic, then Ranged.

> Lissa's Text Box: That doesn't work anymore, I can't Magic Defend and heal at the same time.

Roodg's Text Box: sERIOUSLY. wHAT IS THAT?

Caëlahenãilenŵhei's Text Box: Then the best option we have is to put Mr. Max in the front. There will be Magic that will get through. There is nothing we can do about it. We will just need to be prepared.

White Quest Fairy's Text Box: Being prepared for any quest is the—

Palcath's Interruption Text Box: Agreed, lass. We will just need to remain vigilant.

Roodg's Text Box: nO SERIOUSLY. cOME & LOOK ALREADY!!

Palcath looked towards Roodg's diversionary tactic.

Palcath's Text Box: What is it Roodg? Well, it is obviously…

Palcath became very pale, almost white.

Palcath's Text Box: Son of a bitch. No way, I can't believe it!

Lissa's Text Box: What's wrong dwarf?

Roodg's Text Box: oH i SEE WHAT IT IS NOW!

Palcath's Text Box: They can't be serious. How could I fall for this again?

Lissa's Text Box: You are scaring me! #SpillItAlready. You're not even saying lad!

Roodg's Text Box: iT IS Breaker's DRAGONS! aLL 6 OF THEM!

Palcath's Text Box: Quick, did anyone read the name of this Airship?

Caëlahenãilenŵhei's Text Box: I believe it was called the S.S. PlotDevice. Why does that matter?

Palcath's Text Box: Fuck!

Roodg's Text Box: yEP. tHEY ARE GETTING INTO FORMATION. hERE THEY COME!

Palcath's Text Box: An Airship is a kind of Ship!

◈ Chapter 12 ◈

SPLITTING UP IS FORCED ON YOU

It only took seven rounds.

The first round the Dragons dive bombed the ship with thier elemental breath attacks.

The second round the Dragons combined their breath attacks and hit the Airship's balloon, burning it to cinders.

The third round saw the propellers destroyed by angry claws.

The fourth round had Breaker show up. With a *Stretching Out of His Wings and a Dramatic Movement of his Claws Animation* Breaker simply snapped a pair of his clawed fingers.

During the fifth round the Airship began to Zing.

On the sixth round the Airship had Codexploded. No one had time to even attempt to summon an Administrator.

The seventh round involved various avatars who plummeted towards the ground (in nice little groups no less).

◈ Chapter 13 ◈
THE D TEAM

Gliint opened his eyes with less effort than he thought it would take given the circumstances. He felt pretty well in spite of falling from such a large number of Height Units. He was stretched out and noticed that he had fallen back first on a rock and was nearly bent in half. That made the entire feeling well portion of his wake up unsettle him a little, as he was literally bent in half the incorrect way but felt fine. He stood up feeling lighter than he had remembered. Gliint checked himself over and something was out of place.

His *Backpack* had fallen off; *Backpacks* simply could not fall off, but it was gone. He looked around, paniced. He noticed it was hanging from the branch of a nearby charred tree. It must have either snagged when he fell down or bounced off when he struck the rock. The tree was far too high to climb safely, and it was perched at the very edge of a nasty cliff.

Gliint looked down and the vertigo (or whatever the video game equivalent was) set in, and he could fuzzily see several razor-sharp rocks at the bottom (or possibly just one razor-sharp rock multiple times). He also saw a large D had been stenciled onto the cliff face (there may also have been several cliff faces and multiple stenciled Ds).

At least he knew where he was, at the very base of Mountain D. This was the Air themed area of the world. That would explain all the thunder, lightning, wind, and all the yellow undertones around here.

Gliint trembled as lightning struck every tree in this area randomly. The tree with his *Backpack* had not been hit yet, but it was only a matter of rounds until it was.

He quickly climbed the very dangerously placed tree and shimmied his way across the highest branch in an attempt to reach his *Backpack*.

Success! He reached his *Backpack*! It was safe! He was relieved!

Lightning! It hit the branch he was on and shattered it! He was falling! He was no longer relieved!

Gliint landed hard on the ground, surprisingly he took only minimum damage. He had lost his grip on the *Backpack* and it tumbled away towards the cliff. He scrambled towards it, hoping to not lag while he made his way. He reached it just as it fell over the edge. His hand made it to the strap and the sudden weight nearly ripped his arm right off. With sheer determination alone he managed to slowly pull the *Backpack* back up. Sweating heavily from both exhaustion and nerves, he caught his breath slowly while leaning against the rock he should have broken his back on.

> Gliint's Text Box: Geeze! *Wipe away sweat* That was too close!

Finally calm Gliint noticed a large object hanging from another nearby tree. It looked almost like a big sack of meat. Gliint donned his *Backpack* and slowly moved towards the object. It became clear when it rotated slightly, this was no ordinary sack of meat. It was Mr. Max hanging from his ankle, unconscious.

Getting Mr. Max down from the tree proved much easier than the *Backpack*. A lightning strike hit Max to the ground before Gliint could think about what to do. Gliint checked him over carefully. That was strange. Mr. Max was only at 15% total health. With his higher Levels and Melee Class Type, Mr. Max should have reached full health way before Gliint had recovered. It certainly couldn't have been Gliint's soft landing on the pointy rock.

The area became darker and Gliint had a horrible feeling deep in the pit of his stomach. Something was coming. Something powerful. Something evil. Gliint saw a small indent in the rocks, it wasn't much of a hiding spot but it was something. With much effort, Gliint dragged the beefy avatar over to the hidden indent. Mr. Max was almost heavier than Gliint's *Backpack*, but Gliint had them all hidden just before the something showed up.

It was one of Breaker's Dragons. It landed hard on a large group of scenic rocks. As it landed the background music changed from the light airy music of the area to a very intense instrumental that included ominous Latin chanting. The Latin thankfully did come with subtitles, it was a song about this dragon, and the general theme involved ripping out other creature's organs to practice origami with.

This dragon had changed, significantly. The purple dragon was now at least twice the size of its previous incarnation. It had spikes coming from its back that were twisted and black. Wicked claws grasped the rocks which left visible marks in the geometry. Dark purple energy pixels swirled around the dragon. It was intense, powerful, and broken.

The name had even been changed. This wasn't the purple dragon anymore, this thing was now Assil, the Purple Dragon of Dark. Gliint shuddered as he took in the magnificence, but realized it was no longer an it. Assil, the Purple Dragon of Dark was now a she, there was no mistaking it.

Assil looked around, sniffed the air, and folded a nice origami swan out of the insides of an unfortunate passing Treegull. Assil, the Purple Dragon of Dark flew off to display her swan on her bookshelf. Once the music had switched back, Gliint finally remembered to breathe.

Gliint turned his attentions over to Mr. Max. Mr. Max's Health had only gone up 0.4% during that entire terrifying ordeal, this was going to be a bit of a wait. Gliint didn't have any *Healing Potions* in his full *Backpack*, but guessed that Mr. Max would, and he rummaged through his idol's *Ultra-Mega-Pack-Super Mark 2*. The first thing he noticed was the giant stack of *Bacon*. Mr. Max had claimed to have run out, but still had a secret stash. As Gliint had no food of his own, he took one for tonight's meal and replaced it with some coins. He didn't want to steal it, but he did need it.

Feeding Max the *Health Potions* took a few rounds, but after Gliint thought of the great idea to use a *Funnel* it went by faster. Soon the avatar was awake and he jumped up on his feet like a big beefy cat.

> Mr. Max's Text Box: Wow! that was a harder landing than last time! I miss ocean ships.

> Gliint's Text Box: Hello Mr. Max *Waves*, glad you are alright.

> Mr. Max's Text Box: Well hey there... you!

With only a quick survey of the area Mr. Max had his bearings and a plan. It was even a good plan.

> Mr. Max's Text Box: Okay! We are near Spire D, which was the Air Spire. Equip any Yellow Defence Boosters that you have. Hmmm, it is obvious to anyone with a sense of plot that no one would have fallen near Spire E or Spire F. Those Spires had been mentioned as being locked until A through D were completed. That would not have been mentioned if it wasn't important. So logically there will be... uh?

> Gliint's Text Box: *Maths* There will be three groups of three, and one of two.

> Mr. Max's Text Box: If you say so! Is anyone else here with us?

> Gliint's Text Box: No, *Shrug* I am pretty sure it is just us.

> Mr. Max's Text Box: Interesting. Well fortunately the split was like this then. My higher Level will help to balance out the lack of another

member here. We will need to defeat this Spire, and the two areas before it, with just the two of us. We still have a few rounds until nightfall, let's quickly update our Player Pagers to alert the others.

Gliint's Text Box: *Confused look* How come you are so good at planning out game logic, but can't even remember my name. Especially since I am your biggest fan and run your fan club. Remember we fought all the Gigases after B together side by side? We found out that we needed a full set of Gigas gear to summon the Plague of Shadow together. You promised to go adventuring with me in the Expansion! Flaming Pit, you even signed my ass twice and my tits once!

Mr. Max's Text Box: That wasn't you! The Hero of the Cycle was some Backstabber gnome. I think her name was something sparkly! Something like Fliint or Pliint or something.

Gliint's Text Box: *Sigh* Unbelievable!

Mr. Max's Text Box: Okay, let's venture into that area over there. The Strangely Ominous Empty Field With Lightning Rods Placed Too Far Apart!

Orange Quest Fairy's Text Box: Fellow adventurers, there is one quest located within The Strangely Ominous Empty Field With Lightning Rods Placed Too Far Apart. Be sure and visit the pools on your—

Gliint's Interruption Text Box: Why are those so far apart? It is just lazy construction work on the Level Designers part.

The Strangely Ominous Empty Field With Lightning Rods Placed Too Far Apart delivered exactly what it promised. It also delivered a random jolt of lightning every two to three rounds on a random avatar. The randomly placed too far apart lightning rods would stop the lightning from striking if you were close enough. After getting hit Mr. Max ran at full sprint to the nearest one, but got hit twice more. He barely avoided falling into an unmarked pool of water.

Mr. Max's Text Box: Look out for that pool there, it is full of fish. They might be dangerous.

Orange Quest Fairy's Text Box: The three pools in The Strangely Ominous Empty Field With Lightning Rods Placed Too Far Apart contain fish that are important to a quest that allows you to leave the area. Fellow adventurers, be sure and start The Something Fish—

> Mr. Max's Interruption Text Box: Run little girl!

Gliint tried to run but he simply couldn't. When a bolt came down to hit him the lightning didn't reach, stopping just above his head and fizzling out. Another bolt came down and suffered the same fate.

> Gliint's Text Box: *Laugh* I guess I am just too short for the lightning to strike! That is prett—

Lightning came down and bolted the gnome right out of his Text Box. He slowly hurried to the safe zone, getting both hit and missed twice more.

> Mr. Max's Text Box: What is wrong with you fellow adventurette! Why aren't you running?

> Gliint's Text Box: Uh… Lag I guess. *Shrug* Yeah. Lag.

> Mr. Max's Text Box: I don't recall you ever lagging before. Oh well! Let's heal up before we go to the next pond. I have an idea!

> Gliint's Text Box: I don't have any way of doing that. Can I buy a *Health Potion* from you?

> Mr. Max's Text Box: I clearly remember telling everyone to buy a full complement of essential items! Why don't you have any, you were with us in Onn right?

> Gliint's Text Box: Lag?

After the duo was healed up Mr. Max attempted to execute his plan, picking up Gliint and running for the next rod. When he grabbed the gnome and lifted up he accomplished nothing but falling over himself.

> Mr. Max's Text Box: Holy Maker! Lag is damn heavy! Maybe we should rest for the night and try next cycle.

Gliint agreed and soon the pair had sat down and gotten ready for the night. Once the meal was ready Mr. Max eyed the gnome suspiciously.

> Mr. Max's Text Box: Where did you get *Bacon*? We ran out.

> Gliint's Text Box: Um… Lag? *Wince*

> Mr. Max's Text Box: Makes sense.

Chapter 14

THE C TEAM

Fourni looked around the giant flower he awoke in. The peculiar flower was house-like with its size and shape. There was a single plane of geometry with a likeness of furniture on it. It was a bit unsettling, but looking around he knew that from outside when someone passed by and looked in the cute little window it would look normal. The furniture was nothing compared to the three Zal Finns looking at him with blank stares. They tracked his movements but said nothing as he approached the door, which didn't open.

It took quite a few kicks, but eventually Fournimer kicked out the door and he barely squeeze outside. This door was not built for centaurs. After taking a *Catch Your Breath Animation* he was ready to look around and find out where he was.

The giant decal letter C right beside him was probably some kind of clue, but that was the only one. Fournimer was sure the C spire was the fire one, but this place looked too earthy and full of life to be an active volcano. That was strange.

Stranger still was the fact that there were no less than twenty Zal Finns walking the streets and randomly going about their business. Entering their own flower houses through impossible to open doors, pretending to shop, or doing other random Animations that normal citizens would do. They all talked amongst themselves although no sound came out. Fourni also saw at least seven male Zal Finns amongst the bunch making their rounds.

Fournimer's Text Box: okay, this place is messed up. maybe I broke open my sanity when I fell.

Fournimer thought for a round or two while admiring all the Zal Finns running around on set paths; these were just NPCs, not Zal Finns. If the party was broken up again then that meant he was paired with someone. There was six Spires, that must logically mean six pairs. He wondered who he was with, maybe it would be just him and Dude! How great would that be? Fournimer crossed his fingers and hoped. He though Bro wouldn't be bad either, cuddling with him the last time they got split into teams was pretty damn nice. Just Man would be nice as well, Man was super good at planning stuff.

He had alright odds of getting one of them. If there were 11 other party members… and… he was 1 of them… so there were 9 others… double for Guy… um… so mathematically… getting either Dude or Bro or Man was… 4 in 11… so that was like an 80% chance or something! Awesome. (Math wasn't built for centaurs either.)

Fournimer looked more and more at the Zal Finn that had stopped wandering on its little path in front of him, not able to move again until the centaur got out of the way. There were probably hundreds of them in total in this little village, if you counted all the male ones. This was an NPC town of random flower people that was important to some Quest, but he had no way of figuring out if there were any quests around. Well, no way that wasn't annoying and floating near his head.

Fournimer still couldn't get over how lifelike these NPCs were. The one right in front of him was a particular good example: she almost looked like she had the spark of an avatar insider her. He reached out and touched it, just to see if it was real. He had never touched an NPC before, they had sort of a surreal heat to them, and it was a little disturbing. It almost felt alive.

Zal Finn III's Text Box: Hi Horseymer!

Fournimer's Text Box: holy fucking shitballs!

Zal Finn III's Text Box: What's with you Mr. Jumpyhooves?

Fournimer's Text Box: you scared the crap out of me!

Zal Finn III's Text Box: You were staring right at me for like 20 turns!

Fournimer's Text Box: sorry, I was just thinking. so we are paired together, huh? strange, there isn't any dramatic tension between us. why would we be paired together?

Zal Finn III's Text Box: No tension at all really! You are rad and I am sweet with that. Uh, there would not be pairs though, there would be four groups, if we were allowed to skip spires for the plot we would have just landed on the G spot.

> Fournimer's Text Box: that makes sense The Finnster. if we are in groups, then who else is here?

> Zal Finn III's Text Box: Good point. Let me check.

Zal Finn's eyes turned pink for a single round, and then she darted off as if stricken by *Advanced Serpent Speed*. Just a few steps into the crowd and she was lost until Fournimer saw a Zal Finn picking through a pile of debris.

> Fournimer's Text Box: that was fast! you can check for everyone so quickly?

The Zal Finn didn't answer; it was intent on the mission. Fournimer was pretty sure it was the avatar variety of Zal Finn (at least 90% sure) and helped to clear away the pile. After moving a brick that was made of petals, he saw a flash of bright purple hair and knew exactly who they had found. With a few more rounds of brick pulling Lissa was uncovered. The digger Zal Finn looked very excited, but Fournimer did not. He and Lissa were not exactly on the best of terms. They had many nickname fights during their mutual time here and while Fourni didn't actually dislike Lissa, he wasn't exactly sure if he liked her. There was tension in the group now, joy.

> Zal Finn III's Text Box: Sweet, it's Lissa! Thank the Maker you are okay!

Fournimer nearly wet himself when the voice came from behind him; the digging Zal Finn wasn't the real one.

> Lissa's Text Box: #StomachRebellion. I don't feel well. I think I am seeing doub… trip… um… centennial? Wait, then why is there only one Fournitaur?

> Fournimer's Text Box: just try and get up Chick.

> Lissa's Text Box: How many times do I need to tell… murble… mummf?

Lissa passed out during mid retort. A Zal Finn that Fourni was sure wasn't the real one freaked him out when it stepped forward and picked up Lissa.

> Fournimer's Text Box: okay, let's get out of this town for now and regroup.

The Zal Finn beside the one holding Lissa replied and Fournimer legitimately screamed a little when it happened.

> Zal Finn III's Text Box: Why?

> Fournimer's Text Box: just cause.

Fournimer and six Zal Finns (two of them male) carried Lissa to the outskirts of town to assess the situation. The Zal Finn that Fournimer was absolutely positive was not the real one started to talk.

> Zal Finn III's Text Box: Look at her leg. Her avatar model looks like it got busted. Her foot is hanging on backwards. It looks all unsweet and junk.

Fournimer picked up Lissa's leg. The stimulation made her cry out in pain. The model of her leg was painfully broken. He lifted it again to be sure after remembering being called Fournitaur.

> Fournimer's Text Box: can we *Combi-Fuse* up a cast or something?

The Zal Finn who was beside Zal Finn replied.

> Zal Finn III's Text Box: Neither of us has a *Combi-Pot*. Maybe we can wrap it up with petals? It would at least look pretty.

> Pink Quest Fairy's Text Box: Petalyuna is a sweet city located on Spire C. It is home to the ques—

> Fournimer's Interruption Text Box: true. let's do that. with luck Chick will wake up again and then she can heal herself.

Fourteen girl Zal Finns, seven boy Zal Finns, and Fournimer did a pretty good job of bandaging up Lissa's leg. After a few rounds, and a few worried looks from several Zal Finns, Lissa managed to open her eyes again. A few healing spells did nothing to heal the break.

> Lissa's Text Box: Damn. Well first I should update my Player Pager, so everyone knows where we are.

After clearing her head and seeing the giant C Lissa updated her Player Pager to let everyone know where they were. It was important to keep everyone informed, but only she had remembered that fact with this group. Update completed, it finally looked as though she got the colour back into her cheeks.

> Lissa's Text Box: I feel much better now. I think I can get up.

> Fournimer's Text Box: what about your leg?

> Lissa's Text Box: Magic is useless apparently. Time better damn well heal it or I am going to be really pissed off. Can you help me up Zal?

Lissa held up her hand to the first Zal Finn she saw, but the one beside it replied.

> Zal Finn III's Text Box: Sure! Let me help you up Lissa!

> Lissa's Text Box: Holy fucking shitballs!

> Zal Finn III's Text Box: What?

> Lissa's Text Box: You scared me is all!

Lissa got up and soon had Zal Finn helping her walk down the little cobbled village path. Progress was slow going but they were at the edge of town before too much time had passed.

> Lissa's Text Box: Thanks for the help Zal. I don't think I would have been able to walk on this leg without help.

The Zal Finn beside Fournimer that was not helping Lissa walk replied.

> Zal Finn III's Text Box: No problem!

Fournimer nearly fell over when the Zal Finn replied. Lissa was in such shock that she let go of the male Zal Finn she held and fell to the ground. A Zal Finn that probably was the real one leaned over to help, but another one started to talk, which further startled Lissa and Fourni.

> Zal Finn III's Text Box: Lissa be careful. Let me help you up!

Lissa stayed on the ground, too scared to touch any of the Zal Finns.

> Fournimer's Text Box: let me help you up. we need to get The Flaming Pit out of here!

> Lissa's Text Box: OMM yes! This place is #SoFuckedUp!

Zal Finn patted Lissa on the shoulder and Fournimer on the horse rump and walked towards the next area. The others followed slowly but then another Zal Finn that both Lissa and Fournimer were pretty sure had just left a little flower house down the road replied.

> Zal Finn III's Text Box: Why?

Neither Lissa nor Fournimer would ever admit what happened next. They were holding hands that clenched at the exact same time. They both had legs that crossed at the same time. They both had felt it. They both knew that the other had done it as well. There was no mistaking it, they both just knew. It was a secret that they would keep forever between themselves. They both had been startled so badly by the latest Zal Finn that they had both peed a little.

Chapter 15
THE B TEAM

P alcath's Text Box: Ouch. That hurt!

Palcath rubbed his head and nicely trimmed *#5 Facial Hairstyle* for a few rounds. He finally managed to stand up after the world stopped spinning.

Palcath's Text Box: Lad!

Palcath took a look around, he was currently alone. He was thankful that nobody had seen him make such a fatal role-playing mistake as forgetting to include lad in a Text Box.

It was snowing. Even before he saw the large B engraved on the mountainside Palcath knew where he was; he had taken proper notes! This was the Ice Spire, and his notes indicated that he was just outside Huge Confusing Snowfield Full of Random Warps. That was just perfect, 122 cycles of being in Onn Forest and its confusing warps hadn't been annoying at all, so another place filled with random warps would be great.

As there had been four Spires that made up the first step of the puzzle, that had to mean there would be four groups. Fate would never allow them to skip Spires after such a big plot twist and Palcath knew it. That meant there would most likely be three groups of three, and a single group of two. Hopefully, whichever group had two would include either Mr. Max for his increased Level support, or Lissa for her healing support.

Palcath did the *Smile Animation*. What if he was paired up with just Lissa again? It was all too exciting. He had dreamed of her every night since he had been forcibly used by her to gain a 3% bonus chance to kill Breaker (even if he had been forced to finish up in Anders). He knew that she must feel the same way too. He could already imagine reading the excerpt from a few Chapters from now, probably like Chapter 28 or so. Maybe even as early as Chapter 22 if he played his cards right.

'Palcath was awakened in the middle of his sleep animation when he felt something touch him. He felt himself do the Smile Animation when he felt a pair of warm half-elf arms around him. They squeezed him tightly and Palcath knew that they would never let him go. The dwarf was so pleased that he didn't even comment on how Lissa had completely destroyed the ground of his Portie Tent while she had spent countless rounds dragging her immovable purple bed next to his yellow one. She must have used nothing but passion and love to do so!

She kissed him deeply and giggled a little when his #5 Facial Hairs tickled her face. They explored each other's bodies for countless rounds until the dwarf finally entered her while on the slowest setting. They spent all night deeply joined, never once feeling the need to use the Ultra setting. The next cycle they woke up late and exhausted but defeated all evil everywhere together instantly with their intense love for each other. They had saved the world with nothing but their love!'

That is exactly how it would be written, Palcath just knew it. His hot little dwarf body almost melted the snow with his thoughts alone. It was time to get up and look for Lissa! Then he saw terror. With his new higher perspective there it was, written in the snow, clear as day.

> Palcath's Reading Box: bACK IN 10 MINS.

> Palcath's Text Box: Oh fuck me!

Palcath changed his mind. This wasn't a happy dream anymore. He had died and was being punished for something he didn't remember doing. He was obviously in The Flaming Pit.

> Roodg's Text Box: u FORGOT 2 SAY LAD!

Roodg was right. Despite being dead and in The Flaming Pit, Palcath needed to step up his game. No matter who he was with, character traits mattered. Having an attack magic user around wasn't really that bad, even if it was Roodg. At least Roodg had started to use the right element to attack the right monster, most of the time. If Roodg started to get annoying Palcath could always just use some scenery as a distraction.

> Palcath's Text Box: Did you find anything while scouting around Roodg?

> Roodg's Text Box: yES! pASTRAMI ON RYE!

> Red Quest Fairy's Text Box: Neat! The Sandwich Quest can be —

Palcath's Interruption Text Box: So, you haven't looked around yet to try and find other lads or lasses?

Roodg's Text Box: nO. sINCE THERE R 4 GROUPS, & Mr. Max & Gliint R TOGETHER WE HAVE 1 MORE.

Palcath's Text Box: How did you know that Roodg?

Roodg's Text Box: wELL, WITH OUR LUCK WE WOULDN'T BE ALLOWED TO SKIP ANYTHING. sINCE THERE R 4 SPIRES THEMS THE MATH! oNLY Mr. Max & Gliint HAVE UPDATED SO FAR.

Palcath's Text Box: I thought that exact same thing.

Roodg's Text Box: i KNOW RITE? Gliint POSTED ON HIS pLAYER pAGER THAT HE WOKE UP LIKE 3 CYCLES AGO! wE ARE NOT BEHIND THOUGH BECAUSE Gliint HAS SO MUCH LAG! hE & Mr. Max ARE AT sPIRE d. wHICH MEANS WE WILL NOT MEET UP WITH THEM AGAIN UNTIL THE END AT sPIRE g.

Palcath's Text Box: Given the rate of Health Recovery time for his class, that little lad should never have woken up first. But three whole cycles before us, that doesn't make sense at all.

Roodg's Text Box: fELL ON A PILLOW? sOME SORT OF DIVINE INTERVENTION? mAYBE HE LANDED IN A CHEST WITH A *hEALTH pOTION*, & IT WENT UP HIS BUTT?

Palcath's Text Box: Amazingly Roodg, those are the only reasons that make even a little sense.

Roodg's Text Box: nO ONE ELSE HAS POSTED YET THOUGH, OUR THIRD COULD BE ANYONE!

Palcath's Text Box: Well Roodg, I know which avatar I would like it to be!

Roodg' Text Box: tRUE, IF IT IS Lissa U GUYS CAN GET CLOSER. sHE HAS A GRUFF EXTERIOR, & U GUYS DIDN'T GET ALONG AT FIRST. u HAVE GOTTEN CLOSER THRU PLANNING LATELY, SO THAT MEANS BY THE RULES OF STORYTELLING U HAVE REALLY GOOD ODDS NOW!

Palcath turned to *Blush Shade #1*; he wasn't expecting others had know that he had a crush on the purple haired half-elf.

> Palcath's Text Box: Really? You think she likes me?

> Roodg's Text Box: yEAH! bUT SHE DOESN'T KNOW THAT YET, SO DON'T PUSH IT LAD! LoL!

> Palcath's Text Box: Noted. Well thank you Roodg. Now I hope that the third is someone you want.

> Roodg's Text Box: i HOPE IT IS Anders AGAIN!

> Palcath's Text Box: Anders? That lad wasn't who I was going to guess. Why him?

> Roodg's Text Box: tHINK ABOUT IT. Anders IS THE PROTAGONIST! iF IT IS HIM THEN WE WILL BOTH GET MORE SCREEN TIME! MORE SCREEN TIME MEANS MORE CHARACTER DEVELOPMENT & A HIGHER CHANCE OF SOMEONE HAVING AN EMOTIONAL ATTACHMENT 2 US. bE CAREFUL THOUGH IF IT IS HIM NOT TO OVERDO IT, OR WE WILL END UP DEAD AS A SUPER EMOTIONAL STORY POINT! aLSO, Anders HAS A CUTE ELF BUTT OF HOLDING.

> Palcath's Text Box: I never even thought of that. That is probably the most intelligent thing I have ever heard from anylad.

> Roodg's Text Box: sANDWICHES MAKE ME SMART!

> Palcath's Text Box: You know Roodg you are often full of insight and intelligence. Now you have all this knowledge of literary structure. Do you only talk like that to keep a low profile or something?

> Roodg's Text Box: tALK LIKE WHAT? tHE JAM?

> Palcath's Text Box: Never mind, let's just go find that Anders lad and start some serious character development!

Palcath changed his mind. Maybe he wasn't dead and in The Flaming Pit being punished for his sins. Roodg had one important thing going, they were not Kray.

When Palcath stood up and felt the chill hit him everywhere he knew that he was alive. Alive and cold. This was no *Lova Mountains* kind of cold. This was a *Salazarm Desert* at night kind of cold and it chilled him to the core. It was easy to see the imprint of where an avatar had fallen into the snow nearby. It was an elf imprint of some kind, possibly even a half-elf.

Palcath was excited as they hurried over to the imprint. When he looked down he didn't see anything at first, and even thought that this maybe had been Roodg's night elf imprint. He noticed a hand waving, all the white and pale colours of the light elf's outfit, skin, hair, and accents had blended into the snow exactly.

> Palcath's Text Box: Well hello there lass, let us help you up.

> Caëlahenâilenŵhei's Text Box: Thank you.

> Roodg's Text Box: HEY Caëlahenâilenŵhei! hI!

> Caëlahenâilenŵhei's Text Box: Hi Roodg!

> Roodg's Text Box: hI!

> Caëlahenâilenŵhei's Text Box: Hi.

> Red Quest Fairy's Text Box: Hi!

> White Quest Fairy's Text Box: Huh?

Palcath changed his mind again. He was definitely dead and being punished. The Flaming Pit must just have frozen over. He was stuck with both mages? He was going to have to take every single attack for the entire time they were together. Even if Caela was as smart as the *Cracking Whip* she used as a weapon, whenever she talked to Roodg they could do nothing but say 'hI, Hi'. They had both continued to do nothing but say hello during Palcath's entire thought process.

> Palcath's Text Box: Alright then Caela, let's get you up to speed lass.

> Yellow Quest Fairy's Text Box: Okay pals and gals, Up To Speed is a quest loc—

> Caëlahenâilenŵhei's Interruption Text Box: No need, I was listening. How about I fill you up to speed instead? Your Lissa has just posted on her Player Pager. It appears as if she, Centimer, and all the Zal Finns are together. I am not sure what that means. However, they are in Spire C, which means that they will meet up with Gliint and Mr. Max, and not us. I posted so they will know who is near Spire B. That means that through the process of elimination, we will end up meeting with Anders, samuri, and Kray. Not exactly the party I would like to meet with, but it is true, having Ande—

> Caëlahenâilenŵhei's Text Box: rs will mean more screen time for us.

Since I am part of the party that wasn't really important until this Book, I would enjoy more screen time. Now, let's get serious for a round here. We are at the Huge Confusing Snowfield Full of Random Warps, and it is exactly that. While you two were blabbering on over there for countless rounds I was trying to even get past just the entrance to Huge Confusing Snowfield Full of Random Warps. I had no luck. Even the very first snow bank was more confusing than the entirety of Onn Forest. I have been warped—

Caëlahenãilenŵhei's Text Box: back here, conveniently enough back into this hole, seventeen times already. We have our work cut out for us, so thankfully there is my intelligence on our side. I am pretty worn out though from all the climbing out, so I think we should rest for the night. It is getting pretty late after all, so it is a very good plan. Now, speaking of resting for the night, we have both Portie Tents amongst us. While that is unfortunate for others, it doesn't change anything for us. We are still setting both of them up. There will still be both a girl's tent—

Caëlahenãilenŵhei's Text Box: and a boy's tent. Since Lissa is not here, I am afraid I have to go back on the original sleeping arrangements. Roodg is back in … uh… Roodg's original tent. No offence meant or anything, it is just that there are more than enough beds now in your *Portie Tent Ultra* Palcath. I will see you both next cycle so I highly suggest that both of you get some much needed rest. Also, try to keep the chatter down and the rough housing to a minimum. I am afraid that I am a light sleeper and even a little smattering of noise can awaken me. It is my cros—

Caëlahenãilenŵhei's Text Box: s to bear.

Palcath was shocked. Five Text Boxes? Even for someone as long winded as *The Long Wind Tunnel of Bronconus*, that had to be a personal record. He was going to be pushed around by the stuffy light elf for the entire time through this impossible to navigate area. All while freezing his balls off. Yes, it was final. He was dead and The Flaming Pit had frozen over. He had no choice but to agree for now. He could spend the night either thinking up a plan of how to keep control of his new party, or alternately thinking about Lissa holding him.

Roodg's Text Box: bUT… yOU TALK IN YOUR SLEEP Caëlahenãilenŵhei!

Palcath's Text Box: Agreed lass. Let's get some rest. Roodg, good news!

> Thinking ahead, I am just going to stick Kray into Fourni's stable when he joins up. So your old bed is yours again! Feel free to use it.

Palcath and Caëlahenãilenẘhei turned in for the night in their respective *Portie Tents*. Caela to talk in her sleep. Palcath to dream about Lissa holding him tight and to thank the Maker that at least she was in the team with Fourni. Roodg lingered outside.

> Roodg's Text Box: bUT, MY OLD BED IS STILL OUTSIDE THE TENT Palcath! … Palcath?

◈ Chapter 16 ◈
THE A TEAM

This area was so thick with black smoke that Anders could barely see a move unit in front of his face. He had been coughing for so many rounds now that it was amazing that he had recovered any Hit Points at all while he had been sprawled out in a mass of burnt scenic bushes unconscious. This had to be the Spire with the volcano, all the burnt scenery and ground really sold the look.

He tied an *Absorbing Cloth* across his face, (it wasn't the intended purpose of the item but it did cut back the smoke quite a bit). but his eyes burned and he stumbled forward to escape the smoke. When the smoke thinned out he was at a crater of some kind, the back was surrounded by a stone wall. This was a dead end and he would have to go back. At least he could breathe here and attempt to collect his thoughts. He used the *Sit Down on Ground Animation* to reach maximum catch breath effectiveness.

Anders decided that he was going to be smart first and check around for posts in Player Pagers. He didn't want to be surprised again by Roodg (even if he liked Roodg now). Roodg was a lot of fun when paired with. Anders didn't know why but he checked the Magic Mage's Player Pager first. Darn, Roodg was with Palcath and Caela at Spire B. He had to take their word for it because he had no idea what the Rocket Sorceress' full name was and that meant not knowing which page to look up. It was too bad really as all three of them would be good strategists right now.

Team B would also have all the *Portie Tents* with them! Anders full body mirror was lost, for who knew how many Chapters! Back to setting campfires the old fashioned way, the beautiful open sky with thousands of stars, the sounds of wildlife in the distance, regular background music, and peacefully sleeping in the open air. How horrible.

Wow, Palcath's Player Pager was specific. There were four groups, and each should have three people. Except for one group which would have two. That was interesting.

Fourni was the one who Anders wanted to find passed out right near him, and in a group of only two. He checked Fourni's Player Pager next. Loaves, he hadn't posted yet, that was so like him. He probably would never remember to do so, but that was just as much a part of him as giving out nicknames and not using capital letters.

Lissa was secretly nice and she could heal. She would be a good choice. She was at Spire C with Fourni and Zal Finns. Anders wondered why Zal Finn was plural in the post, but decided six typos doing that in a row were just a coincidence. At least Fourni would be away from temptation in that group, so no more worries about him and Max cuddling for a bit, even though Anders wasn't sure how you could cuddle with a horse. Mr. Max was big, so no doubt he would have found a way.

Actually, Max was sort of amazing as well; it wouldn't be bad to be with Max and have him cuddle you instead of a horse. He would keep Anders topped up in Mana at least. Muffins, Max was over in Spire D with Gliint. Anders wasn't going to have any Max temptation either. Well, that was the group of two. Gliint also mentioned that the Breaker Dragons are crazy now, and to look out for Assil, the Purple Dragon of Dark. She was an expert at origami and evil.

Anders was definitely in Spire A then, and if he remembered correctly that would mean meeting up with Team B first. That wasn't bad, he didn't have a crush on anyone in Team B, but they were by far the most level headed in the bunch, even with Roodg.

Who was left then? Who was he with? Anders stopped breathing. Oh no. There were only two others left. He was going to be stuck with Kray and samuri? samuri was a breeze to talk to, plus he was a very good listener. But not Kray, he was nothing of the sort. Anders' *Absorbing Cloth* was quickly absorbing up his tears.

> Anders' Text Box: No, not that skinny bitc… jerk, anyone but him.

That was close. Anders didn't like swearing, not even if it was true. Even almost saying it made him change to *Blush Shade #1*.

There was no reason to put off the inevitable, and Anders decided it was time to face the background music. He got up off the ground, but strained a little. That was way more work that it should have been. He checked himself over his heart sunk a little more, he felt fatter and more miserable than ever before. Mental fatigue had made the *Get Up Animation* more physically straining to his body than normal.

> Anders' Text Box: Pickle Shortcake, I am even acting fatter because of that skinny jerk!

Anders took a few more rounds to compose himself (and to polish off a *Pickle Shortcake* or three), if he was going to travel with Kray he was not going to show even a little bit of emotion. There was going to be no satisfaction given to that pile of burnt bones, no matter what. Anders was going to get tough. Anders also really hoped that Kray was too drunk to remember the compliment orgasm.

After nearly forgetting again, Anders remembered that he should update his Player Pager. First was the most important part, he updated his List.

Anders' List:
1. Scenic Pillars
2. Glades
3. Status Effects
4. Constrict Bars
5. Traps
6. (s) Gear
7. Swarm Beetles
8. Hybrid NPC / Monsters
9. Jumping Puzzle Blocks
10. The Text Box
11. Mysterious Comets
12. Onn / Onn Forest
13. Hair-Dryers
14. Rape then Eat Monsters
15. Skinny Little Jerks!

He took a screenshot and started to update his situation.

> Anders Post, Cycle 129 - 17:55 (New World): *Hello everyone! It appea#s as if I a# on Spi#te # wi## #ray an# s##u#i. ##at? #u#? #h## #s ##in# #n #ere#? #ai#. W## #o#s p#########on ##i## sh#/# #p? ## P##### P#### ## ######?*

The Player Pager began to click and whirr. It did not work anymore. The screenshot Anders had taken of the smoking crater was all pixilated and distorted. Nobody would know what they were looking at. His status was also confusing, it wouldn't help anyone. He needed to try and post again, no matter how many useless #'s showed up.

> Anders Post, Cycle 129 - 17:56 (New World): *##I #####a#########m ####################a########t #S###p#####i##r#########e ######∫¢Ψιℋ³/₈≈A?*

The characters had felt sticky to enter once they stopped being #s. That Interrobang had finally done it though, the Player Pager stopped his post. The little Screen Icon for the Player Pager started to smoke, and then it burst into flames. Once the quick fire was over, Anders was too nervous to click it again. The poor icon was ashes, and even a single click now would probably make it crumble to dust. To make matters worse the fire had spread and taken out the WorldForums icon as well. Communication with the other groups was now impossible.

> Game Explanation Text Box: The Player Pager and WorldForums contest is ### ####. Congratulations to all that tried!

> Anders' Text Box: Sure, the first time I actually remember to use my stupid Player Pager to update my status and the dumb thing breaks! Now how will I talk to the others?

> Green Quest Fairy's Text Box: Actually I can commu—

> Anders' Interruption Text Box: It is hopeless!

Anders covered his face as best as possible and braved the smoke again. There was nothing more to be gained by staying here. While he didn't know where he was going exactly, the plan of just going in a straight line away from the dead end was just as good as any. In only a few rounds Anders was out of the smoke and was standing on lush green grass, rubbing the smoke out of his eyes. Anders stood there confused looking at a very green path.

> Anders' Text Box: What in the map?

> Green Quest Fairy's Text Box: Welcome to the Expansion, the Island of Islana! I am your personal guide and keeper of all things Quests. You can always depend on me! The first available Quests are nearby. You may call me Quest Fa—

> Anders' Interruption Text Box: We covered that already Quest Fairy!

> Green Quest Fairy's Text Box: Camembert! Sorry, I just say that when someone steps on that spot.

This was the greenest and most friendly volcano Anders had ever seen. This was also a familiar volcano. Finally his eyes stopped watering and he saw it in the distance. His suspicions were confirmed, this wasn't a volcano.

> Anders' Text Box: What the ginger snaps? No. It can't be. Not... Onn?

> Green Quest Fairy's Text Box: There are 23 Quests, 19 Quest NPCs and 5 Hidden Quests inside Onn. You have completed 23 Quests and 0 Hidden Quests.

Of all the places to fall he fell right beside the initial port in area. Anders remembered hearing that it had blown up, and now he was standing in the aftermath. There were no Quest Fairy lights in that little cave to tip him off. He wondered where they all had gone.

This was bad. There were only two ways out of Onn. He was standing on one, and the other was through the Airship after Onn Forest. He was now going to be stuck in Onn even longer, maybe even forever.

Anders raised his fist to the sky and yelled his wrath at #12 from his List.

> Anders' Yelling Text Box: ONN! OOOONNNNNNNN!

> Green Quest Fairy's Text Box: There are 23 Quests, 19 Quest NPCs and 5 Hidden Quests inside Onn. You have completed 23 Quests and 0 Hidden Quests.

Anders looked around and saw no other avatars in sight, he knew that he was going to be stuck in Onn all alone. At least Kray wasn't here. He did see something though in the distance. A dragon. One of Breaker's dragons. It had heard his wrath to the heavens and had turned in Anders' direction.

> Anders' Whisper Text Box: Eep!

Thinking quickly Anders dove into a nearby scenic bush to hide. He held his breath and didn't even dare to blink. He had to grab his Green Quest Fairy and hold it close, as it was hovering right above his head, a well lit beacon.

This dragon was different. It was larger and meaner. When it landed the very ground shook. The sun was no longer in Anders' eyes, mostly because the dragon was now blocking out the sun. The music in the area had changed from the *Caution Step* song *Onwards to Onn* (which would have been a pretty big hint to Anders' location if he bothered to think about it earlier) to some ominous Latin chanting. Anders couldn't speak Latin, but he could read the subtitles. The chanters were singing about this dragon's intense love for slowly licking off the skin of foes.

Anders was not sure why this song even existed. A song dedicated to a dragon that shouldn't even be in the Expansion, one that he sort of created and its now broken love of skin eating. The production value was pretty high for a broken song. It had an entire boys choir singing in Latin, as well as a full orchestral accompaniment. All things considered, this song shouldn't have been nearly as spine tingling or well produced.

This dragon in front of him was no normal orange dragon anymore. This was Xam, the Orange Dragon of Light, who enjoyed licking skin until it came off. Xam had three rows of spikes from head to tail and the middle set was longer and was made of bone. Three big horns jutted from Xam's head, the middle one was smaller in this case. It had wings in three segments that were adorned with three wicked boney spikes. It had huge hands and feet that each ended in three big claws.

Anders was almost positive that this Xam character liked the number three. Anders was initially relieved when he noticed that Xam had only two testicles. Then he was shocked. Breaker's dragons never had testicles before. They had been blank lifeless drones that attacked without mercy. For some reason, this Xam fellow was now primed and ready. Anders wasn't sure if Breaker had done that on purpose or not, though he sincerely hoped the answer was not.

Xam, the Orange Dragon of Light, sniffed the air and prowled like a real life predatory animal. This was unheard of for anything in this game. Within just a single round Xam had perked up and looked directly at Anders' clever scenic hideaway, even though it wasn't even in range to aggro or see him. It ran forward and with a horrible grasp pulled out the scenic bush and tossed it aside. He wasn't fooled by a scenic bush? That was two logical breaks in as many rounds. This Xam was serious.

It grabbed Anders in one of the three clawed hands without any problems and held him up for inspection. Xam was a big orange boy, and he grinned with intent to eat. With a flick of his big three pronged dragon tongue Xam gave Anders a quick taste, to taunt his victory over the avatar. Xam had made special care to line up the subtitle that translated to *Lick the skin off, and then lick your bones clean. He is Xam, the Orange Dragon of Light and he is mean.'* with the purposeful lick. The tongue was rough and left a welt. It was barbed and made for ripping skin off.

After the lick, Xam's eyes glazed over. With just one taste of Anders, Xam had decided that he enjoyed elf. Licks started to come quickly, yet none of the new licks contained the barbs from the first one. Xam acted strange, very strange. Xam was now licking Anders all over and taking extreme pleasure while doing so. The Dragon wanted nothing more than just to taste the shocked avatar.

On one particular loving lick of his new stunned Anders brand lollypop Xam happened to lick near the elf's butt. With intense desire Xam had pulled off the avatar's Armour and was licking the area before all else. On one lick the tongue happened to brush against the elf's entrance and it was soon all the dragon could concentrate on.

Anders had no idea why Xam was suddenly infatuated with him. It was really hard to think about the possible reasons with a three pronged Dragon tongue deep inside his ass licking him inside everywhere. He was still getting eaten by the dragon, but at least it wasn't the game ending kind.

Anders tingled with one particularly nice thrust of the tongue and this switched Xam into overdrive. The next round the dragon had Anders bent over the top of a large scenic rock, ass in the air. With a slap of a dragon hand on Anders' ass his special abilities of *Stretch More* and *Stretch More More* activated, with no Magic Point cost to speak of. Anders had just enough time to question why but not enough to think up any possible answers. Xam, the Orange Dragon of Light pushed in his dragon dick (with the three spiky yet strangely sexy bits near the head) with a desperate need.

With two big clawed hands holding him down firmly Anders could do nothing except feel the sensations. When the pair glowed for a round Anders was taken aback. His *Surge* had activated, this dragon must have the special ability *Fill*. The added sensation of linking up had began to make the experience more intense. Both Anders and Xam moaned in synchronized pleasure.

The big dragon dick hit nearly every spot within Anders, which caused many notes of tingle pleasure. Anders desperately wanted it to hit the one important spot it was missing. Great effort combined with a strength he didn't know he possessed allowed Anders to shift upwards and get onto his knees. Now the dragon dick was hitting every spot, and Anders' eyes rolled back in his head despite the situation. The three little spiky nubs pressed upwards, they felt strange to Anders but he didn't mind them in the slightest.

Anders was enjoying the sensations but wanted more. He rocked backwards against Xam with his own counter rhythm. The increased speed worked. Anders felt dragon claws scratch his back; they were probably going to leave marks.

When Xam grabbed Anders' ass hard and pushed forward, the elf knew this was it. With a mighty roar that was combined with a shot of his dragon breath, Xam began to release his dragon seed within the elf. Anders could feel Xam pulse with each shot, the seed caused his stomach to swell a little more with each burst. Xam grabbed harder on each pulse.

The dragon began to *Spling* once he finished and on the next round his body compressed into a little ball of light. Anders had no idea what *Spling* had meant or how he could ever explain it, all he knew was that it was intensely pleasurable. The ball of light flew off defeated, but Anders didn't notice. The bizarre *Spling* of the Dragon leaving him in an instant had pushed Anders over the edge. It was a few rounds before the quivering avatar had even noticed that Xam was gone.

Anders caught his breath and jumped down off the rock exhausted. After spending a few rounds cleaning himself off with the ill fated *Initiate's Jacket*, he looked down at his legs. They were wounded thanks to an overzealous dragon. Xam didn't take away any health, so a *Health Potion* would be useless. He tried to figure out how to use the *Bandages* he had bought in *Onn*. Anders used them to dress his wounds as best as he could. Now he was wrapped up all over, but they stopped the bleeding at least. The dragon had cut his legs and backside a little, but he would recover completely with a good night's rest (for some reason).

Anders contemplated hitting the switch and turning off the game world. Xam had been a bit rapey and turning off the game would certainly put an end to any more of that kind of thing. Anders used the *Determined Animation*. He could run away from everything but if he did he would be abandoning his friends and the entire quest to defeat that jerk Breaker. No, Anders was going to see this through, no matter how many (admittedly sexy) dragon dicks he had to take (Anders was a trooper like that).

As Anders pulled on his *Too Boring to Describe Armour*, he noticed it wasn't fitting as nicely. He had to loosen some straps and noticed his problem. The Xam seed did not seem to be getting absorbed, despite *Surge* being active. That alarmed Anders. He was now a good 5 Weight Units heavier. Maybe it had something to do with the fact that it was Surged inside, hopefully soon it would turn into some Magic Points. Hopefully. It was a good thing that Kray wasn't here to point out how fat Anders looked.

Sighing as he walked with his hands in his Armoured pockets, Anders headed towards Onn. There wasn't anywhere else to go and at least there would be some better hiding places. It took more rounds than normal on account of his legs being so shaky, but at least the scenery was nice. Soon Anders was in front of the gates to Onn and ready to port in.

With a fierce pound of the ground something landed right behind Anders. Nervously he looked behind himself and was stunned. With a hungry smirk in his eyes stood a much starved monster, completely refreshed and ready. A theme song started up with ominous Latin chanting.

Anders' Text Box: Xam?

Chapter 17
THE REAL TEAM A

Kray's Text Box: After that is when he said that I was the better gay elf, kay! It was so true! Anders is such a fool, I pity him and his ample rump.

samuri's Text Box: …

samuri killed a cute Fire Skeetle that was far stronger than its appearance would otherwise indicate.

Kray's Text Box: Kay, I know right? I could barely believe that he finally admitted it. I know he felt that inside, but he wouldn't admit it. Then he did! Good for him! I'm always glad to help with personal growth.

samuri's Text Box: …

samuri used the *Point Animation* directed at a nearby bridge. There was a switch on the other side that only ranged attacks could hit.

Kray's Text Box: It sure is hot here, kay. I mean what is with all this lava? I feel like I'm sweating. It's strange because I don't think I have sweat glands anymore.

samuri's Text Box: …

samuri used his PVP broken ability to attack a rock; it shattered into many pieces.

> Kray's Text Box: Kay, it was really lucky for you that we ended up together!

> samuri's Text Box: …

samuri tossed a total of seven stones until one hit the ranged switch to lower the bridge. He was initially upset when it took a strange bounce, but the stone that hit the switch had banked off a monster's head and killed it. It was a great accidental shot.

> Kray's Text Box: Maybe you should try to keep up though. I feel like you're not holding up your end of this pairing. I am doing all the work here, kay!

> samuri's Text Box: …

samuri killed a group of three Ice Monkeys that were on the other side of the bridge without any help.

> Kray's Text Box: Why are there even ice monsters here? Kay, cause this is a volcano. That doesn't make any sense. There should be fire monsters, right?

> No-Colour Quest Fairy's Text Box: This volcano is called—

> Kray's Interruption Text Box: I mean fire stuff should be here, not ice.

> samuri's Text Box: …

samuri looked over a complicated series of switches. There was a pattern somewhere here.

> Kray's Text Box: I hate puzzles. They require too much thought, kay. Why can't there be like a contest for looking good or something? Oh wait, there was a contest for that, and I won it!

> samuri's Text Box: …

samuri pulled seven levers. The seventh caused a giant red x to show up followed by a buzzer noise.

> Kray's Text Box: Remember? The original Spiderboy totally picked me. I told you that story right? Kay, cause there was this boss and he said that he was coming back for the cute one.

> No-Colour Quest Fairy's Text Box: Yeah well, the Spiderboy is not relevant to any quests.

> samuri's Text Box: …

samuri killed the two bigger Fire Skeetles that showed up. It was a dangerous encounter that took away quite a large portion of his health.

> Kray's Text Box: Geeze, watch it, kay. Those things are tough you know?

> samuri's Text Box: ...

samuri pulled seven levers, but this time a little green circle showed up and it was accompanied by a nice sounding ding noise. He wished he had saw that fainted pictogram sooner.

> Kray's Text Box: Finally, kay. That took forever.

> samuri's Text Box: ...

samuri stepped forward and took out his sword and he brandished it at the boss monster, a Mecha-Taur.

> Kray's Text Box: What is that, kay? A boss I'd wager given the size of the Mecha-Cock.

> samuri's Text Box: ...

samuri slashed at the Mecha-Taur but it cock-blocked the attack.

> Kray's Text Box: Kay, speaking about big cocks, you know what had a really big cock, that Spiderboy who picked the cute one. Have I told you that story yet? Spoiler Alert: I am the cute one!

> No-Colour Quest Fairy's Text Box: Yeah well, the Spiderboy is not relevant to any quests.

> samuri's Text Box: ...

samuri attacked the Mecha-Taur again, but this time was not blocked (cocked or otherwise).

> Kray's Text Box: Kay, so I was in some webs right, and Anders was there as well since I kinda pushed him into the webs earlier.

> samuri's Text Box: ...

samuri attacked the Mecha-Taur a few more times and defeated it with a Critical Hit. Pieces of the Mecha-Taur went flying. Kray dodged out of the way of the severed Mecha-Cock as it flew towards his face. It was the only time Kray had done anything but talk since they had landed here.

> Kray's Text Box: Geeze watch it with that thing, kay! You almost hit

me with that!

samuri's Text Box: ...

samuri filled out the Mecha-Taur's Insta-Wiki entry.

Creature Name: Mecha-Taur
Class: Mecha-Man Beast
Level: 70
Special Attacks: Mecha-Gore, Mecha-Spin, Mecha-Assault, Mecha-Charge, Mecha-Grapple, Mecha-Snatch
Drops: Mecha-Musk
First Player Encounter Notes: ... – samuri

Kray's Text Box: Did you write about how great I was, I bet you did, kay.

samuri's Text Box: ...

samuri opened up the red chest that was in the lava glade.

Kray's Text Box: What is it, kay? Score! It is an *Ultra Snazzy Belt Deluxe*! That is a Level 65 Belt? Nice, I need a new belt, mine is only a Level 50 *Ultra Snazzy Belt*!

samuri's Text Box: ...

samuri had the *Ultra Snazzy Belt Deluxe* snatched from his hands. Kray put on the *Ultra Snazzy Belt Deluxe*, and purposely threw his old *Ultra Snazzy Belt* into the lava, destroying it in a puff of smoke.

Kray's Text Box: This looks really good on me, because I am really skinny. I mean look at it, kay. This thing is pretty *Ultra, Snazzy*, and *Deluxe*. Right?

samuri's Text Box: ...

samuri tightened his very faded Level 3 *Plain Belt* and continued on.

Kray's Text Box: Kay, back to the important thing, my story. Now that you finished up with your rude boss distraction. Maybe you should consider others for a moment, huh? I mean, I was right in the middle of a story. Some avatars with their interruptions and boss fights.

samuri's Text Box: ...

samuri put his hand on his sword and looked at Kray intently. He remembered the promise that he had made to himself and took a deep breath. 119 was enough, 119 was too many. No more. No more. His *Katana-Nata* would have to stay put for now.

> Kray's Text Box: Kay, now where was I? Oh right! So there was this Spiderboy and he had left me and that chubby butt in some webs. Now remember, the important part was that the Spiderboy had said that when he got back he was going to...

> No-Colour Quest Fairy's Text Box: yeah well, the Spiderboy is not relevant to any quests.

> samuri's Text Box: ...

samuri used the *Sigh Animation*.

♦ Chapter 18 ♦
ANDERS, BACKWARDS TO ONN

Anders awoke all snug in his rented Onn Inn bed. He got up from the sheets that never changed in appearance and looked into the half-sized mirror. It was a little upsetting that it wasn't a full length mirror, but he could see what he needed to when he stood up on his tippy-toes.

The scars were gone from Anders' two encounters with Xam last cycle. He noted this with a *Smile Animation*. His *Smile Animation* quickly was re-emoted as a *Frown Animation*. The weight Xam had shot into him, now about ten Weight Units total, was not gone.

Anders had to loosen the straps on his *Too Boring to Describe Armour* before he could even put it on. He was now officially worried. Last night Xam had started to circle only Onn, ignoring the rest of his route completely. Anders was convinced that Breaker had broken Xam with a specific purpose. To target and destroy his arch-nemesis (Anders was convinced that he was Breaker's arch-nemesis).

There was a lot to try and do this cycle though, so Anders could not just hide inside, despite the fact that he wanted to do just that. He bucked up and left the Onn Inn. He was determined to find a way out of Onn. There had to be a way out of here, and Anders was going to find it. He was not going to be stuck here in Onn when everyone else got to the top of Breaker's hidden G Spire spot and defeated that crazy guy!

Peeking out of the Inn cautiously Anders was pleased to not see Xam patrolling the town. The dragon might have finally calmed down and left, despite his persistent last cycle, had Anders not sprinted to the Inn he would have had 15 Weight Units to worry about. Xam was M.I.A., whivh was just fine as Anders had a full schedule this cycle.

The first stop was not going to be a happy one. Anders walked towards the little broken tower with a sad heart. He had wanted to say goodbye to Yallundy and visit her grave ever since he had heard of her death. He took the *Mixed Flower Bouquet* out of his *Ultra-Pack* that he had Combi-Fused out of a *Red, Blue, and Yellow Flower* last night. There was no recipe for it, and normally you could only use two items, but Anders had been very persistent.

Anders turned the corner and dropped his *Mixed Flower Bouquet* in shock. There was a lot of stuff here, but Yallundy was not amongst them. The gravesite was desecrated. There were *Potions* of the *Health, Mana,* and *Stamina* varieties piled up against the side wall. Foodstuffs, mostly *Golden Gribblet Pickles* and bakery goods, were tossed carelessly on the cobblestones. There was a bunch of outdated equipment discarded haphazardly about; this mess included a familiar pair of *Leather Armlets* which Anders used to own. "To Gliint, good luck out there. - Anders." was written inside the right cuff. Gliint must have given them to Yallundy at some point, he was in love with her after all and they did work for all classes. Finally, random monster drop items were scattered on top of hundreds of little *Combi-Fusion Flowers*. What was not here was anything to do with Yallundy, even the gravestone and her Quest Fairy were gone.

Anders had heard that Yallundy's favourite things were also left here, but he couldn't imagine her liking this much random stuff. A thought jumped into his head, this was the contents of a *Backpack*. What if Xam had flown down and stolen the body to bring it to Breaker so he could gloat. Maybe that sick jerk liked doing corpses! The thought made Anders sick, first just metaphorically, but then physically. Anders wasn't sure where that sickness had come from, but he vomited.

Anders shuddered and cleaned out his mouth as best as he could. He collected all of the non puke-covered items strewn about. Fortunately, he had only hit a few *Red Flowers*, which he tossed into the broken house to hide from the public eye. He tucked everything else together into his broken *Ultra-Pack,* since there was no point in just leaving them here. When he found Breaker, and therefore Yallundy's body, he would return her things to her.

It was a bit disappointing, but Anders left the *Mixed Flower Bouquet* next to the only Item he was sure had been Yallundy's, her now worse for wear *Ni Hao Bunny©* journal. He said goodbye to the tall soft-spoken, silver-skinned troll and walked back towards town.

He checked every wall, every alley, every everything. He double checked them. Triple checked. There was simply no other way out of Onn. Deep down he already knew that. He would find no comfort within these walls, only other walls. His Green Quest Fairy was no help, spouting endless dribble about the importance of cats.

The only other option was Onn Forest. Anders knew that they had checked absolutely everything there as well, but they could have missed a secret path. Maybe there was a path behind the Airship, or a hidden warp wall they had walked by that wasn't obvious. Anders had to try, and really had nothing else to do.

Anders hadn't even fully ported into Onn Forest yet and was already being attacked.

> (Red) Spiderboy's Text Box: You little bitch! Nobody escapes me!

With an attack of his *Web Shot*, the Spiderboy had hit Anders and completely bound up the elf's wrists. Anders was now under the Bound (Wrists) Status effect.

> Anders' Text Box: Eep!

> (Red) Spiderboy's Text Box: I've been waiting for you. I could feel you walking around in Onn. I knew it was you! I have *Tremor Sense* bitch! I am going to wrap you up completely in webs, and I am going to give you a good old fashioned fucking. Then I am going to eat most of your little bitch health up and almost kill you. Then I am going to fuck you again. After that I am going to drain you Hit Point by Hit Point until you are in Dire Status. I will line up your head with a big pointy piece of scenery and fuck you again, but really hard and hope that the pointy thing gets you right in the eye and… hey, where did you go?

Anders had only made it to 'waiting for you', as he had left Onn Forest early during the Spiderboy's evil monologue and was now back safely in Onn. He could hear the Spiderboy yell in defeat even from here in the adjacent area. The boss of Onn Forest had gone insane with a lust for revenge. Sure, Anders had killed the Spiderboy's friend and had humiliated him, but why was he holding such a grudge? It didn't make any sense.

Anders had a new problem to add to his list of many. His wrists were still bound and he needed to find something sharp to cut them with. Most of the geometry in Onn was depressingly flat. Anders hadn't noticed that until now. Even the broken rocks near the tower were round and pleasant. He remembered something he had seen a hundred times before while trying unsuccessfully to use his weapons to break the bonds. On the accessible counter of the bakery, right next to the pleasantly plump Zal Finn NPC who sold baked goods, was a scenery object, a knife in a block of cake.

Anders hurried to the bakery and stuck his wrists inside. Even if he stretched toward the knife Anders couldn't quite reach it. He jumped up on the counter, and could just barely reach it. Anders began to slowly cut through the webbing.

> NPC Margarine's Text Box: Welcome to my Bakery Shoppe, hun. How can I help you today?

The Bakery Shoppe Menu popped up, being this close to NPC Margarine and doing an action had activated her. Anders quickly pressed Exit and continued his cutting.

> NPC Margarine's Text Box: Welcome to my Bakery Shoppe, hun. How can I help you today?

The Bakery Shoppe Menu was up again, Anders pressed Exit again. He was getting close to cutting through the webbing and went back to work.

> NPC Margarine's Text Box: Welcome to my Bakery Shoppe, hun. How can I help you today?

The Bakery Shoppe Menu was up yet again. Anders closed it but was annoyed this time.

> Anders' Text Box: Stop that! I don't want to buy anything right now!

> NPC Margarine's Text Box: Welcome to my Bakery Shoppe, hun. How can I help you today?

The Menu opened yet again. Anders pressed Exit again and performed the *Scowl Animation*.

> NPC Margarine's Text Box: Welcome to my Bakery Shoppe, hun. How can I help you today?

Anders was legitimately mad now. He closed the menu for the sixth time.

> Anders' Text Box: Stop that!

> NPC Margarine's Text Box: Welcome to my Bakery Shoppe, hun. How can I help you today?

He closed the menu yet again and sighed.

> NPC Margarine's Text Box: Welcome to my Bakery Shoppe, hun. How can I help you today?

The menu was not closed correctly this time, and Anders purchased a *Grand Fullcake* by mistake, the most expensive item on the menu.

> Anders' Text Box: Come on! That wasn't even called a *Sigh Animation*.

> NPC Margarine's Text Box: Welcome to my Bakery Shoppe, hun. How can I help you today?

Anders only had to exit the Bakery Shoppe Menu twenty-eight more times before he finally got the webbing off and was free (only four of which involved the actual cutting of the web itself). He exited one last time after giving NPC Margarine the *Finger Animation*. It was actually the *Salute Animation* but Anders bended his fingers and proved it otherwise. It was totally worth it even if he had to exit The Bakery Shoppe Menu yet again.

Anders left the Bakery Shoppe and was face to face with the hooded NPC who hung around here. Anders had forgotten all about him and let out a *Gasp in Alarm Animation*.

> NPC Margarine's Text Box: Welcome to my Bakery Shoppe, hun. How

> can I help you today?

Anders exited the menu, and started to run. The hooded bakery NPC followed him closely. Even though Anders was at full sprint and the NPC just walked they stayed the same distance apart. It made no sense and perfect sense at the same time.

Anders ducked into an alley and used his *Stealth*. As a Ranged Style Night Ranger it wasn't his strongest skill, but hopefully he was good enough at it to fool an NPC. Anders was having a bad cycle, because the hooded bakery NPC spotted him without trouble and turned down the alley. Anders headed in the opposite way. He could see the main street from here and could get away. As he approached a different NPC stepped forward and blocked the entrance. It was the Zal Finn that was normally standing right beside the town entrance. She was always holding the signpost with the word 'Onn' in her right hand.

> NPC Greeta's Text Box: Welcome to Onn!

Fortunately, what Anders lacked in *Stealth* skills he more than made up for in Jumping skills. He ran towards NPC Greeta and used her face as a springboard to execute a *Double Jump*. Anders had left a footprint on her face, but had gotten back to the street safely.

> NPC Greeta's Text Box: Welcome to Onn!

Anders looked back and was happy to see that NPC Greeta and the hooded bakery NPC did not leave the alley. They looked too scared to step out. NPCs had never looked scared before and Anders was confused. The NPC pursuers turned and fled, while others Zal Finns in the area began to scatter. Anders felt the ground shake and some hot sticky breath on the back of his neck. Latin theme music started.

> Xam, the Orange Dragon of Light's Text Box: There you are, my little piece of Dragon Candy! I've been worried.

◈ Chapter 19 ◈
UNNECESSARY QUESTING D

Mr. Max's Text Box: Finally fellow adventurette!

Gliint's Text Box: *Wipes away sweat* This is gruelling. We are almost there though, one more push!

Mr. Max's Text Box: What? I was talking about Level 98.99. I just made .99! But yeah, one more big rush and then we are at maximum!

Gliint's Text Box: I am just glad this is almost over!

Mr. Max's Text Box: It's not over yet. I need a bunch more xp until getting to max Level and a secret prize.

Gliint's Text Box: Not that. I mean the area. We are almost through it!

Mr. Max's Text Box: Right, the area. I had forgotten about that. This last section looks to be three times as long as any others, plus it is full of monsters! We are going to get shocked to bits. Actually, you are going to get shocked to bits, I can run much faster.

Gliint's Text Box: *Slight smile* Well thanks for not leaving me behind.

Mr. Max's Text Box: No problem fellow adventurette!

Gliint's Text Box: *Blush* Especially after I lagged right into that pool filled with obscene fish.

Brown Quest Fairy's Text Box: *Waves hands desperately* The three pools in The Strangely Ominous Empty Field With Lightning Rods Placed Too Far Apart contain fish that are important to a quest that allows you to leave the ar—

Mr. Max's Interruption Text Box: Okay, let's make a run for it. I am going to kill all the monsters on the way. You just deal with your lag. We will meet at Zal Finn over there. Hey, that is strange. I thought Zal Finn was with Fourni and... uh... that purple guy. We are supposed to be the team of two!

Gliint's Text Box: We are the team of two Mr. Max! That isn't Zal Finn, that is a random NPC standing near the exit to this area.

Brown Quest Fairy's Text Box: *Pleas* NPC Hugo is in charge of The Something Fishing Quest. This quest requires you to —

Mr. Max's Interruption Text Box: Okay, are you ready to rush?

Gliint's Lag Text Box: *Quick nod* Yes, let's do this!

Max was already out of the protective range of the final too far apart lightning rod before Gliint had even replied. Monsters fell to his mighty and new *6 Handed Sword* all while Mr. Max was getting shocked by large bolts of random lightning. By the time Gliint's lag had finally cleared Mr. Max was completely through the area.

With a single gnome sized step into the unsafe zone the monsters of the region had respawned. Gliint started to run, both slowly and frantically, through the monster infested area. Monsters of all types were closing in quickly, but Gliint was certain he could make it if he just pulled through. With a telltale skip of his step, he knew that a patch of lag was soon going to be upon him. The lag set in, but not before the little gnome had time to get out a Text Box.

Gliint's Text Box: *Panic!*

Gliint was frozen mid step and monsters were quickly closing in. A lightning bolt cascaded from the sky and struck the gnome with impressive force. Mr. Max knew that he was too far away to get to the gnome in time but he dashed towards his lagged out companion anyways.

Mr. Max's Text Box: I'm coming for you fellow adventurette!

Still frozen in place midair, Gliint took a lightning beatdown. It was a particularly long bout of lag, and Max could only watch as he chopped up yet another Venus Volt-Ape. Gliint was nearly out of Health and a wooded/feathered Treegull was poised to strike. This was going to be it for the gnome, he would awaken from his lag skip and would be alarmed to find out he was now dead. The Treegull jumped towards Gliint to get the final blow.

######### #### #### ####### ####

Gliint awoke from his lag with a sharpened Treegull Hook just a single length unit from his heart. The Treegull had a misty look in its eyes that stared at the gnome for a few rounds, perplexed. After a bolt of lightning struck the Treegull it snapped out of its trance. The gnome was picked up by the Treegull in leafy feathered arms. Both Max and Gliint watched in wonder as the Treegull ran towards the safe area and deposited the gnome on the ground. Mr. Max was so startled that it took a random bolt of lightning to the face to snap him out of it. With a few big beefy steps the slightly charred avatar was back with the Treegull, which was nuzzling the confused gnome.

> Mr. Max's Text Box: What in the Flaming Pit just happened?

> Gliint's Text Box: *Shrug* I don't have any idea.

> Mr. Max's Text Box: Now you have some sort of pet. Pets are only part of the Necromancer and Summoner classes, not the Chemist class. How did you manage that exactly? Was it lag again like with the Bacon?

> Gliint's Text Box: *Shrug* I still don't have any idea.

> Mr. Max's Text Box: It really likes you. See, it's getting all cuddly with you.

The Treegull cooed with a barky voice and stroked the gnome with a gentle wing. Despite its best efforts however a hooked claw accidently jutted into the gnome's thigh and put Gliint into Dire Status. The monster was flustered.

######### #### ##X# ####### #O##

With a wave of its wings and branches the Treegull cast *Fullheal* and the gnome was both back at full health and dumbfounded.

> Mr. Max's Text Box: I didn't even know Treegulls could cast spells, they are a melee type monster.

> Gliint's Text Box: *Wide eyed wonder* I am just glad that it didn't kill me, either on purpose or by accident.

Gliint patted the monster on the head, but cut his hand on a sharp feather. Before the gnome could even react, the Treegull had cast *Low Heal* to recover Gliint to full health.

> Mr. Max's Text Box: Exactly Little Bro, now let's go and talk to that NPC, she has a Quest Bubble!

> Orange Quest Fairy's Text Box: NPC Hugo is in charge of The Something Fishing Quest fellow adventurer. This quest requires you to collect fish and must be completed before you can leav—

> Gliint's Interruption Text Box: Little Bro? *Eyebrow raise*

NPC Hugo stood in front of the locked gate which marked the exit of the area. He was not eager to move out of the way.

> NPC Hugo's Text Box: Welcome to The Strangely Ominous Empty Field With Lightning Rods Placed Too Far Apart, a section of Spire D. If you complete my quest, Something Fishing, you will gain #three# rewards. The first will be the key to my gate and access to the next area of Spire D. Collect the three golden ####fish# from the pools by constant fishing.

> Mr. Max's Text Box: You need to complete a quest to get out of this area? One of those pools was right near the beginning! This is horrible! We are going to have to run back to the start? Why didn't anyone ever warn us?

> Orange Quest Fairy's Text Box: …

> Gliint's Text Box: It's too late tonight to run back. Let's just set up camp for the night. *Sigh* I wish we had a *Portie Tent*, sleeping in the rain is getting really old.

> Mr. Max's Text Box: I agree. I am soaked to the bone. I've been chafing on top of other chafes for cycles now.

The duo set up camp and sat by the fire that still somehow worked in the rain. It had been a very long cycle and equipment and Gliint's *Backpack* had been taken off with a thud. The Treegull had curled up near Gliint and cuddled his leg.

> Gliint's Text Box: I hate to ask this, *Shame* but no monsters dropped any food today, can I buy some more since I don't have any in my *Backpack*.

> Mr. Max's Text Box: Of course you can Little Bro. Delicious appliances or *Bacon*?

> Gliint's Text Box: *Bacon*, obviously.

Mr. Max's Text Box: Your loss. I need to ask you something about your *Backpack*.

Gliint's Text Box: Um, *Gulp* sure. What is it?

Mr. Max's Text Box: How come you like *Bacon* better?

Gliint's Text Box: What? *Eyebrow raise* Uh. It tastes better. What does that have to do with my *Backpack*?

Mr. Max's Text Box: Oh, I had forgotten about your *Backpack*. I needed to talk about that as well. Can I see it for a round? Well, I'll need four rounds.

Gliint's Text Box: Why? No! It's mine.

Mr. Max's Text Box: Chill out, I just noticed that you only have a regular *Backpack*, it doesn't have enough carrying capacity for you. I have all the stuff to upgrade it. 1000 carrying capacity is much better than your 200.

Gliint's Text Box: Oh sorry, It's just... well... I don't think it would matter. I have 2500 worth of weight in here, so getting to 1000 isn't going to be nearly enough. Thanks though Max.

Mr. Max's Text Box: You have 2500 weight units in a 200 carrying capacity bag? No wonder you are moving so slow. How did you even get that much in there? Why do you have no food or items? Let's go through that thing and clear it out! I'll hold some of it for you! We can store some things in *My Spiritual Storage Device From The Crags Of Halm*, I don't understand why everyone else doesn't have one, it was a very easy quest.

Gliint's Text Box: It's complicated, but I can't let you hold anything. It's just really important that I do it.

Mr. Max's Text Box: It's not a big deal fellow adventurer, I have 750 capacity left. I am keeping a bunch open in case the Maximum Level prize is really heavy. Just let me hold some of it for you! Here, just let me help otherwise we will be stuck running around this area for another 10 cycles. I don't have the *Health Potions* for both of us to do that!

Both Max and Gliint reached for the *Backpack*. Gliint was unlucky to experience lag and was beaten to the punch. A round later when Gliint came back he grabbed the *Backpack* with a death grip in an attempt to get it back.

> Gliint's Text Box: No! It's mine! *Annoyed grunt*

> Mr. Max's Text Box: I'm just improving it! Calm down.

Gliint wrestled the exceedingly heavy *Backpack* from the much stronger and larger Mr. Max.

> Gliint's Text Box: You mustn't! Please! *Plead*

> Mr. Max's Text Box: Okay, I'm sorry Little Bro. I was just trying to help.

Without warning Mr. Max let go of the gnome's *Backpack*. Gliint was not prepared for the sudden tchange of heart and both he and his *Backpack* went flying backwards. The *Backpack* hit against a rock, opened, and spilled its contents on the ground. However, the gnome hit nothing and flew off a nearby cliff.

########'# #E## ##X# ###I### #O##

Gliint was dangling precariously off the cliff, but the Treegull came to his rescue and pulled him up, albeit painfully due to its razor feathers. Mr. Max would have helped but he was distracted by the contents of the gnome's *Backpack*.

> Gliint's Text Box: It's not what it looks like… *Panic* I just… I just… Couldn't…

To hastily hide what he had done, Gliint threw items back into his *Backpack* despite the fact that they would never all fit again. He grabbed the Constantly-Colour-Changing Quest Fairy and stuffed it quickly inside, not letting it even catch its breath.

> Mr. Max's Text Box: Yallundy?! You put Yallundy's body into your *Backpack*?

> Gliint's Text Box: *Tears* I just couldn't leave her behind. She needed to be with us at the end. She just… needed to be with us.

> Mr. Max's Text Box: It's okay Little Bro, a little serial killer to be honest, but okay. There are a lot of things about this that are creepy, but I understand.

> Gliint's Text Box: You *Wipes tears away*… do?

> Mr. Max's Text Box: Yep! She meant a lot to someone… who did she like again? They would appreciate her being with us at the end. Your heart was in the right place at least, but still it was really creepy. Maybe next time you need to hide a dead body we can do it in a way that isn't

so terrifying to others. Okay, now let's think about this for a round then... How can we do this?

Gliint's Text Box: Do what?

Mr. Max's Text Box: Take her with us in a much less creepy way!

Gliint's Text Box: *Shock* Really?

Mr. Max's Text Box: Of course! Okay, well we probably don't need to keep the *Ornate Tombstone*. That weighs like 500 right there... Yallundy weights... 1200? Wow! Well she was a Troll and pretty tall I guess. Oh, no she weighs 1000. The rest is all the flowers on her. Okay then. If we upgrade your *Backpack* fully you can still carry Yallundy, but nothing else. I can carry her important other things and her random other things we can stash in *My Spiritual Storage Device From The Crags Of Halm*. Perfect!

Gliint's Text Box: Yeah, but *Blush* then she would be naked!

Mr. Max's Text Box: The flowers don't really cover much anyways. We take her naked, or you get zapped by lightning while we run back to go fishing. I'm pretty sure she would understand.

The Treegull was poking around with Yallundy's discarded gear. It was particularly interested in her *String-Harper*.

Gliint's Text Box: Hey you, *Scold* get away from there!

The Treegull was a bit put out, but within a few rounds Gliint's *Backpack* was upgraded fully, Yallundy was naked and safely tucked away, and all of Yallundy's gear was secure from wandering Treegulls. A quick test showed that while Gliint was still a bit laggy, he could now move at a relatively normal speed. Mr. Max also could now hoist the gnome onto his shoulders if needed.

Mr. Max's Text Box: Perfect, now let's get some rest. Tomorrow we get to go fishing!

Mr. Max used the *Stomp Around Excited While Waving Your Arms Around Like a Little Girl Animation*.

~ ~ ~

It was another rainy cycle, but Gliint was in a much better spirit than normal. It was as if 1500 weight units had been lifted from his little *Backpack*. Max had found out his terrible deed and been alright with it, but Gliint was not keen on sharing that particular secret with anyone else. Maybe it was a good thing that the Player Pagers and WorldForums had erupted into flame preventing communication (but probably not).

> Mr. Max's Text Box: You are still lagging, huh?

> Gliint's Text Box: Yeah. *Nods*

> Mr. Max's Text Box: I was hoping the *Backpack* would solve it. Oh well let's try this.

> Gliint's Text Box: *Confused* Try what?

> Mr. Max's Text Box: It's not there yet? It should be. You said you were my biggest fan right?

> Gliint's Text Box: Yes I did say that, I run your fan club… *More confused* but what does that have to do with… hold on someone is at the door. brb.

Mr. Max waited with a *Grin Animation* on his face.

> Gliint's Text Box: YOU BOUGHT ME A WHOLE NEW COMPUTER? *SHOCK*

> Mr. Max's Text Box: Well yes, I couldn't just stand by and watch my biggest fan lag out. It would look bad on me if you got yourself eaten because of lag. I did put some files on there for you first though, like some spreadsheets and my guide.

> Gliint's Text Box: Wow! *Jaw Drop* Graphics programs, video editing software, and music mixing programs. This must have cost a fortune. I can't accept this, it's too much!

> Mr. Max's Text Box: Not a big deal, I get all of that stuff for basically free anyways. I hope you enjoy it. That system is top of the line and it should get rid of that lag right away. Log out and come back.

Gliint used the *Log Out* function and with a *Blip* he had vanished. After as many rounds as it took to hastily set up a new computer, the gnome was back with a *Bloop*.

> Gliint's Text Box: Thank you so much Max! Wow! This thing even has every single song ever recorded by *Caution Step* on it! Even their impossible to find Christmas Album, *Slippery Surface*? They are only the best band ever! How did you know that I am president of their fan club as well?

Mr. Max's Text Box: Same email address on the websites.

Glïint's Text Box: Wow! This is so exciting! *Almost faint* I love their music. They are the reason that I started to play this game! Did you know that they have a licensed song in the main game and two in this expansion?

Mr. Max's Text Box: Three. They have three songs in this expansion. *Theme of the Dragon Rider*, *Coliseum Rockstar*, and *Onnwards To Onn*. One is a hidden Easter Egg though, so you wouldn't know.

Glïint's Text Box: This is amazing, the graphics look so much better! My lag is—

Mr. Max looked at the gnome frozen in place.

Glïint's Lag Text Box: completely gone!

Glïint's Text Box: Dammit!

Mr. Max's Text Box: I don't understand it, that should have worked.

Glïint's Text Box: Well, it's a lot better than it's ever been. So thank you so much!

Mr. Max's Text Box: No problem Little Bro. Now hold on, I'm going to carry you while we run.

Glïint's Text Box: Alright.

Now that they could run, and Glïint could be carried, progress to the first fishing pond was exceptionally quick. It took only a few rounds of high speed sprinting to get there. The pair, and the Treegull, looked around confused but they could see no way of fishing.

Glïint's Text Box: *Blink* Um… So how do we… uh fish exactly?

Brown Quest Fairy's Text Box: To fish you need —

Glïint's Interruption Text Box: These fish… uh… they all look… uh… *Blush*. #Puckerfish#, #Blownfish#, and #Pussyfish#. They are all… broken. Despite the #'s in their names their faces are clearly anuses, mouths, and vaginas. None of these are golden though.

Mr. Max's Text Box: Yes, you are right Little Bro. None of these are golden! We must need to fish until one shows up. Standard fish rules.

Gliint's Text Box: How do we fish?

Brown Quest Fairy's Text Box: We already tried to tell you, but you avatars are always so rude *pout*!

Orange Quest Fairy's Text Box: Yes. No matter what we say you always inte—

Mr. Max's Interruption Text Box: Awe sorry little guys. Please, can you tell us how to fish?

Brown Quest Fairy's Text Box: To fish you need to use a rod. There is a rod loc—

Gliint's Interruption Text Box: But we don't have rods! *Confused look* Where are we supposed to… uh… Max what are you doing?

Mr. Max's Text Box: Getting my rod out!

Mr. Max used the *Flex Animation* and his rod sprung up to full hardness.

Gliint had heard rumors of Mr. Max's rod. It was always big and crammed into his Armour uncomfortably, but actually seeing it released was an experience.

Gliint's Text Box: That's… Gigantic!

Mr. Max's Text Box: I haven't even grown it yet. I am sure this is big enough to go fishing with!

Now on his knees Mr. Max dangled his full sized rod into the pool. A curious #Blownfish# came near and took the bait, it swallowed up about a third of Max's member. With a swift *Thrusting Animation* Max catapulted the fish to the shore and scored 1 Fish Point.

Mr. Max's Text Box: Ha! Take that #Blownfish#! I got a Fish Point! What is a Fish Point?

Orange Quest Fairy's Text Box: Whoever scores the most Fish Points wins a bonus Accessory when the quest is completed. Golden Fish are worth much more than the normal variety.

Mr. Max pulled out another lewd fish with an expert *Thrusting Animation*, this time it was a large #Pussyfish# that scored 2 points.

Mr. Max's Text Box: I am going to win at fishing fellow adventurer!

Gliint's Text Box: That is alright. You can win. I'm just going to watch.

Mr. Max used the *Splash The Stuck Up Gnome With Water Animation*. Amazingly the

Global Use Total was already at 478.

> Mr. Max's Text Box: Oh come on, where is the fun in that Little Bro?

> Gliint's Text Box: Well... *Blush* uh...

> Mr. Max's Text Box: Just whip it out and catch some fish or you are going to lose!

Gliint started to disrobe hesitantly. Mr. Max had an impressive rod, rivaling even some of the most impressive monsters. According to legend, the thing could even grow bigger! But Gliint was a gnome. Gnomes were half the size of humans already, and even though Gliint had never seen another naked male gnome before he was already sure he didn't exactly measure up.

By the time Gliint had taken down his pants Max was already at 14 Fish Points. The little gnome's rod was exposed, and even hard as it was now it was anything but normal for things in this game. His rod would be called by some 'cute', but most others would just call it 'tiny'.

> Mr. Max's Text Box: I thought you said you were my 'biggest' fan? ;)

Gliint very nearly used the *Blush Animation* after he felt Mr. Max's eyes linger on him, but instead resisted at the last instant and changed it to just blushing without the use of the official action. Regardless Mr. Max still let out a moan, grew a few length units, and thrust a #Puckerfish# clear out of the area.

> Mr. Max's Text Box: Whoa, that was one tight little #Puckerfish#!

There was no possible way Gliint could fish with his rod like Mr. Max was, if he was going to do this he was going to have to get into the water. He stepped into the pool and attempted to seduce a nearby #Pussyfish#, but it showed no interest.

> Mr. Max's Text Box: Gliint? Hey is that you, Gliint?! Well hi! It's been so long. I haven't seen you since right after we found out you needed all the Gigas equipment to challenge The Plague Of Shadow! Where have you been Little Bro?

> Gliint's Text Box: Huh? *Eyebrow raise* How do you suddenly remember who I am? If I knew all this time all I needed to do was strip naked, jump into a pool, and fail at attempting to seduce a fish for you to recognize me...

> Mr. Max's Text Box: I recognized my signature on your ass there is all. Who could forget such a tiny little gnome butt like that one?

Gliint had completely forgotten that he never had washed off his first Mr. Max signature. He looked back and there it was, still written on his right butt cheek in permanent marker.

Gliint had to resist blushing again, which lead to Mr. Max growing a fair amount of length units and a #Pussyfish# being thrust so hard that it burst clear through a very far away mountainside. A giant explosion rumbled through the area and little bits of #Pussyfish# rained down over the entire spire.

> Mr. Max's Text Box: These little fish bastards sure know what they are doing! Damn.

The last fish in the pool was gone, forever lost into the mountainside. Mr. Max had gotten 32 Fish Points and Gliint had gotten wet. From the secret depths of the water emerged their goal. The very proud, and very large, Golden #Cockfish# was now filling up the pool with its golden majesty.

Mr. Max reeled in his rod quickly.

> Mr Max's Text Box: I can't do anything with something like that, you can have the points!

The Golden #Cockfish# circled the pool in a predatory fashion. Gliint, who was stranded in the middle of the pool started to panic as the hunter began a course headed straight for the little gnome's signed ass. Gliint began to rush to the edge of the pool, but it was clear that he was going to meet the fish before the shore.

> Gliint's Text Box: No! Help! *Panic* I'm not even gay curious anymore and that thing is bigger than my entire leg!

With gnome butt in its sights the Golden #Cockfish# cut through the water at an alarming speed. It would have reached and penetrated its target except for the fact that the Treegull jumped into the path of the oncoming cock.

###L####'S #E## ##X# ###I#N# #O!#

Gliint was confused and turned around to look. The Treegull's glazed over eyes first cleared, gave Gliint a look of aggression, and finally became crossed as a gnome leg length Golden #Cockfish# was rammed up its Treegull ass. A squishy display later and the Treegull was dead. Gliint gained 30 Fish Points by pulling out the spent Golden #Cockfish#. He raised it over his head in victory, it limply slapped his face a few times.

> Gliint's Text Box: Wow! I'm almost winning now! *Cheer*

> Mr. Max's Text Box: I'm still winning Little Bro!

> Gliint's Text Box: I'm just sad that my Treegull died. *Sad face*

> Mr. Max's Text Box: There are lots of other Treegulls out there, just seduce another one before we get to the next pond.

Mr. Max was wrong, it was not a Treegull but a Light-footed Dancing Yak that fell in love with Gliint. The next pool contained more fish than the previous one. Gliint stayed close to the edge this time, but despite his best efforts could not entice any fish to take his bait. Once the Golden #Cockfish# reared its engorged golden head Gliint started to leave the pool but the Light-footed Dancing Yak stepped forward and offered itself to the cause. After its eyes unglazed it was pounded to death and Gliint pocketed the golden reward. The total Fish Points were now Gliint 60 vs. Mr. Max 72.

Before the last pool the duo was joined by a smitten Venus Volt-Ape. This pool contained the least amount of fish yet, but they were all at least 2 point fish. Gliint did some quick math and determined that if he could catch the Golden #Cockfish# again and just one other fish he could win the challenge. Otherwise Mr. Max was going to win. Gliint didn't know why, but he really wanted to win this now. With a tearing off of his pants that was accompanied by a casting of *Advanced Serpent Speed* Gliint was deep in the water before Mr. Max had even loosened his belt.

> Gliint's Text Box: *Taunt* I'm going to win this!

Mr. Max used the *Flex Animation* in preparation for the challenge and then the *Smile Animation*.

> Mr. Max's Text Box: Good luck Little Bro! You are going to need it!

Gliint saw his target, an attractive #Pussyfish# with really shiny red lips. Gliint waded up to the fish and displayed his cute little rod. The #Pussyfish# however was not impressed with the bait. Other fish were already being thrust out of the pool by Max, but Gliint was not going to give up so easily. Presenting hard in front of his target he wiggled his hips seductively, with no success. Then he cock-slapped the #Pussyfish# several times, with no success. He stuck his fingers into the #Pussyfish# and massaged opened its mouth, with no success. He grabbed the fish by the gills, lined himself up with the mouth and thrust at the lips desperately, with no success.

> Gliint's Text Box: Damn you!

This fish was double broken. Gliint was going to need a new target. He looked around but only two other fish were left and they were both at the other end of the pool and already interested in Mr. Max.

Gliint looked down at his uninterested #Pussyfish#.

> Gliint's Text Box: That's it! You made me do this! *Scowl*

Gliint executed his special small caps THRUSTING ANIMATION at the #Pussyfish#. The gnome's official animation was so sexy when preformed that it could (and would) cause angels to weap salty tears. The fish quivered with intense pleasure and after several multiple orgasms it flopped upside down, completely spent. Gliint grabbed the defeated fish and held it upright victorious.

> Gliint's Text Box: I did it! *Cheer* Go Gliint! I won!

> Mr. Max's Text Box: Good job Gliint. Just catch that Golden

> #Cockfish# beside you and you win!

It was with widened eyes that Gliint realized that he was standing in the middle of the pool, hands high in the air holding a fish, cheering in victory, all while a glistening Golden #Cockfish# was headed straight for his opening.

Two things happened simultaneously: the Venus Volt-Ape had jumped into the path of the Golden #Cockfish#, and Gliint used the **GASP ANIMATION** in surprise.

###L####'S #E#T B#X# ##I#N# #O!#

The Venus Volt-Ape doubled over in pleasure due to the seductive gasp just in time for the Golden #Cockfish# to enter it. Gliint pondered why there were monsters falling in love with him and sacrificing themselves to the god of fish banging to help him win this contest, but after a few rounds of cock thrusting Gliint seized control of the spent Golden #Cockfish# and promptly forgot. He was victorious! That was far more important. Gliint 92 vs. Mr. Max 90.

> Mr. Max's Text Box: Let's go finish that pulsing quest icon! Don't worry little icon! Daddy Max is coming for you and your wonderful xp reward!

Mr. Max fished Gliint out of the pond and was off running to NPC Hugo with a half nude flabbergasted gnome on his shoulders and an armful of lewd fish in his arms. The pair moved far too fast to have another random monster fall in love with Gliint on the way. As they approached the lightning rod glade near NPC Hugo the background music changed into the boss theme. A viscous Silver Sludge dropped into the area and turned itself inside out to reveal its large sludgy penis.

> Gliint's Text Box: Oh great, *Facepalm* I never even put my pants back on! Now there is a boss with a giant cock.

> Mr. Max's Text Box: Just stay on my shoulders and shoot at it with your Gratling Gun. I'll just chop it up and we will be fine Little Bro.

It was hard for the gnome to attack with a ranged weapon while so close to a monster. The large bobbing penis was particularly distracting. It was hard to hold onto Max while he was attacking with all of his special moves. After a particularly gut wrenching move called *Hurt the Triad* the gnome lost his balance and landed ass up in the dirt.

This as a welcome invitation to go to gnometown as far as the Silver Sludge was concerned and it used its turns to pin the gnome down and prep itself for entry. Gliint could not act while pinned and used his turn to become very worried. Mr. Max attacked, and while he got a Sneak Attack the Sludge was not defeated.

On the Silver Sludge's next turn it pressed up against the tight little gnome hole with intent to rape.

###L##D#'S #E#T B#X: ##I#N# #O!#

The Silver Sludge stopped its movements. Gliint had guessed that if the thing had eyes they would have glazed over. The boss music stopped, the battle was over.

> Mr. Max's Text Box: That was strange.

> **Creature Name:** Silver Sludge
> **Class:** Magical
> **Level:** 70
> **Special Attacks:** Lob, Pin, Pin More, Sludge Slam, Smackdown, Lightning Aura
> **Drops:** Silver Goo
> **First Player Encounter Notes:** #o#o#y #e###s w#t# m# G##i##! – ##l###d#

> Gliint's Text Box: That was stranger. *Confused* Why did the Instant-Wiki entry come up?

> Mr. Max's Text Box: It is in love with you Little Bro! You are like a monster love magnet. I don't get it, but don't mind. We still got full experience points for it.

The Silver Sludge was indeed in love with Gliint. It was as big as an elephant (which existed here but only with saddles), but it was cuddling up to Gliint's leg. The contact of sludge on skin shocked the gnome with an intense *Lightning Aura*. The Silver Sludge looked sorry after damaging the gnome.

> Gliint's Text Box: I'm more confused than you are.

> Mr. Max's Text Box: Let's talk to NPC Hugo and complete that quest!

> Orange Quest Fairy's Text Box: NPC Hugo is—

> NPC Hugo's Interruption Text Box: Congratulations little sparks! Here is your first reward! You may now progress to the next area!

The gate out of the area was unlocked and Hugo stopped blocking the way.

> NPC Hugo's Text Box: Here is your second reward! An Accessory for 'insert avatar name'! May the winner with the most Fish Points step forward!

Gliint eagerly stepped forward with a grin on his face.

> NPC Hugo's Text Box: #It is a Mega Strap-On! Enjoy your Sexcessory!#

> Gliint's Text Box: Huh? Sexcessory?

Taking out a *Mega Strap-On* from his invisible supply NPC Hugo presented the reward to Gliint. With a blur of animation the gnome's pants had been pulled down and the *Mega Strap-On*, complete with its interesting belt, were forcibly equipped onto the avatar. Gliint looked down amazed, this thing was glossy and it was impressive in size. It would have made any normal human male very proud had it been their actual member. On Gliint's little frame however it was out of place, it might even be bigger than Mr. Max's in proportion. It was strapped just above Gliint's actual penis, which was absolutely ridiculously undersized now.

> NPC Hugo's Text Box: Your third reward is… *pause for dramatic effect*

NPC Hugo pulled down his pants and revealed himself.

> NPC Hugo's Continued Text Box: My Electro-Shock Cock!

> Mr. Max's Text Box: Thank the Maker. I've been so pent up lately and those damn fish got me so turned on! Finally a pretty girl to unload in! I hope you are worth some good xp!

Mr. Max approached NPC Hugo while pulling down his belt. He used his big muscles and manhandled the NPC. He flipping him over and leaned him against the now unlocked gate.

> NPC Hugo's Text Box: No wait! I was supposed to be the one that… oh? OH! OOOOOHHHHH!

Gliint spent the rounds in which NPC Hugo was getting his reward by attempting to remove the *Mega Strap-On*, but despite his best efforts his brand new Third Accessory Slot item would not come off. You could only replace it with something else according to the description, so for now Gliint was stuck with it on.

> Mr. Max's Text Box: Ah! That's so much better! Nice manhood there Little Bro, almost as big as mine! Time to go into the next area! I can hardly wait, it is so exciting!

Mr. Max was quickly in the new area, it took Gliint a bit longer as he had to step over the collapsed and grinning NPC Hugo.

> Mr. Max's Text Box: Oh my Maker! Hurry up Gliint! I just found Anders!

Chapter 20
◈ ◈
UNNECESSARY QUESTING C

Lissa's Text Box: So it's a jumping puzzle area? #PerfectIrony.

Purple Quest Fairy's Text Box: This area is called The Canyon of the Complicated Jumping Puzzles. #HeyListen! It is advised that before you start to progress through this area that you start the quest Returning The Related otherwise you—

Zal Finn III's Interruption Text Box: Looks like it, Sweet I am all about jumping now. Are you going to need any help Lissa?

Lissa's Text Box: I am feeling much better. I am sure I will be fine.

Taking a flying leap towards the first platform Lissa landed much more gracefully than Fournimer had thought she would. The round after she landed a painful snap could be heard and Lissa screamed in pain. She fell backwards and couldn't catch herself before she rolled off the platform. She screamed as she fell into the bottomless abyss below and disappeared in a star of light accompanied by a twinkle sound effect.

Zal Finn fell to the ground and used the *Scream to the Heavens Animation*.

Zal Finn III's Text Box: LISSA NO!!! You can't be… you just can't!

> Lissa's Text Box: I can't be what?

Lissa was standing beside them, she had popped back into place in a triple flash with about 10% of her Health gone, but was otherwise fine.

> Zal Finn III's Text Box: Oh… never mind.

Fournimer used the *Quizzical Look Animation*.

> Lissa's Text Box: I recommend falling. #BlastingOffAgain. I don't think I want to do it too many more times though.

Zal Finn jumped off the cliff and into the bottomless abyss below. She disappeared in a star of light and came back in a triple flash with 10% less Health.

> Zal Finn III's Text Box: That was sweet! I feel sick!

> Fournimer's Text Box: okay The Finnster, you realize that someone just told you to go jump off a cliff… and then you actually did.

> Zal Finn III's Text Box: Not someone, it was Lissa! Now, let's do this jumping area!

With a *Fantastic Dancing Triple Flipping Double Jump* Zal Finn was off. She completely skipped the first platform and several others past that. Grace, drama, and jumping were important class skills for a Dancing Ninja Assassin. It took only a few rounds until Zal Finn was halfway through the area opening an impossible to get to red chest.

> Zal Finn III's Text Box: Sweet! A brand new *Shag Dancing Carpet*! Hey, are you two coming or what?

Zal Finn was off fantastically jumping again before either Lissa or Fournimer could reply. Fournimer looked over at Lissa, she was lightly sweating and had a concerned look on her face. Almost as if he was nervous about this jumping puzzle. Lissa noticed Fourni's eyes on her and their glances met. For a split round Lissa showed what might have been compassion, but then her eyes steeled over.

> Lissa's Text Box: Nervous much Fourse?

Lissa was absolutely correct. Fournimer was nervous about this jumping puzzle. It had taken him nearly fifty cycles to just get used to walking around as a centaur. Jumping was a little more complicated, and despite all of his secret training back in Onn he still could barely jump over a scenic bush. Even with his unimpressive 37.4% successful scenic bush jumping rate (as calculated by Palcath), there was another problem. All of his successful jumps had involved a running start. Nearly all of these platforms were too small to run on. A few were going to be too small for Fournimer to even stand on. This area was not designed with centaurs in mind.

Fournimer could not show weakness to Lissa. After all, he wasn't the one with a busted up leg.

> Fournimer's Text Box: of course not Chick! you sure you don't need help? we could maybe tie a rope around you or something.

> Lissa's Text Box: Don't count me out yet. I don't need any help Centimer. You sure we shouldn't tie a rope around you? You're probably too big to triple flash back in.

> Fournimer's Text Box: just watch me! I'll jump circles around you!

> Lissa's Text Box: Let's go then!

With only a few more rounds of hesitation the jumping contest began. Lissa started with a barely passable jump onto the next platform. She landed with trouble, but kept up appearances ending with a flourish that would have impressed any gymnastics team. She looked back with a poorly disguised *Smirk Animation* that had obvious traces of a *Grimace Animation*. Not to be outdone Fournimer executed a mighty running jump. He only just stuck the landing (with just another step he would have toppled over the edge). Fournimer got himself ready for the next jump, he turned with much trouble on the small platform, and leapt over. He had less trouble with this jump due to the larger landing platform and looked back at Lissa with a *Smug Animation*.

Lissa returned the *Smug Animation*, but it had traces of the *Understanding Why the Centaur was so Nervous Before About Jumping Animation*. She jumped to the next platform, happy to have enough room this time to land by rolling.

The next platform was just a single Move Unit across. There would be no roll landing for Lissa as that took at least four Move Units, and no ability to stand for Fournimer as he took up two Move Units.

> Lissa's Text Box: You are going down, Fournitaur!

> Fournimer's Text Box: no, it will be you that goes down Chick! and I mean going down as in falling into the abyss.

> Lissa's Text Box: Well obviously, that was implied.

> Fournimer's Text Box: I just wanted to make sure that we were o—

> Lissa's Interruption Text Box: Stop stalling!

> Fournimer's Text Box: I'm not the one stalling! you are the one stalling!

> Lissa's Text Box: I am not stalling!

> Fournimer's Text Box: then jump!

> Lissa's Text Box: #HorseBeforeTheCart!

> Fournimer's Text Box: no, after you! I insist!

> Zal Finn III's Text Box: What are you two doing?

> Lissa and Fournimer's Simultaneous Text Boxes: Huh?

Looking up from their eye lock the stalling duo noticed that Zal Finn was now perched on top of the next little platform.

> Zal Finn III's Text Box: You guys only made it to the second platform? What's taking you so long?

> Fournimer's Text Box: it is just… uh… that… well we were—

> Lissa's Interruption Text Box: We were figuring out the best way across is all.

> Fournimer's Text Box: yeah, what she said!

> Zal Finn III's Text Box: That's a really good idea. We can use that when we cross the next time. Now we need to get back to Petalyuna.

> Pink Quest Fairy's Text Box: Petalyuna is rad. The —

> Lissa's Interruption Text Box: What? Why?

> Zal Finn III's Text Box: We can't leave this area until we complete the Returning The Related Quest, NPC Zreede told me so. We need to talk to NPC Areede to start it. Leaving is one of the three rewards, the others are an Accessory for whoever can complete the quest the fastest and a special mystery prize!

> Pink Quest Fairy's Text Box: Return—

> Lissa's Interruption Text Box: We have to go back to Petalyuna?

> Purple Quest Fairy's Text Box: Peta—

Fournimer and Lissa interrupted the Quest Fairy by executing the *Shudder Animation* simultaneously.

Zal Finn jumped off her little platform and expertly landed on the starting platform. Without missing a beat she was off and back in *Petalyuna*. Fournimer looked over at Lissa and she returned his frantic look.

> Fournimer's Text Box: I don't think I can go back in there.

Lissa's Text Box: What are you scared or something?

Fournimer's Text Box: yes. yes I am.

Lissa's Text Box: Yeah, honestly so am I. It is just too #CloneAttack in there.

Fournimer's Text Box: will... will you hold my hand?

Lissa's Text Box: Only if you hold mine.

~ ~ ~

Blue Quest Fairy Text's Box: the Returning The Related Quest is a fetching style quest that has 27 steps, they are as follo—

Lissa's Interruption Text Box: 27 steps?! #InsaneFairy!

Blue Quest Fairy's Text Box: yes, there are 27 steps. they are —

Zal Finn III's Interruption Text Box: Well, what are they?

Blue Quest Fairy's Text Box: hey, listen! I was just about to tell you, the 27 ste—

Fournimer's Interruption Text Box: so what is the first step exactly?

Blue Quest Fairy's Text Box: ...

Lissa's Text Box: Well? Will you tell us the steps or not?

The 27 Steps For The Returning The Related Quest

1. Take NPC Areede's *Special Wooden Ladle* to NPC Breede.
2. Take NPC Breede's *Golden Feather of Dnaad* to NPC Creede.
3. Take NPC Creede's *11 Secret Medical Spiced Herbs* to NPC Dreede.
4. Take NPC Dreede's *A Cup Of Sugar* to NPC Ereede.
5. Take NPC Ereede's *Only Rat Tail* to NPC Freede.
6. Take NPC Freede's *Last Burned Moose* to NPC Greede.
7. Take NPC Greede's *Pair Of Second Hand Chaps* to NPC Hreede.
8. Take NPC Hreede's *Big Bladder Balloon Beast's Big Bladder* to NPC Ireede.
9. Take NPC Ireede's *Blackened Axe Handle* to NPC Jreede.
10. Take NPC Jreede's *Engagement Ring* to NPC Kreede.
11. Attend NPC Jreede and Kreede's wedding.

12. Take NPC Kreede's *Ungagement Noose* to NPC Lreede.
13. Take NPC Lreede's *Pocket Sized Launchable Cow* to NPC Mreede
14. Take NPC Mreede's *Magical Whistle That You Can't Use* to NPC Nreede.
15. Take NPC Nreede's *Silver Bee In A Jar* to NPC Oreede.
16. Take NPC Oreede's *Wrestler's Mask With Mittens* to NPC Preede.
17. Take NPC Preede's *Alpaca Lips* to NPC Qreede.
18. Take NPC Qreede's *A Single Banana (Instead Of Three)* to NPC Rreede.
19. Take NPC Rreede's *Magical Planting Hoe* and plant the *Summer Corn Seeds*.
20. Win the *Summer Corn* eating contest against NPC Sreede.
21. Take NPC Sreede's *Synthetic Lawn Ornament* to NPC Treede.
22. Take NPC Treede's *Inn Time Clock* to NPC Ureede.
23. Take NPC Ureede's *Knotting Skip Rope* to NPC Vreede.
24. Take NPC Vreede's *The Prism Of Zendrea* to NPC Wreede.
25. Take NPC Wreede's *Secret Caged Emotions* to NPC Xeede.
26. Take NPC Xeede's *A Major Mask to NPC* Yreede.
27. Take NPC Yreede's *Commonly Rare Empty Bottle* to NPC Zreede.

It was a useless fetching quest relay race that would involve a useless jumping puzzle quest at the end. Fournimer didn't like his odds because of the jumping puzzle at the end, however he knew that Lissa was double in trouble as she could barely even walk.

NPC Areede was talked to, her *Special Wooden Ladle* obtained, the timer was started and the avatars were off. "Pitiful as fuck" is the phrase that best described Lissa and Fournimer's success in this race. By the time Zal Finn had finished, which the timer said was 8:22 (not in rounds, but some other kind of time), Lissa had dragged herself and completed up to step 5. Fournimer fared even worse, due to his inability to distinguish the Zal Finns apart he had not managed to even complete step 1. The Centaur had spent more time accidently talking to the real Zal Finn than he had done of actual questing. Defeated, the half-elf and centaur met in the center of town near NPC Areede.

> Text Box: Congratulations to Zal Finn III, winner of heat one of The Returning The Related Quest!

> Lissa's Text Box: Heat one?

> Purple Quest Fairy's Text Box: The winner of The Returning The Related Quest is determined in a best out of five runs competition.

> Fournimer's Text Box: we are going to have to do that four more times?

> Lissa's Text Box: I doubt it. At this rate Zal Finn will win three times in a row. So we will only need to do this twice more.

The Zal Finn that Fournimer was certain was NPC Areede added her thoughts to the conversation.

> Zal Finn III's Text Box: I know! You guys don't stand a chance at this rate! Sweet!

> Fournimer and Lissa's Simultaneous Text Boxes: Holy fucking shitballs!

> Zal Finn III's Text Box: Don't sound so alarmed. What did you guys expect? I am an awesome jumper!

> Fournimer's Text Box: we should stop for the night, it is pretty late. we can start fresh tomorrow.

> Zal Finn III's Text Box: Sweet! We will be all fresh to start next cycle! I'm all full of corn anyways.

The campfire was set up and avatars went about their business.

> Lissa's Text Box: #CommSystemDown. My Player Pager icon and WorldForums have burnt up. We can't post updates anymore.

> Fournimer's Text Box: mine did as well. every night I was checking on Dud... everyone but I can't check anymore. I don't know where they all are.

> Blue Quest Fairy's Text Box: I can tell you that the one you call Dude is loc—

> Lissa's Interruption Text Box: I think that Dude broke them for good with an interrobang. From what I can see the four groups are: D: Gliint and Mr. Max, C: us, B: Lad, Caela, and Roodg, A: Dude, possibly Kray and samuri, they didn't post. Well, samuri posted a '...'.

> Fournimer's Text Box: Poor Du... samuri! poor samuri, stuck with Kray.

> Lissa's Text Box: #ShovelHorseCrap Fony, we all know who you are really worried about.

> Zal Finn III's Text Box: What? Who? Who is he worried about?

> Fournimer's Text Box: we should uh... it... look at the time! bed time!

> Zal Finn III's Text Box: Wait Horseymer! Who do you like?

> Lissa's Text Box: He can't hear you. He is pretending to sleep.

~ ~ ~

Heat two began and the avatars were off. Lissa had managed to make it to step 5 faster this time due to better use of her route. She made sure that Fournimer had seen every single painful step. She stopped trying after Zal Finn had left the area at 4:35. She made pitiful pouting looks at the centaur while doing so. Fournimer had found NPC Breede by following Lissa, although quickly stumbled afterwards being unable to locate NPC Creede. Lissa waved over Fournimer who was shouting at seven different Zal Finns in a desperate attempt to find NPC Creede.

Lissa's Text Box: Okay Foquine, this isn't going to work. Zal is going to keep winning. I am too slow, with this horrible broken and painful leg, and you obviously can't tell your Zal Finns apart.

Fournimer's Text Box: are you telling me that you can tell them apart Chick?

Lissa's Text Box: Of course not, don't be an idiot. Who could possibly do that? I just memorized where they all are.

Fournimer's Text Box: well that's just wonderful for you then. good luck winning Hoppy!

Lissa's Text Box: That's what I wanted to talk to you about Big Old Horse Butt.

Fournimer's Text Box: Big Old Horse Butt? really?

Lissa's Text Box: Sorry, that was Kray's nickname and it was horrible, but I promised I'd use them all, kay. #UpsetWithMyself. I still don't know how I am going to work in samuri's or Anders' suggestions yet.

Fournimer's Text Box: kay, so what did you want to talk to me about Lissaless?

Lissa's Text Box: Lissaless?

Fournimer's Text Box: sorry, I was going for a mix of your name and listless because you can't walk. I didn't really think it through very well.

Lissa's Text Box: You tried I guess. I expected more from the master of nicknames. #TheNameGameLoser. Now, what I am going to suggest may sound crazy, but if we are going to beat Zal Finn I think it is the only way.

> Fournimer's Text Box: why do you even want to beat her?

> Lissa's Text Box: Because there are valuable Accessory prizes for the winner!

> Fournimer's Text Box: good point. okay I'm in. what do we need to do?

> Lissa's Text Box: Stay with me here. I know where all the Zal Finns are, and you can run much faster than her. So, what we are going to have to do is…

She paused, stricken with dramatic tension. Fournimer couldn't take it, he needed to know!

> Fournimer's Text Box: what? for the love of the Maker what?

> Lissa's Text Box: #WorkTogether.

Fournimer used the *Gasp Animation*.

> Lissa's Text Box: I know it is drastic, but I fear it is the only way.

> Fournimer's Text Box: it does sound like the plan of a madwoman, but if it is the only way, I accept. how are we going to do that?

> Lissa's Text Box: You need to let me ride you, Fournimount.

Fournimer used the *Blush Animation*, and turned all the way to *Blush Shade #5*. Lissa reviewed what she had said and upped the ante, turning to *Blush Shade #6* with her own *Blush Animation*.

> Lissa's Text Box: Not like that perv! I know which way those big always visible horse nuts swing. Ride you as in ride you like a real horse. I know where the NPCs are and you can run faster than Zal.

> Fournimer's Text Box: that makes sense, but how do we get past the jumping part? I can't jump at all.

> Quest Explanation's Text Box: Congratulations to Zal Finn III, winner of heat two of The Returning The Related Quest!

> Lissa's Text Box: I have a plan for that part, but we will have to talk later, she will zip in any moment now.

Fournimer was uncertain about the last part of the plan, but used the *Nod Animation* in agreement.

> Zal Finn III's Text Box: Who will zip in?

Both Lissa and Fournimer's hearts skipped a frame when Zal suddenly was an NPC by some discarded *Summer Corn*.

Once the heat was over, at 8:02 this time, Zal Finn was back and ready. The clock started again but this time Fournimer helped Lissa onto his back and followed her instructions. They were almost neck in neck with Zal Finn until step 20. They could eat the *Summer Corn* much faster than she could while working together on one plate. They were quickly out of *Petalyuna* and ready to take on the jumping puzzle.

> Fournimer's Text Box: okay, so how are we going to do this?

> Lissa's Text Box: I heard from Palcath during one of his math lectures that you can jump alright if you have a running start. So all you need to do is not stop running and every time I kick you just jump.

> Fournimer's Text Box: that's crazy? you are going to kick me?

> Lissa's Text Box: I would have pulled your scarf, but now we just have this far *Too Boring to Describe Armour* on.

> Fournimer's Text Box: I really miss my scarf.

> Lissa's Text Box: Me too. #ScarfMemories. It would have added so much needless drama to this whole place. Now mush!

> Fournimer's Text Box: mush? mush is for dogs.

> Lissa's Text Box: Whatever is that you say to horses to make them move.

> Fournimer's Text Box: do you mean giddy up?

> Lissa's Text Box: Yeah that!

Lissa accented her point by spanking her Fournimount hard on the rump, which made him take off involuntarily. Soon they were jumping across platforms at an alarming rate. They reached NPC Zreede just as Zal Finn entered the area, smelling of corn and defeat. The official time was 6:24.

> Quest Explanation's Text Box: Congratulations to Fournissa, winner of heat three of The Returning the Related Quest!

> Lissa's Text Box: Hey! We did it!

> Fournimer's Text Box: go Fournissa!

> Zal Finn III's Text Box: Hey, no fair! I was already full of corn.

> Lissa's Text Box: You'll do better next time.

> Fournimer's Text Box: yeah The Finnster! don't get upset.

Zal did not do better next time; in fact she passed out in a pile of *Summer Corn*. Fournissa (although Lissa insisted that their combi-name was Lissamer) improved their time to 6:06. Once Zal Finn was back to the land of the living she was completely corn stuffed.

> Zal Finn III's Text Box: So... much... corn...

> Lissa's Text Box: It is okay, it will be all over soon. #VictoryAssured!

> Zal Finn III's Text Box: This is not fair! You guys aren't supposed to work together. You hate each other!

> Lissa's Text Box: We don't hate each other! Who told you that nonsense?

> Zal Finn III's Text Box: You told me that nonsense!

> Fournimer's Text Box: wait, we don't hate each other?

Fournimer felt a pain from getting kicked in the ribs and jumped as a reflex action.

> Fournimer's Text Box: ... oh yeah! of course we don't!

> Lissa's Text Box: We are a great team!

> Zal Finn III's Text Box: This isn't over!

> Lissa's Text Box: Yes it is! #EndOfDebate.

Zal Finn stormed off towards NPC Areede.

> Fournimer's Text Box: you are really competitive. do you know that?

> Lissa's Text Box: I am not competitive! I just really hate losing.

> Fournimer's Text Box: I don't think I've ever seen The Finnster upset before, and I never thought she would get upset with you!

> Lissa's Text Box: Why not?

Fournimer used the *Eye Roll Animation*.

The final heat started and everything was near neck and neck until the crucial step 20. Everyone was pretty full of the horrible slow cooker tasting *Summer Corn*, but since Lissa and Fournimer could split their plate progress was much faster on their side of the table. Fourni and Lissa both stopped eating with only a single cob each, but Zal Finn had barely even started and still had twelve.

> Zal Finn III's Text Box: …corn…

> Lissa's Text Box: I don't think I can ever look at another slow cooker.

> Fournimer's Text Box: come on we can do this!

> Zal Finn III's Text Box: …corn…

> Lissa's Text Box: Can't you eat both? Don't you have a horse stomach or something?

Fournimer used the *Stomach Rub Animation.*

> Fournimer's Text Box: I have normal human organs I think.

> Zal Finn III's Text Box: …corn…

> Lissa's Text Box: You think? Don't you know? What is your horse section full of then?

> Fournimer's Text Box: …corn…

> Zal Finn III's Text Box: Please don't talk about corn.

> Lissa's Text Box: It is time to buck up! We just need to eat this last piece and we can move on and never eat slow cookers again!

Everyone took another few bites of *Summer Corn.* Zal Finn's were particularly small.

> Fournimer's Text Box: oh Maker.

> Zal Finn III's Text Box: …corn…

> Lissa's Text Box: We only have half a cob left.

> Fournimer's Text Box: don't give up Lis! we can do this!

> Lissa's Text Box: Only a few bites left Fourn! #NoCorntest!

> Zal Finn III's Text Box: NO!!! STOP BONDING OVER CORN!

Zal Finn suddenly finished her entire cob of corn in a single bite. Then the Zal Finn next to Zal Finn grabbed an ear and she dug in. A Zal Finn behind her stepped forward and started to gobble up his new ear of corn. A pair of Zal Finns grabbed two cobs each and started to munch with extreme speed. Then NPC Sreede who should have been competing against the avatars grabbed one of Zal Finn's cobs and started to eat it with a brand new sense of urgency. After just a few rounds the Zal Finns had finished up all of her corn and all had run off towards step 21 leaving Lissa and Fournimer alone at the *Summer Corn* eating contest table.

> Fournimer's Text Box: huh?

> Lissa's Text Box: Shut up and finish your corn! We can't let her cheat like that and win.

> Fournimer's Text Box: but we are cheating like that!

> Lissa's Text Box: CORN! EAT! NOW!

A few painful and forceful swallows later and the pair said goodbye forever to *Summer Corn* and hurried off after the Zal Finn army. Once they had entered The Canyon of the Complicated Jumping Puzzles they saw that the thirty-seven Zal Finns were not that far ahead. A few well timed jumps showed that the pair could move faster than the army and that within just a few rounds they could overtake them.

The Zal Finns would have nothing of it. They started to break off into groups and block key jumping areas. They adopted aggressive fighting stances. Fournimer had no time to react to the first group and accidently charged right over three of them, pushing them all down into the abyss to twinkle. Lissa kicked Fournimer on so hard that he felt his corn shift.

> Lissa's Text Box: Charge!

Fournimer charged a few more groups of Zal Finns off the platforms, but on the very last platform before NPC Zreede the twenty-one remaining Zal Finns made a stand. Fournimer was forced to stop due to the sheer number of them.

> Lissa's Text Box: Why are you attacking us Zal?

> Twenty-One Zal Finn III's Text Boxes: I'm not attacking you! The NPCs are!

> Fournimer's Text Box: what? aren't you the NPCs or something?

> Twenty-One Zal Finn III's Text Boxes: Nope, I'm over here.

Twenty-One Zal Finn IIIs used the *Wave Animation*.

> Lissa's Text Box: Your entire chorus line over there all waved at the same time! That is #SoFuckedUp!

> Twenty-One Zal Finn III's Text Boxes: Look, it's not my fault if NPCs like me.

> Lissa's Text Box: But using them to cheat on a corn contest? That's the lowest of the low.

> Fournimer's Text Box: really? that's the lowest of the low? chorus line corn eating?

> Twenty-One Zal Finn III's Text Boxes: I didn't tell them to eat the corn. They just did that!

One of the more sly Zal Finns had jumped across to the final platform and was headed towards NPC Zreede who had also been secretly walking towards the group.

> Lissa's Text Box: #TeethLying. Then why are you making a break for it?

> Twenty-One Zal Finn III's Text Boxes: That's not me, I'm over here. Stop that NPC Sreede! Come back here you corn contest bastard!

> Fournimer's Text Box: I'm so very confused now.

> Quest Explanation's Text Box: Congratulations to Zal Finn III, winner of heat five of The Returning The Related Quest! Good luck in your battle against the Land Octo-Squid!

Blessed with the arms of both a Land Octopus and a Land Squid the Land Octo-Squid had an impressive twenty arms. On its first action it changed from *Blush Shade #0* to a *Blush Shade #%*. A move of *Land Grab* and it had a Zal Finn, presumably the NPC Sreede Zal Finn, in its grasp.

> Twenty Zal Finn III's Text Boxes: Get him! Protect Zal Finn III!

A rush of Zal Finns jumped towards the Land Octo-Squid, leaving only one on the platform. There was a good chance that the loner was the actual Zal Finn but Fournimer had been fooled before and didn't want to make any more assumptions. While the Land Octo-Squid certainly had the intent to have its way with all twenty Zal Finns, (and it certainly had enough tentacles to do so) it simply did not have enough actions per turn to deal with the vast numbers of Zals. In the relatively short time it had in this world the Land Octo-Squid only managed to grab three Zal Finns and pull the pants off of another. A death burble signaled that the excitement was over. The extra Zal Finns slowly broke off and went back to their normal everyday scripted lives.

> **Creature Name:** Land Octo-Squid
> **Class:** Land Marine
> **Level:** 70
> **Special Attacks:** Grab, Twenty-Fold, Constrict, Pull, Pull More, Prehensile

Tentacle
Drops: Discarded Arm
First Player Encounter Notes: Take that Land Octo-Squid! - Zal Finn III

Lissa's Text Box: That was #SoFuckedUp, but I have to admit it was pretty cool. Is that a Dancing Ninja Assassin thing or…

Zal Finn III changed to *Blush Shade #3.*

Zal Finn III's Text Box: Not a dancing thing. It's my *Insta-Orgy* ability. I didn't know that the NPC orgy could attack or anything though. You thought it was cool?

Lissa's Text Box: You did just kill a boss with your chorus line of NPCs, how is that not badass?

Zal Finn III's Text Box: You're right! I am badass!

Lissa's Text Box: Go get your reward, I think you've earned it after that display.

Fournimer's Text Box: I still don't know what happened.

NPC Zreede's Text Box: Congratulations little flowers! Here is your first reward! You may now progress to the next area!

The gate out of the area was unlocked and Zreede stopped blocking the way.

NPC Zreede's Text Box: Here is your second reward! An Accessory for 'insert avatar name'! May the avatar with the most heat wins step forward!

Zal Finn III stepped forward looking smug and much like NPC Zreede.

NPC Zreede's Text Box: #It is an Ultra Cock-Ring! Enjoy your Sexcessory!#

Zal Finn III's Text Box: An *Ultra Cock-Ring?* I don't even have a cock!

Taking out an *Ultra Cock-Ring* from her invisible supply NPC Zreede presented the reward to Zal Finn III. With a blur of animation the human's pants had been pulled down and the *Ultra Cock-Ring* looked around confused. It had no cock to attach itself to, so thinking quickly it instead attached itself to the other thing that rings go on, a finger. Zal Finn attempted to change the ring to a different finger, in an attempt to not be married to it, but it wouldn't budge.

Zal Finn III's Text Box: Hey, change fingers you! We are not engaged!

A few rounds of attemped ring removal caused it be stimulated enough to unleash its true power. A full sized cock emerged out of the *Ultra-Cock Ring* and was staring Zal Finn in the face.

> NPC Zreede's Text Box: Your third reward is... *pause for dramatic effect*

NPC Zreede pulled down her pants and revealed herself.

> NPC Zreede's Continued Text Box: My well groomed lady garden!

> Fournimer's Text Box: what?

> Lissa's Text Box: I don't have the tools to deal with that, so you two can fight amongst yourselves for whom gets to snatch up that reward.

> Fournimer's Text Box: again, what?

> Zal Finn III's Text Box: Do you mind if I try this thing out on those sweet lady petals, Horseymer?

Fournimer changed *Blush Shades* several times.

> Fournimer's Text Box: no, uh you have fun. I'm just going... to go... look at the new area I think.

Before he could up the *Blush Shade* again Fournimer stepped through the gate and left forgetting that Lissa was still on his back.

> Lissa's Text Box: Hey, who are you? #NewCharacter?

> Fournimer's Text Box: and why are you looking at me like that?

✦ Chapter 21 ✦

ANDERS, DRAGON CANDY

Xam, the Orange Dragon of Light, had been relentless this cycle. Three times the dragon had cornered Anders and had his way with the poor elf and it wasn't even midday yet. Three additional shots of dragon were now swelled up in the elf's belly. Combined with Xam's previous unloads it totaled six shots, swelling up Anders a total of thirty weight units.

Anders was marked up with scratches, claw marks, and bites. During the last encounter Xam had ripped apart Anders' *Too Boring to Describe Armour*. Without a *Repair-It* to fix the Armour Anders was essentially naked. He could not find a spare *Strand of Dream* anywhere so Combi-Fusion was out of the question, and the NPC who could repair things was a long and dangerous sprint away. As it was now Anders was only dressed in blood splattered bandages, his accessories, and his unbreakable *Frost Gigas Boots*.

Searching in his *Ultra-Pack* Anders took out the only Armour he had not sold to afford the boring set, his custom made unbreakable *Slime Armour (s)*. The stats were not nearly as good as the boring Armour, but they were still better than being naked. Anders had already spent far too much time naked as it was. The *Slime Gloves (s)* and *Slime Helmet (s)* still fit fine, but Anders could not get the *Slime Armour (s)* or *Slime Pants (s)* to fit. They had been custom made for him, but now he simply could not fit inside.

The bleeding marks of Xam would only disappear with a good night's rest at the Onn Inn. While Anders was currently at the Onn Inn he couldn't technically go to sleep yet due to it not being the night portion of the cycle. Anders looked outside the decorative window and his suspicions were confirmed. There was Xam, in the town square, staring up at him. As soon as Anders would try to leave the Onn Inn Xam would snap him up and have his way with him for the seventh time. Maybe even while flying through the clouds again, which would have been amazingly romantic if Anders had agreed to being ridden by the dragon while flying all around the Expansion in the first place.

Anders used the *Sigh Animation* and turned away from the window, attempting to put Xam out of his mind. He absent-mindedly rubbed at his belly as he moved around the Onn Inn. Six perfectly normal and identical little beds, with six little impossible to open nightstands, six paintings of sailboats, and six little side carpets. It was a perfectly nice little room, if you were just here to sleep for the night. Since this was the only place in Onn that Xam couldn't get to, Anders was going to have to live here for now. Making this perfectly nice little room absolutely dreadful.

Anders could not defeat Xam by himself, he had no magic reserves left and everything Xam shot into him wasn't absorbing. It wouldn't have mattered even if he could defeat Xam, the elf obsessed dragon would just be right back to try again anyways. There was only going to be so much that Anders could expand before bursting, and neither *Stretch More* nor *Stretch More More* helped move the weight. Given his previous experience with The Titan Anders estimated that maybe forty or forty-five weight units were his limit.

Sitting down on the bed he liked the best Anders lost himself in his thoughts. An idea popped into his head and he got up and sat down on the bed he liked the least (It was the identical one across from his favourite). He couldn't absorb Xam's seed, but maybe he could find it and remove it through more conventional methods. Anders unravelled a few of the bandages around his midsection, and a few drops of blood fell onto the bed. The bed did not look impressed. Anders did not apologize because if what he planned on happening did happen, the bed was going to be furious with him in short order.

Anders looked through his *Ultra-Pack*. His hand was probably not going to cut it, so he needed to find something longer. There were only two things Anders could think of that would possibly be long enough. His weapons. While he didn't really consider the idea of shoving a sword up his ass for very long, a bow could possibly work. His currently equipped *Fangbow+* looked even sharper than his on hand swords. That was fine, Anders didn't really want to spend the rest of his career using a bow that he had taken internal. He did have an old friend stashed away, it was simple and smooth and lacked anything point related entirely.

Anders took out his good friend the *Elf Starting Bow*. This bow was as tall as Anders, and by far the longest thing he owned. If anything was going to be able to find Xam's secret stash it was this.

He leaned back and closed his eyes, Anders started slowly. There was really nowhere else outside he could go so Anders decided that he might as well do this properly. First he slowly used a finger to play around with and tease his opening. Only after he felt a drip glide down the crack in his ass did he insert his finger. Anders slowly began to rock his finger back and forth, happy to bend the finger as needed. Soon the elf had added another finger and had found his favourite area. He vigorously rubbed at it and started to feel some tingles pop against his hand.

This stimulation caused the elf to moan lightly and the entire side of the Onn Inn to shake. Startled, Anders looked to the window and saw a huge dragon eye peering at him. It almost caused him to *Double Jump* out of the bed. Xam was staring at him from outside, aggroed by the tingles. It was as the dragon had said in earlier encounters: Anders was irresistible to Xam. He was dragon candy.

Xam had tormented Anders for some time, so the avatar decided that it was time for some well deserved payback. Anders inserted all four of his fingers and started to thrust in and out with increased speed. Every tingle felt amazing, and every tingle from Anders caused Xam to blink in time.

Being watched by the desperate Xam was more of a turn on than Anders had thought. The strain against his *Slime Jock-Strap* increased, so he slowly lowered it. Taking extra care for the reveal to be dramatic, Anders arched his back and moaned loudly when his cock bounced into view. Anders heard the dragon make a desperate howl of need from outside. Anders flashed Xam a *Smirk Animation* and continued on.

Unwrapping a few more bandages Anders reached upwards and took one of his nipples in his free hand. While rubbing and flicking his nipple Anders gasped considerably. It was far more sensitive than he had remembered from the last time he had flicked it. It was nice and he continued to use his other hand to finger himself. Every tingle Anders felt caused Xam to get more riled up, and riling up Xam was causing Anders to show off more.

Anders rotated on the furious bed, if he was going to empty out all of Xam's work, he wanted the dragon to have a good view. Now on his back with his ass facing the big dragon eye, Anders lifted up his legs and held them in place with his free hand. He took special care to maintain eye contact with Xam, and reinserted a single finger as far as possible until he felt himself twitch. A single tingle was all Anders allowed himself to feel before he removed the finger completely, smiled at Xam, and started to repeat the slow deliberate process. Anders took special care to only allow a single tingle per entry, and each insertion was taking upwards of ten rounds. Xam was getting really worked up, with each tingle he had started to thrust at the building.

Ready to start his plan Anders changed positions. Kneeling on the bed Anders gripped the *Elf Starting Bow* with his feet and used a hand to position one end at his opening. He was a Ranged Style Night Ranger, so hitting his target with a bow was second nature and he slowly lowered himself down. Special care was taken to both show Xam every single length unit of bow that he took, and to watch the big eye. Anders moaned as the natural curve of the bow pressed hard against his places. A multitude of tingles came over the elf and Xam's eyes began to water.

Anders heard the dragon's big claws scrape against the outside of the Onn Inn. The dragon wanted to replace the *Elf Starting Bow* with his dragon starting cock. Anders started to bob up and down on the *Elf Starting Bow*, the curve of the bow pressed exactly the right places and Anders was disappointed that he had not thought of this amazing use for his favourite weapon sooner.

Tingles came faster now. Anders grabbed his cock and started to match the rough pace of his bobbing. Xam grabbed the building and joined the pace with thrusts against the smooth brick inn. Anders very nearly lost himself in the moment, but remembered that he had a job to do. He shifted his hips and got up on his knees. He grabbed the *Elf Starting Bow*, in the hand that was not holding his cock, and slowly began to thrust it in deeper. Every length unit added more pressure and more tingles. Right before the grip of the bow, about a third of the way down, Anders felt himself bottom out. This was the limit and where he would need to explore.

Anders began to shift the *Elf Starting Bow* around cautiously. Because of the curve of the bow even the slightest movement was causing direct stimulation to Anders' best spots. Perhaps this wasn't the best tool for the job of searching, but Anders was definitely going to remember it for being an excellent tool at perfect stimulation. Each shifting search caused a great many tingles to erupt from inside, but Anders needed to find the built up seed.

Anders laughed at himself a little. The *Elf Starting Bow* would probably have worked better for this if Anders had remembered to unstring it beforehand, as it was now the string kept making him giggle as it tickled his insides.

When an extra length unit suddenly snuck in Anders felt the *Elf Starting Bow* hit something and heard a tink. A shifting inside caused his entire body to tingle with unrivaled intensity. Anders arched his back upwards and his insides tightened up. The *Elf Starting Bow* shot out of Anders and with a deep internal flurry of tingles Anders began to convulse on the bed, shooting his seed out with extreme force. His orgasm was intense, there were even tingles in his eyes. Anders went over to the window, took many rounds to calm down, and looked out at Xam. The elf took great care to clean himself up neatly with the *Initiate's Jacket* with a smile.

Outside Xam was going wild. The dragon had already been chewing on the building some rounds before, but once the elf had started to orgasm the dragon lost control. Xam grabbing desperately at the building with both feet and hands Xam was now attempting to fuck the Inn. After one great thrust (against all odds) his dragon dick burst through the wall, right beside the window. With an smile the dragon used his claws to increase the size of the opening while the elf looked on in horror.

> Anders' Text Box: Oh, Pancakes!

Anders turned to run, but it was too late. Xam's big hand reached inside and soon had Anders held tightly in its grip. Xam turned around and used his tail to enter the hole of the Onn Inn. It took Xam far more rounds than was necessary, it was if he was now the one showing off, and when he was done the Inn was nothing but a pile of rubble. The dragon turned its gaze downwards towards the elf.

> Xam, the Orange Dragon of Light's Text Box: Bad little candy, hiding from me like that. But now the little candy has nowhere to hide anymore. Serves the delicious treat right for teasing me like that. Here is a tip, next time don't tease the dragon that is PVP broken and can smash through buildings with his oversized cock.

The big dragon squeezed his prized piece of candy, causing more painful wounds to be inflicted on the elf.

> Xam, the Orange Dragon of Light's Text Box: You think you were a slow tease up there don't you candy? Getting me all worked up like that. Well, you don't even know the meaning of slow tease.

Flying high above the rubble, Xam relaxed and hovered in the sky like a King Gribblet using *Throne of the Ages*. He placed Anders carefully, making sure that the elf was sitting directly on the head of his big penis. The big dragon did nothing but let the avatar sit there in place, knowing full well that a fall at this height would be disastrous to his prey.

Anders was still spent and his ass did not feel particularly loose after his intense orgasm. Without mana he couldn't cast *Stretch More* or *Stretch More More*, and both would be needed to accommodate the big dragon. However, Xam did not seem to be in any kind of rush. Rounds and rounds ticked by with nothing happening but Xam smiling. Anders had begun to feel the big dragon's heartbeat as the big dick pulsed.

It was well after nightfall before Anders felt anything relax. When it happened it was quick and earned a smirk from Xam. Anders relaxed just enough to allow the very first length unit inside. Xam began to flex his big dick at random intervals, Anders now had to hold onto the dick with his legs or risk falling to the ground.

> Xam, the Orange Dragon of Light's Text Box: There it is my little candy, we have as long as it takes. No need to rush now.

With every flex of the big dragon, the elf felt himself open up just a little more. Anders was all for being open and had started to push back, he felt that the sooner he was opened up, the sooner that Xam would finish up. With a few more flexes Anders had reached what he knew was the limit of his regular *Stretch*.

> Xam, the Orange Dragon of Light's Text Box: Now what did I just tell you? We have as long as this takes candy.

Xam flexed every so often to prove his point. Every flex caused the elf to bob just a little bit up and down on the very tip of Xam. The heat and the heartbeat from the dragon eventually started to heat up Anders as well. It was about midnight when Anders felt himself growing hard. He used his better judgement and did not touch himself, which earned him a 'good candy' from Xam.

When Anders heard the rooster caw he could barely believe it. He had spent all night perched on the dragon. He had stretched far more than he ever thought possible. The constant heat and flexing from Xam had done its job, and Anders had slowly expanded to the point of *Stretch More* without even casting it.

Anders was exhausted, hungry, and painfully erect. Xam was content to just hover and flex. Anders felt his stomach grumble, his eyes grow heavy, and his cock twitch.

> Xam, the Orange Dragon of Light's Text Box: Awe, is candy hungry? Tired maybe? A bit horny? Well, that is what a bad candy gets. You just sit there and think about what you've done.

As more and more rounds passed by in relative silence Anders felt more and more weak. He fell asleep sometime in the afternoon, but was awakened with a powerful flex.

> Xam, the Orange Dragon of Light's Text Box: No sleeping now until you've learned your lesson candy. You've lasted longer than I thought you would. Time to reward candy with a meal. Take something from your pack and eat like a good candy.

Peering into his pack Anders saw many mouth watering appliances, but he also saw something interesting. *Minotaur Musk*. It would help him to relax, and while he was already more relaxed and stretched out than he ever had been the *Minotaur Musk* could be a big help to end this and he selected it as his 'meal'. Uncorking the musk, Anders splashed the contents on his face and felt a familiar haze overtake him. When Anders head cleared he felt himself stretched out to the very max.

With a well timed flex Xam bobbed Anders up, who came down hard on the dick stretching just enough to allow the member inside. Anders screamed loudly at the size of the intruding member. It filled him up painfully and stopped at the same amount of length units as the *Elf Starting Bow* had when it hit something.

> Xam, the Orange Dragon of Light's Text Box: Very good candy. Much sooner than I thought. You did a good job.

Xam slapped Anders hard on the everything with a clawed hand, this activated both *Stretch More* and *Stretch More More* which earned instant relief from the pain of the intrusion. The rest of the dragon dick slipped in, the Xam reserves had slipped up higher to allow full entry. Anders expected Xam to start thrusting now that the dragon was inside, but he did not move. The dragon only hovered there.

When Anders tried to move instead the dragon screamed out in protest and started to fly higher and higher. Anders was forced to hang on as the dragon began to glide around the world. Each wing beat caused a very faint amount of movement, jerking the avatar just slightly on the big dick. This was going to be the way Xam did it, linked up in the air with very minor stimulation between the pair for however long it took. The dragon was not kidding, this was teasing of the highest order.

There was no area of the entire *Island of Islana* that Xam did not fly over several times. Anders was positive that during the course of the cycle that he had spotted Mr. Max, Palcath, Lissa's hair, and in three different locations Zal Finn.

When the wolf howled and signalled night Anders was at his limit. Every single nerve in his body begged for release. He was exhausted and regretted his choice to eat *Minotaur Musk* as his last meal. With every wingbeat Xam would cause a tingle in Anders. The elf felt Xam's heartbeat quicken and knew that the big dragon was almost there, but the dragon refused to let in and release.

It was just past midnight when it happened. The light dragon could not see well in the dark, and after he took a wrong turn into a gaggle of Great Griffons he needed to beat his wings five times in succession to avoid crashing into a raft made of *Iced Creamcones* and *Marshed Mallows* that was sailing across the ocean. That was all it took. The increased very faint stimulation of extra beats pushed Anders over the edge. The elf crossed his legs and with a silent scream he orgasmed. In a tidal wave of pent up tingles Anders shot his seed soundlessly into the night air.

Xam could not take the sudden outburst of tingles. He had barely plucked the Griffon Feathers out of his mouth when the sudden wave hit him. Xam began to come hard while falling from the sky. The ground approached faster and faster as Xam fell. The dragon was just barely able to correct his trajectory and turn towards land before he shoot a double burst of Xam deep into his elf candy. The dragon disappeared into his ball of orange light.

Anders could not disappear. He continued on the crash course and hit the ground rolling. Everything was a blur, but he could not pass out. If he did, Xam would know exactly where he was and could return before the avatar awoke. On the cobbled path he had landed on, Anders desperately tried to pull himself forward. There was an entry to another area just ahead, it looked like a forest of some kind. If he could just reach it maybe that would be enough. It was only a few move units away.

Anders felt his stomach shift with intense pain. The double shot of Xam must have done it. He was finally going to rupture. Anders curled up in a ball and let out a pitiful whimper. He reached out towards the forest in desperation, but he blacked out dramatically instead.

◈ Chapter 22 ◈
UNNECESSARY
QUESTING B

R**oodg's Text Box:** i HATE THIS FUCKING PLACE!

Palcath's Text Box: You're not the one taking every single hit from every single monster Roodg!

Roodg's Text Box: yEAH, BUT i'M BORED! wE HAVE BEEN HERE FOREVER!

Caëlahenâilenŵhei's Text Box: Fighting amongst ourselves isn't going to help.

Palcath's Text Box: It isn't going to hurt either lass!

Caëlahenâilenŵhei's Text Box: Let's just stop and think. We are supposed to be the intelligent group! We have been acting like... well like everyone else.

Palcath's Text Box: You're right, lass, we have been acting like R... everybody else!

Roodg's Text Box: rEVERYBODY ELSE IS SILLY!

> Palcath's Text Box: It is almost nightfall, lass, let's do this properly.

> Caëlahenãilenŵhei's Text Box: Agreed.

Both *Portie Tents* had been set up, even though they barely fit into the designated area and had to be set up several times until they got it just right. Caela could not be persuaded to abandon her idea about the designated tents, she would not be disgraced by entering Palcath's lesser model, nor would she let anyone else into hers. Roodg was still sleeping outside in the broken red bed and didn't really care either which way.

Everyone sat in the provided chairs around Caela's outside fire pit, it was much nicer. Caela was alright with allowing them to sit around her fire, but she did not change the chair colours to match their avatars. Palcath sat in Gliint's brown chair since he thought it was closest to yellow. Roodg sat in Yallundy's chair since the colour changing pattern was nEAT.

> Caëlahenãilenŵhei's Text Box: Alright so I've been thinking a lot about this lately. We accidently reached the end of The Huge Confusing Snowfield Full Of Random Warps on our third try, but then we found out that NPC Jambass was guarding the exit. We have more than enough *White Winter Wolf Pelts*, *Doubleduck Feathers*, *Grizzled Bear Claws*, and *Bewilderberries* now to finish the Complete Collection Quest now, but despite writing down the directions back to NPC Jambass we cannot make it back. So either the way through The Huge Confusing Snowfield Full Of Random Warps changed or—

> Caëlahenãilenŵhei's Text Box: someone foolishly wrote down the directions wrong. Every round on this accursed Spire B feels colder and I for one am getting sick and tired of casting Fire Tongue on myself every few rounds just to keep from freezing into a finely crafted ice sculpture. It is depleting my *Health Potions* and even worse I think my robes are starting to get all sooty. Yallundy had the *Vacuum*. My poor *Portie Tent Ultra+*. What we need is a plan, not some common run of the mill sort of plan. It needs to be something worthy of us being referred to as the smarter gr—

> Caëlahenãilenŵhei's Text Box: oup.

> White Quest Fairy's Text Box: There are so many trigger words in there… I don't even know where to start.

> Roodg's Text Box: wE SMART!

Palcath wisely did not remind Caela that she was the one writing down directions.

> Palcath's Text Box: The problem is that the warps just don't make

sense, lass. You step in one and you are near the base of the mountain, then another and you are in the middle, then near the peak, then you think you are close but end up near the base again. To make things worse half the time the direction you think you should go is blocked by that damn scenic river, and it goes down the whole damn mountain blocking us at every warp. There is no rhyme or reason, it is such poor level design!

Yellow Quest Fairy's Text Box: I keep telling you pal that —

Palcath's Interruption Text Box: Hush you.

Roodg's Text Box: mAYBE WE SHOULD LISTEN TO THEM FOR ONCE?

Red Quest Fairy's Text Box: Listen to who?

Roodg's Text Box: tO THE qUEST fAIRIES!

Palcath nearly dropped his lads at what Roodg had said.

Palcath's Text Box: The Quest Fairies Roodg? Are you mad?

White Quest Fairy's Text Box: But, we know the way through the maze!

Caëlahenâilenŵhei's Text Box: No you don't! We tried your way and keep getting blocked by that river. You don't know the way!

White Quest Fairy's Text Box: I am sorry, but that is the way. That river shouldn't be there so don't blame us. I even double checked the database and those are the correct directions.

Caëlahenâilenŵhei's Text Box: But your directions were wrong and needlessly long winded!

White Quest Fairy's Text Box: It's not my fault that I have been programmed to emulate you! Logically all it shows us is that since I am like you, that you are bad at writing down directions and that you yourself are in fact long winded. So there you go, I am like you. Also, for reference my real name is also needlessly long and unpronounceable!

Yellow Quest Fairy's Text Box: And you pal have forced your silly overacting pals and gals thing on me! Plus I have natural tendencies to force my leadership upon everyone!

Roodg and the Red Quest Fairy watched the unfolding carnage in silence as the two most 'rational' avatars in the expansion and therefore the two most 'rational' Quest Fairies in the expansion cut an emotional swath through each other. It ended abruptly after the White Quest Fairy told Caela that if she wanted to make it over the mysterious river so badly that she could just jump the fuck over it. That caused an intellectual spark to hit the light elf's brain and an idea to pop into her head.

> Caëlahenãilenŵhei's Text Box: Wait, that's it! Good idea White Quest Fairy! Maybe we should listen to you.

> White Quest Fairy's Text Box: Really? I totally agree! We can help each other so much if we only start to combi—

> Palcath's Interruption Text Box: Care to explain that thought a little more lass?

> Caëlahenãilenŵhei's Text Box: That scenic river goes all the way down the mountain and NPC Jambass is at the peak.

> Palcath's Text Box: But we can't enter the river, lass. There is an invisible force field around it.

> Caëlahenãilenŵhei's Text Box: Exactly. That's why it's not a useable idea yet, just a start. We need to think on it.

> Palcath's Text Box: We are good at thinking, lass. How tall do you think the invisible force field beside the river is?

> Caëlahenãilenŵhei's Text Box: I don't know. Roodg try shooting *Fireballs* at it at increasingly higher and higher intervals.

> Roodg's Text Box: yES!

After the sixth *Fireball* they had their answer. The invisible force field was three height units tall.

> Palcath's Text Box: Crap. None of us can *Double Jump* and the only scenery I have seen around here is one height unit tall, lass.

> Caëlahenãilenŵhei's Text Box: Not true. Those trees are at least twenty.

> Palcath's Text Box: We can't climb trees, lass. How does that help?

> Caëlahenãilenŵhei's Text Box: No, but we can walk on fallen scenic logs. If we can knock over a tree we can walk up!. Roodg attack that tree!

Roodg's Text Box: yES!

Many *Fireballs*, *Lightning Blasts*, and *Whirlwind Extras* were cast, and while the tree did have visible blast damage, it did not budge.

Palcath's Text Box: No good, lass, I've seen Roodg kill many kinds of scenery in the past and I know for a fact that tree is not going anywhere.

Caëlahenãilenŵhei's Text Box: Well damn. That was a very good plan. It is too bad we don't have an axe or a PVP broken avatar here to chop it down. Why do you use hammers and not axes? I thought dwarves liked axes.

Palcath's Text Box: I'm not sure lass, but if I'd have to wager I would put money on that it was for us to get blocked by not having an axe at this very moment.

Caëlahenãilenŵhei's Text Box: I'd think you would win that bet. I even saw axes back in Onn, so one of the new classes even uses them.

White Quest Fairy's Text Box: Can we use something that isn't an axe?

Roodg's Text Box: omm! wE HAVE SOMETHING BETTER THAN AN AXE!

Palcath's Text Box: Are you getting mysteriously smart again Roodg? Did you eat a sandwich?

Roodg's Text Box: yES AND YES!

Caëlahenãilenŵhei's Text Box: What do we have then? Don't leave us in suspense.

Roodg's Text Box: a *cHAINSAW*!

Palcath's Text Box: We have a *Chainsaw* Roodg? Wait, are *Chainsaws* even in this game?

Roodg's Text Box: yES! lOOK ITALICS!

Caëlahenãilenŵhei's Text Box: True, I saw one in... That old starting city way back in Gentalia. It didn't work for reference.

Palcath's Text Box: Okay, I need to know. Roodg, where in the Flaming Pit have you been hiding a *Chainsaw*?

Roodg's Text Box: LoL. i DON'T HAVE A *cHAINSAW*! u DO!

Palcath's Text Box: I don't have a *Chainsaw* on me, where do you think I've been hiding it this whole time Roodg? Am I hiding it in my *Backpack*? No! Is it stashed under my bed? No! Is it tucked away in my pants? N…urk.

Roodg used the *Smirk Animation*. Palcath used the *Mortified Expression Animation*. Caëlahenâilenŵhei used the *Confused Blink Animation*.

Palcath's Text Box: Roodg, even if I could… take down a tree, we would just get stuck behind the invisible force field at the top of the mountain.

Yellow Quest Fairy's Text Box: I keep telling you pal, this one area ends in trees which is why there is an invisible wall here, but there isn't an invisible wall anywhere else on the river! It isn't supposed to be here, if you just walked to the next screen you could just walk into the river! But no, you don't liste—

Caëlahenâilenŵhei's Interruption Text Box: I clearly remember that the zenith of the mountain had a small cave beside it with a blue chest. Behind that chest was a scenic mostly open area with a river flowing peacefully in it. Remember when Roodg accidently dropped the *Empty Bottle* from the blue chest and it rolled under the stalactites and into that area? That means then that logic tells me that this river goes through that cave and that the level designer did not put an invisible force field there. Since the stalactites were big icicles we should be able to either hammer or fire magic —

Caëlahenâilenŵhei's Text Box: them off.

Palcath's Text Box: That is a genius plan! Worthy of being a plan from the smartest party lass and Roodg! Quick question though lass, there is a 550 character limit on Text Boxes have you ever considered just using fewer characters in your… you know what, never mind.

Roodg's Text Box: gO US!

Caëlahenâilenŵhei's Text Box: That was much easier than solving the warping puzzle. Alright Palcath, whip out your *Chainsaw* and let's see you chop down that tree!

Roodg's Text Box: yES!

Palcath changed to *Blush Shade #6*.

> Palcath's Text Box: Oh... uh... well...

> Roodg's Text Box: hE IS JUST SHY CAUSE THE *cHAINSAW* IS TOTALLY HIS COCK!

> Palcath's Text Box: Roodg!

> Roodg's Text Box: wHAT? cOCKS ROCK!

Palcath reached deep down and used the *Blush Shade #8* that had been unlocked for the world by Fournimer.

> Caëlahenâilenẁhei's Text Box: I know, I heard all about the settings. I just never would have thought of using it as a *Chainsaw*, very good Roodg.

> Roodg's Text Box: tHANKS Caëlahenâilenẁhei!

> Palcath's Text Box: Lass, who told you that?!

> Roodg's Text Box: hI!

> Caëlahenâilenẁhei's Text Box: Hi!

> Roodg's Text Box: hI!

> Red Quest Fairy's Text Box: Hi!

> White Quest Fairy's Text Box: Why are you stuck in that 'Hi hI' loop as well noble Fairy? That is as foolish as it is annoying. I insist that you stop this instant, for there is nothing as bad as be——

> Palcath's Interruption Text Box: Excuse me for a moment lasses and Roodgs, I'm going to go fuck a tree.

~ ~ ~

> Palcath's Text Box: Does anylad know why this river is full of snowballs?

Palcath's question was answered by a snowball hitting him directly in the face.

> Roodg's Text Box: yES!

> Palcath's Text Box: Hey, you got a bunch in my mouth Roodg.

Roodg's Text Box: i KNOW. i WAS AIMING FOR THERE!

Palcath's Text Box: Why would you do th—

Snowball to the face from Roodg!

Roodg's Text Box: LoL! cAUSE IT IS FUN, WHY DO YOU THIN—

Snowball to the face from Palcath!

Palcath's Text Box: You're right Roodg, that was pretty fun. Thank you for the sugg—

Snowball to the face from Roodg!

Caëlahenâilenŵhei's Text Box: Now now, this is hardly the time *Snowball to the face from Roodg!* or the place to be doing something so *Snowball to the face from Palcath!* childish. We have a mission to accomplish and *Multiple Snowballs to the face from both Palcath and Roodg!* should hurry.

Palcath and Roodg's Simultaneous Text Boxes: ?

Caëlahenâilenŵhei's Text Box: Hey! You hit me in the face!

Palcath's Text Box: Yes we did lass, but how did you avoid getting inter—

Snowball to the face from Caela!

Roodg's Text Box: bUT—

Snowball to the face from Caela!

Palcath's Text Box: It is so on now light el—

Snowball to the face from Roodg!

~ ~ ~

Caëlahenâilenŵhei's Text Box: That was the most fun I think I have had in ages.

Palcath's Text Box: Agreed lass, I am just sad that the river ran out of snowballs. I could have gone on for—

Snowball to the face from Roodg!

Roodg's Text Box: i KEPT ONE.

Caëlahenâilenŵhei used the *Fall To Your Knees Laughing Animation*. It took quite a few rounds until she finally recovered.

> Caëlahenâilenŵhei's Text Box: Okay now that was the funniest *Snowball to the face from Roodg!* thing ever.

> Caëlahenâilenŵhei's Text Box: Hey!

> Roodg's Text Box: i KEPT ANOTHER.

They reached the source of the river with only a few more balls thrown.

> Palcath's Text Box: Here we are, but what in the lad is blocking the entrance to the cave… is that… snowballs?

> Caëlahenâilenŵhei's Text Box: At least we know where they all came from. Roodg hit them with your staff.

> Roodg's Text Box: yES!

Taking Caela's advice Roodg walked up to the snowball packed entrance and swung at it with great effort.

> Roodg's Text Box: nOTHING HAPP—

638 snowballs and 1 giant wave of snow from the clogged up cave entrance to the face!

Palcath and Caëlahenâilenŵhei used the *High Five Dual Animation.*

> Palcath's Text Box: It was so hard not to laugh while Roodg was walking and getting ready to swing lass.

> Caëlahenâilenŵhei's Text Box: Agreed.

> Roodg's Text Box: iT IS EVERYWHERE!

Inside the cave there were large quantities of snow. It was knee deep for the two magic casting elves, but it was waist deep for the dwarf. A natural curve in the wall near the cave entrance swirled the snow crystals around to form the snowballs, and there was no shortage of raw materials.

> Palcath's Text Box: Over there, this lad sees the blue chest.

> Caëlahenâilenŵhei's Text Box: I don't remember there being snow in here.

> Palcath's Text Box: Maybe it is on a cycle, lass. Let's go see if we can break those stalactites.

> Roodg's Text Box: gO!

Fire magic, hammers, and just desperately shaking the stalactites would make them wiggle. Body parts could travel through and even touch the blue chest so there was definite hope. It took a few rounds but eventually a stalactite broke free. With a casting of *Greasespot* Roodg was able to wriggle up through the mess to the higher area of the cave, and open the blue chest to pocket a brand new *Empty Bottle*. Caela attempted to get through, but even with her jiggleless light elf frame there was still nobody skinnier than Roodg. They began work on the next stalactite, which would allow Caela to get through. The stout Palcath was going to need at least a total of four removed.

Midway through the removal of the second stalactite the cave began to rumble and a strange sloshing sound could be heard from above the avatars' heads.

> Caëlahenãilenŵhei's Text Box: What's that sound?

> Palcath's Text Box: Whatever it is, it can't be good, lass. Keep working!

> Roodg's Text Box: sNOW!

From a hole in the roof near the riverside entrance came a torrent of snow, then another, and another. The snow was quickly swirling by the wall and the river entrance was quickly blocked with snowballs as the liquid pulsed into the cave. Bursts of water followed the sudden snowfall and the cave started to fill.

> Caëlahenãilenŵhei's Text Box: It's the river! No, it is more water in addition to the river over there, but quick we need to break through!

Frantically Caela started to rapidly cast fire spells, Palcath started to hammer, and Roodg started to wiggle. The mix of slushy water and snow was rising rapidly, but the second stalactite broke off freeing Caela just as the water reached her waist. Everyone started to use special abilities, larger spells, and more wiggle on a third stalactite. When it broke off the slush had reached Palcath's neck, and squeeze as he might there was no getting through.

> Roodg's Text Box: hURRY!

Palcath was standing on his tippy toes, swimming wouldn't help for very long, the roof was very low. The snow had reached the dwarf's mouth, but the last stalactite was barely a quarter of the way loose.

> Caëlahenãilenŵhei's Text Box: It's no good, we're not going to make it! He is going to drown!

Palcath had just enough time to Text Box one last thing before going under.

> Palcath's Text Box: Oh Flaming Pit!

Caela and Roodg were rapidly trying to shake out the last stalactite, but they knew it was going to be too late. Palcath had gone under, and Oxygen Bars were only so long.

> Caëlahenãilenẁhei's Text Box: Oh no!

> Roodg's Text Box: dWARF LAD!

The stalactite began to shake with such intense speed that the teeth in Caela and Roodg's heads began to rattle. They let go in alarm just as the stalactite shattered into 1,716 pieces. A dwarf hand reached up from the depths and the elves used all of their combined strength (which wasn't much because they were both Attack Magic types) and pulled Palcath (with his pants around his ankles) from the depths.

> Roodg's Text Box: dUH! wHY DIDN'T WE JUST USE YOUR *cHAINSAW* COCK IN THE FIRST PLACE?

Palcath was too busy using the *Pant Animation* to reply.

> Caëlahenãilenẁhei's Text Box: We should leave, the water level is still rising.

The elves helped the still shaking Palcath to the real cave entrance, although neither was sure if he was shaking from the horrible stress of the situation or on his own accord.

> Roodg's Text Box: oH GOOD! lOOK Palcath A BOSS FOR YOU TO FINISH UP IN!

> Palcath's Text Box: Huh?

> Roodg's Text Box: gO! tHIS BOOK NEEDS MORE SEX!

Palcath was not certain what boss he got pushed into until the Insta-Wiki entry came up. All the dwarf knew at the time was that it really liked him, it was big, it was cold, and it was wet.

> **Creature Name:** Frosty Flork Demon
> **Class:** Flork
> **Level:** 70
> **Special Attacks:** Big Flork, Flork Off, No Florking Way, Flork, Flork More
> **Drops:** Flork Drop
> **First Player Encounter Notes:** What was that? What did I just do lads? — Palcath

> NPC Jambass' Text Box: Congratulations sweet treats! Here is your first reward! You may now progress to the next area!

The gate out of the area was unlocked and Jambass stopped blocking the way.

> NPC Jambass' Text Box: Here is your second reward! An Accessory for

'insert avatar name'! May the avatar that collected the most materials step forward!

Palcath's Text Box: You take it, lass. It was your plan that got us here.

Roodg's Text Box: yEAH!

Caëlahenãilenŵhei's Text Box: Thank you. I appreciate that.

NPC Jambass' Text Box: #It is a *Full Ball-Gag*! Enjoy your Sexcessory!#

Caëlahenãilenŵhei's Text Box: A what?

Taking out a *Full Ball-Gag* from her invisible supply NPC Jambass presented the reward to Caëlahenãilenŵhei. The *Full Ball-Gag* spiralled around the shocked light elf for a few rounds but it understood what it was made for and latched onto her face, completely closing off her mouth with a bright red ball. Caela desperately tried to undo the latch but it would not budge.

Caëlahenãilenŵhei's Text Box: Mmmmrrfh! Muummf *slurp* mmmrrr!

NPC Jambass' Text Box: Your third reward is… *pause for dramatic effect*

NPC Jambass pulled down her pants and revealed herself.

NPC Jambass' Continued Text Box: My Sugar Frosted Cooch!

Roodg's Text Box: u BOTH R BUSY. i CAN HANDLE THIS ONE!

Roodg unbuttoned the *Dark Gigas Armour* and revealed both sets of genitalia.

Caëlahenãilenŵhei's Text Box: Moooh? *slurp*

Roodg used *Switch* and traded in a vagina for an extra cock. This earned a smile from NPC Jambass, and Roodg bent her over and went straight to work with an impressive double penetration.

Caëlahenãilenŵhei's Box Text: Oh?

Palcath went ahead to the next area, partially in an attempt to calm down after his intense florking, and partially to give Roodg some space.

Palcath's Text Box: Hey you there… what are you doing?

Palcath's Text Box: And why are you blushing, lad?

◊ Chapter 23 ◊
UNNECESSARY QUESTING A

Kray's Text Box: You are so bad at this, kay. Why?

samuri's Text Box: …

samuri used the *Scowl Animation*.

Kray's Text Box: It's just dancing. How can you be so bad at dancing, kay? The Double Dance Renovation Quest is so much fun!

No-Colour Quest Fairy's Text Box: The Double Dance Renovation Quest is located on Spire A. Yeah well, dance correctly to the flashing coloured arrows and help to renovate the Infernal Library.

samuri's Text Box: …

samuri looked over the stats, he had hit an impressive 99.5% of the dance steps for the current round, he only missed a single blue step. It was a new personal best. Kray had hit only 34%. That was by far Kray's best attempt yet and he had hit 68 of the 200 arrows, this time only missing six blue, four yellow, sixty-five red, and fifty-seven green arrows. He had missed every single red arrow and had only correctly hit one green. His side of the *Infernal Library* had completely fallen into the volcano yet again, so much for M-Z.

> Demon Librarian's Text Box: You have failed attempt 47 in The Double Dance Renovation Quest. Try again and have fun!

> Kray's Text Box: Kay, that was horrible. You're going to need to do so much better or we are never going to get through this!

> samuri's Text Box: ...

samuri had decided that Kray would probably do better dancing if he didn't pay attention to the arrows.

> Kray's Text Box: Kay, I'm going to start this thing again. Try and pay attention this time.

> samuri's Text Box: ...

samuri paid attention this time and scored a new record, 100% steps completed correctly. Kray also made a new record, for his absolute worse attempt at 8.5%. The entire *Infernal Library* slipped into the lava destroyed. This was never going to work.

> Demon Librarian's Text Box: You have failed attempt 48 in The Double Dance Renovation Quest. Try again and have fun!

> Kray's Text Box: That was your worst attempt yet! Kay, what is wrong with you. Don't you know what colour arrows you are stepping on?

> samuri's Text Box: ...

samuri used the *Eyeroll Animation*.

> Kray's Text Box: Don't give me any of that, kay! Just pay attention this time. I am getting really sick of dancing.

> samuri's Text Box: ...

samuri thought for a moment. That was it, his way out! If he could get Kray to not pay attention during the long alternating green and red section maybe the avatar would accidently dance on enough right steps to pass. The little charred legs of his would only need to hit a few more, kay. Curses, now even samuri's internal monologue had 'kay' in it.

The next attempt of the *Double Dance Renovation Quest* was started. The long alternating section was coming up, and samuri was going to need to do something drastic.

> Kray's Text Box: Kay, you are really bad at this part, try and keep up.

> samuri's Text Box: …

samuri used the *Hand Something To Someone Else Dual Animation* to present Kray with the flashingest, most distractingness thing he could find on his person, a *Gilda-Lily* drop item from the Garish Lobster.

> Kray's Text Box: Flowers!? You're giving me flowers? OMM? Really, kay?

> samuri's Text Box: …

samuri watched as Kray used the *Stomp Around Excited While Waving Your Arms Around Like a Little Girl Animation*. He accidently stomped on six green arrows and four red arrows in his attempts to take the flower, but it was enough for the charred elf to score a 37.5%. They passed and the *Infernal Library* finally had a brand new bathroom stall.

Kray sheepishly tucking his brand new *Gilda-Lily* behind his charred pointed ear and smiled. The extra perfect flower beside the extra burnt ear was extra hard to look at.

> Demon Librarian's Text Box: You have passed attempt 49 in The Double Dance Renovation Quest. We hope you had fun!

> NPC Cleft's Text Box: Congratulations little steamers! Here is your first reward! You may now progress to the next area!

The gate out of the area was unlocked and Cleft stopped blocking the way.

> NPC Cleft's Text Box: Here is your second reward! An Accessory for 'insert avatar name'! May the avatar that danced the best step forward!

> Kray's Text Box: That would be me, kay!

> samuri's Text Box: …

samuri tried to beat Kray to the front, but Kray had much better line jumping reflexes when compared to his dance reflexes. samuri used the *Scowl Animation*.

> NPC Cleft's Text Box: #It is a *Jelly Co—*

> Kray's Interruption Text Box: Wait, Jelly? So, like stupid Anders' stupid jelly? I can use this to be like Anders? Finally, I can be as good as Anders! Wait, I mean EVEN better than Anders. Bring it on, kay!

Taking out something from his invisible supply NPC Cleft presented the reward to Kray. Kray wasted no time, snatching it up from Cleft with amazing *Serpent Speed*. The elf had his pants down and the jelly whatever it was inserted up his compartment without a second thought.

> Kray's Text Box: Kay, I am so much better, thinner, hotter, and jellier than Anders now!

> samuri's Text Box: ...

samuri used the *Shrug Animation*.

> NPC Cleft's Text Box: Your third reward is... *pause for dramatic effect*

NPC Cleft pulled down his pants and revealed himself.

> NPC Cleft's Continued Text Box: My hot cock-cano!

> Kray's Text Box: Kay, I so have this one. You stay back samuri. I'll protect you!

> samuri's Text Box: ...

samuri turned his head as Kray walked over to NPC Cleff, bent over, spread his cheeks, and presented himself for insertion.

> Kray's Text Box: Kay! Use my jelly!

> NPC Cleft's Text Box: Sorry, I can't.

> samuri's Text Box: ...

samuri almost turned to look.

> Kray's Text Box: Why The Flaming Pit not? I'm all jellied up and ready to outdo Anders, kay!

> NPC Cleft's Text Box: Because you just stuffed that *Jelly Cock Sculpting Kit* into your ass. It's all sealed up now. You changed the item into a *Jelly Butt-Plug*. Nothing is going in there anymore.

> samuri's Text Box: ...

samuri used the *Smile Animation* and didn't watch as Kray argued with the male Zal Finn with the hot cock-cano. Some attempts by Kray to stuff the cock in anyways had ended in failure, but he was not one to give up.

samuri decided that this was a perfect time to get a few rounds of much deserved silence. He avoided the whole argument cautiously and went into the next area.

> samuri's Text Box: ...

samuri used the *Wave Animation*.

Chapter 24

ANDERS, EATER OF CUPPED CAKES

Anders opened his eyes slowly and with great effort. The elf had no idea where he was and it took some rounds for his eyes to adjust to the light. He felt more than a bit groggy and looked around cautiously.

That entire paragraph felt vaguely familiar to Anders, but so did the entire situation of waking up in an unfamiliar place after passing out due to intense adult situations. He was in a bed, that much was for certain. He was no longer hurt Hit Points wise and had finally lost all his cuts and bruises, but he was still hurting all over.

A wonderful smell filled his nose and reminded him that he hadn't eaten anything in quite some time. It smelled warm, inviting, and yeasty.

> Anders' Text Box: Ugh... Where am I?

> NPC Greeta's Text Box: Welcome to Onn!

> Anders' Text Box: What?

> NPC Greeta's Text Box: Welcome to Onn!

> NPC Margarine's Text Box: Greeta is correct. Hun, you are in Onn. In my Bakery Shoppe to be exact.

> Anders' Text Box: In your bakery?

> NPC Margarine's Text Box: Welcome to my Bakery Shoppe, hun. How can I help you today?

Anders had the Bakery Shoppe menu opened up for him. He closed it with much annoyance.

> NPC Margarine's Text Box: Sorry, hun, I always have to do that if an avatar talks to me.

> Anders' Text Box: That's okay. How did I get inside here?

> NPC Margarine's Text Box: Welcome to my Bakery Shoppe, hun. How can I help you today?

Anders shut the Bakery Shoppe menu again. This time with only a hint of irritation.

> NPC Margarine's Text Box: Sorry again hun. We brought you inside through the window. But then Xam, the Orange Dragon of Light destroyed most of Onn.

> Anders' Text Box: Xam destroyed Onn? Why?

> NPC Margarine's Text Box: Welcome to my Bakery Shoppe, hun. How can I help you today?

Anders closed the Bakery Shoppe menu again. He deserved it that time.

> NPC Margarine's Text Box: First you must be starving, hun. Here eat this *Cupped Cake*, my treat.

Anders took the *Cupped Cake*, he almost said thank you but caught himself. NPC Margarine looked like she knew that he was thankful. He really was starving and the *Cupped Cake* had a delicious Panini press aftertaste. He talked to NPC Margarine on purpose, and bought three more for good measure.

> NPC Margarine's Text Box: After you disappeared from the town square Xam couldn't come back to fill up your unconscious body anymore hun. He was furious and rampaged through the entire town. We are the only ones left.

> Anders' Text Box: Anymore? We? Who are we? … Also I said all of that only to myself.

NPC Margarine used the *Nod Animation*.

> NPC Margarine's Text Box: Yes, anymore. Before we could come to your rescue Xam ravaged you some more, hun. We saved you after a particularly long session involving the town fountain. Xam went crazy

> when he came back to find you missing. He kill killed nearly everyone, and destroyed nearly every building in Onn searching for you hun. We are the only ones topside who made it.

He looked around the small inside of the Bakery Shoppe, and saw the remainder of Onn's NPCs population. First was NPC Greeta, who was holding her 'Welcome To Onn' sign and still had Anders' footprint on her face. Next to her was NPC Margarine, the chubby owner of the Bakery Shoppe, Anders did not linger on her for too long just in case he accidently did something that made her open the shop menu. The next NPC was an unimportant guard named NPC Galapas who would be mentioned near the end of this Chapter, and then never again. There was one NPC left but Anders couldn't see them from behind the large mass of blankets that was sharing his bed.

> Anders' Text Box: Who are you?

> NPC Illiandro's Text Box: YES!!! Finally! Someone talked to me!

> Anders' Text Box: Huh?

NPC Illiandro moved around into view. Anders had not noticed the floating quest icon until it was too late. This was the creepy hooded NPC that hung out near the bakery harassing avatars by looking in their general direction.

> Anders' Text Box: You are that creepy NPC who harassed only a few of us, everyone thought we were crazy. You stalked me around town. I got Xamed because of you!

> NPC Margarine's Text Box: To be fair, much of Onn was Xamed because of you, hun.

> NPC Greeta's Text Box: Welcome to Onn!

> NPC Illiandro's Text Box: I didn't harass everyone, just the ones of you who were Ranged Classes. Only they can see me to start my secret Ranged Class quest. Now you can start my secret quest! How exciting!

> Anders' Text Box: You did all that just so I would start your stupid quest?

> NPC Illiandro's Text Box: No, I did all of that so you could start my secret quest. There is even a really awesome reward if you beat it! The best part is that Xam didn't destroy your Coliseum, so you can still go!

> Anders' Text Box: There is a Coliseum here? We never found the Coliseum.

NPC Illiandro's Text Box: There are four of them! Your Ranged Coliseum is underground and run by the Thieves Guild. There is a secret entrance, but the only way anyone would find it was by me telling you or after killing the Dragon Rider. Well unless some idiot ran around pressing every brick in town, but like that would ever happen. Besides, I have to give you the key to the entrance.

NPC Illiandro handed Anders a Key Item. It was a *Coliseum Key*.

Anders' Text Box: So there is a secret entrance to a secret place, but you will give anyone a key to it and show them where it is?

NPC Illiandro's Text Box: Of course not, that would be silly. Only I can open the door to the Coliseum, but this key opens the secret passage to the optional boss after you complete the rest of the battles. I only give this key to Ranged classes. I wouldn't want the *Super Amazing Hover-Motorbike* to go to just anyone.

Anders' Text Box: The *Super Amazing Hover-Motorbike*?

Green Quest Fairy's Text Box: The *Super Amazing Hover-Motorbike* is the reward for the final secret stage of the quest Coliseum Battle Champion. While any avatar can compete in the Coliseum by first killing the Dragon Rider, only the Ranged class optional boss is located there. To start this quest be a ranged class avatar and talk to NPC Illiandro near the Bakery Shoppe in Onn after you have been in the Expansion for 30 cycles.. The *Super Amazing Hover-Bike* allows an avatar to revisit any area of the Island of Islana that they have already visited.

Anders' Text Box: Great, so a kick-cupcake sounding item that would allow me to revisit Onn, the warp in area beside Onn, Onn Forest, and a smouldering pile of Airship rubble. I haven't been anywhere else on the Island of Islana!

Green Quest Fairy's Text Box: Of the 160 locations on the Island of Islana you have already visited 152.

Anders was confused for a moment, but then he remembered his personal Islana tour courtesy of Xam.

Anders' Text Box: Quick, Illiandro! Take me to the Coliseum. Then I can finally get out of this accursed Onn, no offense, and meet everyone else in the fight against Breaker!

NPC Greeta's Text Box: Welcome to Onn!

> Green Quest Fairy's Text Box: There are 0 Quests, 4 Quest NPCs and 5 Hidden Quests inside Onn. You have completed 23 Quests and 0 Hidden Quests.

Anders got ready to stand up, but failed miserably. He was still feeling the effects of Xam's special tour.

> NPC Margarine's Text Box: Oh no, you are not going anywhere with those conditions young man!

> Anders' Text Box: What conditions?

> NPC Margarine's Text Box: Welcome to my Bakery Shoppe, hun. How can I help you today?

The Bakery Shoppe menu opened up again, but this time Anders used it happily to buy more *Cupped Cakes*. He licked his lips and bit into another delicious Panini press.

> NPC Margarine's Text Box: First of all hun, you are under the nude status effect. You don't appear to be wearing anything except your Sexcessory and *Frost Gigas Boots*. Everything else in your *Ultra-Pack* is broken.

> Anders' Text Box: What, no I have my set of *Slime Armour* on me and even some familiar *Leather Armlets* in my *Ultra-Pack*, with all my other gear and stuff... I say... to NPC Greeta.

> NPC Greeta's Text Box: Welcome to Onn!

> NPC Margarine's Text Box: I'm sorry hun, I looked through your Ultra-Pack for something to dress you in. Besides boring broken Armour there isn't much in there.

Anders' tore open his *Ultra-Pack* and looked. NPC Margarine was right. Nearly all of his own gear was gone, and absolutely everything that Anders had stashed of Yallundy's had been taken. Xam must have taken all he could while Anders was unconscious. Anders took stock of what he had left and noticed a trend.

Items Anders Has Left
- **Ultra-Pack** → All varieties of Backpacks cannot be taken, just melted by acid.
- **Every food item Anders had** → He wouldn't starve. Anders took out a stored *Cupped Cake* to eat while searching through the rest of his *Ultra-Pack*.
- **Pink Goo x999** → This wasn't stored where it was listed, it was no wonder that Xam hadn't found them. Anders couldn't even find them.
- **Golden Combi-Pot** → Quest Items can be displayed in *Portie Tents*, but not traded.

- **Frost Gigas Boots** → Gigas Gear cannot be traded.
- **Broken Set of Boring Armour (No Boots)** → Broken Gear cannot be equipped, if all the other NPCs in town were dead except these four Anders had no way of fixing this.
- **Pink Slime Jock-Strap** → Sexcessories cannot be unequipped, only exchanged for other Sexcessories.
- **Timing Hammer** → One half of the Combi-Fusion recipe for a Repair-It, completely useless without a Strand of Dream.
- **One Vial of Minotaur Musk** → With a note attached that said 'Only use this when you are with me my sweet piece of dragon candy'.
- **Elf Starting Bow** → Freshly salvaged from the rubble of Onn Inn. No bowstring and still slightly sticky.
- **Gray Wolf Pelt** → One half of the Combi-Fusion recipe for a Bowstring, useless without an Old Twine.
- **Key Item** → Coliseum Key, just obtained.
- **186,219 Gold Coins** → Total Weight of a small nation's net worth of coins, nothing. Xam hadn't taken his money, at least he could still buy things... well baked things. All the other NPCs that sold items were dead except Margarine.
- **One Coupon** → Good for a free ass pounding. Valid only when given to Xam, the Orange Dragon of Light. Not usable with any other offers. Coupon has no cash value.
- **Stone Softener** → One of Anders' very first Combi-Fused items. Not even Mr. Max knew what it was used for.
- **Ultimate Prize** → Strange, Anders could finally see it listed but still couldn't find it anywhere, and his *Ultra-Pack* was very empty at this point.

This was just great. Anders had no usable weapons, no crystals to place into equipment to allow the shooting of rainbows, no non-underpants related accessories, and no Armour besides the ass pounding *Frost Gigas Boots*. The only things Xam had left were things to mock Anders, stuff the dragon couldn't find, things that just couldn't be taken, all of his delicious food, and money that could be used to buy more delicious food.

Anders could no longer attack monsters or defend himself. All he could do now was eat and have sex with Xam.

> Anders' Text Box: This is just perfect. I don't see how this could possibly get worse.

> NPC Margarine's Text Box: Well hun, there is your other condition...

NPC Margarine changed the setting on the Bakery Shoppe bed from comfortably holding avatars to dramatic reveal. Anders was so surprised that he nearly choked on his sixth *Cupped Cake*. There he was, filling the bed completely. The elf was now nearly

100 weight units heavier than when he first got to the *Island of Islana*, nearly all of it was swelled up in his giant belly.

Anders used the *Jawdrop Animation*.

> Anders' Text Box: What happened to me?

> NPC Margarine's Text Box: We are not really sure, hun, but all the extra *Cupped Cakes* probably aren't helping.

Anders put down the *Cupped Cake* and his stomach growled in protest. It grumbled louder. It rumbled as it flipped around inside itself. Anders tasted Panini presses and noted in horror that he had another *Cupped Cake* in his mouth, which he threw across the room. After swallowing the last bite his stomach started to lurch around. Anders definitely should have spit and not swallowed that last bite. He had reached his limit and was going to burst. The avatar was now squirming around in intense pain, his stomach turning about itself.

> Anders' Text Box: Urrrgghhh! Help... help me... please...

> NPC Margarine's Text Box: Welcome to my Bakery Shoppe, hun. How can I help you today?

> Anders' Text Box: Please help me with the horrible pain!

> NPC Margarine's Text Box: We will try our best. You're burning up, hun. Let's get these blankets off right now! Greeta, can you get me some hot... well I don't have towels... get me some hot cake.

> NPC Greeta's Text Box: Welcome to Onn!

> NPC Margarine's Text Box: Illiandro and Galapas, see if you can stop him from squirming about. All that movement will only make it worse.

NPC Illiandro desperately attempted to grab Anders' arms, but all the squirming about in agony made it difficult. NPC Galapas managed to grab hold of Anders' feet.

> Anders' Text Box: Ahhhhhh! Make it stop.

A deep grumble came from deep within Anders, who wretched about in agony. The avatar wrestled his arms free of NPC Illiandro, and with a few high kicks was free from NPC Galapas as well. Once free Anders shivered and with a loud popping noise violently released twenty weight units of fluid from his ass, completely coating the unfortunate NPC Galapas.

> NPC Galapas' Text Box: No way, gross!

◊ **Chapter 25** ◊

THE CLEAN BREAK

The sun broke through the little fluffy clouds in the sky with beams of gentle light. Pleasant background music filled with inspirational flute solos drifted through the wings of scenic birds. The gentle wind carried a hint of lavender fragrance that kissed the cheek. It was all just so revolting. Breaker had to hold back his vomit. At least flight was still badass, even if the scenery was unbearably lovely.

Breaker was so bored. He had resorted to sightseeing. It turned out that flying through the sky was pretty boring, but Breaker was desperate. All of the parts of his plan that he could do without the plot progressing had been finished for ages. The idiots were still forever away from getting to any plot points relevant to him, let alone the climax of the story.

There had to be something up here in the clouds to do to kill some time. Breaker used the *Ponder Animation* as he thought. A scenic bird refused to deviate from its set path and flew directly into Breaker's face. He knocked the bird aside with a tap of his clawed hand and it exploded into a cascade of feathers. Here was something to do, innocent bird slaughter.

Breaker darted through the clouds and snatched up the little pink birds to snap in half with glee. It was great to finally do something fun while flying through the clouds, plus the exercise was always welcome. Birds by the bucketful were snapped like the low-leveled monsters named Feathered Twig Buckets.

A particularly cute bird darted into the clouds and Breaker was determined to snap it into bite-sized pieces. Breaker dove into the cloud and broke his nose when he smacked into the solid surface.

> Breaker's Text Box: Son of a cunt!

Breaker held his nose as blood dripped through his claws. Another little pink bird flew through the impassible cloud and Breaker kicked the same spot, only to hear a clunk. Only this one cloud in the entire sky (Breaker checked later) was solid. Breaker flew back and *With a Stretching Out of His Wings and a Dramatic Movement of his Claws Animation* he called down an *Orbital Firestrike*. The smoke cleared and the cloud revealed a different cloud.

> Breaker's Text Box: For fuck's sake.

Breaker pounded his fist against the metal surface, confirming it was what had broken his nose. A metal cloud that looked exactly like the regular clouds, but with one distinct difference. This one had a door. Breaker attempted to open the door, but it was locked with a combination lock.

There was something in this cloud that someone wanted to keep secret, locked with an item that wasn't even technically in this game. Breaker used the *Smirk Animation*. It looked like he had something to do now. Something secret and locked with an impossible key. It was wonderful, finally there was something interesting to do.

◈ Chapter 26 ◈
THE FORESTS OF INTRODUCING D

Gliint's Text Box: Max, *Shakes head* I hate to break it to you, but that isn't Anders.

Mr. Max's Text Box: Of course it is Anders.

Gliint's Text Box: You had me worried for a turn there Max *Relief*.

Mr. Max's Text Box: Why would you be worried Little Bro?

Gliint's Text Box: I had Anders in the Mr. Max remembering name pool, I thought I had just lost all of my buy in. Speaking of which Caela is going to be pissed off when she finds out that you remembered my name.

Mr. Max's Text Box: Who is this Caela fellow you are talking about?

Gliint's Text Box: *Shrug off* He doesn't matter right now. The important thing is that this isn't Anders.

Mr. Max's Text Box: Of course it is, I know Anders like the back of my hand. Let's look at my list of commonly known Anders facts.

Mr. Max's Commonly Known Anders Facts List

1. Class: Healing Magic Type - Sage - Urban Style. New with the expansion. Can debuff enemies and cast healing spells. Anders is always healing us when we are in tight spots.
2. Race: Fight elf. Stronger than a regular elf, but worse with Dexterity, which is why Anders picked it, for Consitution Saves.
3. Primary Weapon: *Flicker Flail.* Anders is always up front with melee attacks.
4. Secondary Weapon: *Big Action Boomerang.* Anders is never using ranged attacks though.
5. *#2 Hairstyle (Dark Blond),* ultra short and no nonsense, same as someone else in the party, me.
6. Gender: Female.
7. Body Type: Body Size 8, Muscular. Biggest and most muscular girl around.
8. Height: Maximum height for females.
9. Sex Power: Ridiculously oversized breasts, set to the maximum level of jiggle. Perfect for using *Fill* on.
10. Armour: Skin-tight, water resistant, and barely there outfit. See how it almost contains Anders' breasts and the peek-a-boo diamond with no fabric in the middle? It is complete with stomach girdle that somehow holds up those giant breasts and an Amazon style leaf skirt. Anders loves her leaf skirts.
11. Gigas Gear: *Wind Gigas Helmet,* perfect for finding your enemies weak points. The same Gigas Gear as Palcath.
12. Eyes: Steel gray. Face is stuck in a permanent scowl expression, Staring at me like I am some sort of idiot
13. Colour green with a single dash of pink secondary accent colour, and a Green Quest Fairy. That doesn't seem right, but maybe she changed it?

> Mr. Max's Text Box: Clearly this is Anders.

> Gliint's Text Box: *Facepalm* The only one of those commonly known Anders facts that you got right is the one that you thought was wrong. This is not Anders!

> Mr. Max's Text Box: No, this is Anders. End of debate.

> Hippolyta's Text Box: This debate is hardly over Max. I am going to have to side with the gnome. This is clearly not Anders.

> Mr. Max's Text Box: So how have you been Anders?

> Hippolyta's Text Box: Honestly, I was much better before you trotted along to my supposed rescue. Typical male chauvinistic views of women needing to be rescued by men when women are more than

capable of rescuing themselves. I am not some useless damsel to be cooped up in some tower awaiting the proverbial knight in shining Armour.

Gliint's Text Box: *Confused* Your rescue? We never said that. Do you need to be rescued?

Hippolyta's Text Box: Of course not! That would be foolish. I need nothing of the sort.

Gliint's Text Box: Then why have you set up a permanent camp here near this lightning rod tower and moved around those scenic rocks to spell out S.O.S.?

Hippolyta used the *Hands On Your Hips and Angrily Scowl Animation.*

Hippolyta's Text Box: Signalling to a specific rescuer you are waiting for and just begging to be rescued by any random passersby are completely different events.

Mr. Max's Text Box: Well we are here to rescue you then Anders! How did you know that we specifically were coming though?

Hippolyta's Text Box: Famous or not, you are still as smart as a sack of bricks Max.

Mr. Max's Text Box: Oh Anders, you kidder you! We both know that A-Sack-a-Bricks is the monster with the lowest Intelligence Score in the game.

Hippolyta's Text Box: Honestly, I didn't know that. I however will stand by that statement. In fact I enjoy it more now.

Mr. Max's Text Box: What's wrong Anders? I don't remember you being this grumpy. Oh, I know, are you pent up? Down on magic reserves? I know I just used that NPC, but you feel so much better. Should we *Surge* together and I'll fill you up proper like?

Hippolyta's Text Box: I beg your pardon?

Mr. Max's Text Box: You know, your magical absorbing love pillo—

Gliint's Interruption Text Box: *Flustered* You will have to excuse Mr. Max… he is… he is just…uh…

> Hippolyta's Text Box: An idiot?

Hippolyta looked at the gnome for some time, but she did not get a reply. Gliint had lost his train of thought while staring at Hippolyta's massive chest.

> Hippolyta's Text Box: Wonderful. Just wonderful. Typical gnome chauvinist perverts, unable to look away from the female form. I can't believe I am being forcibly rescued by Captain Idiot and his sidekick Pervert the Gnome. On second thought, I will just stay here instead and await someone who doesn't objectify women to come by. An impossible to realize dream I know, but that is the game we play in this day and age.

> Mr. Max's Text Box: Captain Who and his what now? Who are those guys?

> Gliint's Lag Text Box: Yeah, a bit, but he's really nice deep down.

> Gliint's Text Box: No wait! Not that! Sorry, I wasn't staring honest!

> Hippolyta's Text Box: Yes, a likely enough story. However, your massive erection gives your obvious intentions away gnome.

Gliint tried to cover up his obvious erection with his *Ni Hao Bunny©* *Text Book*, even though it was the *Mega Strap-On* showing and not his own gnome member. Even if his own little member was rock hard and staring straight at the maximum level of jiggle, that wasn't the point.

> Gliint's Text Box: Hey, that's not even mine!

> Hippolyta's Text Box: Not yours? Did you borrow it from a friend? Typical male excuses for their treatment and objectification of women. That kind of thing does not fly around here!

> Mr. Max's Text Box: He didn't borrow it from me. Trust me, I still have mine.

> Gliint's Text Box: *Blush* It's not my fault!

> Hippolyta's Text Box: What you just have a fake cock permanently strapped to your waist? Put there magically simply just to embarrass you in front of random women you meet in the forest and to ruin all your chances at giving the toast at a fancy royal gala when it bumps your notes in all different directions? So it isn't your fault that you are a pig of a man, of course not, that would be silly. Impossible.

> Green Quest Fairy's Text Box: The Fancy Royal Gala quest involves a few key players that are chosen randomly: 1. The Toas—

> Gliint's Interruption Text Box: *Nod* That is it exactly!

> Hippolyta's Text Box: Typical male reply by a —

Gliint interrupted the amply endowed fight elf by pulling down his pants, exposing the *Mega Strap-On*.

> Gliint's Text Box: See!

> Hippolyta's Text Box: I... I... I see. I am sorry. I know all too well what it is like to be burdened with something oppressive that you never wanted.

Gliint would have accepted the apology but he had lagged out again, again looking directly at the impressive fight elf chest, but this time with his pants down and his hand holding his borrowed package.

> Hippolyta's Text Box: I can't believe that I just apologized to such a little pervert asshole! Here is a little tip for you, my eyes are up here. So if you are talking to me, look at my eyes and not my chest!

> Mr. Max's Text Box: I don't remember you being so confrontational Anders.

> Gliint's Lag Text Box: *Head nod* Apology accepted. Sorry we got off on the wrong foot there.

> Gliint's Text Box: Hey!

Hippolyta used the *Hands On Your Hips and Angrily Scowl Animation*.

> Gliint's Text Box: Well here is a little tip for you, my eyes are down here! So if I did look up when I talked to you the only thing I would be able to see is your giant bouncing breasts!

> Hippolyta's Text Box: Gah!

Gliint stepped back a few move units until he could actually see over Hippolyta's breasts and into her eyes.

> Gliint's Text Box: Better?

The fight elf's steel coloured eyes softened for a moment.

> Mr. Max's Text Box: Your giant bouncing breasts are a little bigger than I remember Anders. Maybe it is that new Armour of yours. Can you

> take it off so I can have a good look at them?

The fight elf's steel eyes reverted back to their original state.

> Hippolyta's Text Box: My breasts are nobody's business but mine!

This was escalating quickly, Gliint decided that the best course of action would be to try and calm things down.

> Gliint's Text Box: Okay, we are sorry. *Formal bow* obviously we got off on the wrong foot here. I apologize, let's start from the beginning. Hello, nice to meet you, I'm Gliint and this is Mr. Max.

Hippolyta was thinking. She used the *Toe Tapping Animation* for a few rounds. Each tap of her toe caused her oversized chest to start jiggling. By the time Hippolyta had made up her mind her large breasts were moving in large rhythmic circles.

> Hippolyta's Text Box: I'm Hippolyta, and I accept your apology. But I warn you gnome, no more funny business or so help me Maker I will slap your sorry ass into the heart of the sun itself.

Gliint couldn't reply. He was frozen in place. This time it was not due to lag, but the fact that the gnome was *Spellbound* by Hippolyta's massive rotating bosom. His eyes and camera angle had been locked with her nipples. Mr. Max was also staring, while drooling.

> Hippolyta's Text Box: Stop ogling my breasts!

> Gliint and Mr. Max's Simultaneous Text Boxes: Gha-lu-lugga-ah…?

Hippolyta's steel eyes were forged in fire. She slapped both of the ogling avatars three times. Once with her hand on purpose and twice accidentally with her big breasts as they followed through her slapping motion.

###L##D#'S #E#T B#X: #LI#N# #O!

The Silver Sludge stepped forward and pushed Hippolyta away from Gliint and Max. Seeing the Silver Sludge snapped both Gliint and Max out of their trances, but put Hippolyta into one of her own.

> Gliint's Text Box: Hey! *Rubbing cheek*

> Gliint's Text Box: Hey!

> Gliint's Text Box: … Hey?

Hippolyta was still caught in the self induced *Spellbound Status Effect*. Gliint used the opportunity to jump up and slap her in the face, causing her breasts to sway back and forth. Even that did not snap the fight elf out of her Silver Sludge stare down.

> Gliint's Text Box: Stop ogling my Sludge!

The Silver Sludge snuggled up close to Gliint and caused severe lightning damage trauma, but the gnome didn't flinch.

> Hippolyta's Text Box: Who is that divine creature? I am too stunned by her beauty to even speak.

> Gliint's Text Box: Her beauty? He just tried to fuck me with his giant cock not fifty rounds ago.

> Mr. Max's Text Box: Then it fell in love with the little guy. A touching story really. Sludge meets gnome. Sludge tries to fuck gnome. Sludge trances out and cuddles gnome. Real blockbuster material right there.

> Hippolyta's Text Box: Please forgive me, beautiful creature for harassing your gnome, even if he is a pig and did deserve it.

> Gliint's Text Box: I am not a pig! I was never staring. I just suffer from acute lag.

That was barely a lie, Gliint rationalized to himself. He had only been staring once; the other times had been lag.

> Hippolyta's Text Box: Jorthan used to suffer from lag all the time, but he never lagged out while staring at someone's breasts! So don't use that as an excuse you little perv.

> Mr. Max's Text Box: Jorthan the Male Troll Warrior? I haven't seen him in ages.

> Gliint's Text Box: Who the Male Troll What? *Confused* How could you possibly know who that is Max?

> Mr. Max's Text Box: Don't you remember Jorthan the Male Troll Warrior? He led a team of adventurers into the starting town of Caelahenailenwhei after Breaker destroyed it. He was the one who reported that NPC Valisha had gone missing.

> Gliint's Text Box: *Head shake* I don't remember any of that, and that's not the name of the starting city in the old map! It's one of our party members that you think is a man.

> Mr. Max's Text Box: I don't know, Caelahenailenwhei sounds about right to me.

> Hippolyta's Text Box: I hate to say this, but I think he is right with that name. For the first time ever no doubt.

Glint's Text Box: *Arms crossed* For some reason I find it hard to believe that you would ever follow a man Hippolyta, or even be in a party with one.

Hippolyta's Text Box: I don't recall saying that I followed him. He is the organizer of our guild nights, nothing more. My party has more women than men, and the men are all ones that I can tolerate, unlike you lot.

Mr. Max's Text Box: Sure you remember Little Bro. The Jorthan's party thing happened when we were going up the Moving Stairway of Clouds on our way to beat up Breaker!

Glint's Text Box: I wasn't with you then!

Mr. Max's Text Box: I think you might be wrong Glint. I clearly remember you being there at The Plague of Shadow.

Glint's Text Box: *Facepalm* I was there!

Mr. Max's Text Box: See, what did I tell you. Why are you so forgetful. Obviously you don't remember Jorthan the Male Troll Warrior either. He and his party were some of the key players when we killed the Gigases the first time. You were definitely there, that's when you got those boots.

Hippolyta's Text Box: He goes by Jorthan The Male Troll Monk now. Not the best of names really, but it does get his point across and he didn't really get the whole naming thing. Why would you remember him, but not other members of that party?

Mr. Max's Text Box: He was the leader, why would anyone need to remember anyone else?

Hippolyta's Text Box: You insufferable…

Glint's Text Box: Wait… *Thinking*

Hippolyta's Text Box: Wait indeed… are you the little gnome that lagged out and then accidently killed the Frost Gigas? Yes you are! I remember you now, we all were forced to go to Lova Mines to get you to Level 20. The hero of the cycle I believe. My how the mighty have fallen.

> Gliint's Text Box: Wait, I remember you as well. You're that elf who yelled at the Wind Gigas for being a typical juvenile male fantasy and then you stabbed her right in the boob! You were less… distinctive then.

> Mr. Max's Text Box: So, Jorthan the Male Troll Warrior changed his class to Monk huh? Still a good choice. How is he nowadays?

> Hippolyta's Text Box: I haven't seen him in game since my team won the second Insta-Wiki Contest and got blasted every which way but directly to the Flaming Pit after porting in.

> Gliint's Text Box: That was you? You killed her!

> Hippolyta's Text Box: What?

Gliint jumped forward with intent to bomb, but he lagged out and only managed to blow himself up. The Silver Sludge tended to his wounds while Hippolyta watched on with interest. By the time Gliint caught up to the world, Mr. Max was restraining the gnome.

> Mr. Max's Text Box: Calm down there my friend, that was Breaker's fault. Anders would never have hurt Yallundy on purpose.

> Gliint's Lag Text Box: *Intense Anger* You will pay!

> Gliint's Text Box: Huh?

> Hippolyta's Text Box: You might have more luck being dramatic and killing me if you got that lag under control.

She was right, and so was Max. It really wasn't her party's fault. It was Breaker's. Gliint calmed down from his adrenaline high.

> Gliint's Text Box: *Sigh* I've tried everything. Better internet package, meditation, asking nicely, thinking positively, asking not nicely, upgrades, video cards, and even a new computer. Nothing works.

> Hippolyta' Text Box: Well Jorthan doesn't lag anymore.

> Gliint's Text Box: How? You have to tell me how!

> Hippolyta's Text Box: I don't know, nor do I care.

> Mr. Max's Text Box: Of course you care Anders. Gliint is your bakery sniffing bud!

> Gliint's Text Box: Please? *Beg* You just have to tell me!

> Hippolyta's Text Box: Fine. But you better not ogle me even one more time if I tell you. Do you agree?

> Gliint's Text Box: I Agree. *Nodding* 100 times over agreed.

> Hippolyta's Text Box: He summoned an Admin about it.

> Gliint's Text Box: Why? *Confused* What did that do?

> Hippolyta's Text Box: Beats me, when that was going on I went to get a taco.

> Mr. Max's Text Box: Taco? You mean a sandwich silly!

Gliint summoned an Admin and didn't have to wait long. A magenta Administrator ball was unfolding on the next round.

> Administrator Owen's Text Box: You haven't found Breaker, why are you calling me?

> Gliint's Text Box: No it's just—

A yellow Administrator ball unfolded beside Owen.

> Administrator Ethelred's Text Box: Breaker we need... wait, where is my introduction? I prepared it earlier.

> Gliint's Text Box: *Wave* He's not here. I just had a quick question. I heard that you know how to deal with lag issues?

> Administrator Owen's Text Box: Not this crap again.

Administrator Owen used the *Sigh Animation*.

> Administrator Ethelred's Text Box: I swear, nobody ever reads the troubleshooting. Okay go to Menu → Options → Display → Then change it from Ultra Smooth Quality to Smooth quality. Did that work? Oh look, my house keys, thank goodness.

> Gliint's Text Box: ... ... ??? !!! !!! *Bwahaha!* It's gone! It's gone! OMFM It's gone! Bwahahahahaha! Thank you! Thank you! Thank you!

Gliint was so overjoyed that he used the **OVERJOYED ANIMATION**, the **ECSTATIC ANIMATION**, and the **JUMP AROUND DELIGHTED ANIMATION** all in the same round. It was something that only Gliint, the fastest of all avatars could do. Now that his horrible crippling lag was gone and his *Speed Code* was active the gnome could officially change his full avatar name to Gliint Lightning from Gliint Doossleer, if he spent gold coins to do so (which he honestly wouldn't do, what a money grab). Both Administrator Owen and Ethelred, who were closest to the gnome, screamed out in pleasure. They quickly took leave of the area to go clean their now sticky robes. The Silver Sludge flattened to the floor and was bucking up and down excitedly while silver goo shot out at different angles. Mr. Max fell to his knees and was pointing his fully expanded arousal at anything that dared to look. Hippolyta stood there in shock, her breasts bounding around excitedly after the instant hardening of her nipples.

> Gliint's Text Box: *Composed look* Sorry, I got a bit too excited.

> Mr. Max's Text Box: Okay Anders, I really need your help now. For some reason I've used *Max More More*. I've just got to use you now. Where do you want it?

Hippolyta used the *Hands On Your Hips and Angrily Scowl Animation*. Her nipples became even harder with anger, as nipples often do. She slapped Mr. Max across the face three times, again only once was on purpose.

> Hippolyta's Text Box: That is it, I am going through this forest and then this spire just so I can get to the Airship Port. Then I will be away from you avatars and your horrible views of women and hopefully back to MY party. How could you treat this Anders woman like a cheap piece of meat just begging for your oppressive man tool. Like she has nothing better to do than service you and your every whim. It is degrading and all women everywhere should be appalled.

> Mr. Max's Text Box: Can you slap me with your breasts again Anders? That was kind of hot.

> Hippolyta's Text Box: I need you both to come with me to unlock the forest gate, since there are four levers. I trust your Sludge can flip switches as well. After that though you are on your own.

Gliint didn't bother to correct Hippolyta's mistake with the real Anders' gender. She had a mission to complete and her help through the *Lightning Tree Forest* would be useful. Even if she wouldn't be using any of her healing abilities on Max or Gliint, she did have a *Flicker Flail* and the aggression needed to use it.

Hippolyta had a unique combat style. First she lowered the monster's abilities with anti-buffs, then she would run up to the enemies who were often hypnotised by the rotating of her breasts during her run cycle. She would hit the enemy hard three times. Once was with her *Flicker Flail*, the other two hits were from her ample breasts as she slapped the monsters accidently on her follow through. The tactic worked wonders, but Gliint was sure that only half of her strategy was on purpose.

Getting through the *Lightning Tree Forest* was easy. The monsters might as well have been Start Rats for all the damage they caused. Mr. Max was over-leveled and shamelessly cock-slapping around everything in his path. Hippolyta was her own combo completion team. Gliint was ramped up to more than triple speed and could place a bomb, retreat, and have it explode in less than a round. Silver Sludge was a boss monster and could hold its own, despite its knees still being shaky after all the orgasms it had experienced after Gliint's sexy Animations.

Four levers stood atop four pillars on the sides of the lightning tree glade. Massive piles of electrical wire littered the glade. This was a puzzle that did not involve brains or tact, just having enough hands (or whatever it was that Silver Sludges had) available to pull levers.

Before the easy puzzle could be attempted the area boss dropped in to visit. The Bellowing Griffon was sheathed in lightning effects and every time its impressive wings moved they created the low rumbling noise of distant thunderclaps. It surveyed the area, feeling very impressed with itself before preening its attractive yellow feathers.

> Game Explanation Text Box: Be wary of wind attacks, some can be so powerful that they can blow you over.

The boss battle had begun, and like all annoying bosses the Bellowing Griffon was the first to act. On its first action it spread its powerful wings in a display of both power and sound effects. The wings switched sides of the model while turning upside down. This gave the Bellowing Griffon an otherworldly and chilling appearance. At the end of its display of power a long penis grew hard from the beast's crotch accented by two tiny but constantly pulsating balls. The beast used his second action not to attack, as would be expected, but instead to gloat.

> Bellowing Griffons' Text Box: Back for more I see? Just couldn't stay away, could you, fight elf? Well don't worry, I know I can make them bigger if I try.

> Hippolyta's Text Box: Not on your life you male chauvinist Griffon! Prepare for the fury of a true Amazon Goddess!

> Mr. Max's Text Box: But Anders, you are a Sage, there is no Amazon Goddess class!

> Gliint's Text Box: Shhh! *Finger up to mouth* You're ruining her dramatic moment.

Blessed with the fury of a true Amazon goddess, or possibly just the fury of a really mad woman, Hippolyta charged at the male chauvinist Bellowing Griffon. Paying attention to only the crotch of the beast, she first unleashed a *Flailing Atonement* to the beast's penis then a *Furious Buster* to his pulsating balls. Both attacks were accidently followed by two damaging breast slaps. Neither Mr. Max nor Gliint commented on how she had technically illegally used two moves in a single round, as they both enjoyed their own crotch equipment intact and did not want to be the next in line for an assault.

> Bellowing Griffon's Text Box: Now is that the way to treat the guy who made you the object of desire for men everywhere? I think not!

Raising his strange backwards wings completely outward the Bellowing Griffon executed a move called *The Bellows*. This caused his tiny balls to grow tenfold, when the beast lowered his wings with force his large balls shot out massive amounts of wind blowing Hippolyta backwards into a large pile of conveniently placed electrical wires. Hippolyta was struggling against the wires, but was trapped. Each struggle caused her breasts to rotate more and more until neither Gliint nor Max were able to do anything but stare at them. The Bellowing Griffon gave a quick *Smirk Animation*, the raging Amazon Goddess had just incapacitated her own teammates with her hypnotic breasts. The beast strutted towards his prize, careful to avoid looking at her ample rotating bosom.

> Bellowing Griffon's Text Box: You were so eager to increase your bust size that you forgot all about my wire traps didn't you? This time I'll inflate those love balloons up for you properly.

> Hippolyta's Text Box: My breasts are nobody's business but mine!

The Bellowing Griffon stepped forward and got ready to insert his slightly bruised, but still-working bellowing cock into the fight elf's mouth. He was going to enjoy pumping her up again. Maybe if he blew enough air into those big breasts he could make the avatar float away.

The Silver Sludge, who was immune to the *Spellbound Status Effect* of the fight elf's *Heaving Bosom*, slapped Gliint out of his trance. Gliint thanked the monster and noticed an annoyed look in its nonexistent eyes.

> The Bellowing Griffon's Text Box: Oh, I am going to enjoy this. Should I use liquid air again or some—

The gnome bravely stepped forward and shot at the Bellowing Griffon, hitting it right in the hindquarters and interrupting the beast's Text Box.

> Gliint's Text Box: Hey! *Scold* Didn't your momma ever tell you that No means No?

Turning away from his prize the Bellowing Griffon looked over at Gliint. The beast stared down the gnome.

> Gliint's Text Box: Let's get him, Mr. Max! Show me what you're made of! You can do it!

> Mr. Max's Text Box: Gha-lu-lugga-ah…?

> Gliint's Text Box: Crap.

> Bellowing Griffon's Text Box: Didn't your momma ever tell you that it is rude to interrupt?

> Gliint's Text Box: *Scold* Leave her alone!

> Bellowing Griffon's Text Box: That is a great idea. I think it might be fun to see what a little rude gnome looks like with giant boobs. Sure, since this will not be your first time your new boobs will eventually explode and kill you, but what the heck.

> Gliint's Text Box: Crap.

The Bellowing Griffon used a very effective tactic. It stepped out of the way and revealed Hippolyta's still struggling form. It walked towards the gnome as the elf's breasts took care of everything.

> Bellowing Griffon's Text Box: Just think how fun it will be finding out how big you will get before you 'pop'!

> Gliint's Text Box: Gha-lu-lugga-ah…?

The Bellowing Griffon positioned carefully. He didn't want to obstruct the gnome's view and ruin his Spellbound Status, but he also wanted to stick his dick in the little mouth to start the inflation process. His careful paces were halted by a powerful *Sludge Slam* and *Smackdown* combo.

###L##D#'S #E#T B#X: ##I#N# #O!

> Bellowing Griffon's Text Box: What in the Flaming Pit are you doing Sliver Sludge? This is my glade! Go find your own gnome to inflate!

A fierce battle between the two bosses broke out. Talons, sludge, wings, more sludge, beaks, and even more sludge were being thrown around. Had any avatars been paying attention to the battle, they would have been impressed. The Bellowing Griffon eventually got the upper talon by using a *Return Gust*. The move hit the Silver Sludge to the ground, and also accidently slapped Gliint out of the Spellbound Status by continuing onward and dealing a glancing blow to his head.

Gliint was over to try and release Hippolyta in a flash, while taking extra care to avoid looking at her breasts. The Bellowing Griffon topped the Silver Sludge and started to use *The Bellows*. As the Silver Sludge grew larger and larger sludge boobs the Bellowing Griffon laughed in triumph. A final gust caused the Silver Sludge to collapse under the weight of the extra chest sludge.

Beaten up but not defeated the Bellowing Griffon turned to look at the gnome.

Gliint had nearly gotten the raging Amazon goddess untied, but the beast was not going to back down.

> Bellowing Griffon's Text Box: That is it. I have had it with you avatars. I try and try to do nice things for you with my dick and this is how you repay me. With boss—

The Bellowing Griffon had been interrupted by a *Sludge Slam*, the move had hit three times yet only the first was on purpose. With crossed eyes the Bellowing Griffon fell over, defeated. Fifteen red chests descended from the sky, in three groups of five.

> **Creature Name:** Bellowing Griffon
> **Class:** Winged Beast
> **Level:** 75
> **Special Attacks:** The Bellows, Return Gust, Wing Flap, Buster Blow, Tornado
> **Drops:** Bellowing Ball
> **First Player Encounter Notes:** Typical. Not everyone wants what you offer, you male chauvinist Griffon Pig. - Hippolyta
> Additional Comments: #o#ody #es##s w#t# m# G##i##! – ##l###d#

> Hippolyta's Text Box: I didn't need your help gnome, I can handle myself.

> Gliint's Text Box: *Smirk* I didn't help you though. I simply didn't want you flying away on your Fury of the Amazon Goddess Breast Airship unless I could hitch a ride.

Hippolyta's first used the *Eyebrows Furrowed and Face Twitch Animation*, but her steel eyes softened, and she changed over to a *Smiile Animation*.

> Hippolyta's Text Box: Well, go pick up your new outfit. Then should we see what the Spire D Castle holds?

> Gliint's Text Box: New outfits? *Happy* Let's do that!

Gliint looted five of the fifteen red chests, the Silver Sludge attempted to loot five as well, but they dissolved. The two avatars and the Silver Sludge crossed the drawbridge to enter the Spire D Castle.

> Gliint's Text Box: I can't wait to try it on.

> Mr. Max's Text Box: Gha-lu-lugga-ah…?

Chapter 27

THE FORESTS OF INTRODUCING C

E. E. Lynn's Text Box: kekeke. |_| R teh C3|\|74|_|R?!

Fournimer's Text Box: pardon?

E. E. Lynn's Text Box: |_| R 70741 teh |-|07|\|3$$!

Fournimer's Text Box: it's like she is talking to me, I just know it.

Lissa's Text Box: Try to read it very slowly. That works for me.

E. E. Lynn stood half as tall as a human. She would have been a gnome (or that other small stature race) if not for her cat ears and tail. She wore something Fournimer had never thought existed here, a *School Girl's Outfit*. The outfit was covered in custom patches and accented with what appeared to be a bloody handprint on her left breast. She was wielding *Nunchakus* as a main weapon and a *Pointy Clock* as her secondary. Her *#13 Hairstyle* was tied up behind her cat ears with an oversized red ribbon, complete with a bell in the center. Strapped to her belt was a gilded cage that housed a terrified Red Quest Fairy that had been bound and gagged.

Mystic was her class, but Fournimer had heard very little about it. Mr. Max had told him once that a Mystic could do a little of everything, melee, ranged, healing, or attack magic, but not be as good at them as any of the regular classes. It was like a multi-class, whatever that was. The only other thing that Max had mentioned about Mystics was that nobody in their right mind would ever pick that class, and he was right.

> E. E. Lynn's Text Box: C3|\|74|_|R$ |-|4\/3 |-||_|G3 C0C|<$!
> ^-^ F|_|C|< /\/\3 \/\/|7|-| |7?

> Fournimer's Text Box: what?

> Lissa's Text Box: It says… Give me a bit… Centaurs… have… huge… oh my!

> Fournimer's Text Box: what? what does it say?

> E. E. Lynn's Text Box: kekeke. N00B. |t s4yz C3nt4urz h4v3 hug3 c0ckz. ^-^ Fuck /\/\3 \/\/|th |t!

> Fournimer's Text Box: oh. no, not going to happen.

> E. E. Lynn's Text Box: I kn0\/\/. U d0n't h4\/3 teh b|ts. Just m3ss|n'. 0nly | h4\/3 4ll s0rts 0f b00ty!

Fournimer tried his best to steer the leering girl's glances upwards but to no avail. When she saw that the Centaur actually had exposed bits her eyes nearly popped out of her head.

> E. E. Lynn's Text Box: N0 \/\/4y! H0\/\/ d|d u g3t th4t? 4\/\/s0/\/\3! \/\/3ll, d0n't just st4nd th3r3 th3n, g3t 4ll up |n /\/\y b|z-sn4tch! D0n't \/\/0rry! | 4/\/\ s/\/\4ll |n teh \/4g, but | h4\/3 b33n pr4ct|c|ng. L0ts.

Before Fournimer could translate E. E. Lynn's latest still confusing Text Box the little catgirl had ducked under his horse section and had started to jack off his cock in her little hands.

> Fournimer's Text Box: hey stop that!

> E. E. Lynn's Text Box: \/\/h4t? ^-~ R u teh g4y 0r \/\/h4t?

Fournimer answered by turning directly to *Blush Shade #4*.

> E. E. Lynn's Text Box: U R teh g4yn3ss? Th4t r0xz0rz. ^-^ G4y b0yz r 3\/3n h0tt3r! |'/\/\ c0n\/3rt|ng u. kekeke.

E. E. Lynn shamelessly stuck the centaur's cock into her mouth and continued to jack it off with both hands. Lissa bent down on Fournimer's back and picked up the little catgirl by her collar and looked her directly in the eyes.

> Lissa's Text Box: Hey, he asked you to stop crazy skirt!

E. E. Lynn replied by sticking her hand under Lissa's belt and feeling around. The catgirl found Lissa's button and pressed it in violently, causing Lissa to go into the ultra setting. E. E. Lynn quickly had several fingers stuffed into the half-elf.

> E. E. Lynn's Text Box: Y3s! Y0u g0t s3>< 2? S0 g|\/3 It up. *4ut0-Fuck Pussy!* ^-~ sc|ss0r /\/\3!

Lissa hashtagged out in shock. Fournimer grabbed the little catgirl out of Lissa's hands and held her at his eye level, before Lissa could clean her *Pointy Clock*. Fournimer spoke through the vibrations he felt on his back.

> Fournimer's Text Box: stop that before someo—

> E. E. Lynn's Interruption Text Box: U r teh g0rg30us! @-@ H0\/\/ l0ng d|d y0u sp3nd 0n y0ur f4c3?

Fournimer could not react in time, the catgirl had grabbed him by the face and kissed him deeply. Sweeping romantic music and little hearts that exploded into valuable experience fireworks soon followed.

> E. E. Lynn's Text Box: U h4\/3 teh t0t4l k|ss pwn4g3! \/\/*0nd3r K|ss3s!* H0\/\/?

> Fournimer's Text Box: stop covering me in your damn *Slutty Kisses!* … oh crap. you're kidding me. *Slutty Kisses* is one of my moves?

E. E. Lynn kissed Fournimer again. Little purple hearts completed his rainbow of kisses (but not his full ability list). The aphrodisiac hearts exploded into increased levels of desire for the recipient. E. E. Lynn mysteriously broke free of Fournimer's grasp (possibly due to her now more arroused nipples) as he tried to block out the memory of his new unlocked ability being called *Slutty Kisses*, and she leaned forward onto a scenic rock. She hiked up her skirt and revealed everything she possessed.

> E. E. Lynn's Text Box: U kn0\/\/, pwn4g3? 0-0 k|ss /\/\3 4g4|n! Th|s t|/\/\3 k|ss /\/\y cunt! kekeke. |\/\/4nt 3xpl0d|ng h31rtz th3r3 2 /\/\4k3 /\/\y /\/\|nd h|t teh /\/\00n r0ck3ts! *Slutty K|ss3s!*

> Fournimer's Text Box: what? no!

> E. E. Lynn's Text Box: r|t3. U g4yb0|. K, k|ss /\/\y 4ss th3n!

> Lissa's Text Box: He will do no such thing to you.

> E. E. Lynn's Text Box: \/\/hy? |s h3 y0ur g4y b0yfr|3nd? N0! | b3t

> C4us3 u w4nt |t huh? L|k3 u 4 b|t 0f \/4g \/\/|th y0ur /\/\34l?
> huh? N0 n33d 2 b teh shy! $-$ L0tz 2 sh4r3!

Zal Finn ported into the area and wiped her fingers clean. She looked over the scene confused.

> Zal Finn III's Text Box: What in the sweet Flaming Pit did I miss?

> E. E. Lynn's Text Box: G0 4\/\/4y NPC n00b! x-x | f|n4lly f0und
> s0/\/\3 r34lz 4\/4t4rs!

> Zal Finn III's Text Box: Hey! I am not a n00b!

E. E. Lynn carefully looked over Zal Finn, her catgirl eyes lit up when she saw the bobbing and still dripping *Ultra Cock-Ring*.

> E. E. Lynn's Text Box: O. Th3n d0n't just st4nd th3r3. C0/\/\3
> f|ng3rb4ng /\/\3 unt|l | /\/\4k3 teh 7:20 tr4|n 2 0-T0\/\/n!

> Zal Finn III's Text Box: What?

> Lissa's Text Box: We will be right back. #ExitStageLeft.

> E. E. Lynn's Text Box: 4n 0rgy? ^-^ \/\/|nn|ng! K33p n0t3s!

Fournimer, Lissa, and Zal Finn carefully walked out of Text Box range. Looking back at the avatar they were going to talk about only greater furthered on the urgency of their situation. E. E. Lynn was already pleasing herself. The *Nunchakus* were buried deep up her ass as she searched in her bag for more delights.

> Lissa's Text Box: She is clearly over #TehMoonRockets insane.

> Fournimer's Text Box: I still don't even understand half of what she is Text Boxing.

> Zal Finn III's Text Box: What do we do then? Can we just leave her there on that rock spreading *Meganaise* on her nipples while she uses that poor bound and gagged Red Quest Fairy as a living dildo?

> Fournimer's Text Box: I'm all for that.

> Lissa's Text Box: #SolidPlan.

The three gingerly stepped by the awkward scene and continued into the forest. They all felt a little tinge of guilt when the Red Quest Fairy saw them sneak by it shot them a look that just begged for assistance. They didn't look back, poor Red Quest Fairy or not.

Fournimer's Text Box: thanks for standing up for me back there Fair Maiden.

Lissa's Text Box: Not a problem Bhrose. You stood up for me as well after all.

Fournimer's Text Box: well yeah, but that is because I am supposed to look after you.

Lissa's Text Box: You were supposed to look after me? What do you mean by that?

Fournimer's Text Box: I uh… oh nothing?

Lissa's Text Box: No, it is not nothing! What do you mean by that?

Fournimer's Text Box: nothing!

Lissa's Text Box: You mean something! #SpitItOut!

Fournimer's Text Box: hey, do you girls think that everyone is okay? I am really concerned for Anders and Max. I hope they are okay.

Lissa's Text Box: I am sure they are fine in Spire A and D, stop changing the subject! What are you talking about?

Purple Quest Fairy's Text Box: Actually, #BigMistake, Anders is not on Spire A, he is—

Fournimer's Interruption Text Box: hey look! levers!

It didn't take long to get through the Lush Earth Forest since it wasn't as lush as advertised. It was also a great distraction that Fournimer wanted to use.

Zal Finn III's Text Box: Unsweet. Looks like we need four avatars to hit those switches. We need to go back and get that crazy cat girl.

Fournimer's Text Box: please no. maybe I can hit two at once if I kick?

Lissa's Text Box: I don't think so Horseymer. They are pretty far apart. Now back to the important thing, why are you looking out for me?

E. E. Lynn's Text Box: \/\/h4t r \/\/3 \/\/4|t|ng f0r? ^-^ L3t's pwn teh gl4d3 & g3t |n 4 bl4/\/\!

E. E. Lynn stepped forward and the boss fell from the sky. It was a Groaning

Manticore. It had the head of a human and the body of a lion. A tail and a mane made of wicked spikes instead of fur accented the beast. It spent the first action rotating every spike it owned exactly 46° and she grew a new set of spikes around her newly formed vagina. She spent her second action running as far away from E. E. Lynn as she could, She cowered in the corner and trembled. This was the distraction that stopped Lissa's train of thought.

> Game Explanation's Text Box: Be carefu—

> E. E. Lynn's Interruption Text Box: H| 4g4|n. kekeke!

> Groaning Manticore's Text Box: No please. Not again, I beg you! I did everything you asked me, just leave me alone!

E. E. Lynn used the *Crazy Kitty Face Animation* and stepped towards the Groaning Manticore. The catgirl hoisted up her skirt and was already teo knuckles deep.

> Groaning Manticore's Text Box: No! Don't! I'm warning you... I'll.... uh... Maybe..... no... um... or... what can I do? Something! I'll do something!

> E. E. Lynn's Text Box: D0 |t! ^-^ /\/\0r3 fun th4t \/\/4y!

The Groaning Manticore panicked, and did something that she wasn't even sure that she could. She contacted an Administrator and clicked harassment as the reason. On the next round two Admins had unfolded, one was cyan and the other orange.

> Administrator Ivy's Text Box: You're not at Breaker yet... wait... it says here that a monster just summoned us?

> Administrator Allen's Text Box: A monster? Impossible! Out of the question! Unfeasible! Monsters can't even summon us, can they?

> Administrator Ivy's Text Box: I don't think they can. Must have just been a glitch or something. Let's go.

> Administrator Allen's Text Box: Approved! Settled! Decided! When you three avatars and your giant walking hotdog get to Breaker remember to call us first alright?

> Groaning Manticore's Text Box: No wait! Please I beg you!

The Admins had folded themselves up and left as quickly as they arrived. E. E. Lynn dropped the giant hotdog held tight in her grip and looked back to her target.

> E. E. Lynn's Text Box: Gr8. 4ll 4l0n3. #-# kekeke! |'/\/\ gunn4 g3t 4ll up |n y0ur b34st-sn4tch!

E. E. Lynn descended upon the Groaning Manticore with a perverted fire in her eyes and a *Kitty Smirk Animation* on her face. Taking some bondage materials out of her *School Backpack*, the catgirl had the boss bound, gagged, and on her back helpless within just three rounds.

Fournimer, Lissa, and Zal Finn watched the scene caught in a strange silence. They had never seen a boss terrified of an avatar before, usually the bosses had taken a dominate roll in the encounters. This time E. E. Lynn was calling the shots and her forcefulness with the boss was making the others wince. E. E. Lynn was fucking the Groaning Manticore's spiky pussy with her entire arm, reaching in as deep as possible.

> E. E. Lynn's Text Box: L00s3n up b|tch!

E. E. Lynn did not give the Groaning Manticore much time to comply. The avatar ripped her arm out and had replaced it with her leg in short order. Squirming in pain the spiked beast could only feebly struggle as E. E. Lynn continued to boot fuck her. No longer content to just cause severe pain to the boss, E. E. Lynn kicked in her other boot. Hiking up her skirt the avatar began fucking the beast with her entire lower body. Rubbing her little cunt up against the spiky Manticore clitoris, E. E. Lynn moaned loudly as she stuck the entire bulbous mound inside herself.

The catgirl rode the clit and double leg fucked the boss until both started to climax. Jumping down hard with her legs and digging in with her fingernails, E. E. Lynn bucked around wildly. Just as her climax was winding down she leaned forward and bit the Groaning Manticore hard, which caused the avatar to start climaxing again. Several more waves of biting commenced until both avatar and boss passed out. The spectators noted grimly as the Groaning Manticore faded away that it had far more bite marks than this one encounter could have produced.

> **Creature Name:** Groaning Manticore
> **Class:** Spiked Beast
> **Level:** 75
> **Special Attacks:** Groaning Spike, Truespike, Screaming Groan, Tail Spike, Mane Spike
> **Drops:** Thick Spike
> **First Player Encounter Notes:** kekeke. | pwnzorz F|_|C|<'d teh |\|00b.
> - E. E. Lynn
> **Additional Comments:** | r b0r3d |\|0\/\/.– E. E. Lynn

> E. E. Lynn's Text Box: D0n3. N3><t!

E. E. Lynn led the way, and had ported into the Spire C Castle without even so much as a courtesy rinse off. Fifteen red chests descended into the area.

> Zal Finn III's Text Box: There are... chests... should we go get her

and let her hav—

Lissa's Interruption Text Box: Fuck no!

Fournimer's Text Box: I'm... scared.

Lissa's Text Box: We all are Fourn, we all are.

Chapter 28
◊ ◊
ANDERS, BIG SHOT

NPC Margarine's Text Box: What do we do? What do we do?

Anders' Text Box: Please help me! I'm going to burst.

Green Quest Fairy's Text Box: Does anyone have any good ideas?

NPC Greeta's Text Box: Welcome to Onn!

NPC Illiandro's Text Box: I am freaking out here!

NPC Margarine's Text Box: Okay everyone, we need to keep calm.

Green Quest Fairy's Text Box: We need some cheddaring help here!

NPC Margarine's Text Box: Genius! Let's call an Administrator. Maybe they can help.

Green Quest Fairy's Text Box: Brie! Can we do that? You are NPCs and I am a framing device.

NPC Margarine's Text Box: He is in no condition to summon one. We

> need to try!

The NPCs attempted to summoned an Admin while Anders started to roll around on the bed in pain.

> NPC Margarine's Text Box: You need to calm down there hun.

> NPC Illiandro's Text Box: I think he's tightening up. Do we have anything to help?

> Green Quest Fairy's Text Box: I'll see what we have.

> NPC Margarine's Text Box: No, you need to stay loose hun!

Sticking her hand up Anders' ass, NPC Margarine massaged inside in an attempt to prevent Anders' from tightening.

> Anders' Text Box: Ahhh!

An Administrator was folding into the area. Anders could see that it was female and glowing a soft lime green. This was the only sometimes there Administrator Yvonne. Her glowing symbol was of a kickass firebird holding a cigar and surfing down a volcano on a long board, which Anders did not see coming in the slightest.

> Administrator Yvonne's Text Box: Okay I was already trying to not wa… I mean, hi. How did I get summoned by an NPC? Maybe Ivy was right about the Admin contacting being broken.

> NPC Greeta's Text Box: Welcome to Onn!

> NPC Margarine's Text Box: No, I summoned you! We need your help.

Yvonne looked around the room. On the bed there an avatar, who was a good 80 weight units over normal, writhing around in pain. A Green Quest Fairy was rifling through an *Ultra-Pack* spilling the contents all over the room. One NPC with a footprint on her face was just staring at her being creepy. Another NPC was running around blindly in panic. The last important NPC had her hands buried deep in the writhing avatar's ass.

> Administrator Yvonne's Text Box: I don't know what you all are doing in here, but you are on your own, I'm not watching this anymore. I am going out of the office for lunch and getting a really good sandwich. I think I've earned that after this.

Administrator Yvonne folded herself up quickly to leave, with a slightly disturbed look on her face.

> Green Quest Fairy's Text Box: That didn't work!

NPC Margarine's Text Box: Wait, I think I have an idea, what is my quest again?

Green Quest Fairy's Text Box: NPC Margarine is involved in the Quest, Letters Spread From Margarine. You must deliver three letters to her children and—

NPC Margarine's Interruption Text Box: That's it! I know what to do!

Green Quest Fairy's Text Box: Really? Even NPCs interrupt us?

NPC Margarine's Text Box: Sorry, but find some towels, I need real towels and all I have is cake!

Green Quest Fairy's Text Box: All I can find is this *Gray Wolf Pelt*... will that do?

Anders no longer had a *Gray Wolf Pelt*.

NPC Margarine's Text Box: Better than cake at least.

NPC Margarine patted Anders on the shoulder, the avatar was holding his breath.

NPC Margarine's Text Box: Okay hun, you're going to need to breathe. We need a way to keep the pace for his breathing.

Green Quest Fairy's Text Box: All I can find is this *Timing Hammer*... will that do?

NPC Margarine's Text Box: Perfect! Greeta, use this and keep time. Every ding means you need to take a deep breath hun.

NPC Greeta's Text Box: Welcome to Onn!

Anders nodded and no longer had a *Timing Hammer*.

NPC Margarine's Text Box: It's no good. We are going to need to relax him more.

Green Quest Fairy's Text Box: I have this *Minotaur Musk*... will that do?

NPC Margarine's Text Box: Let's try it.

When his vision returned Anders was barely more relaxed and no longer had a *Vial of Minotaur Musk*. His scarce item supply was quickly dwindling.

NPC Margarine's Text Box: No good. Okay, I know it hurts hun, but you are going to need to try and relax as best as you can. Can you do

> that for me?

Anders barely had the strength needed to nod, but tried.

> NPC Margarine's Text Box: No good, it's starting and he's only 5, maybe 6 length units dilated. Can you do anything more hun?

> Anders' Text Box: Yes... I can...

Anders used the last bit of Mana he had been saving and cast *Stretch More*. NPC Margarine was relieved.

> Ander's Text Box: What's starting?

> NPC Margarine's Text Box: Don't worry about that hun, you just work on your breathing okay.

Anders tried to keep pace with his *Timing Hammer* schedule, but the intense pain had started to contract through his entire body. They felt as though they were getting closer and closer together.

> NPC Margarine's Text Box: I can see it starting to crown, okay hun you are going to need to start pushing.

> Anders' Text Box: Why?

Anders did not get an answer to his question. A powerful urge to push as hard as he could overtook him. Anders screamed, sweated, cried, and crushed NPC Illiandro's hand as he pushed.

> Anders' Text Box: You did this to me!

> NPC Illiandro's Text Box: My hand! Stop! You're hurting it.

Anders could feel something coming. Even with *Stretch More* active this thing felt as though it was splitting him open. It just kept growing and growing and Anders' legs were spread apart wider than what would have been possible for any other avatar.

> NPC Margarine's Text Box: I can feel it go smaller right after this. Okay hun, one more big push should do it!

With one more big and painful push, that had caused Anders to both scream out and to nearly break NPC Illiandro's hand, the stretching stopped. It was followed by a satisfying wave of relief and goo.

> NPC Margarine's Text Box: Congratulations hun.

> Anders' Text Box: What... is it?

> Green Quest Fairy's Text Box: The *Ultimate Prize*, a special item gained

by being the first avatar to defeat NPC Narbenock. Keep warm for 364 cycles to mature. To decrease the amount of cycles needed just bathe the Ultimate Prize in a defeated dragon's essence.

Anders' Text Box: What is that all supposed to mean?

NPC Margarine's Text Box: It means that you've just given birth! You are a dad!

Anders' Text Box: WHAT?!

◈ Chapter 29 ◈
THE FORESTS OF
INTRODUCING B

> **P**alcath's Text Box: This cave is full of water lass, Roodg, and new lad. The river goes right inside so it must connect to the one we got trapped in while in the last area.

> Roodg's Text Box: yEP!

Caëlahenãilenŵhei used the *Nod Animation*, she was upset that she could not verbally voice her opinion.

> Palcath's Text Box: So, new lad, you have obviously been camped here for some time. Do you know the schedule for when the river floods?

Caëlahenãilenŵhei used the *Raise Your Hand Animation*. She knew how she could talk. Taking the tail end of her *Cracking Whip* she started to write in the snow.

> Caëlahenãilenŵhei's Snow Box: Using the time between the flood in the cave and the snowball fight in the river, then factoring in the residual amount of snow we saw in the cave it would lead me to believe that the river floods approximately 3.4 times a cycle. Without more accurate data I cannot give an exact amount.

> Palcath's Text Box: Does that sound about right lad?

Palcath looked over at the new sprite elf and questioned the outrageous amount of elf types in this game. There was only one kind of dwarf, but personally he already knew about four different kinds of elves, five if you counted half-elves. He was already journeying with a night elf and a light elf, he didn't need a sprite elf as well. To make things even worse this sprite elf was a Geomancer. Now he had three elf attack magic users in his party.

Trev Terra turned to *Blush Shade #6*, he had already long been at *#5*. His *#9 Hairstyle* was a little shaggier than a normal *#9 Hairstyle* and was a mousy brown. He needed a haircut, somehow, even though hair didn't actually grow. Beads were strung in his hair leading Palcath to believe that they were a helmet. He was dressed in a brown tunic covered in quasi-tribal patterns. Geometric patterns of blue and obscure chunks of liquid metal accented the outfit, especially on one shoulder. It took Palcath a round to place it, but realized that this was the *Dark Gigas Armour*, but unlike Roodg's, it had the fabric. The sleeves were oversized and ended in large white sections. The avatar's thumbs came out of the sleeve in a small gold rings, and the sleeve went on for at least six length units past that point. The tunic ended abruptly near the top of his thighs and the pants portion of his outfit seemed to be missing entirely, possibly hiding under his far too high boots. Besides the *Dark Gigas Armour*, this was clearly an (s) outfit. Even with the lack of coverage the outfit looked warm, Trev wasn't shivering like everyone else.

The sprite elf was armed with a *Felling Axe* (of course, an axe user now that they didn't need an axe anymore) and a *Slotshot Slingshot*. Palcath had looked over the new classes carefully, he knew that the Geomancer was like another new class called the Sage. Both had limited ranged attack abilities and better melee skills than others from the types. They were sort of like reverse versions of their magic counterparts. Sages debuffed monsters instead of buffing allies and Geomancers used elements on allies, to either bolster their defences or attacks with magical properties. Perhaps this Geomancer wouldn't be so bad, Palcath would now be able to wave around a thundering hammer while sheathed in dramatic flames.

Palcath could tell that this Trev fellow was shy and that he liked the colour blue. Palcath knew that he was shy because they hadn't even been talking to him that long and he was already blushing at maximum levels. All the poor lad could seem to do was stutter and stall, avoiding the conversation entirely while befuddled. Palcath knew that he like blue because all of his accent choices and his Quest Fairy were blue.

> Palcath's Text Box: Well lad, does that sound about right?

> Trev Terra's Text Box: Well... it's just that... you see... the thing is... well... rather I... well um... so... I suppose... that... uh... gosh!

> Palcath's Text Box: It's okay, don't hurt yourself lad.

> Trev Terra's Text Box: Yes... thank you.

Roodg's Text Box: hEY IT IS Stutters! wHERE DID U COME FROM?

Trev Terra's Text Box: I won a contest and then I... well my party and I rather... well we came here. When we ported in... we all codexploded... then everyone went everywhere. After that we all... got broken by... well... gosh uh... after that we got split up rather. Four of us... all but Jor... well all but our leader Jorthan I meant to say... we don't know where he ended up compared to us, where is Desserted Island, so many pies and cakes? All the rest of us ended up trapped in forests by spires.

Palcath's Text Box: Stutters? Who is that? How do you know that Roodg?

Roodg's Text Box: cHECK YOUR NOTES.

Palcath's Text Box: My notes? Hey, look at that! Jorthan. I just checked my notes, I thought that sounded familiar. Jorthan the Male Troll Warrior ran into me way back when during that time when everyone and their dogs were running into me. That lad also lead a team into Chrysanthemum after Breaker destroyed the place. Was that you lads?

Trev Terra's Text Box: That was us lads yes. Well... I mean not all lads... Hippolyta would skin me alive if I called her a lad... sorry Hippolyta! So us members... yes. He is a Monk now. Jorthan I mean. Jorthan is a Monk now and is looking for me... and the rest of our party... his party. With the Airship, by looking for it. He is the leader.

Palcath's Text Box: He will not have any luck, the Airship was destroyed.

Trev Terra's Text Box: It was... but how will he... Jorthan... how will he find me? Us rather! I mean us! How will he find us? Can Jorthan stop... no? Well okay, keep paddling.

Palcath's Text Box: I don't know what you are really asking lad, but we have members on every Spire since the Airship crashed. We are all going to meet in the centre Spire to take out the guy that blew up your party. We are not that far from joining up with Party A. You should come with us. It is better than just staying here alone and you will probably meet someone you know in party A, and the rest soon after that no doubt.

> Trev Terra's Text Box: Really? That is awfully nice of you guys... er... guys and... uh... one guy and... ah a girl... and... um... I mean that is really nice... uh what is the Magic Mage... I mean... it's not my business never mind.

If he could blush more, Trev Terra would have.

> Roodg's Text Box: i'M A Roodg!

Using Trev's obvious confusion about what a Roodg was as a distraction, Caëlahenãilenẇhei tapped Palcath on the shoulder and then started to write in the snow. Roodg and Trev continued to talk; well, Roodg talked and Trev stumbled over his words.

> Caëlahenãilenẇhei's Snow Box: Do you think that it is really a good idea to bring him with us? He does seem to talk an awful lot while not saying much of anything. Besides, we should really be concentrating on characters new in this book, adding a bunch of others midway through this one is pissing me off. I am supposed to have lots of character development this time, but now I am getting pushed to the side. Flaming Pits, I can't even talk anymore. I know Anders will be with us soon, but still that doesn't excuse the fact that I am getting pushed to the side for this new meat right now. Even you and Roodg are getting pushed away for this guy.

> Palcath's Snow Box: Wow, a Snow Box doesn't have a character limit! About this Trev lad though, he seems pretty shy. I think he is just going to blend in with the background anyways. Besides, what if we run into a four lever puzzle like in the Lova Mountains again?

> Caëlahenãilenẇhei's Snow Box: You're right! There is no character limit in a Snow Box... We are almost out of snow, but that's about it. Also, you are right about lever puzzles. I was stuck tasting like cherry for over two cycles. Let's take him with us for now and then we will know more about this lat—

Caëlahenãilenẇhei ran out of snow.

> Palcath's Text Box: Agreed!

> Roodg's Text Box: u AGREE WITH ME THAT TREV IS A CUTE ELF GUY? i HAD NO IDEA YOU FELT THAT WAY!

> Palcath and Caëlahenãilenẇhei's Simultaneous Text Boxes: What?

> Roodg's Text Box: tHAT IS WHAT WE WERE TALKING ABOUT. wELL HE WAS TRYING TO BLUSH. i WAS TALKING.

> Palcath's Text Box: No, I don't like lads like that. You know that Roodg.

> Roodg's Text Box: oF COURSE NOT.

Roodg used the *Wink Animation*, and Palcath turned to *Blush Shade #1*.

> Palcath's Text Box: Let's continue on lads, lasses, and Roodgs. Hopefully this Snow Covered Tree Forest isn't as horrible as Huge Confusing Snowfield Full of Random Warps.

> Yellow Quest Fairy's Text Box: The Snow Covered Tree Forest does not contain any quests or puzzles pals and gals!

> Roodg's Text Box: gO!

~ ~ ~

> Palcath's Text Box: The puzzle in this Snow Covered Tree Forest is awful!

> Yellow Quest Fairy's Text Box: But pal, the Snow Covered Tree Forest does not contain any quests or puzzles. There is a four leve—

> Palcath's Interruption Text Box: Lies! All lies. What the Flaming Pit do you call all these frozen lakes if not a puzzle? A lad steps on one and skids all the way to the other side. No control at all. We only have gotten past one, and I can't count how many others are ahead of us. There is just no way past this second one! No random logs to stop us and change directions. Just one way to walk, over to that little platform surrounded by rocks over there and only one way back. To right here! So enough of your lies Quest Fairy!

> Yellow Quest Fairy's Text Box: I don't understand it pal... my records show nothing here.

Caëlahenãilenẅhei started to write in the snow, but only after she made sure that everyone was looking at her snowpad.

> Caëlahenãilenẅhei's Snow Box: We are not thinking about this problem like intelligent avatars anymore. Since the way is blocked by this obviously impassible puzzle we need to think about a different way of getting through this that doesn't involve using the puzzle. I already have a great idea, but I welcome the opportunity for others to voice their opinions.

> Palcath's Text Box: Good point lass. I was thinking earlier since we have two axes we can chop down some trees. That would get us past the first few frozen lakes at least.

> Caëlahenâilenŵhei's Snow Box: Exactly! One *Golden Glitter Star* for Palcath!

Caela took a *Golden Glitter Star* out of her sleeve and stuck it to Palcath's *Wind Gigas Helmet*.

> Palcath's Text Box: A what, lass?

> Caëlahenâilenŵhei's Snow Box: Drop items from I only give them to party members who have good ideas.

> Roodg's Text Box: aWE! i WANT A gOLDEN gLITTER sTAR! i THOUGHT OF USING Palcath's cHAINSAW!

> Caëlahenâilenŵhei's Snow Box: Alright Roodg, you can have one as well. I will take one for my plan earlier. Then we are all even.

> Trev Terra's Text Box: Well… what about me… I mean just… well never mind.

> Roodg's Text Box: tHANKS, Caëlahenâilenŵhei.

Caëlahenâilenŵhei used the *Smile Animation*.

> Roodg's Text Box: hI!

> Caëlahenâilenŵhei's Box Text: Hi!

> Red Quest Fairy's Text Box: Hi!

> Palcath's Text Box: Come on Trev, once they start to 'Hi, hI' they will be awhile. We have trees to chop.

> Trev Terra's Text Box: You have a hammer… how do… well… what I mean is…

Cutting down enough trees proved more strenuous than cutting down the monsters that kept respawning. By the time night fell they had cut down enough trees to cross three frozen lakes. Future lakes down their set path did not contain large enough trees for their strategy to continue working. They settled down for the night and conversed between their two *Portie Tents*.

> Caëlahenâilenŵhei's Snow Box: I'm exhausted.

> Palcath's Text Box: You're exhausted lass? We cut down all the trees!

> Caëlahenâilenŵhei's Snow Box: Do you know how exhausting it is to calculate a scenic tree's trajectory on an uneven plain?

> Palcath's Text Box: Good point lass, I do know how hard that is.

> Caëlahenâilenŵhei's Snow Box: There isn't much snow here, so I'll explain my plan in the open next cycle. Everyone else think up your plan and we will pick the best to try.

> Palcath's Text Box: Your secondary weapon is a Book lass. Why don't you just write in that?

> Caëlahenâilenŵhei's Snow Box: Are you kidding? Then it wouldn't be in mint condition anymore! I wouldn't have a complete set of Rocket Sorceress equipment! I accidently sold one thing in Onn when trying to buy a *Cupped Cake*, I am still mad that I ruined my complete set of gear. I can't buy a new one in Chimmichillinchi since it blew up. I wish I still had my *Initiat—*

Caëlahenâilenŵhei ran out of snow.

> Palcath's Text Box: Let's get some sleep then everylad.

Palcath was dead tired, but he would be staying up late. He needed to think up a *Golden Glitter Star* winning plan for tomorrow.

~ ~ ~

Roodg groggily opened tired eyes. It was just past midnight and Roodg simply did not wake up early, ever. Something had stirred Roodg from slumber in the little private outside red bed. Roodg surveyed the area. It wasn't a something that woke up Roodg, it was a someone.

Trev Terra was sneaking away from camp nervously, constantly on the lookout for someone following him. Roodg decided to comply with the Geomancer's wishes for secrecy by following him, but by doing it secretly. Taking great care to step directly in Trev's snow prints, Roodg followed at a distance. They travelled over a ridge, down a path, between some trees, and finally up to the shore of a frozen lake. Trev obviously wanted to keep whatever he was up to a secret by going this far away, and Roodg was thrilled. Roodg loved secrets.

Near the shore of the frozen lake Roodg hid behind a mound of snow and watched Trev. The nervous Geomancer looked around carefully, and again to make sure that he was alone. Roodg was getting more and more excited. Finally content that he was alone,

Trev went to work. He closed his eyes and pulled the front of his tunic up over his head, leaving his chest exposed but sleeves and back covered. He took his stiffening cock in one hand and shyly began to pull on it.

Roodg nearly used a *Eyebrow Raise Animation*, but knew that Trev could have read any executed Animations. Why was the sprite elf going to all this trouble just to jack off. Roodg had already secretly masturbated three times earlier in the red bed tonight. Trev has started to nervously moan, and had bit his bottom lip after he had grabbed his balls to massage them. Pace quickening, breath shortening, and moans loudening, Trev was close to the edge.

The suspense was killing Roodg, but it was also a turn on. There would be a fourth time tonight for the red bed if it asked nicely. Trev arched his back, squeezed his nuts hard, and started to cum in his own unique fashion that amazed even Roodg.

> Roodg's Internal Text Box: nEAT!

~ ~ ~

It was just before dawn and Roodg had woken up early for the first time ever. Roodg was a little upset at the early hour, but it was for a good cause. Trev had woken up early and was sneaking out of Palcath's *Portie Tent Ultra*, just as Roodg suspected. It had been worth it to wake up so early. Roodg waited until just after Trev snuck by to speak up.

> Roodg's Text Box: eARLY RISER 2 HUH?

> Trev Terra's Text Box: Gosh! Hi... I mean... yes, I have always been a really early riser... That's me... early to bed and early to rise... and early awake and always to bed on time... that is me!

> Roodg's Text Box: Palcath & Caëlahenãilenẁhei ALWAYS SLEEP IN! tHOSE 2 I TELL YOU!

> Trev Terra's Text Box: They don't seem like the type... I mean rather... um... they both seem like the type to wake up early... but if they don't then well... uh... so... if they... yeah.

> Roodg's Text Box: sURE WHY NOT. wANT TO START MAKING BREAKFAST?

> Trev Terra's Text Box: Oh... sure, that sounds alright... actually no it doesn't. I always... uh... go for a walk in the morning so... yeah... I'll help with breakfast, but first I'm going to go for a walk first... if that is okay with you.

> Roodg's Text Box: sURE! sOUNDS LIKE FUN! lET'S GO FOR A WALK.

> Trev Terra's Text Box: Oh… I meant by myself… I mean well if you want to come I guess we could go together… for a walk I mean.

~ ~ ~

Palcath put down the *Double Danish* after eating only half. He was really hoping that at least one of the new monsters on this Spire would drop *Bacon*, but no luck so far. He had stayed up far too late working on his plan, but despite that he could just never sleep in.

Caëlahenãilenẇhei sat across the way, she was trying to choke down a *Cupped Cake*, with very little success. The *Full Ball-Gag* made eating nearly impossible for the light elf. Palcath wasn't sure how long it was going to take until she broke down and tried to eat something through her nose. Palcath's guess was in three more cycles.

> Palcath's Text Box: I'm full I guess lass. Should we try to drag those sleepy heads out of bed?

Caëlahenãilenẇhei used the *Point Animation* directed at a 'y' from one of her previous Snow Boxes. The pair went up to Roodg's outside bed but found it empty. Caëlahenãilenẇhei went back to her Snow Box and pointed to a '?'. Before they could panic Roodg and Trev walked up over a ridge.

> Palcath's Text Box: What are you doing up already Roodg, it isn't even noo—

> Roodg's Interruption Text Box: i WENT FOR MY EARLY MORNING WALK. Trev Terra CAME 2. hE LIKES WALKS LIKE ME!

Caëlahenãilenẇhei used the *Point Animation* at the '?' again.

> Roodg's Text Box: oH. u GUYS ALREADY ATE! u KNOW THAT i ALWAYS MAKE BREAKFAST. sILLY BOOTS!

Palcath used the *Point Animation* at the '?' this time.

> Palcath's Text Box: Well… um… okay. Sorry Roodg, we forgot?

Caëlahenãilenẇhei used the *Point Animation* at a 'w', then a 't', then she looked for the next letter she wanted and couldn't see one anywhere in her last night's Snow Boxes so she changed the 't' into an 'f' and pointed at it.

> Roodg's Text Box: iT'S OKAY! lET'S GO PICK A PLAN. wE CAN EAT IN THE FIELD.

Palcath's Text Box: Yeah, sure thing Roodg. Let's go do that?

~ ~ ~

Palcath's Text Box: Okay, so who wants to go first?

Roodg's Text Box: mE! mE! i HAVE THE BEST IDEA! wE CAN SKATE!

Palcath's Text Box: That is a great idea Roodg. What do we use as skates?

Roodg's Text Box: oH. i FORGOT THAT WE WOULD NEED SKATES TO GO SKATING.

Palcath's Text Box: Okay, good try Roodg, next plan.

Roodg's Text Box: cRUD. wELL WE COULD ASK AN ADMIN TO HELP! i'LL CALL ONE!

Administrator Umple's Text Box: Please don't.

Roodg's Text Box: nEVERMIND. i'M DONE.

Palcath's Text Box: My plan, lads, lasses, and Roodgs, is to do the puzzle almost as intended. We take other pieces of scenery that we can break and set up a path that will work.

Caëlahenâilenŵhei's Snow Box: I like that idea. Let's try it out.

Palcath's Text Box: Thank you lass.

~ ~ ~

Palcath's idea worked fine but it was time consuming. It took until about noon to cross the next frozen lake, and they discovered another problem. They had run out of scenery that they could get Roodg Scenerybane to break.

Caëlahenâilenŵhei's Snow Box: Sorry dwarf. It was a solid plan but we are stuck again.

Palcath's Text Box: I guess it is time for your plan lass.

Caëlahenâilenŵhei's Snow Box: It is similar to your plan, mine involves taking larger scenic trees that we have already chopped down and bringing them to new lakes.

Palcath's Text Box: Solid idea. We should try it. Let's go get some logs.

Trev Terra's Text Box: Okay... I'll just go and find... some trees. Trees to bring back here. I'll be right back.

Roodg's Text Box: k! i'LL HELP U!

Roodg followed a reluctant Trev and the pair went off to find some trees to drag over.

Palcath's Text Box: What is going on with Roodg today?

Caëlahenãilenŵhei's Snow Box: I don't know. I was going to ask that myself. Roodg hasn't let Trev out of ... um... I think the term is hir... sight.

Palcath's Text Box: Is that what the term is? I tried to look it up once but never found it lass. I've been avoiding that topic for some time now.

Caëlahenãilenŵhei's Snow Box: Yes, I think so. The terms are 'hir' pronounced 'here' instead of 'his' and 'her', and 'ze' pronounced like that instead of 'he' or 'she'. It really depends on how Roodg wishes to identify though.

Palcath's Text Box: Roodg keeps insisting that they are a Roodg whenever asked though.

Caëlahenãilenŵhei's Snow Box: Maybe we should just stick to using that...

Palcath's Text Box: Probably, I mean the parts switch around and everything.

Caëlahenãilenŵhei's Snow Box: I was convinced at first that Roodg was a boy, but now that I know otherwise I am still pretty sure that Roodg at least started as a boy.

Palcath's Text Box: Really? I knew Roodg before Roodg became a both. I had no idea even back then. If I had to guess though, I would have said that Roodg started as a girl.

Caëlahenâilenŵhei's Snow Box: Really? A girl? Too bad we can't take it to a vote or ask Yallundy.

Palcath's Text Box: Nah, that would ruin Roodg's mystery I think, lass. We should just leave it at this and not talk about it again. I am curious though, why Yallundy?

Caëlahenâilenŵhei's Snow Box: She just seemed to know everything about everyone. I am sure it was her 'power'.

Palcath's Text Box: Really? That is interesting, like 'empathy' or something. Speaking of which, we never really talked about powers as a group, it might have been helpful to know everyone's power beforehand. I guess some lasses and lads might have been shy. Speaking of which, what is you—

Caela pulled off an impressive feat. She interrupted a Text Box by writing.

Caëlahenâilenŵhei 's Interruption Snow Box: Wait. We got off topic. What is going on with Roodg today?

Palcath's Text Box: You're right. We did. Back on topic then. I don't know what is going on, but that Roodg has been confusing ever since Level 2. Probably even Level 1, but we met at Level 2. What do you think, lass?

Caëlahenâilenŵhei's Snow Box: It is confusing. Roodg is sticking to Trev like glue. Oh no. Do you think Roodg has a crush on Trev?

Palcath's Text Box: I don't think so, lass. The obvious signs are not there for that. I think Roodg likes someone else anyways.

Caëlahenâilenŵhei's Snow Box: Someone else? Who? Roodg has obvious signs?

Palcath used the *Eyeroll Animation*.

Palcath's Text Box: Let's just watch them for now lass. I am almost convinced that Roodg is secretly very intelligent, so maybe there is a plan in the works?

Caëlahenâilenŵhei's Snow Box: Okay, we should go and get a tree, so we don't look susp—

Caëlahenâilenŵhei ran out of snow.

~ ~ ~

Caëlahenãilenẇhei's plan worked just as well as Palcath's. It also suffered from the exact same problem. It was time consuming and they eventually ran out of trees. By nightfall they had crossed another two frozen lakes but three still loomed in front of them. Everyone was thoroughly exhausted and went to bed in relative silence.

~ ~ ~

Roodg slept with one very freaky *#36 style eye* open. Just after midnight the tactic paid off, when a quiet Trev attempted to sneak by.

> Roodg's Text Box: uP LATE HUH? i ALWAYS STAY UP LATE. lATE TO BED, EARLY TO RISE. tHAT'S MY MOTTO.

> Trev Terra's Text Box: Oh! You scared me there. I was just… uh… what was I doing… I couldn't sleep is all… so I was just… sleep walking… no, going for a walk rather. Oh… hurting. That is what I was doing. Going on a walk… in the night air… for a refreshing night time midnight walk at night… right?

> Roodg's Text Box: gOOD IDEA! lET'S GO FOR A WALK!

> Trev Terra's Text Box: Oh… you want to go again… well… okay, alright. Let's go then.

> Roodg's Text Box: k

~ ~ ~

> Caëlahenãilenẇhei's Snow Box: Don't eat breakfast dwarf. Roodg cooks for us now remember?

> Palcath's Text Box: I almost forgot lass. I am both scared and curious to see what Roodg considers to be cooking. Especially since you don't even need to cook the food here. Gourmand is such a wasted skill, who would ever put ranks in it?

> Caëlahenãilenẇhei's Snow Box: As soon as those two get back from their morning walk, Roodg is going to cook and we will find out.

> Palcath's Text Box: Morning walk? I heard them come back last night from an evening walk.

> Caëlahenãilenẇhei's Snow Box: The plot thickens. I have an idea. Since we are both tied for *Golden Glitter Stars* now, whoever figures out what is secretly going on first gets 5 *Golden Glitter Stars*.

> Palcath's Text Box: Interesting idea, lass. Alright, I accept. Do you have any ideas about the final three pools to cross?

> Caëlahenãilenẇhei's Snow Box: I completely forgot to think about that! I thought all night about what was going on so i could win 5 *Golden Glitter Stars* first.

> Palcath's Text Box: That contest hadn't even started yet though, lass.

> Caëlahenãilenẇhei's Snow Box: I know, pretty smart huh? I deserve a *Golden Glitter Star* for that one.

> Palcath's Text Box: I think you do, lass. I should have done that, the only other plan I could think of involved a rope and Roodg, then throwing those things together like a grappling hook.

> Roodg's Text Box: i LIKE THAT IDEA! iT SOUNDS LIKE FUN! cAN WE TRY?

> Palcath's Text Box: Sure, why not! After breakfast let's do that Roodg!

> Roodg's Text Box: bREAKFAST? oH YEAH. i SORT OF FORGOT ABOUT THAT.

~ ~ ~

Breakfast was something. No one, neither Palcath, Caela, Trev, nor even Roodg had tasted anything even close to that before. It wasn't unpleasant, just different. Roodg had transformed the taste of the food from appliances into power tools. They had enjoyed a breakfast of cordless power drills, ban saws, and a wood spinning lathe. Caela tried desperately to eat with no luck, and she was becoming sunken in with hunger. After breakfast she went into her *Portie Tent Ultra+* to change out of her pajamas and came out finally looking full. Palcath had another mystery to solve it seemed as her nose looked fine.

The throw Roodg like a grappling hook plan did not work, but Palcath had great fun trying it out again and again. It was noon by the time the dwarf finally gave up.

> Palcath's Text Box: Back to the drawing board then lads, lasses, and Roodgs.

> Trev Terra's Text Box: Actually, well… no never mind… rather, that would just be… urgh…

> Palcath's Text Box: Don't hold out on us, lad. If you have a plan, you need to tell us.

> Roodg's Text Box: yEAH!

> Trev Terra's Text Box: Well… I was just thinking that if we could… that maybe… no it would be really… well, what I mean rather… is that we could… I don't know though, it wouldn't be very nice… but maybe we could swim?

> Palcath's Text Box: Swim? How could we do that lad?

> Trev Terra's Text Box: There are three attack mages here and well… I mean I could cast fire spells on your hammer then all four of us could… melt the stuff?

> Roodg's Text Box: sAWESOME. LoL. lET'S DO THAT.

> Palcath's Text Box: That is genius. Someone give that lad a *Golden Glitter Star*!

Trev's plan worked like a charm. Four avatars using high powered fire attacks melted the frozen lakes to a swimmable slush in just a few rounds. Fortunately, Roodg had a stash of *Absorbing Cloths* on hand so nobody had to walk around dripping wet in the snow. Roodg claimed past experiences while split up with water as the reason for carrying around so many. Whatever the reason, the *Absorbing Cloths* earned Roodg a *Golden Glitter Star*.

Soon they were at a glade with four levers. This was the boss area.

> Trev Terra's Text Box: Careful… there is a nasty boss here… I mean, well there probably is a boss here. Well, there is like a glade… so you know what I mean right? Gosh, bosses are in glades… so, well, there is probably a boss… right?

Palcath and Caela exchanged a look. Palcath scratched his *#5 Facial Hairstyle* and Caela was twirling her long *#24 Hairstyle* with a finger.

The boss had fallen into the area, and as suspected it spent its first action doing sparkling cartwheels. The next action it looked over at Trev Terra and used the *Grin Animation*.

> Game Explanation's Text Box: Be careful, some monsters can create new monsters with special attacks.

> Palcath's Text Box: Interesting, noted.

> Planting Treant's Text Box: Back again little one? What can I do for you this time?

> Trev Terra's Text Box: Nu... nu... nothing. I am... well we are rather.... just here to get by you. I... well... what I mean is us... well, we really... we don't want any trouble. Please?

> Planting Treant's Text Box: Where is the fun in that little one? How about we double up?

The Planting Treant rooted over towards Trev and grasped his foot with a branchy hand. The avatar was dangling upside down, helpless.

> Palcath's Whisper Text Box: If we just let the monster do over Trev, it would provide some answers no doubt.

> Caëlahenäilenŵhei's Whisper Snow Box: Nah, I like a challenge. Let's interfere.

Palcath scanned the Planting Treant with both his eyes and his handy *Wind Gigas Helmet*.

> Palcath's Text Box: It is interesting tree lad, that you are so resistant to fire. Given the fact that you are a tree, one would think otherwise. You are however very vulnerable to air magic, which I would never have guessed.

> Planting Treant's Text Box: What? How did you know that?

> Palcath's Text Box: Alright lads, lasses. and Roodgs. Let's see what three attack mages and a dwarf with a lightning hammer can do to something with a severe air magic vulnerability.

The Planting Treant did not last long, especially since the first round of attacks all counted as Sneak Attacks. Once the lightning smoke finally cleared the Planting Treant was nothing but a smouldering pile of ash.

> **Creature Name:** Planting Treant
> **Class:** Tree Beast
> **Level:** 75
> **Special Attacks:** Branch Swipe, Tree Grab, Pain Planter, Seed Planting, Plant Plow
> **Drops:** Smouldering Ash Pile
> **First Player Encounter Notes:** Ahhh! Well... what I mean rather is... uh...

ouch full. - Trev Terra

Additional Comments: Mumble mumble murrb… meh. – Caëlahenãilenŵhei

Trev Terra's Text Box: Thank you for saving me from that… well helping me to kill that… thanks.

Roodg's Text Box: nO PROBLEM!

Palcath's Text Box: Sure thing lad.

Trev Terra's Text Box: You… you guys can go ahead, I want to… to say goodbye to the boss? Yes… to do that.

Fifteen Red Chests dropped into the area.

Roodg's Text Box: sTUFF!

Trev Terra's Text Box: On second thought… um… you stay here I will scout ahead.

Roodg's Text Box: k, LET'S DO THAT, i GOT MY IMPORTANT NEW STUFF ALREADY. oH Palcath, PICK THAT LAST ONE UP, IT'S FOR A PLAN!

As Roodg and Trev left the area, Trev used the *Sigh Animation*, and he walked uncomfortably into the new area.

Palcath's Text Box: Any ideas yet lass?

Caëlahenãilenŵhei's Snow Box: A few, but I don't think any are right.

Chapter 30

THE FORESTS OF INTRODUCING A

> Kray's Text Box: OMM! They are twins, kay. That is so cute! Even if they are girls, it's still cute.

> samuri's Text Box: …

samuri looked over the two new avatars.

In'ferni was a demonian, with matte black skin. A small pair of silver horns were visible on her forehead accented by her long flowing white *#22 Hairstyle*. She had pointed elfish ears and white lips, hiding a pair of fangs. Fire burned in her red eyes. A small pair of demon wings came out of her *#4, average sized frame* which caused her to float in place just above the ground. She was wearing a purple vest, a hint of barely-there purple *Bikini Armour* with orange accents, and glittery *Light Gigas Pants* with white accents, not at all suitable for an attack magic type Necromancer. She had a Purple Quest Fairy. Strapped to her belt was a *Susan the Scythe* and a *Clear Chime*. A large skeletal cat, called the Nine Circles of Hellcat, was at the avatar's side, being aggressive.

De'vini was a celestian, with glossy white skin. A small golden halo was visible above her forehead accented by her long flowing black *#22 Hairstyle*. She had pointed elfish ears and black lips, hiding a set of braces. Water swirled in her blue eyes. A small pair of angel wings came out of her *#4, average sized frame* which caused her to float in place just above the ground. She was wearing an orange vest, a hint of barely-there orange *Bikini*

Armour with purple accents, and glittery *Light Gigas Pants* with black accents, not at all suitable for a healing magic type Summoner. Strapped to her belt was a *Hedging Shears* and a *Jongle Bells*. A large angelic dog, called the All Seeing Eye Dog, was at the avatar's side, being protective.

They were two different races and two different classes. Although they were completely different in every way, they were completely the same. samuri used the *Nod Animation*. They were indeed twins. Demonic and angelic twins that were both dressed and ready for a day at the beach, but were too busy kissing each other passionately to have left to get to the beach before dark.

> Kray's Text Box: Kay, so I am Kray. I am the hot thin one for your reference. This is Sami-Guy, he is the tall, gray, and handsome type. Don't get any ideas though lesbians about going bi because he is now spoken for. If you will take note of my engagement *Gilda-Lily*.

In'ferni and De'vini used the *Kiss Passionately Dual Animation*.

> samuri's Text Box: …

samuri used the *Shake Your Head Animation*.

> Kray's Text Box: Good. That is settled then, kay. Where are you girls from? We won the Insta-Wiki Contest way back then crashed here after the Airship fell to Breaker's dragons, that Breaker guy is the one that made me so thin and hot.

In'ferni and De'vini used the *Sweeping Embrace Dual Animation*.

> samuri's Text Box: …

samuri used the *Shrug Animation*.

> Kray's Text Box: Great, kay. You can come with us then. Try to actually help in battle, unlike Sami-guy here. Don't worry Sami-guy, you have really nice hair so it's okay that you aren't good in combat.

In'ferni and De'vini used the *Inappropriate Grope Dual Animation*.

> samuri's Text Box: …

samuri used the *Scowl Animation*.

> Kray's Text Box: Let's get through this Flaming Tree Forest then, kay. Hopefully there are no dancing puzzles. Sami-Guy isn't good at dancing, but that's okay he is really sweet otherwise. Don't you two touch him, he's mine.

In'ferni and De'vini used the *Nipple Twist Dual Animation*.

> samuri's Text Box: …

samuri used the *Point Animation*.

> Kray's Text Box: My Sami-guy, I tell you. Always in a rush, kay. Let's go then twins, Mr. Bossy is on a schedule. You are such a cute little slave driver, Sami-guy.

In'ferni and De'vini used the *Loving Fondle Dual Animation*.

> samuri's Text Box: …

samuri slashed at a Wolpentinger, but only scored a glancing blow. The All Seeing Eye Dog deflected an antler aimed at samuri. The puppy cast a variety of buffing spells on tall, gray, and handsome. The Nine Circles of Hell Cat finished off the Wolpentinger by first slicing off its head and then eating its face.

> Kray's Text Box: Which way do we go, kay? This place is like a maze or something.

In'ferni and De'vini used the *Ear Tickle Dual Animation*.

> samuri's Text Box: …

samuri looked down the only path in the entire *Flaming Tree Forest* and used the *Eyeroll Animation*. He and the two party members that participated in battle, the All Seeing Eye Dog and the Nine Circles of Hellcat, carved up several Wolpentingers, Wampahoofuses, and Wild Carrots. The skeletal cat was the only one that attacked, but both certainly had a taste for faces.

> Kray's Text Box: Oh hey, kay. Look! A glade is coming up. That means a boss. So everyone use your A game for once. I mean we are the A Spire Team after all.

In'ferni and De'vini used the *Super Kiss Dual Animation*.

> samuri's Text Box: …

samuri and the two pets prepared for battle. A Welder Sphinx dropped into the area. It was female given her pair of barely-concealed Sphinx breasts held secure by only a thin strap of welded metal. As her first action she shifted her thin strap down, exposing her nipples. For her second action she looked around the area and settled on the *Super Kissing* twins.

> Welding Sphinx's Text Box: There are far more this time, a much better challenge! Who can answer my riddles? The correct answer will earn rewards. Riddle me this. I have a pair of everything, and yet I share a pair. While I am two, I am never apart. What am I?

> Kray's Text Box: I am all about rewards. So, kay, I got it. Um… the Spiderboy? No, wait, he had four pairs of legs and eyes, kay. He didn't

> share me with anyone since he liked me the best!

> No-Colour Quest Fairy's Text Box: Yeah well, the Spiderboy is not relevant to any quests.

The Welding Sphinx shot Kray with a blast of *Magma-Flare*.

> Welding Sphinx's Text Box: Wrong!

In'ferni and De'vini used the *Spit Swapping Dual Animation*.

> samuri's Text Box: …

samuri half guessed and used the *Point Animation*, directed at the twins.

> Welding Sphinx's Text Box: Correct!

10,000 Gold Coins popped into existence in front of samuri. He pocketed the coin and used the *Smile Animation*.

> Welding Sphinx's Text Box: Riddle me this. To you, rude would I never be, though I flag my tongue for all to see. What am I?

> Kray's Text Box: Kay, I got this one. It is a Tonguer Llama!

The Welding Sphinx shot Kray with another blast of *Magma-Flare*.

> Welding Sphinx's Text Box: Wrong!

In'ferni and De'vini used the *Light Spanking Dual Animation*.

> samuri's Text Box: …

samuri used the *Point Animation*, this time directed at the All Seeing Eye Dog.

> Welding Sphinx's Text Box: Correct!

A *Large Sparkling Ruby* popped into existence in front of samuri. He pocketed the gem and used the *Cheer Animation*.

> Welding Sphinx's Text Box: Last one. Riddle me this. I get wetter the more I dry. What am I?

> Kray's Text Box: Kay, I know this one for sure. It is my hair-dryer.

The Welding Sphinx shot Kray with a final blast of *Magma-Flare*.

> Welding Sphinx's Text Box: Wrong!

In'ferni and De'vini used the *Hard Spanking Dual Animation*.

> samuri's Text Box: …

samuri searched through his gray *Backpack* and found his pink *Ni Hao Bunny*© *Beach Towel*. He used the *Point Animation* directed at it.

> Welding Sphinx's Text Box: Correct!

The Sphinx's Riddle Belt popped into existence in front of samuri. It had amazing stats. He put it on quickly before Kray saw it and used the *Stomp Around Excited While Waving Your Arms Around Like a Little Girl Animation.*

> Welding Sphinx's Text Box: Your team has answered all the riddles correctly, no welding punishment is necessary this time. Have a nice cycle.

The Welding Sphinx jiggled her bosom for effect before she flew off defeated.

Creature Name: Welding Sphinx
Class: Riddle Beast
Level: 75
Special Attacks: Magma-Flare, Riddle Swipe, Flaming Smash, Welding Crush, Pop Quiz.
Drops: Nothing. Correct riddle answers yield rewards.
First Player Encounter Notes: I got all the riddles wrong. So did I. Hey, why are you talking at the same time I am? I dunno, why are you talking at the same time I am? - In'ferni and De'vini
Additional Comments: … – samuri

> Kray's Text Box: Those riddles were really hard, kay. Ouch.

In'ferni and De'vini used the *Dry Humping Dual Animation.*

> samuri's Text Box: …

samuri thought for a round. He couldn't believe it. When he had first seen two new avatars he had been excited. There would be someone to break up Kray's constant chatter and someone to help him with battles he had thought. But he had managed to find the two avatars that spoke less than he himself did, and helped out even less than Kray. Kray didn't actually help himself, but at least Kray's No-Colour Quest Fairy talked. The twin's Purple and Orange Quest Fairies only flew near their avatars while constantly making out with each other.

The twins reached out desperately with their feet, and managed to flip both of their puzzle levers without needing to take a break from kissing. Ten red chests fell from the sky.

> Kray's Text Box: Oh look, kay. There is stuff! It is so stats and cute!

In'ferni and De'vini used the *Sorry I Needed To Stop Fondling You for a Round While I Flipped That Lever Dual Animation.*

samuri might be happy to have some new gear, depending on how cute it was.

Hopefully not very cute.

The best part of this cycle was that he now had the help of the All Seeing Eye Dog and Nine Circles of Hellcat. samuri scratched behind their ears. The neglected pets of the twins enjoyed finally getting some much needed attention and wagged their tails. samuri made a mental note to collect some monster faces to feed them as treats. They were just so cutie-ootie, yes they was. Yes they was!

◈ Chapter 31 ◈
A QUICK BREAK

Breaker looked over the pile of plundered items. Given the fact that many of these items were usable by Anderses only Breaker had a good idea who they belonged to. Xam, the Orange Dragon of Light had told him that they belonged to Anders, but that particular dragon seemed to have problems remembering names so it didn't hurt to double check.

There were many things here to tamper with. Nearly everything looked like it had emotional relevance to Anders, that just made the whole thing better. It wasn't the ideal avatar's items to have, but that was what back-up plans to back-up plans were for. Always be prepared.

Breaker looked at a secondary stash of items. Xam had said that these items had been kept separate from the others. They all were junk, some old any class armlets, potions, food items, and the like. He spotted something written on the inside cuff of the right *Leather Armlet*. 'To Gliint, good luck out there. - Anders.' Interesting, for some reason Anders had a bunch of Gliint's personal items stashed away. Breaker could manipulate items like potions or food, why not experiment with them as well? A back-up plan to a back-up back-up plan? Why not.

Xam ported into the area, still pleased with himself.

Breaker's Text Box: Did you find anything belonging to Mr. Max yet?

Xam, the Orange Dragon of Light's Text Box: Sorry boss, the only avatar I can seem to find is Anders.

Breaker's Text Box: Well at least you brought me more than enough of his items to use, thank you Xam.

Xam, the Orange Dragon of Light's Text Box: Sure thing boss! I gave you everything I had taken from him. Every last thing! All of it, every bit!

Breaker's Text Box: That was strangely reassuring. Care to elaborate?

Xam, the Orange Dragon of Light's Text Box: I didn't secretly keep something, if that is what you are asking.

Breaker's Text Box: Okay, then. Good.

Breaker eyed the newly broken dragon. He was doubled in power, could understand more complicated commands, and even had gotten one of the better Latin theme songs, but damn was this one stupid.

Xam, the Orange Dragon of Light's Text Box: Good, he didn't notice.

Breaker avoided replying to that. Whatever, so Xam had kept a *Yellow Flower*, or a lock of hair, or something else not important. It was too small to be a weapon, a piece of Armour, or even a potion since the dragon had it concealed. Nothing that small could accept code anyways. If it made the dragon try harder to find Max, he could keep it.

Breaker's Text Box: Alright, go back to scouting. Tell me if you find anything.

Xam couldn't believe Breaker hadn't noticed his clever ruse. The big beefy dragon lumbered away stroking his prize. Xam didn't have an inventory, so he had no idea what this thing was called. He did know that it was a little bronze key. Xam was convinced that this was the key to his tasty candy's heart. If his constant vigorous ass poundings were not enough to win over the heart of Anders then this key would certainly unlock it and let him in. Xam cuddled the little bronze key one last time and ignored Breaker's orders. He flew off to look for his candy. Max wasn't important right now.

◈ Chapter 32 ◈
ANDERS, SINGLE WORKING PARENT

nders had not felt this great, or looked this skinny, since before the expansion. Amazingly, Kray had been right. Anders had been getting fatter and fatter ever since he had gotten here, although Anders would be loathe to ever admit that fact to the skinny burnt jerk.

If you wanted to get back to your creation weight, giving birth to a sixty weight unit silver speckled egg was the way to do it. Anders viewed the egg closely.

Item Name: The Ultimate Prize
Description: A special item gained by being the first avatar to defeat NPC Narbenock. Keep warm for 270 cycles to mature. To decrease the amount of cycles needed just bathe the Ultimate Prize in a defeated dragon's essence.
Time Left Until Hatching: 0.02 Cycles

Anders finally knew what had happened. NPC Narbenock had been defeated in an unconventional way and had dropped his drop item deep into Anders. Like the *Pink Goo* that was in there, Anders couldn't find it in his *Ultra-Pack*, even if it was listed as being inside.

Anders had a pretty good idea what defeated dragon essence was, that would explain all of his sudden expansion after meeting Xam. The egg had been maturing. This probably also explained his morning sickness, tender nipples, and strange food cravings.

It didn't look like a humanoid shape was floating around in the egg, that was a big relief. Whatever was inside would hatch soon, so it was a good thing that Anders had given birth before it broke out.

The egg shook once, twice, then a third time. The shell showed a single crack line, and exploded open. That was good, at least the egg followed the logical rules for how eggs should act in video games. Inside was a little dragon. When the dragon jumped into Anders lap, he estimated that it weighed in at about thirty weight units, (which meant that the egg did not need to be that large or hurt that much coming out).

The dragon was only about as big as a cat, so it was dense and its wings and claws were too large for its small size. It had matte gray scales which gave it a bland appearance. When Anders changed the accent colour to green only the eyes changed colour. It was still boring to look at and out of proportion, but Anders loved it anyways. It was his baby. It purred around on the sheets above Anders' lap before it jumped up and nuzzled Anders' face. Finally, it bit Anders affectionately on the ear, hard. Anders was now bleeding but didn't care, he loved it anyways.

> Ultimate Prize's Text Box: Please choose a gender for your dragon.

Anders briefly hovered on female, but eventually decided on male. Both models looked the same anyways.

> Ultimate Prize's Text Box: Please choose a name for your dragon.

The default name was The Ultimate Prize but Anders rightfully decided that was a horrible name for a dragon, even if it was accurate, and deleted it. Anders needed a name, and he didn't want to upset any avatars he knew by using a name that started with their letter of the alphabet. That would just confuse things. Anders had twelve letters to pick from, thirteen since 'w' was free again thanks to warrior's change to samuri. He decided to use 'D' because the name that popped into his head right away sounded the most dragony of all the names that popped into his head. It was also very original.

> Anders' Text Box: His name is Draganders.

Draganders chirped happily. Either he liked his name or his coding made him do that after getting named. Anders hoped it was the first one.

> NPC Margarine's Text Box: You two boys are welcome to hide and rest here anytime.

Anders replied, knowing full well that he would have to close a shop menu afterwards.

> Anders' Text Box: Thank you for your help Margarine.

After Anders closed the menu, she replied.

> NPC Margarine's Text Box: No problem, hun. Oh, before I forget...
> I... found something else up there with the egg. You should probably take it.

Anders turned to *Blush Shade #2*. He was both grossed out and relieved when he took the item. It was the *Elf Starting Bow*'s string. it must have gotten lost up there when Anders was showing off to Xam. Anders could attack now at least, even if it was with a low powered weapon that was slightly goopy.

Anders sprung up out of bed feeling great.

> Anders' Text Box: I feel like I could take on the whole map!

> NPC Illiandro's Text Box: Perfect! I haven't seen Xam for cycles, so let's start my quest right now. I'll show you the secret way to the Coliseum. I'm so excited I could just burst!

> Anders' Text Box: OMM yes! Let's go Draganders!

Draganders chirped excitedly.

It was a good thing NPC Illiandro knew where he was going. Nobody would ever be able to find the hidden brick switch needed to open this place. Anders walked down the long hallway and spotted some red graffiti on the wall. 'Roodg WAS HERE!' Anders wasn't surprised in the least.

NPC Illiandro unlocked the door at the end of the hallway. It wasn't a door, it was a slide up painting over a port in area. That probably had confused Roodg. A trick door after a trick door.

The first thing that Anders saw were Zal Finns, hundreds of them, sitting in the stands. They were low polygon count NPC Zal Finns, who were constantly cheering no matter what was going on, but they were Zal Finns none the less.

Anders heard the background music. This was one of the licensed song he had not even heard was in this game! *Coliseum Rockstar* by *Caution Step*! That made this area great, *Caution Step* was his favourite band, and all of the members were really cute in their own way.

> Anders' Text Box: Okay Illiandro, what do I need to fight first? Can you give me any tips?

> NPC Illiandro's Text Box: I have no idea, I've never gotten to see my quest before. Good luck though.

> Anders' Text Box: That's not your fault I guess. I'll just have to wing it. Come on Draganders!

Anders stepped into the battle arena, ready for the first battle. Draganders tried to step in but was blocked by an invisible force. Draganders paced back and forth looking both upset and lonely.

> Coliseum Text Box: Only Summoner and Necromancer pets are allowed to participate in normal Coliseum battles. No other pets,

> mounts, or vehicles are allowed according to the rules.

> Anders' Text Box: Awe, man. Come on jerk game!

> NPC Illiandro's Text Box: I'll watch him for you. You go fight.

Anders nodded and stepped forward.

The First Battle: Anders vs. the XIII Elite.

Anders didn't need to think about what 'the XIII' was for long. A door on the other side of the Coliseum opened and out came thirteen gladiators. They were all identical in appearance, except each was brandishing a different weapon and had on a different style of full helmet, blocking their facial features from view. The Armour they were wearing did look almost like something a gladiator would wear. They had bronze chest plates, red brushes on their shoulders and leather strapped skirts finished with metal studs. Then Anders placed it: this was what Roman soldiers wore, not gladiators.

> Gladiator I's Text Box: Prepare for battle against the XIII Elite, knave!

> Gladiator XIII's Text Box: Wow! Look at how naked he is.

> Gladiator I's Text Box: Did I say that you could talk XIII? Nobody would be stupid enough to challenge the Elite XIII naked.

Anders looked down at himself while the gladiators mumbled amongst themselves. In all of the excitement he had forgotten that except for his *Frost Gigas Boots*, *Pink Slime Jock-Strap* sexcessory, and *Ultra-Pack*, he was pretty naked.

> Anders' Text Box: Apparently, I am stupid enough!

> Gladiator I's Text Box: What are you using for a weapon? An *Elf Starting Bow*, nothing else? We are going to cut you up into ribbons.

> Anders' Text Box: Yes, most likely.

> Gladiator I's Text Box: Where is the challenge in that? I thirst for combat, for challenge. We have been waiting for this first battle for way too long, and now it is going to be a *Grand FullCake* walk.

> Gladiator XIII's Text Box: I have an idea.

> Gladiator I's Text Box: What did I tell you about talking?

> Gladiator VII's Text Box: Just because you are the leader and you made XIII the team bitch, it doesn't mean that you get to be a jerk to him all the time.

Gladiator X's Text Box: Yeah I. Let the boy talk. I want to hear his idea.

Gladiator I's Text Box: Okay fine. What is it XIII?

Gladiator XIII's Text Box: Well… we don't need to kill him, we can still use him for a Competition.

Gladiator I's Text Box: I never back down from a Competition nor have I ever lost one! So bring it on!

Gladiator XIII's Text Box: First I have a new rule!

Gladiator I's Text Box: Oh do you bitch? Let's hear it.

Gladiator XIII's Text Box: The winner of the Competition will become the new Gladiator I.

Gladiator I's Text Box: Oh really? What of the losers? The runner up? What happens to them?

Gladiator XIII's Text Box: The losers? Nothing. They all keep their positions in our complicated gladiator hierarchy. But the runner up will become the new XIII.

Gladiator I's Text Box: A possible new XIII bitch for me, huh? I like that idea, but it isn't really fair to everyone else. They all worked hard to get their numbers.

Gladiator XIII's Text Box: Alright then, if I get anything but first place in this Competition I will stay as XIII and everyone else will stay their number, but if I happen to win then second place becomes my number XIII.

Gladiator I's Text Box: I accept those terms on one condition. If you get anything but first then you become number XIV. That's even worse than XIII. You will be everyone's bitch to use whenever and however they want. Forever. What say you?

Gladiator XIII was nervous, but nodded his head in agreement after some thought.

Gladiator I's Text Box: What say you all?

Gladiator II through XII's Simultaneous Text Boxes: We accept the rules of the Competition!

Gladiator I's Text Box: I have the best stats here and have never lost a Competition yet. You have your work cut out for you XIII bitch, or should I say soon to be XIV. Shall we begin?

Anders' Text Box: I hate to interrupt whatever the deep and complicated subplot going on here is, but what exactly is a Competition and why is it capitalized?

Gladiator XI's Text Box: True, we should probably explain. Competitions were implemented after cycle 20. It was so dreadfully boring down here waiting for someone to battle, so we took matters into our own hands, so to speak.

Gladiator III's Text Box: It is off the charts! We take a *Double Danish* and stand around it.

Gladiator VI's Text Box: We all jerk off until we cum on it.

Gladiator IX's Text Box: The first one who cums loses and has to eat the *Double Danish*.

Gladiator XII's Text Box: That's usually me, am I right guys?

Gladiator II's Text Box: The twist is that the winner gets to use the runner up as his fuck bitch.

Gladiator VII's Text Box: Except I always wins and XIII was the runner up so many times in a row that Gladiator I made XIII his permanent bitch.

Gladiator XIII's Text Box: Not this time! He isn't going to win!

Gladiator IV's Text Box: Once we started doing this, we pretty much stopped training for battle. This is way more fun!

Anders' Text Box: Okay, so if XIII wins at your jack off contest then he doesn't have to be the permanent team… uh… loser anymore?

Gladiator VIII's Text Box: Correct!

Anders' Text Box: Why exactly am I here then?

Gladiator I's Text Box: We ran out of *Double Danishes*.

Anders realized that the XIII Elite had slowly been forming a circle around him the entire time. Their strange Competition rules had distracted the elf from noticing that their gladiator skirts had been doing a really bad job of hiding their erections for some time now.

> Gladiator I's Text Box: No interference either, elfboy.

Gladiator I pushed Anders to his knees and the elf was quickly head to head with all of the members of the XIII Elite. They all pushed their skirts to the side and took hold of their excited cocks with their left hand. Pumping them as slow as the rules of the Competition allowed (one pump per round as far as Anders could figure out), they began their battle. Anders could only watch as thirteen stiff dicks were waved and jacked just mere length units from his face (he could also get hard).

Anders thought about joining the fun but eventually decided against it. He didn't want to accidentally become a contestant in this Competition and become the runner up. The elf was content just to take in the sights.

As predicted, Gladiator XII was the first to break down. Almost immediately he was no longer able to follow the rhythm and excitedly pumped his shaft. Anders turned to look just in time to watch XII scream and shoot his load all over Anders' right cheek. XII bowed out of the circle, took out a *Double Danish* to eat, and sat on the benches to watch the rest of the show. Anders wasn't sure which he was more upset with, the fact that he was getting used as the target in a gladiatorial jerk off Competition, or the fact that the gladiators had obviously lied about running out of *Double Danishes*.

> Gladiator I's Text Box: Round two!

The pace doubled for round two. Each turn the gladiators took two precise pumps. This round lasted much longer than round one. As the crowd cheered on the gladiators started to develop a thin misting of sweat and the smell of men filled Anders' nose. The man smell did not last forever. Gladiator X screamed out and shot a big stream that mostly hit right above Anders' upper lip. Now all the target could smell was gladiator spunk.

> Gladiator I's Text Box: Round three!

Round three involved the switching of hands. Anders had wondered why they were all left-handed, but now he knew that none of them were. What a ingenious ruse. They had all just started with the wrong hand for extra challenge. Gladiator IV was the one who cracked first. Anders was expecting it to be someone with a higher number and only noticed after he felt the shot hit the back of his ear.

> Gladiator I's Text Box: Round four!

This round involved another speed increase. Now the gladiators were pumping at a pace of three a turn. Rounds passed, with only a few little sporadic grunts to break the silence. Anders was now taking personal bets. He was sure that the next would either be VII or VIII, both were sweating hard and had closed their eyes in concentration. Anders was almost right, they both came at the same time. Each covered one of Anders' cheeks before bowing out of the circle.

> Gladiator I's Text Box: Straight to round six!

Anders wasn't certain which round added what, but the gladiators were now going at a pace of four pumps per turn, what most would consider a normal pace, and twisting their pumps for added stimulation at the tip. Gladiator IX was soon at his limit and bowed out of the Competition after hitting Anders on the forehead, with just a little in his hair for good measure.

> Gladiator I's Text Box: Round seven! The Lightning Round!

The gladiators increased their speed to thirteen strokes per turn. Their hands blurred at that speed and their faces twisted under the denial of release. It only took ten rounds until III caved under the speed stroking. The load hit Anders on his neck, with a single drop finding its way onto his stomach.

> Gladiator I's Text Box: Round eight!

The pace slowed down to five thrusts per turn, but the shortness of breath after the lightning round took their toll on Gladiator VI. His pace had slowed down for too many consecutive turns and he was disqualified. The other gladiators took a break from their own members and turned their full attention to VI who only stood there helpless. Five sets of hands worked over the body of VI, all while positioning his target exactly. A set of hands held Anders' mouth open as VI did his best to shoot inside, but he had horrible aim. Much landed on Anders' lips, but he did taste the distinct flavour and knew that at least a little had hit the target.

> Gladiator I's Text Box: Round nine!

This was the longest lasting round since round two. The break from stimulation had given the remaining contestants a second wind. It also helped that round nine had added a new element: every five turns the gladiators would stop pumping and spent the round shaking their cocks. Anders enjoyed this added element, as it was really hot to watch. During one particularly lively shaking turn, Gladiator V started to spray. Anders was surprised that all of it had somehow landed on his face.

> Gladiator I's Text Box: Round ten!

Round ten involved stopping your own actions, grabbing the gladiator to your right and jacking him off instead. There no longer were any solid rules for pace, just that you only used your hand. It was Gladiator XI who fell under the expert handling of II. The gladiator shot more spunk than any previous contestants. Only a little had hit Anders in the face, right on the nose. The rest did a great job of covering his chest. It was Gladiator XI's personal best placing.

> Gladiator I's Text Box: Round eleven!

Anders never saw the new rule for round eleven. Only three gladiators were left and two of them were locked in a fierce emotional battle. Gladiator II panicked. He did not want to be the new team bitch and grabbed Anders by the pointy elf ears and shoved his cock into the shocked sperm coated mouth. After a few desperate and fast thrusts Gladiator II screamed out in relief. The first shot hit the back of Anders' mouth, but Gladiator II knew the rules and finished up on Anders' chin.

Only Gladiator I and Gladiator XIII were left. XIII had a look of strained discomfort on his sweat drenched brow, while the smug Gladiator I had not even broken a sweat. His stats must have been very impressive. Anders felt sorry for the poor oppressed XIII and decided to do something about it. Anders really didn't like bullies.

> Anders' Text Box: Final round! Special guest judge rules!

Anders reached out and grabbed the remaining contestants. Both moaned out in surprise, and Gladiator I started to complain. The cheers out from II to XII at the twist stopped Gladiator I from stopping the elf from pumping the cocks. Anders was still fresh and could put a lot more effort into his actions than the gladiators, at least into the actions on his left hand. While the pace was identical his pressure was not. Anders was putting far more strength and flourishes into his hand job treatment of Gladiator I.

Anders had taken up the cause for the downtrodden Gladiator XIII in his hands. Literally. XIII had noticed the differences in treatment but only smiled thankfully at the elf with the open mouth and both pumped cocks pointed squarely at his tongue. Gladiator I did not notice the differences, he was far too busy concentrating on unsexy thoughts.

Anders felt the cock in his right hand begin to stiffen. Even with the gentle stimulation XIII was getting close to the edge. Taking a risk Anders pumped the left handed cock and took extra care to make sure each down stroke also caused the tip of Gladiator I's cock to flick against his tongue. The gamble was paying off, the cock in his left hand was now stiffening and throbbing as well. It could now be anyone's game, but that wasn't good enough for Anders, he wanted XIII to win for all the oppressed gladiator jerk off competitors everywhere.

Anders had a really naughty idea and did the *Smirk Animation*. He abruptly stopped his pumping and licked the index fingers on each of his hands. He reached between the legs of both gladiators, abruptly shoved the now slick fingers into their tight holes, and pressed down hard on their buttons. Both gladiators screamed out in alarm, but it was Gladiator XIII who had experienced the feeling many times before as Gladiator I's bitch who could resist. Gladiator I came, coating Anders' tongue with impressive stats in defeat.

Gladiator XIII had won for team bitches everywhere but Anders decided that he needed a special reward for finally winning a Competition.

> Anders' Text Box: Special bonus round!

Anders swallowed the last member in one swift action. With the elf still pressing down hard on the inside of Gladiator XIII it didn't take long for Anders to taste the much deserved victory shots. Nearly every gladiator, and member of the watching crowd, cheered out in excitement as XIII came.

Gladiator I was terrified as his named changed to Gladiator XIII. The last competitors Text Boxed through their panting.

> New Gladiator XIII's Text Box: That's not fair… the elf…

> New Gladiator I's Text Box: Calm down. Unlike you I am not a total asshole. My second action as Gladiator I will be to forever abolish the bitch factor of being the runner up in Competitions. The winner will still get to fuck the runner up of course, I'm not crazy, but they will not be looked down upon or treated like filth ever again.

> New Gladiator XIII's Text Box: That is surprisingly kind of you all things considered. Wait… why is that the second action? What is the first?

> New Gladiator I's Text Box: My first action is declaring that for the entire next cycle you are to be called Gladiator XIV and you will be used as everyone else's bitch as they see fit. I can still be a bit of an asshole if I want to.

All the gladiators cheered except for XIV, who got his ass spanked several times by the other gladiators as they walked away. The New Gladiator I looked back at Anders and mouthed the words 'thank you' before disappearing.

A red chest descended into the area, but Anders had something important to take care of first. He looked down at his straining member, still fully charged with sexual energy and started to give his much neglected erection some attention. Licking his lips to remember the taste of the gladiators, Anders spent a few rounds enjoying the feeling of his hand working his own cock. He was so charged up that it didn't take Anders long to release, shooting up with an impressive aroused force.

> Anders' Text Box: Oh my Maker! Ahhhh! Ow! Son of a bunt!

After the pain subsided Anders opened his eyes, the left was now red and irritated. He couldn't help but laugh at himself. Fourteen guys had just shot cum on his face at they only jerk insensitive enough to get any of it in his eyes was himself.

Anders reached into his pack to take out the well used *Initiate's Jacket* to clean himself off with, but it was gone. He had forgotten that Xam had stolen it. He needed to clean himself off somehow. He spotted a recently purchased *Double Danish*. If they were good enough for gladiators, they were good enough for Anders. The *Double Danish* was surprisingly absorbent and soon Anders was fresh and clean again. He put down the

Double Danish in the centre of the Coliseum for the gladiators to find later; there was no way Anders was going to keep it.

There was a more important thing to worry about here than limp Danishes, there was a red chest! Inside the chest was a shining pair of *Gladiator Gloves (s)*. These gloves single handilly restored Anders' faith in (s) gear. Not only were they nearly comparable in defensive power to Gigas Gear, they also increased Anders' Dexterity by 50 points. That was unheard of in a piece of Armour and would make even his *Elf Starting Bow* (with the goo covered string) do some significant damage. These were definitely (s) as in sawesome, not (s) as in slutty.

They looked great, metal plates were strapped on with sexy leather straps. The right side had plates that went to the shoulders and the left to the elbow. Even if the *Gladiator Gloves (s)* didn't contain actual gloves but only had metal hand covers, they were still nice.

The absolute best part was that you could change both the accent colour and the main colour. Anders switched both to green right away, but they were now too green. Anders couldn't decide between blue or orange accents, and instead decided that black straps were by far the best option to go with.

Only the Insta-Wiki entry was left to do before going home to the bakery, where he could rest, cuddle Draganders, and think about how next time there might be even more gladiators needing to release their frustrations.

Creature Name: XIII Elite
Class: Man Team
Level: 75 (I), 60 (II-XIII)
Special Attacks: I, II, III, IV, V, VI, VII, VIII, IX, X, XI, XII, XIII, Lightning Speed
Drops: Gladiator Gloves
First Player Encounter Notes: Am I allowed to redo this battle again later?
- Anders

◈ **Chapter 33** ◈

OUTFITS, D ELEMENTALS, SECRETS, AND YELLOW DRAGONS

A ccording to a Text Box, all of the Armour from these chests had a theme. They were all based on the season of spring. Given the amount of rain on Spire D, that made a lot of sense.

Gliint twirled around, this new *Slick Armour (s)* set, was just that, slick. His new overcoat would open at a dramatic angle due to how diagonally the front was cut. It had more straps holding it closed than were necessary for a hundred *Slick Overcoats (s)*, but that only helped the appearance (he decided). You could barely even tell he had a permanent fake erection on under the coat (at a few select angles anyways). His gloves and pants matched the extreme level of straps, as did the boots he didn't need to wear, due to having *Frost Gigas Boots*. The absolute best part without a doubt was the helmet. They were a pair of *Too-Dark Shades*, set to black.

He switched the entire set to a brown, and made half the accents green and the other half blue (since he could not switch them to teal in honour of Yallundy). The gnome admired himself. The glasses were a little less cool when coloured brown and made everything he saw sepia tone, so he switched them and their accents back to black. He looked wicked now, there was no doubt.

Mr. Max had put on his new *Spring Armour (s)*. The outfit took the term spring in a different direction than Gliint had anticipated. Gears, pistons, and springs covered the plate Armour and spun with an animation that would have definitely made Gliint lag out last cycle. On the chest piece was a giant clock face that kept accurate time, down to the milliround. Diligent springs desperately tried to contain Mr. Max's manhood in a brand new codpiece, which had not yet given up on trying to do its job. The main colour had been set to orange, there was no surprise there, and the accents to brown. Gliint felt pretty good about Max using brown as an accent, even though Max actually hadn't used brown and that was just what the real colour looked like as seen through a pair of *Too Dark Shades*.

> Gliint's Text Box: Why don't you get treasure boxes Hippolyta?

> Hippolyta's Text Box: I already did when I was here before. Apparently, this skin-tight waterproof bodysuit with a peak-a-boo chest is some male jackass developer's perverted fantasy idea of what a 'spring' outfit is. Unfortunately my other Armour exploded during my first encounter with that chauvinist boss or I would be wearing it into the castle.

> Gliint's Text Box: What do we know about Spire D Castle anyways?

> Brown Quest Fairy's Text Box: Spire D Castle is the final area before the Connector and Airship Sub-Station D. Heavily themed on the air element it contains no notable quests or puzzles. Stronger monsters dwell in this area as well as the d Elemental.

> Mr. Max's Text Box: We know all of that Little Bro!

> Gliint's Text Box: Yeah, I guess we do. Quest Fairy, what is an Elemental?

> Brown Quest Fairy's Text Box: Now that you need something you want to talk to me?

> Mr. Max's Text Box: Well yeah.

> Brown Quest Fairy's Text Box: I don't care why, *Fist Bumps* I'm just so excited you finally care! The Elementals are six powerful monsters that are the servants of The Dragon Rider. Each has powerful attacks tied to their element. Similar in power to the Gigases of Gentalia, they require 100 avatars to be present to fight. Being present during the defeat of a Elemental will earn you a *Spire Key* that both allows you to return to any area in the Spire and also to leave the castle. Whichever avatar deals the killing blow will gain a special item.

> Hippolyta's Text Box: So we need 100 avatars to be here so we can take on that thing or we can never leave? Figures!

> Brown Quest Fairy's Text Box: Summoning an Elemental is not a tas—

> Mr. Max's Interruption Text Box: It's okay Anders, we will not need to have 100 avatars here. You already know that!

The Brown Quest Fairy did the *Scowl Animation*.

> Gliint's Text Box: We don't? *Quizzical look* Why not?

> Mr. Max's Text Box: That's right! You were only around Gigases with me before getting broken. Like a Gigas, an Elemental will show up anyways since we are broken, but be confused at first and then want me to fuck it. Just like before.

> Hippolyta's Text Box: Like before? I dare not ask, but must.

> Mr. Max's Text Box: Yeah Anders. Don't you remember what the Frost Gigas did to you to give you that *Wind Gigas Helmet*?

> Hippolyta's Text Box: Yes, of course. How foolish of me to forget.

> Mr. Max's Text Box: Let's hurry fellow adventurers!

> Gliint's Text Box: *Cheer* Yeah!

> Hippolyta's Text Box: Anything to get away from this conversation.

The monsters here were air powered and stronger than anything they had faced before, but with the combined power of Max's levels, Hippolyta's triple slaps, Gliint's badass shades, and Silver Sludge's new triple slaps they were progressing with relative ease. By the end of the cycle they had completed over half of the map.

They set up camp and ate happily while Gliint and Max bragged about Max's accomplishments. Max had just finished a retelling of his famous story about the six Flork Demons of the Crags of Halm when the background music changed to a theme song with Latin Chanting. Mr. Max and Hippolyta exchanged confused looks but Gliint knew better.

> Gliint's Text Box: Quick! *Panic* We need to hide. It is one of Breaker's new and improved dragons!

> Htaclap, the Yellow Dragon of Air's Text Box: Fear me. For I am Htaclap, the endless tormentor!

The yellow dragon's look was heavily influenced by ultra thin spiky scales that resembled hair. His face, shoulders, and tail were covered in whisker scales not unlike that of a Porker Pine.

> Hippolyta's Text Box: Yes, the subtitles in your song told us that.

> Htaclap, the Yellow Dragon of Air's Text Box: My quarrel is not with you fight elf, so silence your sharp tongue before I rip it out. I am here for Mr. Max.

> Mr. Max's Text Box: For me? Why just me?

> Htaclap, the Yellow Dragon of Air's Text Box: Give me a piece of your equipment Mr. Max or I will rip out your soul and fashion it into a hat. It's all there in the subtitles.

> Mr. Max's Text Box: Um… you can have this *Spring Gloves (s)*. I don't need them.

> Htaclap, the Yellow Dragon of Air's Text Box: Bwahahahaha! I am finally victorious! Bye!

Htaclap had grabbed the *Spring Gloves (s)* before Mr Max had even finished signing them. The dragon was gone in even faster than a flash.

> Hippolyta's Text Box: Some endless tormentor he was. He left before his theme song was even in the second verse.

> Gliint's Text Box: *Confused* What was that all even about? Why did that dragon want your stuff Max?

> Mr. Max's Text Box: That was a dragon? I just thought he was another fan looking for a signature.

After a debate about dragons, signatures, and keeping a better night watch they turned in for the cycle.

~ ~ ~

> Gliint's Text Box: Are we ready to take on whatever this Elemental is?

Mr. Max used the *Flex Animation* to its full extent.

> Mr. Max's Text Box: I sure am Little Bro!

> Hippolyta's Text Box: We should just get this over with.

They stepped forward and the Wind Elemental materialized in with wisps of gray smoke. She was ethereal and her hair flew wildly in the wind that she herself created. Her clothes floated dramatically and had the same transparent appearance as her hair and skin. Her face was twisted in a look of permanent agony.

> The Wind Elemental's Text Box: Fear my ethereal visage, for I am the

mighty…

Mr. Max's Text Box: Wind Elemental!

The Wind Elemental's Text Box: Where is everyone?

Mr. Max's Text Box: We don't need them to fuck you.

The Wind Elemental's Text Box: Oh. You are those kinds of avatars. I get you.

The Wind Elemental used the *How You Doin' Animation* and assessed the party. Hippolyta did not press the Wind Elemental's buttons and the monster looked over both Max and Gliint with her shocking yellow eyes. She grinned with agony while staring at Gliint, she had made her choice.

Game Explanation's Text Box: Some monsters can use Possess. Be careful if your allies are Possessed, they will attack you without holding back, the save is based on your Intelligence Score.

Gliint's Text Box: *Groan* Perfect.

Gliint readied himself for battle, but the Wind Elemental used her next turn to surround Mr. Max with her transparent hovering sheets. As the avatar screamed out the boss flew inside his mouth. Mr. Max looked over at Gliint with a wild expression in his now yellow eyes. He stepped towards Gliint while unspringing his *Spring Pants (s)*.

Mr. Max's Text Box: Look out! I've been put under the Possess Status Effect! I can't be trusted Little Bro!

Mr. Max was chasing Gliint around the once huge wind castle glade that was now far too small for the gnome's tastes. Gliint was exceptionally fast while running scared, but Max was incredibly beefy while running horny. One miss-jump from Gliint was all it took for Max to have the gnome in his clutches. Gliint struggled but it was pointless, he simply could not succeed in an opposed strength check against the big piece of beef. With a look of malice in not his eyes Mr. Max pulled down Gliint's pants and gave the little gnome's butt a firm spank right on the Mr. Max signature.

Mr. Max's Text Box: Sorry Little Bro.

Gliint's Text Box: Please Hippolyta, *Desperate plea* cast that spell that removes status effects on Max!

Hippolyta's Text Box: Sorry, Sages don't get that one. Not that it matters, your ass clearly belongs to Max as it is. Note the signature.

No longer content to just spank the gnome's exceptionally small butt, the possessed

Max tried to stick in a finger with very little success. After a few failed attempts the Wind Elemental succeeded with a pinky thrust. Gliint screamed out as Mr. Max was forced to prostrate Gliint against a pillar. The Wind Elemental cast *Confining Storm* and Gliint was put under the Bound More Status Effect. He could no longer move. Max lined up the far too large to ever fit in the gnome without causing permanent damage Mr. Maxum at the little gnome hole.

> Gliint's Text Box: Stop! *Beg* Please!

The Wind Elemental only smiled through Mr. Max's eyes and kept a tight hold on the gnome.

> The Wind Mr. Max Elemental's Text Box: You are not going to enjoy this gnome, I am going to really enjoy this though.

The Wind Elemental started to press forward into the screaming Gliint. The Silver Sludge rushed towards the scene and used *Sludge Slam* three times (only once was on purpose) on Mr. Max so hard in the side that the avatar fell to the ground.

###L#ND#'S #EXT B#X: #LI#N# NO!

> The Wind Mr. Max Elemental's Text Box: What in the Flaming Pit are you doing here Silver Sludge? This is my glade! Go back to yours and find your own gnome to fuck!

The Silver Sludge and the Wind Mr. Max Elemental started to fight. Goo, lightning, and oversized sludge breasts were flying through the area and both Mr. Max and the Silver Sludge were taking heavy damage. The Wind Elemental's Hit Points were protected while possessing an avatar. While Hippolyta was casting healing spells on the Silver Sludge, her lower versions of the classic healing spells were not enough to keep the Sludge alive while the over-leveled Mr. Max hacked at it. The intense battle finally ended with a *Supreme Shock*, which took the last of the Silver Sludge's health. As the Silver Sludge dissolved into a *Silver Goo* drop item, the Wind Elemental turned Mr. Max's attention back to Gliint.

> The Wind Mr. Max Elemental's Text Box: Now where were we? Don't bother to reply, I know the answer already. Right at the part where I split that little gnome ass of yours in half with this giant stud.

Max approached the still trapped Gliint with the intent to impale, but was knocked over by an invisible force.

#A#L#ND#'S #EXT B#X: #LI#NT NO!

The invisible force and Mr. Max wrestled on the ground. Mr. Max's eyes first changed from yellow to violet and then back to the avatar's original green. Max screamed out and in the process evicted the Wind Elemental. Mr. Max was free from possession and quickly decided to kiss the ground.

> Mr. Max's Text Box: Oh thank the Maker, I am free.

> Wind Elemental's Text Box: I am *pant pant* not going to lose *pant* that easily. Your little ass is mine!

Turning most of her floating clothes into a sword with a move called *Lightning Sword*, the now nearly naked Wind Elemental rushed at Gliint's still exposed ass. Her sword was aimed at his little gnome hole.

#A#LUND#'S #EXT Box: #LIINT NO!

The invisible force tackled the Wind Elemental. The boss thrashed about on the ground, fighting for her life. Whatever had her was not giving up. Swirls of teal light surrounded the Wind Elemental as she screamed out in pain. The lights entered the monster and its eyes shifted from the cold yellow to a pale violet. The Wind Elemental's face softened into a more gentle expression and what was little was left of her gray clothing and accents shifted towards a gentle Constantly-Colour-Changing palette. Floating in the air was a nude female form, she was far taller than a human with hair that flowed in its own wind, constantly changing colours. Only a long shawl of transparent teal fabric with a hint of brown accents covered her shoulders and stretched out behind her, as a pair of cloth ethereal wings.

> Hippolyta's Text Box: She is the absolute vision of everything that I have ever seen that could be described as lovely. Who is that floating goddess?

The Wind Elemental had the tables turned on it and been possessed. The new softer visage screamed a final scream expelling a mass of inky black pixels with shocked yellow eyes. In a last desperate attempt at life the little inky mass crept slowly towards the helpless gnome, ready to attempt a possession.

> #ALLUND#'S Text Box: #LIINT NO!

The ghostly visage rained lightning down on the remains of the Wind Elemental, taking away the last bit of fight it had left. With the Wind Elemental dead Gliint was released from his Bound More Status Effect.

> Gliint's Text Box: *gasp* Do my eyes deceive me... How can it be... is that...

> Mr. Max's Text Box: They don't deceive you Gliint! It is true! I can barely believe it myself!

> Gliint's Text Box: Yallundy?

> Yallundy's Text Box: GLIINT NO!

> Mr. Max's Text Box: It is true, I made it to level ##...! No wait, level

✪ ✪! I'm not even a number anymore! Ninety-nine isn't a thing in this game!

Yallundy's Text Box: Gliint No!

Text Box: Congratulations to Mr. Max, winner of the Level Contest, enjoy your prize!

Yallundy's Text Box: Gliint… No?

Mr. Max's Text Box: What is my prize? I'm so excited!

Yallundy's Text Box: Gliint… Yes!!!

Gliint rushed towards the ghostly visage that was now Yallundy and attempted to jump into her arms. He passed right through her and fell down on the ground hard. She floated down and looked at the gnome right in the eyes.

Gliint's Text Box: Yallundy!!!

Yallundy's Text Box: Gliint!!!

The two avatars locked lips as best as they could. They couldn't feel each other physically due to Yallundy being ethereal, but they both felt it mentally.

Yallundy completed the Wind Elemental's Insta-Wiki entry quickly to get it out of the way, she was going to be very busy for the foreseeable future making out with her gnome.

Creature Name: Wind Elemental
Class: Elemental D
Level: 98 (Requires 100 avatars to be present to Spawn)
Special Attacks: Confining Storm, Supreme Shock, Lightning Sword, Possess, Scream, Elemental D
Drops: Spire D Key, the Heart of Wind (Only for avatar that gets last strike)
First Player Encounter Notes: Nobody messes with my Gliint! – Yallundy

◈ Chapter 34 ◈
OUTFITS, C ELEMENTALS, SECRETS, AND GREEN DRAGONS

Fournimer looked over the girls who had now been outfitted with the theme of autumn. Zal Finn now had a decorative *Harem Dancing Outfit (s)*. Many layers of leafy fabric swirled around in every which way. She had a puffy silk pair of pants with a decorative sash belt. Her delicate shoes were pointy and whisper quiet. Much of her torso was visible but her breasts were covered by a thin fabric binding. The lower half of her face was covered by a veil of fabric, whivh accented her normal brown eyes. Zal had switched the main colour to pink, even though it didn't make much sense for leaves to be pink, and the accent leaves to purple. Fournimer thought he would probably be able to recognize her in a crowd now (probably).

Lissa looked sharp in her new *Fashonista Outfit (s)* threads. Her thigh length jacket was zipped open, revealing a beaded bodice underneath. Her *Fire Gigas Necklace* rested on her again perky cleavage. She was wearing a pleated skirt that didn't go very far past the thigh length jacket. She had leather gloves and knee high boots both blessed with many buckles. The outfit was accented by a really cute knitted cap. Lissa quickly changed the main colour to purple, but it took her longer to settle on an accent colour. Fournimer watched as the colours cycled through. Black, gray, blue, and white all looked pretty good but when Lissa got to yellow, Fournimer knew she would stop. The yellow looked gold on all the buttons and buckles and popped against the purple.

Fournimer was mostly happy with his new duds, which he had changed to blue before even putting on. He couldn't decide on an accent colour and eventually settled on using both orange and green depending on the piece. The *Fall Battler Outfit (s)* had stylized metal chain gloves accented with metal plates that resembled leaves. His *Light Gigas Pants* still looked the same on the centaur, mostly a big belt with some sections of poufy material on his four legs and horse crotch exposed. His new *Battler Helmet (s)* was better described as a half tiara, but with the delicate leaf work Fournimer decided that it was pretty manly. The new gloves and horseshoes were even pretty nice, with some turtleneck sweater with an ugly fall scene embroidered on the front. Fournimer did not like his ridiculous sweater or the scene of kittens playing in leaves. He had been hoping for a scarf.

> Zal Finn III's Text Box: Wow! We look sweet… except for that sweater, sorry Horseymer.

> Fournimer's Text Box: I know! it is an awful sweater isn't it?

> Lissa's Text Box: I am sorry for your sweater, but at least this theme explains those new *School Girl Clothes* on … I need a nickname for her. Fourn, that's your shtick, what do you got?

> Fournimer's Text Box: I was already thinking of that Lis. my suggestion is E. E. Loon.

> Lissa's Text Box: #LoveIsSplenderous!

> Zal Finn III's Text Box: Are you two being nice to each other again?

Zal Finn III used the *Quizzical Look Animation.*

> Fournimer and Lissa's Simultaneous Text Boxes: No!

Zal Finn III used the *Sigh Animation.*

> Zal Finn III's Text Box: Not sweet. I was afraid this was happening.

> Lissa's Text Box: What is happening?

Zal Finn Text Boxed with tears in her eyes.

> Zal Finn III's Text Box: You are bonding again! First you really didn't like each other and were fighting all the time. Now both of you are working together and even having fun while doing it. Heck, you are even riding him around Lissa! Now you have all but stopped using mean nicknames for each other and are calling each other by the special nicknames 'Lis' and 'Fourn'. You have obviously started to get over your hatred for each other, and soon you will… you will…

> Fournimer's Text Box: we will what?

Zal Finn III used the *Sad Cry Animation.* Comical spurts of cartoon tears arced from her eyes.

> Zal Finn III's Text Box: FALL IN LOVE!

Both Fournimer and Lissa used the *Burst Out Laughing Animation*. Zal Finn was hurt, you could tell from the number of times her lower lip quivered.

> Lissa's Text Box: Oh Zal, you are hilarious! There is absolutely no way that we are falling in love with each other.

> Zal Finn III's Text Box: There isn't?

> Lissa's Text Box: Of course not, he is already involved in a complicated love triangle that I have nothing to do with.

> Zal Finn III's Text Box: HE IS? With who then if not you Lissa? Is it Caela? Me? There aren't that many girls… um Roodg? Wait, is Roodg a girl?

> Lissa's Text Box: It isn't any of those avatars, #TrustMeOnThis.

> Zal Finn III's Text Box: What? How come? All of those girls are really hot!

> Fournimer's Text Box: well first of all, I'm gay.

> Zal Finn III's Text Box: YOU'RE GAY?!

> Lissa's Text Box: How could you not know that?

> Fournimer's Text Box: now that I think about it, The Finnster has never been around during any conversation that involved which side of the fence my hooves jumped over.

> Zal Finn III's Text Box: I didn't know that. I guess it makes sense now.

> Lissa's Text Box: So we are not falling in love. I do admit that we got off on the wrong… hoof though.

> Fournimer's Text Box: yes, we did. I'm glad we talked about this. can we be friends now 'Lis'?

Lissa used the *Smile Animation*.

> Lissa's Text Box: I would like that 'Fourn'. Thank goodness, I was never going to be able to use some of those suggested nicknames.

> Zal Finn III's Text Box: Sweet! That is a big relief. I was scared for awhile there.

> Lissa's Text Box: Why?

Zal Finn III turned directly to *Blush Shade #6*.

> Zal Finn III's Text Box: Uh because…

> Lissa's Text Box: Because what?

> Fournimer's Text Box: go on. tell her.

> Lissa's Text Box: Tell her what?

> Zal Finn III's Text Box: But…

> Fournimer's Text Box: she isn't good at recognizing it, nobody in this story is for some reason when it is directed at them. you're going to have to tell her.

> Lissa's Text Box: Recognizing what? What are you two going on about? #SoapOperaDramaLevels!

Zal Finn threw caution into the wind. It was now or never.

> Zal Finn III's Text Box: Recognizing that… I… I AM IN LOVE WITH YOU LISSA!

Lissa used the *Shocked Animation* and returned the *Blush Shade #6*.

> Lissa's Text Box: Oh… I'm flattered Zal, but I don't like girls like that.

> Zal Finn III's Text Box: Do you think I don't know that already? I saw how you looked at Vendimm and how upset you were when The Feaster consumed most of him, in Book 1 but off screen. I've seen how you look at other guys now. But this has been tearing me apart since I first met you, I just needed to finally say it! I think!

Lissa got off of Fournimer's back and hobbled over to Zal Finn, taking great care to show how painful each step was. Lissa gave Zal a big hug and kissed her on the forehead.

> Lissa's Text Box: Oh Zal, you have always been and always will be one of my closest friends here. Your death at the Hydra was the worst moment for me in this game. Honestly, it was even worse than Vendimm's death. It meant that I was alone. I was so happy when I saw that you had recreated yourself so we could talk again, I had really

> missed you. So I do really love you, as my dearest friend.

Zal Finn returned the hug and both girls were crying, their mascara running.

> Zal Finn III's Text Box: Oh Lissa, thank you! I don't need to use purple accents anymore in a desperate attempt for you to like me, any suggestions?

> Lissa's Text Box: Try complimentary colours, it worked great for me. Green on the leaves will look nice with pink flowers.

Zal began to switch to green, but black was in-between the colours, and with the leaf pattern it was too sweet looking to scroll past. She left the leaf nearest her heart green.

> Zal Finn III's Text Box: Black? Never would have thought I would like it! Done!

> Fournimer's Text Box: awe, shucks. secret accent colour love, that gets you right in the heartstrings.

Fournimer joined the hug, it was a special moment.

> E. E. Lynn's Text Box: | kn3\/\/ | t! x-x

> Fournimer, Lissa, and, Zal Finn III's Simultaneous Text Boxes: Holy fucking shitballs!

> E. E. Lynn's Text Box: U r h4\/ | ng 4n0th3r 0rgy \/\/ | th0ut /\/\3!

> Fournimer's Text Box: we were not!

> E. E. Lynn's Text Box: N0t y3t 4t l34st! kekeke. ^-^ K, g4yh0rs3 u fuck /\/\3 \/\/ | th teh h0rs3c0ck, NPC y0u st | ck th4t r | ng up /\/\y 4ss. \/ | br4t0r, u rub up 4g4 | nst /\/\y n | ppl3s 4t full sp33d!

> Lissa's Text Box: #L8r. We should get through that spire first.

> E. E. Lynn's Text Box: k. t h3r3 | s 4n 3l3/\/\3nt4l 4t teh 3nd & 4 dr4g0n fly | ng 4ll 0v3r.

> Fournimer's Text Box: four dragons?! there are four dragons in there?

> E. E. Lynn's Text Box: N0 u | d | 0t. 4 dr4g0n! C0/\/\3 0n.

E. E. Lynn went into the spire castle, both of her hands were down the front of her skirt, busy at their task

> Zal Finn III's Text Box: I don't want to go, she's crazy!

> Lissa's Text Box: The sooner we get through these spires, the sooner we can get rid of her.

> Zal Finn III's Text Box: Good point Lissa! Let's go.

> Fournimer's Text Box: but there are four dragons in there!

~ ~ ~

> Zal Finn III's Whisper Text Box: There it is. I can see the green dragon flying in the distance. If we keep quiet and walk slowly it probably will not see us.

E. E. Lynn used the *Wave Animation*.

> E. E. Lynn's Yelling Text Box: H3y! 0\/3r h343!

The green dragon spotted them and changed direction for an interception course.

> Lissa's Text Box: What is wrong with you? Why did you do that?

> E. E. Lynn's Text Box: Dr4g0ns r teh h0tn3ss! H3 |sn't 3v3n |n teh g4m3, ho\/\/ h0t! | b3t h|s c0ck |s b|gg4r th4n m3!

> Fournimer's Text Box: we are trying to avoid the four dragons in here, not attract them!

> E. E. Lynn's Text Box: \/\/hy d|dn't u s4y s0? D|3 dr4g0n! kekeke. ^_^

The background music had changed, the green dragon's theme song was starting. E. E. Lynn turned to the dragon and held her hands up beside her eyes. Small dots of light came from them and appeared on the green dragon's hide. E. E. Lynn opened her eyes wide and out came two smiling missiles with Ni Hao Bunny© faces that shot out towards the green dragon. The missiles hit and the green dragon spiraled out of control, crashing into a rock face and exploding into a ball of green light destined to return to Breaker. The Latin theme song stopped before the subtitles had even gotten to the dragon's name.

> Zal Finn III's Text Box: Holy crap!

> Fournimer's Text Box: you have laser guided bunny eye missiles? no way!

> Lissa's Text Box: #RunningGagPayOff. I didn't even think that was a real thing!

E. E. Lynn's Text Box: |'/\/\ just th4t f4nt4st|c.

Lissa's Text Box: Perhaps we have misj——

E. E. Lynn's Interruption Text Box: L3t's g0! | \/\/4nt 2 s33 c3nt4ur g3t m0unt3d 4nd p\/\/nfuck3d by th3 34rth 3l3/\/\3nt4l!

Lissa's Text Box: Never mind.

It was a quick trip to the Earth Elemental's glade. All the random encounter monsters avoided E. E. Lynn, as word had gotten around. The Earth Elemental dropped into the area. He was a centaur, and he was 52% larger than Fournimer. His body was sculpted of different kinds of crystal.

Game Explanation's Text Box: Be careful some monsters can cause the ground to shake and make every avatar touching the ground fall.

Earth Elemental's Text Box: Beware adventurers, I am the Earth Elemental and... uh... where is everyone?

E. E. Lynn's Text Box: H| 34rthy! | br0ught u 4 c3nt4ur 2 pwn!

Fournimer's Text Box: hey!

Earth Elemental's Text Box: Dear Maker. Not you again. Please, you already have a *Spire C Key* so just leave me alone! I beg you!

E. E. Lynn's Text Box: 4w3! But h3 is cut3 4nd l0v3s d|ck. ^-~ | just \/\/4nn4 \/\/4tch! H3 |s hung l|k3 4 g|r4ff3!

Fournimer took a mental note. Hung like a giraffe. He would need to remember that and tell Anders later.

Earth Elemental's Text Box: He is pretty cute. I've never fucked another centaur before. Only if you watch though. You have to promise to keep your hands to yourself!

E. E. Lynn's Text Box: D03s h4nds |n /\/\ys3lf c0unt?

Earth Elemental's Text Box: Close enough. Okay centaur get over here.

Fournimer's Text Box: no way. I never agreed to that.

E. E. Lynn's Text Box: D0n't b3 such 4 \/\/|/\/\p! |t's just a b|g c0ck. |f | c4n t4k3 |t, y0u c4n h0rs3 butt. B3s|d3s, y0u r teh g4y! ^-^ Y0u l0v3 teh c0ck!

> Zal Finn III's Text Box: Just because Horseymer is gay that doesn't mean he runs around fucking every boy monster he sees!

> Fournimer's Text Box: yeah!

> Earth Elemental's Text Box: If he doesn't want to I don't really want to force him.

The little catgirl stomper her feet and pouted.

> E. E. Lynn's Text Box: \/\/h4t |s \/\/r0ng \/\/|th y0u 3arth 3l3/\/\3nt4l? Y0u r 4 b0ss! |t |s y0ur j0b t0 fuck br0k3n th|ngs r3/\/\3/\/\b3r? N0\/\/ g0!

> Earth Elemental's Text Box: You know what? You're right! Get over here right now centaur boy and take my cock or I will knock your ass to the ground and beat you into submission. That way I can just force you to take my cock!

> Lissa's Text Box: You'll have to go through me first!

> Zal Finn III's Text Box: And me!

> Earth Elemental's Text Box: Okay purple hair, I'll fuck you too. I don't mind, girl avatars are really hot. But no to you NPC, I've fucked my share already.

> E. E. Lynn's Text Box: Y34h! ^-^ H4ppy!

> Lissa's Text Box: Crap! #PlanBackfire.

> Fournimer's Text Box: thanks for trying.

> E. E. Lynn's Text Box: \/\/0uld s0/\/\30n3 hurry up 4nd fuck teh b0ss!

> Lissa's Text Box: If you want someone to fuck the Earth Elemental so bad, why don't you just do it?

> E. E. Lynn's Text Box: G00d |d34!

E. E. Lynn jumped at the Earth Elemental, arms wide open, and crazy skirt completely off. Before she had the Earth Elemental bound and gagged to use as her personal fuck slave the poor monster managed one last Text Box.

> Earth Elemental's Text Box: No! You promised.

Zal Finn III's Text Box: Wow. Look at her go.

Lissa's Text Box: How does someone so small take so much? That is #SoFuckedUp.

Fournimer's Text Box: even though he was going to rape us, I still feel bad for the guy.

Creature Name: Earth Elemental
Class: Elemental C
Level: 98 (Requires 100 avatars to be present to Spawn)
Special Attacks: Earthquake, Magnitude 8.8, Soil Sword, Knockdown, Saddle Prod, Elemental D
Drops: Spire C Key, the Heart of Earth (Only for avatar that gets last strike)
First Player Encounter Notes: $|_|p3r |-|0t c3|\|74|_|R c0c|<! – E. E. Lynn
Additional Comments: $33 4b0\/3. - E. E. Lynn

Chapter 35

ANDERS, DRAGON HUNTED

Anders wiped the sweat from his brow. The strenuous half cycle Coliseum battle was finally over, and now the promising shine of a red chest was all Anders could see. He bent over to check the contents within.

Anders' Text Box: Of course you are!

This had not been a good cycle so far. First, Anders had discovered that all the baked goods here tasted awful now that he was no longer with child. He had traded all of his *Bacon* reserves long ago, and now would be stuck eating nothing but appliances for the foreseeable future.

Second, Anders had heard strange pounding noises coming from the direction of Onn Forest. They were faint, but after a distant tree fell over they got just a hint louder. Anders was sure that the Spiderboy, who was not relevant to any quests, was trying to break into Onn through a different way than the forest entrance that he couldn't use.

Third, Anders had come excited to the Coliseum for round two but had ended up facing the Harpy Sisters Three. Before they were even broken they had shown female nudity. Even if the female nudity did not seem out of place here, flying women with sharp claws and big bouncing breasts did not excite Anders in the least. Fortunately, all three of them had eyes for Anders and they mostly had fought amongst themselves. That was the only saving grace of this cycle so far, he had managed to kill them without needing to resort to alternate methods.

Finally, now that the red chest had resulted in a pair of *Gladiator Boots (s)* Anders was livid. They not only had less defence than his *Frost Gigas Boots*, they also (for some reason) would increase his Intelligence. Intelligence was a completely useless stat for a Night Ranger. These boots were useless, even if they were pretty. Anders put them in his *Ultra-Pack* to keep them safe to play dress up with later.

At least he could come back next cycle and be on round 3 of the *Coliseum*. Anders left the ring and was greeted by Draganders and Illiandro. Draganders perched on Anders' neck and chirped happily, biting Anders' ear affectionately. Even if the bites of the little dragon hurt, they did cheer up Anders and he rubbed the dragon's favourite place, under the chin.

Anders petted Draganders as they left the secret entrance to the Coliseum and headed towards the Bakery Shoppe. Half way there the sun was darkened and the background music changed. Anders stomach sunk. It was Xam's song. The ground shook as the dragon landed behind the avatar. Illiandro had already bolted but Draganders had stepped between Anders and Xam and adopted a protective stance, he chirped in a do not mess with momma manner.

> Xam, the Orange Dragon of Light's Text Box: There you are candy. I've been searching everywhere for you! Wow, look at how skinny you are now. I was sort of wondering if you'd pop, but I'm glad that you're going to be around much longer.

This was the icing on the *Grand FullCake* for this cycle, an encounter with Xam. Anders spat on his hand with a look of annoyance in his face as he turned away from the dragon. Anders stuck his spit coated fingers up his ass and started to get himself lubed up as he cast *Stretch More* and *Stretch More More*.

> Anders' Text Box: Okay Xam, let's just get this over with.

> Xam, the Orange Dragon of Light's Text Box: Normally, I would love to candy, but I am just here to tell you something.

> Anders' Text Box: What? I don't believe you.

> Xam, the Orange Dragon of Light's Text Box: It's true candy! I swear!

Anders noticed that Xam was acting strangely. The dragon looked around nervously, even the background sound effects made him jump. Dragon sweat poured down his brow. Anders watched the dragon carefully as Xam fidgeted with something he was hiding in his front claws. Xam looked exhausted, and tattered around the edges, perhaps he was telling the truth.

> Anders' Text Box: Okay, I'll listen. What did you want to tell me Xam?

> Xam, the Orange Dragon of Light's Text Box: It's Breaker. After he found out that you were stuck in Onn he has ordered all the dragons

> to come find you. We are supposed to bring you to him.

> Anders' Text Box: That's perfect. I want to find Breaker. Can you bring me to him now Xam?

> Xam, the Orange Dragon of Light's Text Box: No. I know you are looking for him. But I will not let you go to him.

> Anders' Text Box: Then why are you here warning me about the other dragons coming to bring me to Breaker?

> Xam, the Orange Dragon of Light's Text Box: I'm not. As I said already, I'm here telling you, not warning you. You are mine. Not Breaker's, not another dragon's, mine. If I ever see you talking to any other dragons or going to Breaker I will use my secret Anders' controlling item on you to keep you forever. So watch yourself carefully candy, because I will.

After the warning Xam flew off. Anders was confused. Whatever the dragon was fiddling with nervously earlier was his new secret Anders controlling item, but what could be so powerful it could take over an avatar permanently? Was even such an item possible? Maybe there was, if anyone could make such an item it would be Breaker. That would explain why Xam was so nervous. Had the dragon stolen something from Breaker's personal reserve of broken items? That must be why Xam wouldn't take Anders to Breaker, Xam was avoiding his boss. Perfect, now he had an obsessed stalker dragon with an item that could take him over at a moment's notice.

Anders was going to have to keep a close watch out now. All six of Breaker's dragons were coming here to look for him. This was not only a horrible cycle, it was one of the worst. His two best options were to find a dragon that wasn't Xam and hope that Xam didn't notice and take control of him permanently, or to finish the Coliseum as fast as possible and get the Flaming Pit out of Onn. The second plan seemed like the better of the two, and Anders rushed back to the Bakery Shoppe while keeping a close lookout for dragons, Xam or otherwise.

~ ~ ~

Anders was determined this cycle. If he already had the *Gladiator Boots (s)* and *Gloves (s)* that only left a helmet, pair of pants, and suit of Armour. With the secret battle for the *Super Amazing Hover-Motorbike* that might be a total of four more battles to win at the Coliseum. He thought that if he was lucky, there would be less, maybe two items would drop after a single battle. If he was unlucky, there could be up to five extra battles thanks to the possibility of primary weapons, secondary weapons, and three accessory slots. Anders was hoping that he would get lucky.

Anders sprinted to the Coliseum entrance with a watchful Draganders and a terrified Illiandro. They made it inside without incident. Anders left Draganders in Illiandro's care and stepped forward.

The Third Battle: Anders vs. the Gladiator Brothers.

Out from the shadows they came. Wearing similar clothing to their little XIII Elite friends, the Gladiator Brothers were the elder brothers in the family. They didn't follow the normal avatar sizing rules and were so tall and muscular that they made Mr. Max, the beefiest avatar around, look like the tiny gnome Gliint. Their hard muscular bodies were covered in battle scars that they wore with pride.

The Gladiator Brothers started by showing off for the crowd, flexing this way and that in a variety of masculine poses. The pair enjoyed the attention of the screaming crowd. They adopted battle stances and began a well choreographed battle amongst themselves. One fought with a giant two handed axe, the other with an even bigger two handed hammer. They added at least triple the amount of necessary flourishes and were using double volume sound effects. With each practiced near-miss the pair looked to the crowd and smiled, they were hamming it up, and loving every moment of it. A big finish of swishes and pounds caused the pair to look to the crowd, rise their arms, give a big thumbs up, and earn a giant cheer from everyone watching.

Their display over, the Gladiator Brothers turned to look at their competition. It was a dumbfounded drooling elf with a mouth that was gaping wide open, crossed eyes, and a twitching bulge in his cute jock-strap. The Duo glanced at each other and both used the *Fist Bump Dual Animation*. They approached the elf, pushed him down to his knees, unbuttoned their skirts, and presented their offerings.

With two independently bobbing members in front of his face, Anders could finally uncross his eyes. They were not long, as Anders had suspected they would be, but a relatively normal length. What they were, however, was thick, Anders could only just get his mouth down the 'little' brother, and Anders could only get the jaw breaking 'bigger' brother's head inside. The elf wasn't one to back down from a challenge though and worked diligently despite the obstacle. The crowd watched on and erupted into thunderous fapping.

The bigger brother appreciated the elf's attempts and returned the enthusiasm during one of the elf's valiant tries. He lifted the elf up to all fours with the help of the *Ultra-Pack's* straps. Flat and powerful hands came down hard on the elf's backside (with double volume sound effects and triple the amount of necessary flourishes), which earned a loud but muffled moan.

Anders stopped what he was doing with the big brother and looked up with a cock filled grin. The elf set his target lock on the little brother, working diligently at his new task. The big brother went around back and bent down to get a better view. He spread open the elf's cheeks and dove in with his tongue. Muffled moans indicated that the elf enjoyed the thorough licking,, a squeak indicated that the thick finger that shortly followed was also appreciated.

The big brother knew it would take some time to relax the elf to fit properly on his thick member, but he didn't mind spending the rounds. Some experimenting revealed that the entire hand of the gladiator could easily fit in thanks to Anders constant practice, so the big brother wasted no time in trying the hole out for real. It was wet and his thick member felt a tingle of pleasure when he bottomed out.

Anders enjoyed the work of the brothers, he shuddered as he got spit-roasted. For a moment Anders wanted to tell the brothers that if they just stepped a few length units closer to each other each that every thrust wouldn't need to cause an entire new penetration. The elf decided after a few rounds to keep his stuffed mouth shut, the constant penetration was a thrill ride and would even allow him to breathe on occasion.

One brother had his hands on Anders' hips, the other had his tightly gripped on the elf's ears. They started a tug-of-war, alternating their insertions. Anders was banged back and forth on the brothers as they pulled him every direction and it was surprisingly exhilarating. Everyone was doing well in the tug-of-war, but the crowd cheered on one combatant before all others. There was the clear winner of the competition and everyone knew it, it was the rope. A hush fell over the crowd, they were edging on their seats.

Every combatant was sweating, moaning, and putting on a great show for the spectators. A firm slap released a barrage of tingles. The big brother started to shudder and the rope knew that the pumping Gladiator was close. Given the size of the nuts that were slapping, it was going to be a big load. The crowd's champion pressed back firmly, as he wanted to feel it shoot inside and to absorb some of the wonderful sweat coated magic.

The last thrust was the only thrust that the bigger brother managed to miss the target. He slipped out of the hole, resting in the crease outside, and caused thick ropes (of the hot cum variety) to land all over the excited rope (of the tug-of-war variety) and it pooled in the small of the rope's back. It dripped and rolled as the thrusting continued, coating the front of the rope before the last traces fell to the arena floor.

Seeing his older brother get off caused a stirring in the loins of the young brother who shot his big load as well. He grabbed the rope's ears and pulled, missing the mouth by just a fraction of a length unit. The load erupted past the *#6 Hairstyle* and further helped to coat the rope in hot and sweaty seed. The smell of the sticky man cum combined with the with the residual tingles of pleasure set the rope off, causing his rope to shoot out different happy ropes. Thanks to the jock-strap holding his penis upright with only the head peeking out from under the waistband, the rope got every drop on his own chest, hitting many of the areas the brothers had missed. The crowd screamed out in a final spurt of applause (mixed with the spurts of their orgasms).

The brothers gave a final pose to the crowd, a *High Five Dual Animation* to each other, and a shy kiss to their rope. They left the arena while both of them waved the red cum covered tug-of-war flag (that the rope hadn't noticed had been tied around his midsection for the entire encounter).

The red chest offered Anders to a new pair of *Gladiator Pants (s)*. This initially made Anders excited, he didn't expect to find pants so soon in the Coliseum process. The pants caused a sigh when Anders looked at them. They were only thigh coverings, nice thigh coverings, but still only thigh coverings. The chest piece was what he actually needed to find for this set to cover his shame. The elf was going to be stuck with his ass in the open breeze for longer, even if it was a crisp refreshing feeling in the morning. He would try them on after cleaning up; he didn't want to get them all sticky.

> Anders' Text Box: Danishes, I don't have nearly enough *Double Danishes* to clean all this up.

Creature Name: Gladiator Brothers
Class: Man Team
Level: 78 (both)
Special Attacks: Flashy Show, Big Deal, Tug o' War, Double Team, Flag Roaster
Drops: Gladiator Pants
First Player Encounter Notes: Am I allowed to redo this battle again later?
- Anders

Chapter 36

OUTFITS, B ELEMENTALS, SECRETS, AND BLUE DRAGONS

For an outfit called the *Metal Parka (s)*, Palcath had been pleasantly surprised. It didn't look ridiculous— except for the awful helmet, which Palcath didn't need to wear. Otherwise, this Armour was a smart set, trimmed with the warmest of furs. It showed a lot of skin given that it was *(s)*, but it was far warmer than it looked. Palcath changed the main colour to yellow, and the accents to purple. It would be a desperate attempt to get Lissa to notice him when they met up later, but he was going to try it, even if it meant having purple fur trim on his outfit.

Palcath understood at least one of Roodg's strange plans. The treasure that was left over held a chest piece of Armour from Roodg's new outfit. It was a *Winter Fun Scarf (s)*, and since Palcath opened the box it was now for melee classes. Roodg wouldn't need a new body piece thanks to a *Dark Gigas Armour*, so this scarf was going to be a gift for Fournimer. Palcath added a check to his list under the 'Roodg is smart' side, and even added an entire new column for 'Roodg is nice'. When Palcath remembered the Flork shoving earlier he added another column for 'Roodg is a jerk'.

The rest of the *Winter Fun Armour (s)* was presentable on Roodg, the long mittens, boots, snowpants, and hood almost looked exactly like the old Armour the avatar was wearing but more wintery and fun. It was covering only obvious gender signs. Roodg had set the colour to red and the accents to white, combined with the charcoal skin of the avatar it was just beaming with contrast.

Caela had on her new *Finest Furs (s)*. Stunning and set to white, they glistened like the newly fallen snow. She was showing a lot of her non-existent cleavage with the

Finest Fur Bodice (s), as well as most of her midriff, but it made the outfit sophisticated due to her demeanour. She was struggling on a colour to pick for an accent, so her new fur lined cloak, dress, and trimmings were still set to white, making her near invisible in the snow. Her new *Finest Fur Muffs (s)* did make Palcath use the *Smirk Animation*, the earmuffs did a bad job at covering any part of her oversized ears.

> Caëlahenãilenŵhei's Snow Box: I simply am unable to decide on the accent colour of this outfit. Never knowing that I would ever have the choice of two different colours is weighing heavily on my mind.

> Palcath's Text Box: Yellow might look nice lass, if the accents change to look golden.

Caela changed the accents to yellow, giving her the distinctive appearance of being covered in yellow droplets. Caëlahenãilenŵhei used the *Shake Head Animation*.

> Caëlahenãilenŵhei's Snow Box: Not happening, it looks like yellow snow.

> Trev Terra's Text Box: Blue might be, well what I mean is, blue is nice with white… right? And yellow, cause yellow is good with blue, which is why I use yellow accents with my blue. Jorthan… is yellow. Why not blue?

Caela tried blue, which had a soft hue and a frosty appearance. The colours were nice on the eyes, especially on the cape, but to make the decision harder so did pink, purple, green, and orange.

> Roodg's Text Box: wHY NOT TRY RED? iT IS VERY HIGH CONTRAST WITH WHITE!

> Caëlahenãilenŵhei's Snow Box: Excellent idea Roodg, contrast is what I need! All of this pale stuff is attractive certainly, but I want to stand out and be noticed. However, there is better contrast between white and black, the highest possible in fact, so I am going to try that combination.

Black made Caela grin with copious amounts of *Full Ball-Gag* drool. Next to the lightness of her platinum blond hair, pale blue eyes, and milky white skin, the black caused her to pop out of the snowy scenery like a black reindeer nose. No other accent colour could have done a better job of seeing through a winter snow (except perhaps a red reindeer nose). With a black inside lining to her cloak and distinctive trim Caela was ready to speak up and declare herself as an important character (if she had any snow left to write on). She did assign her boots with red trim as they looked 'festive'.

> Roodg's Text Box: oR BLACK… yEAH CONTRAST!

> Palcath's Text Box: Lass, you look great now! Let's take on that castle, all while looking great in our new duds! Even if we are showing far more skin than before, at least these are warmer!

Caëlahenãilenŵhei used the *Nod Animation*, Roodg the *Cheer Animation*, and Trev Terra used the *Nervously Chew on Lips Animation*.

The *Spire B Castle* was a spiralling expanse of solid ice, reflections on every surface caused even the best processors to quiver in fear. The level design was not complicated, it was one long corridor, one very long possibly several cycles of walking long corridor. There was ice everywhere, the ceilings, the walls, the scenery, and even on the floor. This area did lack something important from the other winter environments, snow. Caela was not going to be able to write on the ground anymore, unless she thought up a clever new trick. Unable to do so, at this moment at least, she resorted to just pointing at things.

Caëlahenãilenŵhei used the *Point Animation* directed at the ice.

> Palcath's Text Box: I don't know lass, hold me and I'll check.

Palcath took a practice step, the ice on the floor wasn't slippery like the stuff on the frozen lakes. There went their idea of taking one step and playing a nice game of cards while slipping down the corridor.

> Palcath's Text Box: I guess we walk then lads, lasses, and Roodgs.

~ ~ ~

> Roodg's Text Box: tHIS IS SO BORING!

> Palcath's Text Box: I know Roodg, we have been walking for over a cycle already and we are not even half way. It wouldn't be so bad if there were some Makerdamn monsters to kill or some chests to open or some barrels to smash!

Caëlahenãilenŵhei used the *Point Animation*.

> Roodg's Text Box: i KNOW! i NEED TO DO SOMETHING!

> Palcath's Text Box: I agree Roodg, any kind of something would be better than this!

Caëlahenãilenŵhei used the *Point Animation*.

> Roodg's Text Box: tHERE ISN'T EVEN ANYMORE SCENERY TO BLOW UP / *CHAINSAW*! BTW, I ABSOLUTELY LOVE WHAT U DID WITH THAT LAMP.

> Palcath's Text Box: Thank you Roodg, so do I! I think that I'm going

> to display it in my section of my Portie Tent!

Caëlahenãilenẁhei used the *Point Animation*.

> Roodg's Text Box: sAWESOME! i WAS GOING TO SUGGEST THAT!

> Palcath's Text Box: You should put that scenic ice crystal sculpture up in your part!

Caëlahenãilenẁhei used the *Point Animation*. Caëlahenãilenẁhei used the *Point Animation*.

> Roodg's Text Box: i DON'T THINK I GOT HER NOSE RIGHT!

> Palcath's Text Box: Really? It looks just like her though. I really like it.

> Trev Terra's Text Box: Um… well uh… I don't want to interrupt…

> Roodg's Text Box: i LIKE YOUR DECORATIVE LAMP BETTER.

> Palcath's Text Box: Can we trade? I would love to trade Roodg!

Caëlahenãilenẁhei used the *Point Animation*. Caëlahenãilenẁhei used the *Point Animation*. Caëlahenãilenẁhei used the *Point Animation*.

> White Quest Fairy's Text Box: Not nice being ignored, huh? How do you like it?

> Trev Terra's Text Box: Guys… er well guy and… um… well you two should. Uh…

> Roodg's Text Box: OMM YES! tRADES!

> Palcath's Text Box: Huzzah!

> Reminrouf, the Blue Dragon of Ice's Text Box: What do I get in this trade exactly?

Reminrouf's theme song started, he was the dragon coloured blue, he was the dragon of destruction, and he was the dragon who was all about his fancy ice soul patch. It was all there in the subtitles.

> Reminrouf, the Blue Dragon of Ice's Text Box: I was thinking your heads on a silver platter would be a great trade. I will let you keep your bodies in return. That's fair right?

> Palcath's Text Box: I know that I should be terrified right now dragon lad, but I just have to ask before you try and sever off our heads…

> What is with your name? Reminrouf, seriously?

> Roodg's Text Box: LoL! iT SOUNDS LIKE A TALKING DOG IS SAYING LEMON LOAF! rELP Ralcath, RIT'S RA RHOST! rA RHOST! rEHEHEHE.

Caëlahenâilenŵhei used the *Point Animation* directed at the 'f' in Reminrouf's name.

> Trev Terra's Text Box: I think I agree with that... we are pretty much f'ed here.

Caëlahenâilenŵhei used the *Sigh Animation*.

> Reminrouf, the Blue Dragon of Ice's Text Box: Curse you! My name is radical! It says so right there in the third verse of my song. See? Right there! 'He will kill you with frozen flame, and his name isn't lame. It's Reminrouf, ♪♫ the blue!

> Roodg's Text Box: hOW DID YOU TYPE THE MUSIC NOTES?!

> Palcath's Text Box: I can read the words, but it's not helping lad. It's a pretty bad name. I don't think I can find it in me to even fight. I just feel bad for you.

> Roodg's Text Box: wOULD YOU DO IT FOR A DWARFY SNACK?

Caëlahenâilenŵhei used the *Point Animation*, directed at the subtitle for the word 'lame'.

> Trev Terra's Text Box: Well... Yeah it is sort of, what I mean to say is, well it's not that bad... Okay, it is pretty bad. Gosh, that is a bad name. How can you deal with having such a bad name?

> Reminrouf, the Blue Dragon of Ice's Text Box: You guys are all jerks! I'll make you suffer! I'll make you pay!

> Roodg's Text Box: r U CRYING?

> Reminrouf, the Blue Dragon of Ice's Text Box: Yes? No! Shut up!

The blue dragon held back his tears as best as he could and took to the skies. As he flew away a single tear escaped from the big dragon and fell to the ground. It froze into a shard of ice and it embedded into the ground with a scritch when it hit. Cracks in the ground scritched outwards and when two lines met, the ground fell inwards. The speed of the scritching was steadily increasing, and more and more floor was falling into the newly created void.

Caëlahenâilenŵhei used the *Point Animation*.

> Palcath's Text Box: I see it lass, the entire area is falling apart! We need to run and we need to run now!

> Reminrouf, the Blue Dragon of Ice's Text Box: I, *sniff* totally meant to do that!

The party ran from the quickly expanding void towards the end of the area. They were now thankful for the lack of monsters and boring level design. The distance left to cover was vast, but they had an ample reserves of *Stamina Potions* and motivation. They reached the spire glade only about twenty rounds ahead of the expanding void of certain death.

A bridge at the far side of the glade that hung precariously over a chasm was the only way out of the area.

Caëlahenãilenẘhei used the *Point Animation*.

> Palcath's Text Box: Quick everylad! Make for the bridge!

> Game Explanation Text Box: Be careful. Some monsters have attacks that can freeze you solid.

> Ice Elemental's Text Box: Beware adventurers, I a—

> Roodg's Interruption Text Box: nO TIME iCE eLEMENTAL! wE ARE FLEEING!

> Ice Elemental's Text Box: Fleeing? From what?

Caëlahenãilenẘhei used the *Point Animation*.

> Ice Elemental's Text Box: Oh my Maker! It's all falling apart! What do we do?!

> Roodg's Text Box: rUN! bRIDGE!

> Reminrouf, the Blue Dragon of Ice's Text Box: Need that little old bridge jerks? Well too fucking bad! I am so spiteful, for a reference please see verse six in my song.

The poorly named dragon dropped from the sky and thought unhappy thoughts. He cried over the bridge and shed scenery destroying tears, critching the bridge into pieces. Reminrouf used a claw and pulled down his eyelid while sticking out his tongue. He flew off, into a different Chapter.

> Palcath's Text Box: The bridge is out lads, lasses, elementlasses, and Roodg! That's the only way across!

> Ice Elemental's Text Box: OMM! I am freaking out here! That chasm

is like wicked deep! What do we do?

Palcath's Text Box: I don't know lassemental!

Caëlahenâilenŵhei used the *Shrug Animation*.

Trev Terra's Text Box: Nobody here knows either!

Roodg's Text Box: i DO! i HAVE A PLAN!

Palcath's Text Box: Listen to Roodg no matter what! Roodg always has the best and most insane plans!

Roodg's Text Box: k. pART 1. sO Trev Terra NEEDS 2 STAND HERE BY THE CHASM & Palcath BEHIND HIM. Caëlahenâilenŵhei & Ice Elemental NEED 2 STAND BESIDE Trev. i STAND HERE!

Caëlahenâilenŵhei used the *Quizzical Look Animation*, but after reassurance by Palcath everyone had themselves in position with ten rounds before death left to spare.

Roodg's Text Box: pART 2. Caëlahenâilenŵhei & Ice Elemental GET EVERY ICE SPELL YOU HAVE & START CASTING WHILE Trev Terra PULLS UP HIS *dARK gIGAS aRMOUR* OVER HIS HEAD & JERKS OFF.

Trev Terra, Caëlahenâilenŵhei, and Ice Elemental's Simultaneous Text Box: WHAT?

Roodg's Text Box: oR WE CAN ALL DIE IN 9 ROUNDS.

Palcath's Text Box: You heard Roodg, Go!

Trev Terra's Text Box: But... I...

Roodg's Text Box: 8 ROUNDS!

Caëlahenâilenŵhei used the *Point Animation*, focused on the word 'Go' in Palcath's last Text Box.

Ice Elemental's Text Box: Please gay elf, can you save us?

Trev Terra's Text Box: How did you know I was gay? Wait... I guess I just told you that right now. Still...

Trev Terra reluctantly closed his eyes, set his *Blush Shade* to #6, told everyone to look at their own screens, and lifted up his Armour. The elf sheepishly wrapped his hand around his soft member.

Roodg's Text Box: 7 ROUNDS!

> Trev Terra's Text Box: I'm too nervous… I don't think that I can, what I mean is… well… everyone is watching and…

Caëlahenäilenŵhei used the *Point Animation*, focused on the word 'Go' in her last animation.

> Roodg's Text Box: 6 ROUNDS!

Trev had started to masturbate but was having little success, his balls were quivering with anticipation thanks to Roodg's constant harassment over the past few cycles. He had a desperate need to release, but despite that could not overcome his intense shyness.

> Palcath's Text Box: Hurry up lad!

> Trev Terra's Text Box: I am trying, but it is… well… this isn't something I just can do with others around. I can hardly even do this when I'm with a … um… never mind.

> Roodg's Text Box: 5 ROUNDS!

The sprite elf was trying, but had started to grow softer.

> Trev Terra's Text Box: I'm so sorry everyone… but…

> Roodg's Text Box: i KNEW i WOULD NEED TO HELP. dON'T YOU DARE SHOOT ME.

With a strange grace and a quick swallow Roodg executed a masterful deep throat in no time flat. Roodg broke lip-lock only to say important advice.

> Roodg's Text Box: 4 ROUNDS! hELP HIM CUM Palcath!

> Palcath's Text Box: What? But how would I… Oh no, not again. I'm not going gay again Roodg.

> Roodg's Text Box: oR DIE?

Palcath used the *Sigh Animation* and reached around to Trev and grabbed the elf's balls tightly and started to massage them, it made the elf cry out in alarm and pleasure. The balls were surprisingly heavy, weighing far more than Palcath hand anticipate they would. Caëlahenäilenŵhei used the *Point Animation*, focused on the word 'again' as she followed up with a *Quizzical Look Animation*.

> Roodg's Text Box: 3 ROUNDS! hELP BETTER. *cHAINSAW* HIM!

> Palcath's Text Box: But… Flaming Pit!

Palcath looked behind himself and saw certain death only three rounds behind. He looked forward at the gay elf's butt. It was either gay elf butt or death, Palcath swallowed his pride and choose life (also gay elf butt). He could not believe that he was going to have to bang a guy again to live, this game was messed up. The dwarf pulled down his pants, set both of his settings to ultra, grabbed the elf's hips with his free hand, and pushed his *Chainsaw* inside.

> Trev Terra's Text Box: Holy fuck! I'm not normally a… well what I mean is, gosh. That is way nice. Wow. So wow. Sorry! It's not like that, we need to. Sorry, but… Oh my! ♥

> Roodg's Text Box: 2 ROUNDS! wORK THAT BOY ELF BUTT Palcath!

Neither Palcath nor Trev paid attention, they both were concentrating. Trev was focussing on the intense pleasure of the dwarf *Chainsaw*, his elf balls were shaking in the squeezing hand of the dwarf. Palcath was concentrating on pretending to be somewhere else.

> Roodg's Text Box: lAST ROUND! sHOOT!

> Trev Terra and Palcath's Simultaneous Text Box: YES!

Palcath could not stop himself, the combination of the vibrations, his ultra settings, and the sudden tightening of the elf was enough to make him climax. Trev twisted a nipple and his nuts began to pulsate rhythmically. Roodg stopped sucking and ducked for cover. The sprite elf used his free hand to grab the dwarf and pull him in deeper just as he began to ejaculate. The denial of the previous cycles combined with the vibration hitting home caused the elf to expel hard and quickly. Each burst caused an actual river of ejaculate to emanate from the elf, whose little but near infinite balls could no longer hope to contain. Each shot passed through the ice spells and as they hit the chasm floor froze into a quickly rising frozen pool.

> Roodg's Text Box: jUMP!

The party landed on the ice lake and slid across the now full chasm just as the other side collapsed, ending the scritch. The Ice Elemental, the light elf, and the night elf wiped the sweat and other fluids from their brows. Trev was still latched onto Palcath, shooting forcefully into the scenery. Even after Palcath had left the elf and zipped up, the Geomancer was still shooting off countless rivers, now aimed into the void.

> Palcath's Text Box: I think you can stop now lad.

> Trev Terra's Text Box: I can't until… it's all gone… he… she… Roodg made me keep it too long. Rivers of it. So much of it. Ugh!

Trev shot a few more lakes into the void but lost his footing due to the full force lake shots and was forced to fall backwards. He released one final burst straight into the air. The Ice Elemental thought quickly and shot off an *Elemental C* which caused the torrent to change from liquid, which would have flooded them off the narrow edge, into harmless falling snow. The avatar collapsed in exhaustion after the incredible release of pent up fluids.

> Roodg's Text Box: nEAT.

Palcath and Caela tied in their challenge. They both had realized what had been going on at the exact same moment, which was right now as the elf snow fell on their lips.

> Caëlahenâilenẁhei's Box Text: Oh sweet Maker.

> Palcath's Text Box: Everything… the river we walked up, the snowballs that we fought with and got in our mouths, the cave flooding that we nearly drowned in, and even all the frozen lakes that we eventually melted and swam through… they were all huge floods of elf… oh I think I'm going to be sick.

> Ice Elemental's Text Box: I'm not, that was sick!

◈ Chapter 37 ◈

OUTFITS,
A ELEMENTALS,
SECRETS, AND
RED DRAGONS

K ray's Text Box: Oh my Maker I was so right, this outfit is cute, kay!

In'ferni and De'vini used the *Lipped Locked Dual Animation*.

samuri's Text Box: …

samuri looked over Kray's new *Beachcomber Outfit (s)*. It was a bit too revealing for samuri's tastes, even if it was designed for the beach area. Kray was now wearing *Flan Flops* (of the Royal Flan variety), *Jammy Bracelets* (seventeen on his right arm, three on his left), a *Shlarkjaw Necklace* (that only sported a single tooth), a pair of *Water Goggles* (on the forehead that could not be moved to protect the eyes if swimming), and a pair of *Swim Briefs* (which had the *Serpent Speed* symbol on the side).

Kray's Text Box: Kay, I've changed all the colours and accents now. Do they remind you of anything?

In'ferni and De'vini used the *Turn Away Dual Animation*.

samuri's Text Box: …

samuri needed to close his eyes. The colour choices Kray had made were just that hideous. Nothing matched in the slightest. Somehow Kray had managed to use ten of the eleven colour choices, including black, but all of them were in the absolute worst places. The only colour the avatar had missed was red, and that was already present due to the avatar's bright red flip #4 *Hairstyle*. samuri had no idea what this was supposed to remind him of except perhaps a pile of colourful unicorn vomit.

> Kray's Text Box: Kay, give up Sami-guy? It's you! I made my colours look like you since we are engaged!

In'ferni and De'vini used the *Laugh Hysterically Dual Animation*.

samuri was so speechless he couldn't even say '…'. How in anyway did he resemble colourful unicorn vomit? His new *Bushido Beach Wear (s)*, which was the absolute perfect thing for any samuri to wear to the beach while remaining completely covered and modest, was all set to gray in both colour and accent. samuri did not have time for the ridiculous accent colour descriptions that had been going on in previous Chapters. They were a waste of everyone's time, and overall just felt like filler text. Even if in reality they were an elaborate foreshadowing code that no one would every pick up on about multiple different events that happened in book three of the series, samuri thought they were pointless (even if he had inadvertently participated by not picking an accent colour).

> Kray's Text Box: Your outfit could show a little more skin though Sami-guy, kay.

In'ferni and De'vini used the *Inside Joke Dual Animation*.

> samuri's Text Box: …

samuri would have been showing much less skin if he had his way. The fact that his ankles were showing was a little too risqué for his tastes.

> Kray's Text Box: Kay, this Spire Castle A is such a bore, we are over half way done and nothing has happened yet!

In'ferni and De'vini used the *Butt Squeeze Dual Animation*.

> samuri's Text Box: …

samuri chopped a passing gang of Firegers into pieces with a series of mighty blows from his *Katana-Nata* and help from his new companions. The All Seeing Eye Dog and the Nine Circles of Hell Cat were each tossed a fresh *Fireger Face Treat* (that had fallen to the volcano floor, searing in their juices) and they showed their appreciation with happy tail wags. samuri kept the rest of the faces as treats for later. The pets of the constantly kissing Necromancer and Summoner twins deserved all the faces they could eat, but samuri didn't want to spoil them too much at once.

> Kray's Text Box: More boring monsters. Like yawn, kay. Oh look, there is the dragon boss, strange this isn't the glade… At least something will happen now.

In'ferni and De'vini used the *Quiet Kiss Dual Animation*.

> samuri's Text Box: ...

samuri used the *Shh Animation*.

> Kray's Text Box: What? It's the boss, don't you know anything. You need to fight it or we can't leave. What's the big deal, kay.

In'ferni and De'vini used the *Double Shh Dual Animation*.

> samuri's Text Box: ...

samuri used the *Head Chop Off Animation*.

> Kray's Yelling Text Box: HEY BOSS, COME DOWN HERE, KAY!

In'ferni and De'vini used the *Mega Gasp Dual Animation*.

> samuri's Text Box: ...

The red dragon changed its flight trajectory to an intercept course with the party. The background music changed to ominous Latin chanting. The subtitles told everyone that this was Gdoor, the Red Dragon of Fire. Further verses chanted of Gdoor's abilities as a master negotiator and intense love of baking muffins.

> Gdoor, the Red Dragon of Fire's Text Box: Fear my presence simple mortals, for it is I, Gdoor, the Re—

> Kray's Interruption Text Box: Like major yawn boss. We just want to fight you so we can leave here, kay.

> Gdoor, the Red Dragon of Fire's Text Box: I am not a mere boss, kay. I am Gdo—

> Kray's Interruption Text Box: Yeah, yeah, whatever, kay. Just fight us already.

> Gdoor, the Red Dragon of Fire's Text Box: I will fight you insolent worm an—

> Kray's Interruption Text Box: Kay, then fight already and stop blubbering on.

> Gdoor, the Red Dragon of Fire's Text Box: Blubbering on? Is this guy for real, kay? I am not blubbering on, I am setting th—

> Kray's Interruption Text Box: Kay, you are more blubber than a chubby gay elf butt that isn't mine. Both vocally and in the butt. Just look at you, how thick are your hips anyways?

Gdoor, the Red Dragon of Fire's Text Box: Hey, kay! I will have you know that I am the skinniest of all of—

Kray's Interruption Text Box: Let me guess, kay, skinniest of all of the kids at fat camp?

Gdoor, the Red Dragon of Fire's Text Box: Kay, I never went to fat camp! ... Why am I saying 'kay' anywa—

Kray's Interruption Text Box: I can tell you didn't go, I could see your big dragon butt jiggling from a thousand move units away.

Gdoor, the Red Dragon of Fire's Text Box: I am not f—

Kray's Interruption Text Box: Fasting? Doing Free Weights? Finger purging? Kay, obviously not chunko.

Gdoor, the Red Dragon of Fire's Text Box: Why are you so mean? You know what, you can kill yourself you big meanie. I'm leavi—

Kray's Interruption Text Box: Are you crying? You are crying! Kay, what a big baby. A big fat baby!

Gdoor, the Red Dragon of Fire's Text Box: Shut up! Just shut up!

Taking to the sky while holding back tears Gdoor left the area, emotionally beaten. samuri wasn't certain if he should congratulate Kray for getting Gdoor to leave, or smack Kray for causing the dragon to cry out flaming tears that turned the entire area into a blazing inferno with random chunks that burnt the world into nothingness. As the party sprinted down the monster infested corridor while dodging newly created void spots, samuri was pretty sure it was that second one.

Kray's Text Box: This fire is stupid, kay.

In'ferni and De'vini used the *Skip and Run While Holding Hands Dual Animation*.

samuri's Text Box: ...

samuri used the *Point Animation* directed at the glade at the end of the area. There was not a visible way to get across the chasm spanning through the middle of the glade. The fire spawned from the tears of Gdoor was quickly destroying the Fire Castle as the real boss for the area exploded in.

Game Description's Text Box: Be careful. Some monsters have attacks that can decrease your size.

Fire Elemental's Text Box: Beware ad—

> Kray's Interruption Text Box: No time for intro speeches, kay. Busy running.

> Fire Elemental's Text Box: Running? What are you running from?

In'ferni and De'vini used the *Frantic Pointing Dual Animation*.

> samuri's Text Box: ...

samuri used the *Point Animation* directed at a burst of fire that caused a section of floor to dissolve into fragments of code.

> Fire Elemental's Text Box: What the fuck is that? OMM! What the fuck do we do?

> Kray's Text Box: Duh, fire, kay.

In'ferni and De'vini used the *Sneaky Feel-up Dual Animation*.

> samuri's Text Box: ...

samuri used the *Shrug Animation*.

> Fire Elemental's Text Box: I know! Lower the bridge, quick! Normally you need to defeat me to get the codes, but since my glade is on fucking fire I'll let it slide! Just use a ranged attack on the buttons in the order I give you.

> Kray's Test Box: Kay, I am all over this. Ranged attacks, yes! Which do I hit first?

In'ferni and De'vini used the *Kiss in the Flames Dual Animation*.

> samuri's Text Box: ...

samuri listened for instructions.

> Fire Elemental's Text Box: Don't hit the wrong ones or pieces of scenery fall away, and only 20 pieces are not on fire right now! The order is: Green, Red, Red, Yellow, Blue, Green.

> Kray's Text Box: Oh uh... yeah, I am so on that. I'm the only one here with ranged attacks after all. So everyone just step back and let me get to work hitting those buttons in that order, so, kay, I'll just get to aiming an—

> Fire Elemental's Interruption Text Box: Remember, the entire glade is on fucking fire! Think you could speed this up a tad?

In'ferni and De'vini used the *Panicked Spit Swap Dual Animation*.

samuri's Text Box: …

samuri looked across the chasm as the buttons flashed and got two different sinking feelings. One in his stomach when he looked over at the very dance style buttons, and again after Kray shot the red button and caused the piece of scenery samuri was standing on to fall into the abyss. samuri was glad he was a good jumper.

Fire Elemental's Text Box: Green button! Hit the green button first!

Kray's Text Box: Uh… I just slipped, kay.

In'ferni and De'vini used the *Green-Eyed Monster Dual Animation*.

samuri's Text Box: …

samuri used the *Eyebrows Furrowed and Face Twitch Animation* several times as Kray hit both the blue button and yellow button before he finally hit the green button. They were down to 17 pieces of floor now. The buttons swapped colours on the wall.

Fire Elemental's Text Box: Red next!

Kray's Text Box: Kay, got it!

Kray promptly hit the green button, which used to be the red button and lost another piece of floor. This reset the puzzle.

In'ferni and De'vini used the *Double Shrug Dual Animation*.

samuri's Text Box: …

samuri used the *Speechless Animation*.

Fire Elemental's Text Box: The red one! Red!

Kray's Text Box: I know, kay, Green, Red, Red, Yellow, Blue, Green. I'm on it.

After many more attempts, they were down to only four pieces of floor, though fortunately In'ferni and De'vini could share one. The All Seeing Eye Dog and Nine Circles of Hellcat were pressed up against samuri nervously.

Fire Elemental's Text Box: What is wrong with you? GREEN! RED! RED! YELLOW! BLUE! GREEN!

Kray's Text Box: It's not my fault, kay. Your button order is like so wrong!

In'ferni and De'vini used the *Confused Spank Dual Animation*.

samuri's Text Box: ???

samuri used the *OMMWTF Animation*.

Fire Elemental's Text Box: No it isn't! You keep hitting the wrong buttons!

Kray's Text Box: Nope, kay. Wrong order. End of discussion. Simple as that.

Fire Elemental's Text Box: Just do them one at a time. Hit GREEN!

In'ferni and De'vini used the *Possible Last Kiss Dual Animation*.

samuri's Text Box: !!!

samuri used the *Close Eyes Animation*. Kray let an arrow fly, and hit the green button. After what samuri decided could only be a miracle, Kray had accidentally hit red, red, yellow, and even the blue buttons all in the right order.

Fire Elemental's Text Box: Green! Hit GREEN and we are done!

Kray's Text Box: Green huh? Easy as pie, kay.

In'ferni and De'vini used the *Potential Last Kiss Dual Animation*.

samuri's Text Box: !!!!!

samuri used the *Massage Eyebrows Animation*.

Kray's Text Box: Any moment now, kay. I'll hit the green button and save us all. You'll see. Savior of the cycle and all that.

Fire Elemental's Text Box: No rush, we aren't on fire or anything here.

Kray's Text Box: The fire just makes it more dramatic, kay.

In'ferni and De'vini used the *Probable Last Kiss Dual Animation*.

Kray's Text Box: Enough with being dramatic you two, I am totally going to handle this green button thing, kay. Just watch.

samuri's Text Box: !!!!!!!

Kray's Text Box: Don't worry Sami-guy. I'll save you. One green button press coming up, kay.

samuri used the *Come on Already Animation*.

Kray's Text Box: Aiming isn't easy you know, you can't rush something like that, kay.

samuri's Text Box: !!!!!!!!!

Kray's Text Box: Yeah, I know, kay. I'm getting ready.

samuri used the *Toe-Tapping Animation*.

> Kray's Text Box: Don't rush me, kay. Buttons are a lot of pressure. Geeze Sami-guy, why are you always in such a hurry, I don't get it.

> samuri's Text Box: !!!!!!!!!!!

> Kray's Text Box: There you go again, rush, rush, rush. We still have like a third of our hit points left not yet burned in the fire, so just keep your Sami-pants on and I will shoot the green butt—

> samuri's Interruption Text Box: SHUTH HUP!

In'ferni and De'vini used the *Cover the Mouth Dual Animation*. The Fire Elemental turned to *Blush Shade #6*. Kray just stood there blinking with his mouth wide open. samuri picked his body length tongue up off the floor and continued his speech.

> samuri's Text Box: Allth hyou do ith talth, talth, talth! I can'th thandle ith anymorth! Ifth I didn'th makth a pledgth to never kilth againth I would hath cuth hyou in halth cthycle onth. So shuth hup! Shuth hup! SHUTH HUP!

Kray's eyes started to well up with tears, his heart now beat painfully in his stomach.

> Kray's Text Box: But... but... the flower...

> samuri's Text Box: Now do thomething uthful for a changth and hith the thucking greeth butthon!

samuri grabbed Kray by the scruff of his *Swim Briefs* and threw the avatar across the chasm. Kray finally hit the final green button after so much delay (with his face) and fell to the ground below. The puzzle keys shattered, and disappeared into a mass of pixels, forever removed from the game. The bridge descended as samuri started to roll up his tongue to put back in his mouth. In'ferni and De'vini stopped kissing for the first time that samuri had seen and turned their heads towards him. They shared a pair of lips, welded completely on one side. Until now that fact had been covered by their constant kissing. The sight of it fazed samuri so badly that he dropped his tongue and would need to start over.

> In'ferni and De'vini's Simultaneous Text Boxes: Oh my Maker thank you. I didn't think he would ever shut up. Yeah, I was thinking the exact same thing. I could hardly hear myself think over all his chatter. Neither could I. I couldn't get a word in edgewise! Me either! We should celebrate the silence! We should! How about we make out? YES!

◈ Chapter 38 ◈
ANDERS, DOUBLE DRAGONED

nders left the Coliseum with a *Smile Animation* on his newly helmeted face. The *Gladiator Helmet (s)* was not much of a helmet. It was a simple red bandana with some gray metal sections, that had quickly been changed to a green bandana with black metal sections. Anders had suspected that it would have been a full helmet like the gladiators he had fought. Maybe a full helmet was for the non (s) version, but the bandana was easy to see out of, so Anders didn't complain.

He was a bit upset that the Empusa had dropped the helmet and not the Armour, but he had seen that coming. At least the Empusa had fallen in battle with relative ease. Anders was immune to all of her seduction techniques, leaving her disappointed. Several sneak attack arrows to the compellingly attractive female torso with one donkey leg was all that it took to finish her off.

As Anders approached the Bakery Shoppe cautiously he heard more of the banging noises coming from Onn Forest. Given the distance covered thus far he had about three cycles before the Spiderboy broke into Onn. Still woefully lacking on mana reserves, (since all the gladiators had managed to cum on him and not in him) Anders was not looking forward to having the Spiderboy lurking around Onn as well as Xam and the other dragons. He had more than enough to worry about without another obsessive monster stalker he couldn't possibly defeat with only his *Elf Starting Bow*.

Anders also had a Draganders, but Anders hadn't seen Draganders do much of anything yet except bite on his ear affectionately and chirp. Draganders could probably fight since he was a dragon, even if he was the size of a winged cat.

Three cycles was going to be more than enough time, Anders hoped. After resting tonight he should only hopefully have an Armour battle and the secret battle left in the Coliseum. A full cycle for each battle should be more than enough. He just hoped that there wasn't some additional battles thrown in to mess with him.

Anders turned the last corner in the alley before the Bakery Shoppe and was met with an obscure sight. A wall of ice crystals had formed in front of the door to the secret entrance, while the other side of the alley was aflame. Hidden in the shadows, Anders questioned what it could possibly mean.

> NPC Illiandro's Text Box: What do you think that is all about?

Anders tried to do the *Shh Animation*, but was too late. Two long dragon necks looked down from their building perches.

> Gdoor, the Red Dragon of Fire's Text Box: *sniff* Well what do we have here?

> Reminrouf, the Blue Dragon of Ice's Text Box: Another jerk probably? No, no it's just NPC Illiandro.

> Gdoor, the Red Dragon of Fire's Text Box: Pity, we are not allowed to eat him, stupid rules.

> Reminrouf, the Blue Dragon of Ice's Text Box: I know, I would love to eat an NPC right about now. Eating makes the pain go away. Wait, Illiandro said what do 'you' think. Someone else is down there. Someone with *Stealth*! Perform another spot check!

> Gdoor, the Red Dragon of Fire's Text Box: There! I see him. A little half naked elf, not being all that stealthy beside that wall. He really should have hid in that scenic bush instead.

> Anders' Text Box: Flatbread.

Gdoor picked up Anders and brought him up to the building tops, placing him square in-between the blue and red dragon's feet. Their Latin theme songs were getting all muddled up and the subtitles were too confusing to read.

From up here Anders could see that both spire A and B were completely gone, only their little connecting bridges held up by nothing on one side remained. Anders was very concerned, some of his best friends were in those spires. Well, in spire B at least, Anders didn't really care about what happened to Kray.

> Reminrouf, the Blue Dragon of Ice's Text Box: Crap. It's an avatar.

> Gdoor, the Red Dragon of Fire's Text Box: I am so sick of jerk-ass avatars. Constantly interrupting me and calling me chubby! I am

> NOT fat! I am the skinniest of Breaker's dragons! You stupid colour-uncoordinated jerk, kay!

This Gdoor had met Kray, Anders noted.

> Reminrouf, the Blue Dragon of Ice's Text Box: You think you had it bad Gdoor, I got double-teamed by a two jerks making fun of my name. My name is super! If I ever see that man who can't stop saying lad or that guy who types in caps lock again I'll tear them both to pieces.

This Reminrouf had met both Palcath and Roodg, Anders noted. He also had to agree with his friends and not the dragon, Reminrouf was a terrible name.

> Gdoor, the Red Dragon of Fire's Text Box: Neat. I just checked Reminrouf. It says here that the avatar Anders is on our list of special things to acquire.

> Reminrouf, the Blue Dragon of Ice's Text Box: Darn! We can't eat him either.

> Gdoor, the Red Dragon of Fire's Text Box: No, but he is listed under 'Bring to Breaker, dead or alive' and not under 'Bring to Breaker, alive and unspoiled.' So we can kill him and spoil him as much as we want before bringing him to Breaker.

> Reminrouf, the Blue Dragon of Ice's Text Box: Perfect! That dude is just what I need to make me feel better. A little hole to use up. Look at him, he is pretty much begging for it already, bare ass exposed like some kind of elf hussy.

> Gdoor, the Red Dragon of Fire's Text Box: Don't forget, we can respawn and be back here in a flash. He will be stuck up here on the rooftop thanks to the invisible walls surrounding it. We can fuck our worries away for some time before bringing him to Breaker.

This wasn't what Anders needed. Two new crazy dragons to terrorize him. He wanted to get taken to Breaker, not get stuck up in the roof and used as a slave.

> Anders' Text Box: Can you just bring me to Breaker right now instead? I need to talk to him.

> Reminrouf, the Blue Dragon of Ice's Text Box: Nope Dude, we are pretty set in the fact that we are going to sex up your dead corpse for awhile.

Anders assessed the blue and red dragons. They were not even half as large as Xam in size. Where it really counted they were not even as big around as Xam combined. Anders had an awful plan, but it was still a plan.

> Anders' Text Box: Hmmm, tell you what. Let's make a bet. I bet that I can handle both of you at the same time without being killed. If I win, you come back here after you respawn and take me to Breaker. If I lose, well you can sex up my corpse as long as you want with my consent. I'll even die with a sexy look on my face.

> Gdoor, the Red Dragon of Fire's Text Box: I don't know…

> Anders' Text Box: I will also sign a letter that says Reminrouf is the best name ever derived in all of fiction and that Gdoor is super skinny!

> Reminrouf, the Blue Dragon of Ice's Text Box: Deal!

> Gdoor, the Red Dragon of Fire's Text Box: Are you sure that is a good idea?

> Reminrouf, the Blue Dragon of Ice's Text Box: Of course it is Guy, it's not like he has a magical butt. Let's split this Dude apart.

Anders preparing himself and motioned for Reminrouf, the Blue Dragon of Incredibly Bad Name, to lie down. Anders *Double Jumped* up and began to stroke the dragon's member to full erectness. After a few rounds of good strokes, with licks thrown in for encouragement, the blue dragon was hard and dripping icy ejaculate with anticipation.

Anders positioned himself at the head of the beast and started to rub it against his entrance. He made a good show of it and pretended that it would never fit. He winced and squirmed with pretend discomfort.

Reminrouf used a *Smirk Animation* in triumph and grabbed the elf by the hips with a hard spank. The dragon spank activated *Stretch More* and *Stretch More More* just as it had with Xam. With a great pull and a wholehearted chuckle the dragon impaled Anders in one strong thrust. Anders looked up and returned the *Smirk Animation*, with a round to concentrate on the pleasure he let forth a flurry of magical tingles.

> Reminrouf, the Blue Dragon of Ice's Text Box: Oh my Breaker!

> Gdoor, the Red Dragon of Fire's Text Box: What? How did it do that?

Anders looked back at Gdoor, the Red Dragon of Equally Really Bad Name, smiled, and wiggled his already impaled ass seductively. Gdoor took the bait, stepped forward, placed red dragon hands on top of the blue ones, and thrust its member into the hole already occupied by the blue one. This earned a moan from all participants of the encounter and a chirp from Draganders who watched with vacant eyes.

> Gdoor, the Red Dragon of Fire's Text Box: The tingles… I can feel them all the way up in my vajayjay!

Anders looked back with interest. This Gdoor indeed had an additional set of genitals, and even sort-of-there dragon breasts. Well, good for her… him… uh…

> Reminrouf, the Blue Dragon of Ice's Text Box: This dude is magic! He does have a magic butt. That sly little thing.

The combined thrusts of two different patterns and temperatures accelerated Anders much faster than he had thought possible. The avatar came after a double thrust hit him hard in the right spot, which unleashed a flurry of tingles. The dragons both resisted, as they were not keen on ending this encounter as quickly as the avatar. They continued their poundable efforts even as Anders finished his shots onto the blue dragon's stomach.

Anders still felt the pleasure of both dragon's efforts, but had gone soft after his orgasm. As the rounds went by it was become uncomfortable and he started to tighten up. Despite the pleasure, he wasn't going to get erect again and he wanted these dragons to finish up. During the next deep double thrust Anders clenched down hard. The two dragon dicks pressed firmly against each other and the dragons both screamed out with sudden stimulation.

Draganders chirped happily as the two bigger dragons thrust hard into his avatar mommy. The Green Quest Fairy was happy to have been forgotten about right now. The red and blue dragon cum combined in Anders and he felt it absorb, but strangely not into his magic point reserve. Both dragons finished and *Splinged*, as dragons did after being defeated, into balls of coloured light. Anders fell to the ground and quizzically looked over at the excited chirp storm next to him.

Draganders was going wild with an intensity that Anders had never seen in the normally docile little matte gray dragon. Draganders jumped into the air and tackled the ball of red light to the ground, with just a few savage bites the ball that was Gdoor was devoured. The matte scales of Draganders' head changed into a fiery red. The dragon switched his attention to the ball of freaked out blue light. Reminrouf tried to flee, but Draganders took swiftly to the air and grabbed the blue dragon after it ran into an invisible wall. Draganders swallowed the light in one bite, and the scales near his hind quarters switched to a brilliant blue.

Anders noticed that his own main colour on his Armour had changed. No longer default green, it had started a gradient effect. Now he had red changing to green then to blue accents. His status page even now listed his selected colour as ????.

Anders stared in shock at his dragon as it came back to cuddle, Draganders had grown a little after his meal. The dragon chirped happily and cuddled with his master, then painfully bit the elf's ear, which also caused fire damage, ice damage, and almost a swear word. According to the status page, Draganders had taken the magic reserves from the shooting dragons and could now do magic ice or fire attacks.

Creature Name: Gdoor, the Red Dragon of Fire
Class: Breaker Dragon
Level: 98
Special Attacks: Breaker's Special Fire, Breaker's Special Flame, Breaker's Special Burn, Switch Hitter
Drops: Nothing! Suck it bitches!
First Player Encounter Notes: Chirp! – Draganders

Creature Name: Reminrouf, the Blue Dragon of Ice
Class: Breaker Dragon
Level: 98
Special Attacks: Breaker's Special Ice, Breaker's Special Freeze, Breaker's Special Cold, Wonder Kisses
Drops: Nothing! Bite me!
First Player Encounter Notes: Chirp! – Draganders

Anders looked over the Insta-Wiki entries that showed up and Draganders could fill out. This meant that Gdoor and Reminrouf had been defeated. Not just defeated to return to Breaker, this meant they were defeated defeated. They couldn't return to Breaker to respawn and Breaker could no longer summon them to protect himself. Anders felt a *Smile Animation* come on. His Draganders in the hole could permanently get rid of Breaker's Dragons in the hole. Anders ran over and playfully tackled Draganders to the ground and play wrestled. This made the not-as-little anymore dragon happy.

Without a dragon army, Breaker was just an overpowered avatar-turned-monster. Anders had stumbled upon a great plan, now all he needed to do was get off this impossible-to-get-off of roof!

Chapter 39
THE BREAK ROOM

The combination lock fell to the cold cloud floor. Finally, after giving up on being sneaky about it and just trying 6,968 other combinations first the four digit combination lock was defeated. Breaker kicked the foul thing for good measure and stubbed his toe.

> Breaker's Text Box: Of fucking course!

The door to the cloud was set to *Slowly Swing Open*, but Breaker would have nothing of it. He pushed the fuck out of that door and barged inside the secret room, he had no patience for dramatic reveals. The room held firm and was extra dramatic as it revealed itself, the shit.

The background music stopped completely, which was unsettling. Even the most unimportant areas in the world had at least a drumbeat or a penny whistle solo to set the mood, but this area had nothing. Having absolutely no mood setting music set the mood better than Breaker would have thought— to creepy. The walls were hazy, like they were not really there. When Breaker went to touch them he found they were hidden from even his advanced game senses. They didn't match the world's in-game physics.

A custom item maker's dream workshop of tools and gadgets took up every conceivable surface. There were things Breaker had never even thought of using to alter items, tables of them. There were stacks and stacks of crafting materials littering the floor, and boxes of fragments of code to pound into those items. Cans of customization options Breaker had never dreamed of, red dyes, yellow enamel, and team changing blue markers. There was even a hammer. Not a *Hammer*, but a real actual hammer.

Breaker felt his perky breasts. This was perfect. He could finally hammer out the *Boobplate Armour* that he had pilfered from that idiot boss off-screen and make its amazing boss stats match his masculine physic. Before getting his hammering on, a spray-can near the wavering wall caught Breaker's attention. A small patch of wall appeared as if it hadn't been fully painted into another reality. Breaker picked up the can to make sure his eyes didn't deceive him, was this simple can something that could solve one of the most important problems he faced?

> Breaker's Reading Text Box: *Deflective Meat Paint*. Use to keep Asshat Bastards from finding me.

Breaker tested the spray on a scrap of plaid fabric. The swatch slipped into another reality, just like the walls. This item was perfect. This can could stop all those Asshat Bastards from finding him. What he had tried to create for cycles had fallen into his hands. Whoever owned this room sure knew their stuff, it was inspiring.

> Breaker's Text Box: This *Deflective Meat Paint* is the best find in the history of finding shit! I can't wait to—

Breaker interrupted himself when he saw the ultimate display that was the back of the room. A sheet was covering something in a locked cage, but Breaker instinctively knew that whatever it was that it was worth a thousand cans of *Deflective Meat Paint*. He knew this only because it had a security system. A security system in an impossibly locked, impossible to get to, impossible to detect room. Yes, whatever was in there was good. He approached the control panel and activated it.

> Computer Terminal: What is your name?

The blinking underscore demanded an answer. Breaker took a guess.

> Entry: Breaker?

> Computer Terminal: Incorrect. What is your name?

Breaker used a *Crack Neck Animation*. He had a secret base to hide and a code to crack. It was going to be a long night, but it was going to be worth it.

◈ Chapter 40 ◈
UNNECESSARY
QUESTING F

Gliint's Text Box: *Joy* I'm so excited to see you again Yallundy, but why can't I stand up anymore?

Yallundy's Text Box: I don't know, I'm too scared that if I try to help you up, I might accidently possess you.

Mr. Max attempted to help Gliint up. It was a struggle but there was just enough strength to complete the task.

Mr. Max's Text Box: You are over your weight limit again. The only explanation is that you have picked up an item. Since Yallundy defeated the Wind Elemental it only makes sense that she picked it up. Yallundy, can you see your inventory?

Yallundy's Text Box: Yes, I can but it is all frayed and strange, I don't have a weight limit anymore. The only thing in here is a *Heart of Wind*. It is a third accessory slot item.

Mr. Max's Text Box: Can you equip it?

Yallundy equipped *The Heart of Wind*. It didn't show anywhere on her floating visage, but it made her immune to all earth attacks, which she thought was great because after possessing the Wind Elemental she was weak to them. Glint was no longer overweight and could move at full speed.

Mr. Max's Text Box: Interesting. Do you think we could try an experiment?

Yallundy's Text Box: I guess, what?

Hippolyta's Text Box: Wait a round, what is going on here? When did Mr. Man become so enlightened?

Mr. Max's Text Box: My name is Mr. Max, Hippolyta.

Hippolyta's Text Box: What? Why do you know my name now suddenly? Why am I not the Anders lady anymore?

Mr. Max's Text Box: It's strange, I spent so long trying to be the best, to win, to reach the top. It was all that I really worried about. Now that I am level ✪ ✪, my mind is so clear, so free. I feel so liberated from concentrating on the game, but I don't know why.

Glint's Text Box: So, now that you are level ✪ ✪ you have a clear and focused mind and no longer think that Hippolyta is Anders?

Mr. Max's Text Box: Of course not. Hippolyta is the healer type in Jorthan's party. She was originally a Mendicator with absolutely no cleavage to speak of. I do need to ask though, who is Anders?

Glint's Text Box: Well, *Sigh* some progress is better than nothing I guess. Level ✪ ✪ got you a prize right? What is it?

Mr. Max's Text Box: Oh I almost forgot about that. I laughed out loud when I found out what it was. I didn't need that, so I had them send it to you instead Glint, I hope that is okay.

Glint's Text Box: You didn't need it? *Confused* What was it?

Mr. Max's Text Box: Little Bro, where is the fun in that? You will have to wait and see! ;)

Glint was busy pouting. He didn't use a real *Pout Animation* because he would cause ripples of sexual excitement to all around him, but he was still pouting. He wanted to know now, not later.

Mr. Max's Text Box: Oh, before I forget. I made a bet with my real world friends. We wanted to see who could design something better.

I thought that I could do a really good job at design, which is why I forced them to take the bet in the first place. But it turns out, all of mine look like crap. I loved the graphics on your fan websites, I was wondering if you could help me out.

Gliint's Text Box: *Nod* Sure, of course I will help you, you're Mr. Max remember?! What do you need?

Mr. Max's Text Box: I made the bet that I could do a better job at the cover art for an album.

Gliint's Text Box: A pretend cover art challenge, huh? *Thinking* Sure, I do those all the time with my friends. What album?

Mr. Max's Text Box: *Caution Step's* new album of course.

Gliint's Text Box: But their new unnamed album is on hold until guitarist / tech guru *Ashler Waldenmyer* gets out of rehab!

Mr. Max's Text Box: He will get out soon I hope, so the album will be allowed to drop, I just know it.

Gliint's Text Box: I already have a bunch of pretend album covers for them, what is the name of the album you guys are making? *Smile* I'll put it on some of them for you.

Mr. Max's Text Box: We decided on *Mind the Gap.*

Gliint's Text Box: That is an awesome name, *Caution Step* would so pick something like that!

Mr. Max's Text Box: I know! I'm pretty proud of the name, I thought it up myself.

Gliint's Text Box: I love it! *Grin* I already have the perfect font picked out!

Yallundy's Text Box: I don't want to be a bother, but can we maybe try out Mr. Max's plan and stop talking about *Caution Step* for now?

Gliint's Text Box: Oh yeah! *Sheepish grin* Sorry Yallundy.

Hippolyta's Text Box: Boy bands. Who cares? Let's help the floating goddess.

Mr. Max's Text Box: Alright, so what just happened is that Gliint became overweight because Yallundy's *Backpack* is inside his. Once she equipped the *Heart of Wind* it no longer was against his carrying capacity. What I suggest we try is to place some items in Yallundy's *Backpack* and see if she can use them. That does mean we will have to take Yallundy out though.

Yallundy's Text Box: I'm alright with that, I'm already floating around naked as it is. Everyone has seen my nipples.

Hippolyta's Text Box: Nipples… Gha-lu-lugga-ah…

Gliint opened his *Backpack* and with Mr. Max's help they had dragged Yallundy out. On the lifeless avatar's chest was a glowing yellow gem shaped like a heart. A short of breath Constantly-Colour-Changing Quest Fairy came out of Gliint's *Backpack*, frazzled.

Hippolyta's Text Box: Whoa, whoa. Not cool. Are you telling me that the entire time we have been travelling together you had the corpse of a dead girl in your *Backpack*? You absolute creep! That is such a typi—

Yallundy's Interruption Text Box: It's not like that! Okay, it was a bit like that. It was really creepy, but I was there watching him, even if he didn't know it. It was a very sweet/creepy gesture. Besides, it wasn't my body, it was just my character model.

Hippolyta would have nothing more to do with the conversation, but she did leer quite a bit at both of Yallundy's naked forms when she thought no one was watching.

Mr. Max's Text Box: Okay, let's try this idea out.

Mr. Max stuffed Yallundy's *Backpack* full of her own equipment and goods. Yallundy tried a *Health Potion* first. The lifeless body showed the numbers that symbolized regained health, but otherwise was unchanged. Yallundy tried to equip her boring Armour set and the lifeless avatar became dressed. Mr. Max lifted up the avatar which earned a few quizzical looks.

Mr. Max's Text Box: Just as I thought. Things she has equipped don't weigh anything. You never should have undressed her Gliint. Alright, I have one more idea, but it might be risky. I want to try something else first though. Ghost Yallundy, you can possess things now right? Do you think you can possess Dead Yallundy?

Yallundy's Text Box: I can try.

Despite her best efforts, Ghost Yallundy could not possess Dead Yallundy.

Mr. Max's Text Box: Okay, can I try one more thing? I am 99% sure it will work.

Yallundy's Text Box: Well, nobody knows more about this game than you Max, if you think it will work, please try.

Mr. Max's Text Box: Okay, here goes nothing then fellow adventurette!

Mr. Max took a swing at Yallundy's corpse and deftly used his PVP brokenness to sever her *Backpack* from her model. This earned a worried look from Gliint. Mr. Max took Yallundy's Corpse and stuck it into Yallundy's *Backpack*. Mr. Max lifted up the *Backpack*, it didn't seem to weigh much of anything. Max handed the *Backpack* to Gliint.

Mr. Max's Text Box: You keep her safe, Little Bro.

Gliint's Text Box: Don't worry, I will never let her *Backpack* go!

Yallundy's Text Box: I'll make sure of it.

Mr. Max's Text Box: I didn't think *Backpacks* would weigh anything, I was right. Can you see yourself in your *Backpack* Yallundy?

Yallundy's Text Box: Yes! There I am... I am... Special Monster Armour?

Mr. Max's Text Box: That is not what I suspected, can you equip yourself?

After a few frayed menus Yallundy equipped herself. Her ghost form shifted until it looked like her normal form. While she did move awkwardly like a badly controlled puppet, she could move herself again.

Gliint's Text Box: *Pray* It's a miracle!

Mr. Max's Text Box: No, it's just very lucky that Yallundy possessed the one monster that can possess avatars, the coding must just place possessed avatars in the Monster Armour slot for ease of programming. If she unequips herself she will be the Wind Elemental again and could probably equip someone else. That is just too cool.

E. E. Lynn's Text Box: S0 n34t! ^-^ | d|dn't kn0\/\/ th4t /\/\0nst3r p0ss3ss|0n \/\/4s 3v3n p0ss|bl3. | gu3ss teh C0d3>< p0s|0n th4t br0k3 teh \/\/0rld \/\/4sn't pr0p3rly c0d3d. N00bzors. But \/\/0\/\/z3rs!

Hippolyta's Text Box: Dear Maker, leet.

Gliint's Text Box: *Blink* You scared the crap out of me. Where did you come from?

E. E. Lynn's Text Box: Sp|r3 C. ^-~ Y0u r s|tt|ng @ teh c0nn3ct0r sp0t s|lly. kekeke.

Hippolyta's Text Box: Perfect, we are at the connector, but since the Airship was destroyed we can't get out of here. Not telling me about the airship crash just to control me, bah.

Yallundy's Text Box: They didn't tell you about the Airship being destroyed Hippolyta?

Hippolyta's Text Box: Of course they didn't. But I have my own ways of finding out. Typical men needing to control their women. Having me follow them all this time, just letting my goddess anger boil over.

Mr. Max's Text Box: If you are at the connector little... Catgirl? E. E. Lynn, Catgirl isn't a race, did you use a code to get that. Well, no matter, does that mean Zal Finn III, Fournimer, and ... oh hey look there they are with Lissa!

Lissa's Text Box: LISSA? #HearingInfection. Did you just use my name Mr. Max?

Gliint's Text Box: He did! *Nod* It's crazy! Mr. Max actually had character growth! He remembered me earlier! Why are you riding Fournimer like a horse?

Lissa's Text Box: Broken leg. Wow, I'm shocked. So I guess Caela is out for him remembering you, and Anders is out for him remembering me. The Mr. Max bet narrows huh?

Mr. Max's Text Box: Who are Anders and Caela?

Gliint's Text Box: *Nose tap* My theory is that he needs to see them to recognize them.

Lissa's Text Box: I better make sure he sees samuri last then.

Mr. Max's Text Box: Who?

E. E. Lynn's Text Box: | b3t th3y 4r3 4ll teh h0tn3ss! | d0n't c4r3 th0ugh. R|ght n0\/\/ | \/\/4nt gh0st b|tch!

Zal Finn III's Text Box: Ghost bitch? What is that?

Fournimer's Text Box: no way! look. ghost bitch is Lundy!

Yallundy's Text Box: That sweater is absolutely dreadful Fourni.

Zal Finn III's Text Box: Yallundy?! Sweet, no way.

Yallundy's Text Box: Do you want me to look at your broken leg Lissa?

Lissa's Text Box: No, uh that's okay. My leg is fine. I'm more curious about how you are alive!

Yallundy's Text Box: I'm not alive. See, first I was a ghost and I stopped lightning from hitting Gliint, then I accidently possessed a little monster to protect Gliint from getting hit. I possessed more monsters to protect Gliint from fishing. Next, to save Gliint from getting sludged I possessed a boss. After the Elemental possessed Max to split Gliint I attacked the Elemental and possessed it. Now I am a monster, but have myself equipped and am using my corpse like a puppet.

Zal Finn III, Fournimer, and Lissa's Simultaneous Text Box: What?

E. E. Lynn's Text Box: | s0 g3t |t. N0\/\/ gh0st, plz t0 p0ss3ss teh c3nt4ur 4nd fuck m3 w|th h|m! ^-^ g0! H3 |s s0 hung!

E. E. Lynn jumped towards Yallundy, but was stopped when Hippolyta stepped in the way and preformed the *Stop Animation*. The sudden movement and animation caused her ample bosom to being rotating.

Hippolyta's Text Box: Not on your life. You will not lay a finger on that beautiful creature.

E. E. Lynn's Text Box: \/\/0\/\/.

Zal Finn III's Text Box: They... are... beautiful... and... hypnotic.

Fournimer's Text Box: what are?

Lissa used the *Shrug Animation*, while Mr. Max, Gliint, Zal Finn, and E. E. Lynn could do nothing but stare at Hippolyta's rotating bosom and drool. This, as expected, did not impress Hippolyta.

Mr. Max, Gliint, Zal Finn III, and E. E. Lynn's Simultaneous Text Boxes: Gha-lu-lugga-ah...?

Hippolyta's Text Box: Stop ogling my breasts!

Yallundy's Text Box: They can't. Haven't you ever read the description under your *Heaving Bosom* sex ability? I never wanted to *Empathy* reveal someone's ability, but you have been pissing me off with this lady. Avatars and monsters that enjoy breasts can be put under the Spellbound Status Effect if they fail an opposed Wisdom Check against you. Since you are a Sage, your Wisdom is through the roof so they always lose. Lissa and I are immune because we like boys, and Fourni is more of an ass man. ^_~

Fournimer changed to *Blush Shade #2*.

Hippolyta's Text Box: Oh. I just assumed they were being male chauvinist pigs. Men always are.

Lissa's Text Box: Well it was all you, so just calm your tits lady.

That earned Lissa a Laser Guided Bunny Eye Missile Death Glare from Hippolyta.

Hippolyta's Text Box: I beg your pardon?

Fournimer's Text Box: remember when we talked about starting off on the wrong foot Lis?

E. E. Lynn's Text Box: \/\/4|t! Gh0st h4s 3/\/*p4thy*? NFW! ^-^ | \/\/4nt3d 2 try th4t 0ut! S\/\/33t! |'/\/\ g0ing t0 c0/\/\3 f|ng3r y0u, y0u us3 3/\/*p4thy* 0n /\/\3 s0 | c4n f33ls |t!

Yallundy's Text Box: How did you break out of being Spellbound?

E. E. Lynn's Text Box: Duh. |'/\/\ 4 /\/\yst|c. | h34rd y0u us3 3/\/*p4thy* s0 | st0pp3d. 3/\/*p4thy*. |t's teh h0tn3ss.

Yallundy's Text Box: Mystics can do that?

Mr. Max's Text Box: A Mystic? No, they can't do that. Besides, nobody in their right mind would ever pick that class. Since they do a bit of everything, they excel at nothing!

Yallundy's Text Box: Now, how did you break out of being Spellbound?

Mr. Max's Text Box: Hippolyta's tits listened to Lissa and calmed themselves down.

Hippolyta's Text Box: What?!

Zal Finn III's Text Box: Don't listen to them. I think your tits are

> sweet! You need to own them!

Hippolyta then did something she never thought she would ever do. Hippolyta turned to *Blush Shade #1*.

> Hippolyta's Text Box: Pardon? Own them?

> Zal Finn III's Text Box: Of course! Look at what you just did. You put four avatars, one of which is the strongest in the entire game, completely out of commission just by jiggling! That is wicked sweet awesome.

> Gliint's Text Box: She isn't going to slap me again then? *Worried look* Please don't let her hit me again.

> Mr. Max's Text Box: Please do let her hit me again!

> Yallundy's Text Box: Gliint! Wait! We got distracted earlier, I need you to come here right now! It's important!

> Gliint's Text Box: *Confused* Yes, sure thing. What is it Yallundy?

> Yallundy's Text Box: This!

Yallundy grabbed Gliint in her arms and pulled him to her lips, kissing him passionately. She used *Empathy* and both felt each other's touches and emotions. It took Gliint so off guard that he accidentally used a **SHOCK ANIMATION**. This caused both avatars to collapse to the ground screaming with an intense orgasm due to how sexy Gliint's animations were. Every single frame would make an avatar shudder with excitement, the longer the animation, the stronger the inevitable orgasm.

> E. E. Lynn's Text Box: N0 \/\/4y! H3 h4s teh *4n|/\/\4t|0n(s)*? | th0ught h3 h4d *M4x3d c0ck*!

> Mr. Max's Text Box: No, that's me.

> E. E. Lynn's Text Box: | ♥ y0u guys! |*nst4-0rgy* t|/\/\3!

> Zal Finn III's Text Box: No, that's me.

> E. E. Lynn's Text Box: Duh! Th4t's \/\/hy y0u l00k l|k3 4n NPC! *_* |'/\/\ st00pid. I th0ught y0u \/\/4s just 4 sm4rt NPC!

> Zal Finn III's Text Box: I look like NPCs? I didn't know that I looked like them too, this is awful. Why did no one ever tell me that? I thought they just really liked helping me. That explains everything. No wonder

> people keep thinking I am an NPC!

> Hippolyta's Text Box: You look nothing like one. You are an exquisite goddess of a creature! I would never mistake you for a simple NPC.

Zal Finn changed to *Blush Shade #2*.

Fournimer considered warning Hippolyta not to promise too much since Zal Finn was sneaky with her NPC friends, but he hadn't quite thought up a good nickname for her yet that wouldn't end in him getting slapped. He instead decided to bring up a topic that had been bugging him since he first came into the area.

> Fournimer's Text Box: isn't anyone else curious about the giant racetrack over there? I sure am.

> Hippolyta's Text Box: I hate racing games, they promote the male dominated vid—

> Lissa's Interruption Text Box: #3.2.1.go!

> Mr. Max's Text Box: An unnecessary racing quest I gather, am I right Orange Quest Fairy?

> Orange Quest Fairy's Text Box: Sure, whatever. I don't care anymore.

~ ~ ~

After the first of seven races everyone understood why Hippolyta hated racing games so much. It was because she was terrible at them, and spent most of the time accidently racing in reverse. She was also a hazard, not because of racing backwards, but because of her *Hypnotic Bosom*. As soon as her Giant Racing Chicken started to move, the animation caused her breasts to rotate, which made Gliint, Mr. Max, E. E. Lynn, and Zal Finn equally horrible racers. It was interesting to come to a section of racetrack with a backwards running racer and four kamikaze drooling avatars running every which way after becoming *Spellbound*. It was a much better attack than you could find in those little *Rotating Race Cubes*.

Even with having much more experience riding a mount than the other two competitors that could even hope to finish, Lissa had a distinct advantage over each of them. She was not still learning to control the corpse puppet of herself, and she wasn't a horse who was forced to try and ride the Giant Racing Chicken that was smaller than a horse.

> Fournimer's Text Box: it's only circuit two and she's already bragging.

> Yallundy's Text Box: I never knew Lissa was so competitive. She does

have every right to brag though, she is beating the pants off everyone. It just makes me want to try and beat her on the principal of the thing.

Fournimer's Text Box: this isn't fair, Sparkle. we are the only two that could hope to beat her, but I can't ride that stupid bird. this game is not built for centaurs! so why did they include them at all as a choice? it is starting to piss me off.

Yallundy's Text Box: I know what you mean, Fourni. I can't even hope to compete in this puppet body.

Fournimer's Text Box: didn't you say that you possessed a bunch of little monsters? why don't you just possess your mount instead of riding it?

Yallundy's Text Box: If your mount is smaller than you, why don't you just put it on your back instead?

Fournimer and Yallundy both used the *Grin Animation*. After losing four races in a row Lissa did not use any of the friendly animations in return. The score was tied, Yallundy, Lissa, and Fournimer all had 2 gold place, 2 silver place, and 2 bronze place ribbons. Gliint had one participation place ribbon after running the track blindfolded. Everyone else was devoid of ribbons.

Lissa's Text Box: That is it! You all are going down this time or my name isn't Lissandra Collinswood!

Mr. Max's Text Box: Lissandra Collinswood, wait... Is that your real name?

Lissa's Text Box: No Meatbone, that's my avatar's name.

Mr. Max's Text Box: Never mind then. My mistake.

NPC Plainchant's Text Box: Ready, set, go!

The race was on and Lissa was determined to win. She had a plan, by grabbing a *Spellbound* Mr. Max and keeping him riding in front of her she stuck behind Fournimer and Yallundy in a solid fourth place. She picked up every *Rotating Race Cube* that she could find, and shot off every power-up once the power-up rotate animation stopped. Finally on lap three she found what she wanted, the rare *Rotating Race Cube* power up. Mr. Max was kicked to the side (and into a lake). Lissa used all of her pent up boost power to catch up. She used her hard worked for power-up, a *Blue Tortle Shell*, at the last moment and it exploded on Yallundy and Fournimer who were tied for first. Lissa ran past the carnage and scooped first place, laughing diabolically as she did so.

NPC Plainchant's Text Box: Congratulations little rays! Here is your first reward! You may now progress to the next area!

The gate out of the area was unlocked and Placicant stopped blocking the way.

NPC Plainchant's Text Box: Here is your second reward! An Accessory for 'insert avatar name'! May the winner with the most Race Points step forward!

Lissa stepped forward with a smug look on her face.

Gliint's Text Box: *Confused* I don't understand why you all tried so hard to win, the Sexcessory things are awful.

Yallundy's Text Box: I forgot all about that.

Lissa's Text Box: They are awful?

Gliint's Text Box: Mine is annoying and it doesn't come off!

Zal Finn III's Text Box: They don't come off?! Crap, it doesn't!

Lissa's Text Box: #CtrlAltDel!

NPC Plainchant's Text Box: #It is a set of *Dragon Nipple Piercings*! Enjoy your Sexcessory!#

Taking out a set of *Dragon Nipple Piercings* from his invisible supply NPC Placicant presented the reward to Lissa.

With a blur of animation the half-elf's bodice had been pulled down and the piercings were forcibly equipped onto her avatar. Hippolyta ogled Lissa's breasts the entire time, Zal Finn only peeked.

NPC Plainchant's Text Box: Your third reward is… *pause for dramatic effect*

NPC Placicant pulled down his pants and revealed himself.

NPC Plainchant's Continued Text Box: My Lightly Legendary Longarm!

E. E. Lynn's Text Box: Sh0tgun!

NPC Plainchant's Text Box: Crap no! Not you again! Leave me alone, you promised!

Lissa's Text Box: These are pretty cool.

Gliint's Text Box: Hey, no fair! *Pout* Mine sucked.

Lissa's Text Box: I think I want a set for real, can someone help me take a close up screenshot?

Fournimer's Text Box: you want real nipple dragons, seriously?

Lissa's Text Box: No, to put in my ears silly.

Fournimer's Text Box: oh, well then sure.

A session of Fournimer taking close up pictures of Lissa's breasts occurred. It was something no one had ever anticipated happening. Hippolyta stood and watched from afar, drooling as if effected by her own *Rotating Bosom*.

Fournimer's Text Box: those are pretty cool, I sort of want one now.

Lissa's Text Box: I'll probably make a few spares while trying to get them to match, I'll put one on hold for you Fourn.

Fournimer's Text Box: really? thanks Lis! I don't actually have piercings though.

Lissa's Text Box: I can make one into something else.

♦ Chapter 41 ♦
ANDERS, DRAGON HUNTER

Anders' Text Box: Oh yeah, Htaclap. Do me.

Anders held back a *Yawn Animation*. He could tell by the thrusts intensity that the yellow dragon was almost finished. The Latin theme song wasn't even through the second verse yet.

Htaclap, the Yellow Dragon of Wind's Text Box: You like that huh? Don't you! Fill up that little elfbutt good.

Anders' Text Box: Yeah, it feels so good. Don't stop.

Htaclap, the Yellow Dragon of Wind's Text Box: Here it is boy! Urgh!

Anders was pushed forward on the chimney he was bent over. Htaclap was coming and Anders hadn't even gotten hard yet. Draganders licked his lips and tackled down the ball of yellow light almost faster than the dragon had finished up. Draganders gained a few weight units, yellow front legs, and lightning attacks, while Anders gained some yellow to his main colour, even his map marker arrow was changed.

Anders' Text Box: Some endless tormenter he turned out to be. That entire encounter only lasted 12 rounds. More like Htaclap, the quick shooter.

Creature Name: Htaclap, the Yellow Dragon of Wind
Class: Breaker Dragon
Level: 98
Special Attacks: Breaker's Special Bolt, Breaker's Special Wind, Breaker's Special Tornado, Vibrato Penis
Drops: Jack All!
First Player Encounter Notes: Chirp! – Draganders

Anders scratched Draganders' chin affectionately and got a triple blast of elemental ear pain in return. At least Draganders wasn't biting as hard anymore. That was a good thing with his much larger mouth.

Anders' Text Box: That's strange Draganders, I don't remember Htaclap having a *Vibrato Penis*. He also has a bad name doesn't he?

Draganders chirped happily in agreement.

Anders' Text Box: That makes three with really bad names. Reminrouf the blue, Gdoor the red, and Htaclap the yellow.

Anders read over his Text Box after he wrote it.

Anders' Text Box: Wait a round. There is Xam the orange and Gliint said the purple one was named Assil.

Draganders chirped happily in indifference.

Anders' Text Box: Breaker, you and your opposite party nonsense again! That would mean that the green one is going to be named —

Sredna, the Green Dragon of Earth's Interruption Text Box: Sredna. At least that sounds cool, thanks Anders for not being named Gabehcoud or Hcnumssa.

Anders' Text Box: No problem. Hmm, not that impressed with your song though.

Sredna, the Green Dragon of Earth's Text Box: I don't like it either, 'He is a lucky little b*tch that never should have beat me, Killing The Plague of Shadow in a lame-@$$ staring contest. Probably spreading his legs for any monster that wants to f*ck him, he is an unimportant little gay slut.' But you know, with swearing. It doesn't make any sense, follow musical timing or even rhyme.

Anders' Text Box: That is Breaker being an jerk. He is making fun of me.

Sredna, the Green Dragon of Earth's Text Box: Oh it's about you and not me! That makes me feel better. I was feeling really bad about myself.

Anders' Text Box: Glad I could make you feel better...

Sredna, the Green Dragon of Earth's Text Box: Perfect! I was all self conscious, but you are the little gay slut and not me! I feel so great that I think we should fool around.

Anders' Text Box: What? But that's weird, isn't it? You are based off of me.

Sredna, the Green Dragon of Earth's Text Box: Crud! So you are a total gay bottom with a tingly stretchy magical butt as well?

Anders' Text Box: No, I'm a gay versatile bottom with a tingly stretchy magical butt! Why does that matter?

Sredna, the Green Dragon of Earth's Text Box: Really? Perfect! Wait here, I'll be right back.

Anders waved as Sredna flew away. He was going to wait for the dragon to get back, mostly because he was stuck on the roof and couldn't go anywhere else. Anders had been stuck up on the roof for nearly two entire cycles now. That silly Spiderboy would break through Onn Forest sometime next cycle, and Anders still had no real way to fight him when he showed up. It was nearly nightfall by the time Sredna returned. The Dragon landed while Anders thought he was still long off in the distance. Sredna was now about the size of the average avatar.

Sredna, the Green Dragon of Earth's Text Box: Sorry, it took me longer than I thought it would to find the Fire Elemental.

Anders' Text Box: Look at you. You got all cute and tiny.

Sredna turned to *Blush Shade #D*.

Sredna, the Green Dragon of Earth's Text Box: Yeah, now this will work better.

Sredna bent over and exposed his slightly bigger than average dragon butt while he looked back at Anders with a desperate need.

Anders' Text Box: That is really... different. Hey, I know, can we maybe go somewhere a little more romantic? This roof is a little bit drab. I know of a really nice spot by the port in area, it would be really pretty at sunset.

Anders was off the roof! Sredna had unknowingly freed him. They flew to the romantic lake spot. It was still near a cloud of sickly black smoke, but Anders didn't point that out. Sredna got into the sexiest pose that he could muster.

Anders had become skilled in monster trickery, it was no wonder he didn't need to use the *Gladiator Boots (s)* for their Intelligence Boost. He was off the roof and free to go, but couldn't stop from staring at the dragon bubble butt that was inspired by his own. It was only inspired right? This was still weird, but it smelled of enticing *Pink Goo* and promised tingles.

Sredna, the Green Dragon of Earth's Text Box: Be gentle okay? This is my first time.

Anders didn't care if this was strange anymore. He had to try it, this was a once in a playtime opportunity. The elf stepped forward and accepted this situation. Being careful Anders first only played with the scaly dragon opening. Anders felt the dragon tighten up with anticipation. Anders wanted to make sure that nothing hurt the virgin dragon, he was a nice guy as well after all. He abandoned the dragon hole for now. Anders helped Sredna lie on his stomach. Anders straddled the dragon and began to massage Sredna's tense shoulders, and earned himself some happy chirping dragon noises. It took a lot of strength to rub through the dragon scales but Anders had lots of experience with his bow and had great hand strength.

Anders rubbed down the dragon's scaly back in a sensual pattern, he took great care to skip the dragon's butt completely and massaged the legs. Anders really didn't have any idea how to massage a tail or wings, but did so anyways. The sun had set and a wolf had howled before Anders was satisfied with his back massage.

Anders' Text Box: Roll over.

Sredna rolled over without a hint of hesitation. He sported a modestly sized erection and was aroused. Anders skipped anything sexual and started to massage the chest, the stomach, and the legs of the now elf sized dragon. The stomach massage caused a few giggles.

Sredna chirped and moaned happily while getting massaged. Anders caused a gasp when he deftly swallowed the dragon to the hilt in one swift action.

Sredna, the Green Dragon of Earth's Text Box: Ahhh!

Anders bobbed away happily, he turned his hands towards the dragon's internally contained balls. They were different to work with, but Anders tried all the same and Sredna did not file any complaints. The dragon's legs were guided upward and Sredna was instructed to hold them in place. Anders took a finger and started to tickle against the dragon hole.

Sredna, the Green Dragon of Earth's Text Box: Please be careful.

> Anders' Text Box: I promise.

Anders experimentally used his bendable index finder to apply the lightest of pressure against Sredna's opening. With a gasp of the dragon Anders' entire hand was taken inside. Inside was goopy and felt oddly familiar, a single tingle of pleasure traveled through Anders' finger, continuied along his hand, arm, shoulder, chest, stomach, and finally the pleasure core of his crotch. It nearly made Anders pass out in euphoria, and he understood with a single tingle why monsters loved using him so much. There was no longer any doubt as to why he was dragon candy. He was amazing! Anders removed his hand, he wasn't going to need to be gentle if he worked with what was essentially himself.

He positioned himself to dominate the dragon and Anders hesitated just long enough for Sredna to begin to inquire what was going on. Anders interrupted the Text Box with a determined thrust and impaled the dragon. A barrage of wonderful tingles hit the avatar, they felt a hundred times better from this end, and they were already pretty nice to start with.

Anders began to thrust into the dragon, and he felt remarkably good. Each and every thrust would release a tingle from the dragon that Anders could feel everywhere. Anders wanted more and more tingles, but he took it slow. The Coliseum was closed at night anyways, so he had nowhere to rush to.

Sredna wrapped his legs around Anders, and his arms followed suit. Finally, Anders felt himself get tightly wrapped up with a tail. While the dragon's arms and legs could seem to do nothing but desperately grip his elf lover, his tail was a different story. The dragon flicked and rubbed his tail all over the elf, but when a stray spank hit the elf's ass it caused Anders to buck and thrust in harder than ever before.

Anders saw a *Strange Animation* appear on Sredna. It was an Animation that blatantly expressed that if the dragon was based on Anders and Anders was a versatile bottom, maybe Sredna could defy what he was programmed to accept and become one as well (at least that was how Anders interpreted it). He turned out to be correct as the dragon manoeuvred his tail and used it to impale the elf in a move that Anders really should have anticipated. This caused a wave of tingles from both ends.

> Sredna, the Green Dragon of Earth's Text Box: Oh my Breaker! That's what those feel like?

> Anders' Text Box: I know, I had no idea either.

> Sredna, the Green Dragon of Earth's Text Box: Please, fuck me more!

> Anders' Text Box: I don't swear, remember?

> Sredna, the Green Dragon of Earth's Text Box: Oh sorry. Make love to me more.

> Anders' Text Box: Only if you make love to me more.

Both dragon and elf increased their efforts by a factor of 7.8. There were so many pleasure tingles being exchanged that even after two hundred full intensity rounds neither side could climax due to the over stimulation. Both were exhausted and neither could keep up the pace, so at round two hundred one they both collapsed into a sweaty heap. They desperately tried to catch their breath as the build up of tingles slowly subsided. Twenty rounds of heavy pants yet no tingles allowed Anders to catch his breath, he shifted himself and got ready to thrust anew. A single feeble thrust caused a shift of Sredna's tail, which caused Anders to release a single tingle. This single mote of pleasure caused Sredna to shiver and release one back, which traveled to Anders and in turn caused two to travel back to Sredna. Both just stared at each other as a chain reaction of tingles overtook them. Each round caused the amount of tingles to increase by one. It was round 32 that did Sredna in, he started to pulsate frantically and he squirted out his dragon seed combined with 64 bonus tingles to Anders. It was more than Anders could take, and he joined the massive tingle induced orgasm.

The tingles continued and decreased round after round until 64 rounds later two exhausted and well drained lovers collapsed in a happy pile of sparkling essence.

> Sredna, the Green Dragon of Earth's Text Box: Thank you lover.

> Anders' Text Box: No thank you.

Anders kissed the green dragon on the nose, and Sredna softly *Splinged* into a ball of satisfied green light. Anders watched as it travelled happily down the path towards Onn and was unceremoniously ambushed by Draganders who brutally ripped it apart. Every panicked bit was consumed by the hungry dragon, and Draganders' abdomen scales turned green. Anders stared in shock at the scene as the green that was already in his colour became more intense.

Creature Name: Sredna, the Green Dragon of Earth
Class: Breaker Dragon
Level: 98
Special Attacks: Breaker's Special Shake, Breaker's Special Avalanche, Breaker's Special Rumble, Stretch Butt
Drops: Nothing, nothing, and more nothing!
First Player Encounter Notes: Chirp! – Draganders

> Anders' Text Box: I forgot Draganders would eat and permanently kill you. I'm really sorry dragon me!

Draganders chirped happily, licked up any residual dragon essence in the area, and loudly burped out a mist of green acid.

◊ Chapter 42 ◊
UNNECESSARY
QUESTING E

P alcath's Text Box: Hey, where is that Anders lad?

samuri's Text Box: …

samuri used the *Shrug Animation*.

Roodg's Text Box: aWE, BUT i MISS Anders!

Palcath's Text Box: You know, it's funny Roodg.

Roodg's Text Box: i KNOW RITE? LoL. wAIT. wHAT IS?'

Palcath's Text Box: Here we are, travelling together with six other lads and lasses and we are the only ones that talk. Those lesbian twin lasses only want to kiss each other, samuri only ever says '…', Trev is too shy to say much of anything, Caela desperately wants to talk but has been shut up against her will, and for some reason I will never understand but am completely grateful for, Kray hasn't said a single word since we found him.

Roodg's Text Box: tHAT IS FUNNY. i NEVER THOUGHT i

WOULD BE TALKING TO YOU AND LIKE IT.

Palcath's Text Box: Me either, Roodg. I used to really dislike you, but now I can't help but like you.

Roodg's Text Box: uH OH! bE CAREFUL!

Palcath's Text Box: Huh, why Roodg?

Roodg's Text Box: yOU ARE SUPPOSED TO FALL IN LOVE WITH Lissa, NOT ME! LoL!

Palcath couldn't help but *Laugh Animation*.

Palcath's Text Box: You crack me up now, Roodg.

Roodg happily returned the *Laugh Animation*.

Roodg's Text Box: yOU MAKE ME LAUGH NOW 2! i DON'T HATE YOU ANYMORE EITHER.

Palcath's Text Box: Careful, don't fall in love with me, Roodg! You already have a love interest as well.

Roodg's Text Box: LoL. i KNOW, BUT i DON'T KNOW IF THEY LIKE ME.

Palcath's Text Box: I'm sure they do, just tell the lass how you feel.

Roodg's Text Box: tHE LASS? wHO ARE YOU TALKING ABOUT?

Palcath's Text Box: Uh, I thought that was obvious. I'm talking about Caela. You both get all giggly whenever you are near each other. Heck, you are the only one that even knows her actual full name, except Mr. Max, but he thinks she is a town.

Roodg's Text Box: oH. i NEVER THOUGHT ABOUT Caëlahenäilenŵhei LIKE THAT. rEALLY, SHE LIKES ME? wOW! nOW THAT i THINK ABOUT IT, i THINK i LIKE HER.

Palcath's Text Box: Yes, I am pretty sure the lass does.

Roodg's Text Box: nEAT! wAIT. oH CRAP. vINE sWINGING PUZZLE UP AHEAD!

Palcath's Text Box: So what,? It looks super easy.

Roodg's Text Box: i AM SUPER LANKY. i DON'T SWING WELL. cAN WE GO AROUND?

Palcath's Text Box: That way will take twice as long Roodg.

Roodg's Text Box: pLEASE? iF YOU MAKE UP SOMETHING ABOUT IT BEING DANGEROUS THEY WILL ALL LISTEN TO YOU!

Palcath's Text Box: You know what? Sure, Roodg! Providing of course you stop pushing me into monsters!

Roodg's Text Box: bUT THEIR VAGINAS NEEDED HOT DWARF ACTION!

After a fake reason from the dwarf about Vine Swinging Puzzles taking twice as long as walking if there was six or more avatars, which Caela tried to prove wrong but was ignored, the Vine Swinging Puzzle was avoided. The new enemies turned friends resumed their conversation.

Palcath's Text Box: Wait, Roodg. Who were you talking about liking? If I can ask?

Roodg's Text Box: oH YEAH SURE ASK. i'VE TOTALLY BEEN CRUSHING ON Anders SINCE i GOT PAIRED WITH HIM BEFORE.

Palcath's Text Box: I could see that now that you mention it. He is a great guy, I know why everyone likes him so much, especially the horses. That elf lad is really nice. I'm confident enough in myself to admit it. If I was gay, I'd be gay for Anders.

Roodg's Text Box: oH GOOD POINT! i ALSO LIKE Fournimer, HE IS SO NICE. Lissa IS GREAT. Mr. Max IS A FUN GUY, THEN THERE IS THAT CUTE GNOME BUTT, OR YOU NOW THAT WE ARE TALKING, OH AND —

Palcath's Interruption Text Box: Maybe just concentrate on one avatar at a time Roodg.

Roodg's Text Box: LoL. gOOD IDEA. cAN WE DROP BACK AND TALK TO Caëlahenãilenŵhei THEN?

Palcath's Text Box: Sure thing, Roodg.

Roodg's Text Box: hI!

Caëlahenãilenŵhei used the *Point Animation* directed at Roodg's Text Box, and again at the *Heart of Ice* floating above Roodg's breastbone.

Roodg's Text Box: oH. tHE iCE eLEMENTAL GAVE ME IT FOR MY PLAN. samuri GOT A FIRE ONE FOR HIS. iT MAKES ME IMMUNE TO FIRE ATTACKS.

Caëlahenãilenŵhei used the *Point Animation* directed at Roodg's *Belt*, then *Necklace*.

Roodg's Text Box: a THIRD SLOT aCCESSORY!

Caëlahenãilenŵhei used the *Point Animation* directed at her *Full Ball-Gag*.

Roodg's Text Box: i CAN'T TRADE IT SORRY!

Palcath's Text Box: No, but the Dark Elemental here will have the *Heart of Dark*! If we make sure that Caëlahenãilenŵhei lands the killing blow the lass will get something to replace the *Full Ball-Gag* with. Good plan lass.

Caëlahenãilenŵhei used the *Point Animation* directed at NPC Muurg.

Roodg's Text Box: oR MAKE SURE SHE WINS THE NEXT UNNECESSARY QUEST! tHE NEXT ITEM MIGHT BE SOMETHING LIKE EDIBLE CANDY PANTIES, A FRUIT LEATHER BRA, INSERT BANANAS, OR SOMETHING DIFFERENT WE CAN JUST EAT AWAY! i REALLY HOPE WE CAN EAT IT.

Caëlahenãilenŵhei used the *Nod Animation* happily.

Palcath's Text Box: Listen up everylad and everylass! Caela is stuck with the horrible *Full Ball-Gag*. If she wins Muurg's quest or kills the Dark Elemental she will get a different third slot Accessory and be able to get it off and talk again. Please let the lass win the quest!

samuri's Text Box: ...

samuri used the *Nod Animation*.

Trev Terra's Text Box: Yes, of course I will let her, rather allow her to, and let her... gosh. She will win.

In'ferni and De'vini used the *Double Nod Then Caress Dual Animation*.
Kray used the *Finger Pyramid of Evil Contemplation Animation*.

NPC Muurg's Text Box: Welcome to The Very Very Dark and Suspicious Plateau, a section of Spire E. If you complete my quest,

> Puzzling Puzzles, you will gain #three# rewards. The first will be the key to my gate and access to the next area of Spire E. Be the first to complete the series of 10 Puzzle Block Puzzles to win a special reward! Remember, the yellow blocks can be destroyed!

> Palcath's Text Box: Now they tell us, stupid yellow blocks lads.

> Roodg's Text Box: fUCK YOU YELLOW BLOCKS!

Everyone got into position, and the timer started. Caëlahenãilenŵhei was a natural at brain puzzles and got off to an early lead. It didn't hurt that everyone else just watched. Everyone but Kray that is, who desperately smashed random colours of blocks together. First green blocks, next blue, an attempt at red, then orange. Finally, the avatar smashed three yellow blocks together and exploded them. Caela was already on stage three, but now Kray knew which symbols were on the yellow blocks and he was catching up fast. By the time Caela had moved to stage six, Kray had just started stage five.

> Palcath's Text Box: What are you doing lad?

> Roodg's Text Box: yEAH! Caëlahenãilenŵhei NEEDS A NEW ITEM!

> samuri's Text Box: …

In'ferni and De'vini used the *Lean Against Yellow Puzzle Blocks Dual Animation.*

> Trev Terra's Text Box: Yeah… she asked… well they asked for her I mean, they asked for us to let her win… and we are… right? I am good at puzzles, but… I'm not good at ball-gags so… She helped me, us rather to get here.

Kray didn't say anything. He was busy with the puzzle blocks. It was midway through stage eight before Caela even noticed that Kray was her competition. She used the *Point Animation* to point at a 'w' in Palcath's Text Box, then an 'T' in Roodg's. and finally a 'f' in Trev's. Kray still didn't stop, even using her question as a way to pass her. Caela frantically tried to catch up to Kray, and while she could have beaten Kray if she had known he was competing in the beginning, the sudden realization that her *Full Ball-Gag* removal plan might fail had frazzled the light elf. She messed up the last grouping of yellow blocks by trying to rush and in doing so allowed Kray to win.

> Palcath's Text Box: What is wrong with you lad?

> Roodg's Text Box: yEAH YOU BIG JERK! Caëlahenãilenŵhei NEEDED TO WIN!

> Kray's Text Box: Maybe she wasn't the only one who is stuck with a Sexcessory she didn't want. Did that ever occur to you, kay? Maybe

someone else was stuck with something, but did you even think about asking? No, of course not. Kray isn't important, kay! He isn't the gay elf Night Ranger we like, no. His Jelly isn't the good Jelly! Well, Kray is important. I won fair and square, so deal with it, kay.

In'ferni and De'vini's Simultaneous Text Boxes: Oh great, he is talking again. I know, I'm upset as well. I'm really disappointed, I was liking the silence. So was I!

Palcath's Text Box: Those lesbian lasses are sharing a single mouth! Which one said what?

Roodg's Text Box: nEAT! tHEY BOTH DID!

samuri's Text Box: …

samuri used the *Disappointed Look Animation*.

Kray's Text Box: It's okay, kay. I forgive you Sami-guy! I just can't stay mad at you. Now I will get a brand new Sexcessory and we will be able to be together! Don't worry, we are still engaged. Oh Sami-guy, I really can't wait to try out your sex power on our wedding night. It is going to feel so good!

Palcath's Text Box: What is with the name Sami-guy? They are engaged? You are engaged to Kray? Lad what is wrong with you?

samuri's Text Box: Weth thare noth engagthed!

Palcath's Text Box: The lad can talk?! Wow, look at that tongue!

Roodg's Text Box: nEAT! tHAT IS THE BEST TONGUE EVER!

Kray's Text Box: Sorry Sami-guy. I know an engagement *Gilda-Lily* when I see one. My Sami-guy, always such a kidder.

Kray went over and gave his Sami-guy a *Big Hug Animation*. samuri used a *Scowl Animation*.

Kray's Text Box: Awe, don't pout Sami-guy, kay. Soon you will be able to unleash that tongue in me!

Roodg's Text Box: sHOULDN'T IT BE sami-guy SINCE HIS NAME DOESN'T USE A CAPITAL LETTER?

NPC Muurg's Text Box: Congratulations, little shades! Here is your

> first reward! You may now progress to the next area!

The gate out of the area was unlocked and Muurg stopped blocking the way.

> NPC Muurg's Text Box: Here is your second reward! An Accessory for 'insert avatar name'! May the winner with the fastest Puzzle Time step forward!

Kray stepped forward, pleased with himself. Caëlahenâilenŵhei used the *Scowl Animation*.

> NPC Muurg's Text Box: #It is a *Risqué Tattoo*! Enjoy your Sexcessory!#

Taking out a *Risqué Tattoo* from her invisible supply NPC Muurg presented the reward to Kray.

> Kray's Text Box: No thanks, I'm not really into ink. Hopefully the Dark Elemental has something better, kay.

Caëlahenâilenŵhei used the *Scowl Animation*.

> NPC Muurg's Text Box: Your third reward is… *pause for dramatic effect*

NPC Muurg pulled down her pants and revealed herself.

> NPC Muurg's Continued Text Box: My Dark Empty Void!

> Kray's Text Box: Kay, not it!

> Caëlahenâilenŵhei's Whisper Box Text: You jerk.

Chapter 43

ANDERS, DRESSED TO IMPRESS

Anders thought that if he hurried and beat the next Coliseum battle quickly, he might just beat the appearance of the Spiderboy. Despite having many encounters lately, the avatar still had no Mana Point reserves to execute a charged shot, and his *Elf Starting Bow* would not make much of an impact. If the Spiderboy had been breaking down scenic trees for over a week to get here, he had to be serious.

NPC Illiandro opened the Coliseum secret door and allowed Anders entry to the fifth battle of the Coliseum. The headline that flashed offered hope, this was going to be the final battle. The headline also delivered interest, this was not a female monster.

The Final Battle: Anders vs. the Mandusa.
A Medusa in folklore is a creature that is so hideous that she can turn anything to stone that even glimpses at her. Her frazzled hair is composed of vicious vipers that can both poison and attack her foes and her skin is made of rough scales. She otherwise had a normal humanoid shape.

So as expected, this Mandusa was a beautiful man with flawless skin accented with a few choice scales. He was topless with fabulous pecs, of course, and his snake hair consisted of well behaved snakes that made a cute haircut with a single snake serving as facial hair to make a soul patch. In place of legs, he had a long serpent tail. A sash of cloth was barely hiding presumed serpent sex organs.

Despite the fact that this Mandusa was not even in the least bit hideous, the first thing he did was use *Hideous Glance* on Anders and it turned the avatar into a stone statue. He had failed his Constitution save, as per usual for elves. Even though he was stone, his gear was not, and the avatar was still well aware of what was going on in the area. He just couldn't move his petrified limbs. Anders wished he had been frozen in a more flattering pose.

The Mandusa slithered up to Anders with a look of triumph in his reptilian pupils. He placed his hand on Anders' chest and the avatar felt a firm and slightly scaly hand touch him. The Mandusa traced his finger down Anders' stomach in a slow and deliberate manner. As his finger got lower and lower, Anders grew more and more aroused. The Mandusa paused when he reached the *Pink Slime Jock-Strap*. He leaned into Anders and started to nibble his neck. He deftly slipped his hand under Anders' waistband and began to feel up the now stone privates of the avatar.

Anders would close his eyes or roll them backwards, if he could move. As it was, he could only watch as the snake man began to kiss his lips, press his scaled naked form against his chest and massage his stone testicles. The serpent lowered the *Jock-Strap* and exposed the avatar, and began to stimulate the stone shaft. Anders was in a trance, if he could do anything he would be doing so right now.

> The Medusa's Text Box: Come on Mark, you know he really isn't into it, leave the poor guy alone.

> Mark the Mandusa's Text Box: Awe Constance, but I am having fun!

> Constance the Medusa's Text Box: Now now, he is a boy. Everyone knows that boy gamers like curvy female forms.

Anders looked over at the Medusa, she was styled similarly to the Mandusa but had a soft form, longer but similarly styled snake hair (without a single snake serving as a soul patch). She was far too attractive to be considered an ugly monster. As the snake woman slithered towards him, Anders couldn't help but get slightly alarmed.

> Constance the Medusa's Text Box: See, he saw me slithering over here and is already getting hard.

> Ander's Text Box: …

Mark was beginning to pout.

> Constance the Madusa's Text Box: Just let me handle him okay?

> Mark the Mandusa's Text Box: But I'm so horny for cock!

> Constance the Medusa's Text Box: The Gladiator Brothers have had their eyes on you, why not go stone them?

> Mark the Mandusa's Text Box: Good idea! They are super hot. I'll go

> stone them good!

The Mandusa slithered away with an excited look on his comely face. If Anders could move to follow the Mandusa he would have.

The Final Battle: Anders vs. the Medusa.

The Medusa sized up Anders while using the *Tail-Tapping Animation*. She was deciding on what to do with the stoned avatar. The snake woman had used her *Hideous Glance* on Anders, but only looked at the elf's crotch. Anders stone crotch became rock hard, despite his best efforts to resist. Curse you Constitution!

This was going to happen and Anders could do nothing but watch. So much for his gay gold star. If it was for a greater cause though he would have to accept it, others he knew had done so in the past. If Palcath could go gay for the team, Anders could as well (but straight).

The Final Battle lowered her coils and viewed the stone erection. She grabbed it firmly in her grasp and flicked it with her long forked serpent tongue. The tongue darted back and forth with amazing *Serpent Speed* and provided stone Anders with a unique and not unpleasant sensation. The Medusa stuck the head into her fanged mouth and started to playfully dart her tongue to and fro.

Anders almost moaned, but couldn't. The serpent tongue playfully teased the slit and Anders tried to gasp as he felt the tongue try to enter his shaft. She was very good at this, even Anders had to admit that, but her tongue was just too large to enter. The Medusa would not take defeat so easily and looked at Anders some more. When she stopped just looking and used *Hideous Glance* Anders felt himself turn to stone, but more so. Anders painfully grew almost another length unit of stone flesh as he grew harder. The Medusa did not stop there, after a few more glances Anders was up to a size he never would have imagined on himself, 8 whole length units. The Medusa's head moved quickly back to Anders' shaft, lips pressed the stone member and tongue tentatively attempted to go inside. With a jolt of intense strangeness, Anders' shaft was penetrated by the tongue. It licked him internally and exploring all the way down. After many strange and blissful rounds the Medusa stopped, which would have earned a whimper from Anders if he could.

The Medusa wrapped her tail around Anders. Now cencircling the avatar and hanging upside down, Constance continued her happy work on the avatar's member. The boss was now lined up to allow the stone avatar to participate, in a manner of speaking. The Medusa's serpentine opening slid against Anders' still frozen and surprised mouth. It was fortunate that the elf currently did not need to breathe, as the lady serpent's placement would have prevented the flow of air.

Anders could feel the tongue go deeper and deeper with each flick. It was a bizarre sensation that was quickly bringing the avatar to orgasm, but despite the fact that he needed to release, the tongue had stopped Anders from being able to do so. The Medusa cooed and gave a wicked *Glance Animation*. She enjoyed the delay.

Anders kept on trying to release, but he just couldn't. He was relieved when the Medusa removed the tongue for a split round. He wasn't sure how it was going to work exactly, but he felt his abdomen tighten and a concentrated wave of pleasure. It was stopped quickly when the Medusa grabbed the base of Anders' stone shaft tightly, which would have earned a yelp. Constance used a *No No Finger Wave Animation*, Anders was sure she wasn't ready to end this yet.

Constance shifted her tail and lined up her entrance with Anders' stone shaft. This was no longer just college experimentation, this was the real thing. The Medusa was exceptionally tight, almost as if she was gripping down on Anders' shaft with her snake slit (which she did). She slid down the shaft completely, all while she prevented Anders from release. She didn't stop just at the base, her exceptional cloaca tightness relaxed somehow while remaining vice tight and took in Anders' stone testicles as well. Constance used a *Smile Animation* and started to slowly move up and down on the stone shaft, constantly squeezing with her impressive kegel prowess.

Anders could only watch as his hands were filled up by two full bouncing serpent breasts with perky green nipples. He could only remain breathless as the Medusa slid up and down his member with impressive tightness and stimulation.

The Medusa bounced away, with Anders inside her. After one exceptionally long and deliberate bounce Constance began to quiver. Anders wasn't exactly sure what that meant, but it was something he never had felt before. The quiver was a wave but only managed to make the entire entrance even tighter as it shuddered. The Medusa's tail constricted Anders and her thrusts became more powerful. With a final thrust the Medusa released her serpent grip with a powerful orgasm and Anders' pent up seed cascaded into her with the force of at least a *Double Shot*. The avatar felt it gush through his stone shaft as he shot more than ever before into the snake woman.

After a wet, salty, and forked kiss the Medusa slithered away, cheerfully defeated and full of her reward.

> Stone Softener's Text Box: Would you like to use your *Stone Softener*? y/n

Anders selected yes and the use of the *Stone Softener* was revealed as his stone body changed slowly back into flesh and his size returned to normal. He could move again, and the *Stone Softener* was consumed. He didn't know why it didn't work until after the encounter was over, though. Silly items.

> Creature Name: The Medusa
> Class: Snake Woman
> Level: 85
> Special Attacks: Hideous Glance, Serpent Speed, Serpent Grip, Snake Hair Tango

Drops: Gladiator Armour
First Player Encounter Notes: Am I allowed to redo this battle again later? If
I want? - Anders

Anders couldn't wait to try on his *Gladiator Armour (s)*. As he suspected, it did have
a little gladiator style skirt, but it did completely cover up his butt at certain angles. His
Armour had much less coverage than the other *Gladiator Armour* he had seen, but it
made him look and feel very tough and manly, even though it was a skirt.

He was finally fully dressed and ready to go find his *Super Amazing Hover-Motorbike*.
After a quick lunch. All this sexual experimentation had made him hungry. He wasn't
sure if he would try out snake ladies again, but he wasn't sure if he wouldn't either.

Chapter 44

THE BREAK IN

Entry: 45 6c 61 6e 6f 72 65

Computer Terminal: Wait, what? How?

Breaker's Text Box: Don't try to lock out someone with a computer terminal password system when that avatar has access to the game's code and can just hack it.

Computer Terminal: Fair enough, honourary mistress. Enjoy!

Breaker used the *Sigh Animation*. The mistress? Right after he discovered what was locked behind this caged door, he was going to need to remember to pound out the metal boobs on his pilfered *Boobplate Armour*.

The sheet that covered the mystery was removed by Breaker *With a Stretching Out of His Wings and a Dramatic Movement of his Claws Animation*. It was an open metal pod that would have better fit in a sci-fi deep sleep section. Lights blinked, levers glinted, and dials just begged to be twisted. A smudged plate revealed the name of this device (once Breaker gave it a quick clean).

> Breaker's Text Box: *The Device*? How original.

A tube shot out of *The Device* and impaled Breaker in the arm.

> Breaker's Text Box: The fuck?

> The Device's Text Box: Acquiring sample. Target: Breaker

A few drops of fluid travelled up the clear tube. Lights beeped as pixels flowed out of *The Device*. Breaker watched in awe as the pixel swirled and gathered into a familiar form. It was black, had claws, scales, and a distinctive mole. This was Breaker's own arm, cloned.

Breaker was not terribly impressed. He didn't really need this arm as he had two already, *The Device* was a bit of a letdown after so much build up. The terminal that had required a password hummed awake. Breaker left the useless arm alone to investigate. The touch-screen showed his arm and a variety of sliders, buttons, and check boxes. Breaker slid a slider to the right casually and the claws on the cloned arm nearly doubled in size and damage output potential. A button flashed on the screen called *Make Change Permanent?* and Breaker clicked yes without hesitation. His own claws grew to the size of the cloned one. He was suddenly giddy.

The Device wasn't a lameass cloning machine, it was something that could do things that he had only ever dreamed about. Adding abilities to your code was one thing, but alterations were impossible, until now. *The Device* could alter the code of your character in countless ways, turn you into whatever you could dream. *The Device* was the Holy Grail of character code editing.

Breaker could use *The Device* to become everything he had ever dreamed of. He would first need to find a new place to hide this wonderful machine (since his own secret base was full) and perform all kinds of experiments with it. He could become a God.

> Breaker's Text Box: It is about fucking time.

Chapter 45

FORESTS, SECRETS, AND LIGHT ELEMENTALS

Gliint's Text Box: *Look away* She is freaking me out, but she is really good at bondage and handling the bosses.

Lissa's Text Box: I agree with you. Did you see how she sandwiched that Twinkle Hippogriff? I didn't even know that Hippogriffs could bend so much. #AnatomyLesson.

Fournimer's Text Box: I don't think they can. but at least the crazy Catgirl has fallen asleep for a bit. maybe. she might be pretending to be a cat again. she does that.

Mr. Max's Text Box: Wait, did you say sandwich?! That reminds me, I am going to go get a sandwich!

Lissa's Text Box: That really isn't a reminder, it's a statement, Meatbone.

Yallundy's Text Box: He is really honestly trying now Lissa. He is genuinely interacting with everyone and caring about what they say for the first time ever. Maybe you should cut him some slack.

Lissa's Text Box: No, I've grown enough with my interactions for a while. Just look at how good Fourn and I are getting along! Now mush, horse!

Fournimer's Text Box: horses don't mush, Lis.

Lissa's Text Box: Right. Giddy-up!

Lissa kicked Fournimer in the flank and he jumped.

Yallundy's Text Box: Are you sure I can't look at your leg Lissa? I have a better healing skill than you, maybe I can fix it.

Lissa's Text Box: Not right now, uh, maybe tonight, okay? #TopicChange. If we hurry we can get out of here before Meatbone gets back or E. E. Loon wakes up.

Gliint's Text Box: Wait, it's here! *Joy* I'll be right back!

Zal Finn III's Text Box: What is here?

Lissa's Text Box: Awe man. I don't want to leave Gliint behind, I like Gliint.

Gliint's Text Box: OMM! I can't believe it. How could Max not want to keep this? It is the best prize ever for getting to level ✪ ✪!

Yallundy's Text Box: Don't keep us in suspense. What is it?!

Gliint's Text Box: It is the official artwork for *Caution Step's* last album! It's framed, and wow it isn't just blown up but someone really painted it. This is the original artwork!!! You know the album right, *Out of Service: Use the Stairs*? That is the album with all the songs for this game on it! This is so mind blowing, it is signed by all of the band and says 'Congratulations for being the best at Annals of Gentalia!' I am going to hang it above my television.

Zal Finn III's Text Box: Sweet! No way!

Fournimer's Text Box: that is pretty great. I'm jealous Gliint. why wouldn't Bro want that? It is a great prize.

Lissa's Text Box: Maybe he doesn't like *Caution Step*?

Gliint's Text Box: Who couldn't like them? They are only like the best band ever.

> Lissa's Text Box: I don't like them, #OverratedMuch.

> Hippolyta's Text Box: I agree, boy bands are not my thing either.

> Gliint's Text Box: Overrated? They actually won an award for being the best underrated band! It's why they suddenly became so mainstream.

> Lissa's Text Box: Well whatever, they are jerks is all.

> Gliint's Text Box: Hardly. I heard that their singer, *Trip Hazard*, donates almost all of his time and money to charities. Their drummer, *Gunner M. Jefferies*, was voted second nicest drummer in modern music. Heck, even *Ashler Waldenmyer* had that hit reality show where he built houses for multi-lingual orphans before he had to go to rehab.

> Lissa's Text Box: They just are jerks okay? #EndOfStoryNoEpilogue!

> Fournimer's Text Box: how do you know they are jerks? do you know them? it sounds like you know them or something.

> Lissa's Text Box: Fine, okay. Yes I know them. We went to high school together and they are jerks. Can we just drop this already?

Gliint stood there in shock. He used the **GASP AND POINT WHILE YOU OPEN YOUR MOUTH AND CROSS YOUR EYES WITH A SUDDEN REALIZATION ANIMATION.** E. E. Lynn, who was right beside him triple orgasmed in her sleep due to the exceedingly long and sexy Animation from Gliint. If she had been less accustomed to intense and bizarre orgasms it would have easily ripped her apart instead.

> Gliint's Text Box: Oh my Maker! You said your avatar's full name was Lissandra Collinswood?! You are… no way! You are *Eliza*—

> Lissa's Interruption Text Box: No, I am not!

> Gliint's Text Box: No! *Shock* You have to be! You're *Elizabeth Collins*! Their first hit song, *Authorized Personnel Lizzy* is all about you! OMM, you are the girl 'With the purple streaked hair and fists clenched with jeweled tags'. Of course you are. You have purple hair and a spunky disposition! You are Ashler's first girlfriend! You, oh my Maker, then you totally went and chea—

> Lissa's Interruption Text Box: Okay, fine! I admit it. I am *Elizabeth Collins*. Can we drop it already? #NobodyCares!

> Gliint's Text Box: You are like famous! I love that story about how the

> band almost broke up. How you and *Gunner* —

> Lissa's Interruption Text Box: Please, can you drop it already?

> Gliint's Text Box: But… but… you are like…

> Fournimer's Text Box: wow! no way. we play games with *Lizzy Collins*! I need to tell Man right away!

> Lissa's Text Box: No you do not! So help me Maker you do not!

Lissa stomped her foot and her face gave a literal furious expression. A hushed silence took over everyone. It lasted for all of one round.

> Mr. Max's Text Box: Hey, I'm back and I have both peanut butter and bananas. What did I miss?

> Hippolyta's Text Box: Some interesting things I would say.

> Zal Finn III's Text Box: Sweetdiculous things!

> Lissa's Text Box: Nothing! Absolutely nothing.

Lissa accented her statement with fierce eyes. She would have used *Laser Guided Bunny Eye Missile Eyes*, but now that those were a real thing she was scared that missiles might actually shoot out of her face.

> Gliint's Text Box: Yeah, nothing. Oh, but thank you for the framed *Caution Step* poster Max. *Heart* I love it.

> Mr. Max's Text Box: I knew you would Little Bro.

> Fournimer's Text Box: I thought that I was your Bro, Max Bro.

> Mr. Max's Text Box: You're right Fourni Bro! So much has been going on I nearly forgot to say hi!

Mr. Max jumped over to Fournimer and gave the centaur a great big hug, he even lifted the centaur (and his charge) up off the ground.

> Mr. Max's Text Box: I missed you Bro! We need to talk, make yourself open for later okay?

Fournimer changed to *Blush Shade #3*.

> Fournimer's Text Box: yeah, sure thing Bro.

> E. E. Lynn's Text Box: \/\/0\/\/! ^-^ Gr34t n4p! 4lr|ght, t|/\/\3 f0r /\/\3 2 g0 fuckz0rz teh L|ght 3l3/\/\3nt4l! | c4n't \/\/4|ts, h3

h4s 1|k3 4 cOcks!

Fournimer's Text Box: a cock? just one? that's not unusual.

E. E. Lynn's Text Box: N0 n3\/\/b. 4 cOcks! 4!

Fournimer's Text Box: what?

E. E. Lynn's Text Box: S33, th3r3! 4! 4!

Fournimer's Text Box: wow look, he has four cocks!

E. E. Lynn's Text Box: |d|0t.

Chapter 46

ANDERS, OBJECT OF DRAGON DESIRE

Anders slammed back the *Cupped Cake* so quickly that he nearly choked. He said goodbye to Margarine before buying a large supply of *Cupped Cakes* (which tasted the least awful) and *Double Danishes* (which were the most absorbent). He grabbed everything he had scattered in the Bakery Shoppe and got ready to leave Onn forever. On his way out the door he said hello to Greeta.

Anders grabbed Illiandro and sprinted out the door. Taking great care to watch the skies the elf made his way to the secret entrance to the Coliseum. He pressed the button for the secret wall and was catapulted across the town and into the Onn city wall by an explosion from behind the secret entrance. Barely able to stand, Anders looked around to see what had happened. From the rubble of the broken entrance stepped a furious Xam.

> Anders' Text Box: What the peanut butter blossoms?

> Xam, the Orange Dragon of Light's Text Box: I am so very disappointed in you candy. I give you special rules and what is the first thing you go and do? Break the darn rules.

Trying to keep from falling over a desperate Anders was attempting to reason with his dragon stalker.

> Anders' Text Box: I... but they—

> Xam, the Orange Dragon of Light's Interruption Text Box: No excuses candy. I am afraid that I am going to have to use your special item and control you forever.

Xam fiddled with the necklace that he had strapped his item on, concealing whatever it was beneath his hand.

> Anders' Text Box: No, you don't understand. The other dragons they att—

> Xam, the Orange Dragon of Light's Interruption Text Box: What other dragons? Don't tell me you have been talking to the other dragons as well!

> Anders' Text Box: Uh… no?

> Xam, the Orange Dragon of Light's Text Box: Good. Then you would be in real trouble. I am talking about you going to Breaker. I told you not to go to Breaker, and that is exactly what you are doing.

Anders couldn't fault the Dragon's logic. That was exactly what he was trying to do by getting the *Super Amazing Hover-Motorbike*. At least Xam had no idea that four of his brothers (three brothers and one brother/sister mix) were dead. The stalker dragon Text Boxed through wet weeping tears as he clawed at the ground in a state of rage.

> Xam, the Orange Dragon of Light's Text Box: You forced me to do this candy! I will control you forever now. We will be together forever and ever!

Xam ripped off his necklace and held the item up high. He was getting ready to activate the item. Anders needed to think fast or he was going to be the permanent sex slave of the insane dragon.

> Anders' Text Box: Wait!

> Xam, the Orange Dragon of Light's Text Box: Why?

> Anders' Text Box: Good question. Let's see. Why? Oh, I know! I have this coupon for a free ass pounding from Xam. I want to use it before I lose my free will. You know, for old times' sake.

Xam's expression changed from intense rage to pure delight.

> Xam, the Orange Dragon of Light's Text Box: Really? You mean it? All emotional and junk! Well, okay candy. Since you are using the coupon I'll let you keep your free will until this is over. It will be a story we can tell our grandchildren.

Anders decided that this dragon was 100% certified nuts. Instead of telling Xam that fact, Anders just pulled up his manly skirt and tried to entice the dragon further. Hopefully Anders could get Xam to finish up quickly before he used the controlling item.

The noise from Onn Forest indicated that there were not going to be many rounds left until the Spiderboy broke into Onn. Anders was hopeful that it would happen before Xam was finished, since Xam would probably rip the Spiderboy to bits, or after Xam was finished and Anders was far away from here.

Xam stepped up to his avatar with a great sense of entitlement. He was in control here and he wanted Anders to know it. He entered forcefully and began to plunge in and out of his candy with slow and careful movements. Anders tried to move a little to increase the speed, but powerful claws grabbed him and held him tightly. Xam was going to take his time, and he didn't care what Anders' thoughts on the matter were.

Each slow thrust by Xam was echoed by the loud thumping noise coming from Onn Forest. Eventually without even realizing it, Xam's pace had changed to match that of the thumping. Each pound got Xam a little closer to finishing and the final trees blocking the new entrance to Onn Forest a little closer to falling.

Anders was unable to move under the big dragon, but there was something he could do to make this encounter end faster. Enjoy himself. If he concentrated hard on every single thrust from Xam and felt every length unit that he could, Anders could maximize the number of tingles that he released. He closed his eyes and concentrated on the thrusts of his dragon partner. Anders entered a Zen like state of meditation. As each stroke entered he moved with it internally and thought of the pleasure it could bring him and his partner.

As the rounds progressed Anders felt more and more at one with himself, his abilities, and the game universe. The exposure earlier with Sredna's tingles had given Anders an entire new concept of his tingles and abilities. With sudden enlightenment Anders opened his eyes, his irises had changed from their normal green colour to thousands of pixel points of multi-coloured light. Anders understood what he was capable of, he had gained a new ability under *Stretch* that was not part of the regular move set. The move came in just as Anders unleashed it.

Ten Thousand Tingle Torrent caused every pixel of the elf to temporarily shift into a node of pure pleasure. Xam, who wasn't even nearly close to his long drawn out abuse of the avatar *Splinged* so forcefully at the pleasure that his light exploded over the entire area in a hundred little balls. Anders popped back into solid form with a strange sense of fulfillment, at peace with himself, the game universe, and his abilities.

Anders heard a 'tink' noise from behind him, Xam's special item had fallen to the ground. Anders reached down to pick it up while Draganders was happily flying around Onn gobbling up the big *Splinged* idiot. It was a small bronze key, Anders' old *Auto-Trap Release*. Anders flipped it around in his hand, there was nothing at all special about this. Nothing that would have ever controlled Anders. It was just a simple item that looked like a key. Anders pocketed the item as he wondered where Xam had gotten such a foolish idea that this could control an avatar.

> **Creature Name:** Xam, the Orange Dragon of Light
> **Class:** Breaker Dragon
> **Level:** 98
> **Special Attacks:** Breaker's Special Beam, Breaker's Special Flash, Breaker's Special Sunburst, Maxed Cock
> **Drops:** Don't tell Breaker I kept the key to Anders' heart.
> **First Player Encounter Notes:** Chirp! – Draganders

Draganders chirped happily as his neck changed to orange. The once matte gray dragon was almost completely rainbowed up now and very nearly fabulous, as was Anders' Armour colours. All they needed now to complete the look was the color purple, but seeing as how Assil was a girl dragon Anders was fine with leaving it incomplete for now. Besides, Anders had more important things to worry about, he needed to get out of Onn before the last—

Anders plans to escape Onn before the last tree fell were interrupted by the last tree as it fell. Anders prepared himself for battle but was startled to not see the Spiderboy but someone else entirely.

> Anders' Text Box: Oh, hi.

$\diamond$ **Chapter 47** $\diamond$

FORESTS, SECRETS, AND DARK ELEMENTALS

Kray's Text Box: Finally you guys killed that Terror Kelpie. I was getting bored, kay.

samuri's Text Box: …

Palcath's Text Box: Well it might have helped if more of you lads and lasses had been attacking the damn thing!

Roodg's Text Box: yEAH! tHAT DOG AND CAT DID WAY THE fLAMING pIT MORE THAN YOU DID!

Kray's Text Box: Well excuse me, kay. I thought that shooting it in the face and killing it was something.

Palcath's Text Box: It technically is yes. But that is the only time you fucking attacked it lad. Otherwise you just sat there! You ninja scooped the bonus xp!

Kray's Text Box: Sat there 'looking good', kay. You forgot the looking good part.

Caëlahenãilenŵhei's Whisper Box Text: Unbelievable.

Kray's Text Box: What was that little miss stuffy britches? Care to speak up, kay?

Caëlahenãilenw̃hei's Text Box: Mumble mumble…

Kray's Text Box: Kay, I didn't think so.

Palcath's Text Box: Whatever, it's over now. I expect that kind of thing from you Kray, but I'm more disappointed in Trev and those twins. Why didn't any of you do anything?

Trev Terra's Text Box: What? Oh sorry… there was a battle? Oh, I'm so sorry, rather I apologize, I mean. We were distracted… I feel really bad now, we are all sorry, right? Yes? We are sorry!

In'ferni and De'vini's Simultaneous Text Boxes: There was a battle? I'm sorry. I'm sorry as well! I was distracted by the gossip. I can't believe it. I know right that is so cool! I agree. I can't wait! Me either.

Palcath's Text Box: What could possibly be so cool over there lasses?

Roodg's Text Box: LoL. yEAH! yOU ARE ALL JUST STARING AT A WALL!

Trev Terra's Text Box: It's not the wall. We are not looking at the wall, well actually I guess we are looking at the wall, that's sort of funny, rather no, it's just that well, something was going on and we wanted to hear. It was pretty scandalous, and we are sorry. Here we are appearing to be doing nothing and just looking at a wall. We didn't help here, I'm sorry. We should continue into the castle then. Sorry.

After continuing into the *Spire E Castle*, the conversation continued.

Roodg's Text Box: i LOVE THINGS! wHAT WAS IT?

In'ferni and De'vini's Simultaneous Text Boxes: That girl with the purple hair, I just can't believe it. I know neither can I! Apparently she is Lizzy. You know, like only from our special song. I love our song. Me too!

Palcath's Text Box: Lissa? What about her? Please tell me!

Trev Terra's Text Box: She is Elizabeth Collins apparently. You know the one, well maybe you do, from that song, *Authorized Personnel Lizzy*.

> Roodg's Text Box: nEAT!

Palcath got wide eyed before replying.

> Palcath's Text Box: Lissa is Lizzy? The 'Girl who made my heart with chains only to break it apart again?' No way! The lass is… famous!

> Roodg's Text Box: nOTORIOUS. nOT FAMOUS, NOTORIOUS.

> In'ferni and De'vini's Simultaneous Text Boxes: I know, isn't that cool? I know it is. I want to go meet her now and tell her we always make out to that song. So do I! Can we hurry up and get to Spire G? Yeah, can we please?

Caëlahenâilenŵhei was concerned. How on earth could they have found out that by staring at the wall. She desperately looked for things to point at after getting Palcath's attention. It took her some time, Palcath apologized for the delay and said he had gotten an important phone call that confirmed suspicions. It was going to have to be a round of Charades to get people to guess.

> Palcath's Slow Text Box following Caëlahenâilenŵhei's finger: Gliint? No? Why are you making Gliint attack the air… oh… so Zap? Socko? Blamo? Pow? Yes, Pow. Yeah I like how his attacks make words in the air as well! It is great fun. Next? Er *Flork Hooves*? Mix? Make into. *Hoof Drink*? No. Gelatine? No. Glue? Yes! Okay, the next one is Dumbass! Yeah, I thought you would like that lass, it's obviously Kray! Hmmm. Shoe? No. Foot? No, oh that's Toe! Scenery? Monster? Um…

> Roodg's Text Box: bAT! tHAT IS BAT!

> Palcath's Text Box: So we have… Pow glue Kray toe bat? What does that mean lass?

Caëlahenâilenŵhei used the *Sounds Like Animation*.

> Palcath's Text Box: Um… Pow. Is it bow, cow, dow… wait dow isn't a word, stop me if I get it, gow, how?

Caëlahenâilenŵhei used the *Point Animation* directed into the distance.

> Palcath's Text Box: Far away? What? So like you mean zow, or yow? What do you mean lass?

Caëlahenâilenŵhei used the *Point Animation* directed beside Roodg.

> Roodg's Text Box: mE? i DON'T RHYME WITH ANYTHING. wAIT. dO i? i NEED TO THINK ON THAT. cAN YOU NARROW IT DOWN?

Caëlahenãilenẁhei used the *Stop Animation*, then the *Frantic Arm Waving Animation*, and finally the *Point Animation* directed at the Dark Elemental that nobody but she had seen.

> Palcath's Text Box: Okay lass, I am so lost now.

> Roodg's Text Box: iS IT *Better Homes & Orphans*? i LOVE THAT SHOW!

Caëlahenãilenẁhei watched in silent terror as the stealthy Dark Elemental raised her *Wicked Scythe* and got ready to cleave Roodg's head clean off. She couldn't just stand there while avatars thought she was still doing Charades. She ran forward and pushed Roodg out of the way of the sneak attack.

> Caëlahenãilenẁhei's Box Text: Roodg, look out!

The light elf took the brunt of the attack. She fell silently into the arms of the Dark Elemental, a floating female form completely covered in inky black robes. With a tip of the hood and a hand wave goodbye, both the Dark Elemental and Caela were gone in a portal of darkness.

> Roodg's Text Box: nO! Caëlahenãilenẁhei!

> Game Explanation Text Box: Be careful, some monsters can set up ambushes and kidnap your party members.

> Palcath's Text Box: Thank you for the heads up ever informative Text Box lad.

> Roodg's Text Box: cOME ON! wE NEED TO SAVE HER!

> Kray's Text Box: Kay, does anyone else notice that stuffy-no-tent letting-in, self righteous bitch talks an awful lot for someone that has a permanent Full Ball-Gag in her mouth?

> samuri's Text Box: …

samuri used the *Glare Animation*.

> Kray's Text Box: Thank you for agreeing with me, kay. My Sami-guy! He's so great.

The group ran down the corridor towards the Dark Elemental's glade, except Kray who walked at a leisurely pace. They came upon a partially disrobed Dark Elemental. She squeezed her inky black breasts. Her nipples were shooting out thick strands of inky milk completely covered Caela's tied up and naked form. This made the once nearly all white light elf completely black, from head to toe. Caela's Armour was strewn about the area, smudged with ink. The Dark Elemental noticed the party's entrance, she had been expecting them.

> Dark Elemental's Text Box: Sorry, this one is mine now. I like her. You all are free to go through as long as you leave her.

> Caëlahenãilenẘhei's Box Text: Oh Maker, it's everywhere. Ink on all of my stuff!

> Roodg's Text Box: nO WAY! u CAN'T HAVE HER! sHE'S MY rOCKET sORCERESS!

> Caëlahenãilenẘhei's Box Text: Your Rocket Sorceress?

> Roodg's Text Box: dAMN RIGHT! nOW GIVE HER BACK!

> Dark Elemental's Text Box: Uh, let me think about that for a round. Nope! I want her. I've even marked her with my breast ink.

> Roodg's Text Box: tHEN YOU DIE TONIGHT!

A fierce battle broke out between Roodg and the Dark Elemental, after a few rounds everyone else remembered to join in. Each attack against the Dark Elemental caused a splash of ink to jet forth, and all of her attacks involved squirts of ink. Roodg had tackled her and squeezed her jumblies to drain out all of her ink, with the thought that maybe the Elemental would dry up if it was all gone. As the battle progressed less and less could be seen of the party. When Kray finally showed up all he could see was six blobs of human sized ink, one blob of four legged hovering ink, and a blob of bigger Dark Elemental ink.

> Kray's Text Box: Sweet! It's almost dead, kay. Ninja Snipe!

With one sneak attack it was over and Kray, who was still completely ink free, had managed to kill the Dark Elemental, much to everyone else's annoyance.

> **Creature Name:** Dark Elemental
> **Class:** Elemental E
> **Level:** 98 (Requires 100 avatars to be present to Spawn)
> **Special Attacks:** Ink Shot, Blot Out, Darkness, Squirt, Rub Out, Elemental E
> **Drops:** Spire E Key, the Heart of Dark (Only for avatar that gets last strike)
> **First Player Encounter Notes:** |-|3r ||\||< 74$73$ 1||<3 8|_|773r$0tC|-|! ^-^ Y|_|/\/\! - E. E. Lynn
> **Additional Comments:** Totally rocked that one, kay. - Kray

> Short Husky Sized Ink Blob's Text Box: What is wrong with you lad?

We were just about to untie Caela so she could land the killing blow.

Really Skinny and Lanky Ink Blob's Text Box: yEAH! dIDN'T YOU READ THE PLAN?

Tall Silent Type Ink Blob's Text Box: …

Two Stuck Together Ink Blob's Simultaneous Text Boxes: That was pretty low man. I agree.

Nervous Jittery Ink Blob's Text Box: That was pretty bad, well what I mean is, it wasn't nice. Isn't she your friend? Why would you scoop her on that?

Kray's Text Box: Because now I have a *Heart of Dark*! I can finally get rid of this *Jelly Butt-Plug* so that Sami-guy and I can be together! Not everything is about you, kay!

Stuffy No Jiggle Ink Blob's Box Text: Kray, you already got the *Risqué Tattoo*. It was black. You would never have even seen it on your skin because you are black now! You didn't need to take the *Heart of Dark* as well. That was beyond self-centered.

Kray's Text Box: No way, kay. Did you see that *Risqué Tattoo*? It was of a lady! An almost naked lady! I didn't want that on my arm! I threw it away!

Short Husky Sized Ink Blob's Text Box: Well, it's too late to worry about it now, lass. There should be one more quest on Spire G that Caela can win. So, let's just get cleaned off and go. We are right by there anyways.

Nervous Jittery Ink Blob's Text Box: Yes, and the other team is already there… they are waiting for us.

Short Husky Sized Ink Blob's Text Box: How many *Absorbing Cloths* do you have left Roodg?

Really Skinny and Lanky Ink Blob's Text Box: oNLY NONE!

Short Husky Sized Ink Blob's Text Box: Maybe we can use something else lads and lasses to get clean. Water? Do we even carry water? Wait, do we drink things?

Really Skinny and Lanky Ink Blob's Text Box: Trev Terra CAN SPRAY US ALL OFF! LoL!

Nervous Jittery Ink Blob changed to *Blush Shade #Ink*.

Stuffy No Jiggle Ink Blob's Box Text: I suspect that a *Grand Fullcake* would work. It appears to be made of, and definitely tastes like, a sponge.

Short Husky Sized Ink Blob's Text Box: That does work lass. Good call.

Really Skinny and Lanky Ink Blob's Text Box: oKAY Caëlahenâilenŵhei, i AM GOING TO CLEAN YOU UP, WITH CAKE!

Stuffy No Jiggle Ink Blob's Box Text: No! Wait! Untie me first! Please!

Really Skinny and Lanky Ink Blob's Text Box: i ALREADY STARTED THE *Cleaning You Off With Cake Animation*, i CAN'T STOP IT. wHY DOES IT MATTER? yOU ARE PRETTY!

Stuffy No Jiggle Ink Blob's Box Text: No, please. Everyone look away... it's...

Kray's Text Box: See, she was totally being a cunt and didn't need to win the *Heart of Dark* thingy, kay. She has a perfectly functioning Mouthgina right there to talk out of.

Caëlahenâilenŵhei's Box Text: Damn.

◈ **Chapter 48** ◈

ANDERS, CROSSING JORTHAN

Jorthan the Male Troll Monk's Text Box: Bonjour mon petit lutin. Me, I am the only player in my amis that had not landed in forests. All of them were stuck in the wooded places. Not moving forward cause to levers or backwards cause to NPC. That is when I make a raft out of *Banane Splits* to leave Desserted Island and voyage across the world to get here to the Onn place. To use the Airship, she would be helping me find my long lost amis.

Somewhere Anders remembered hearing that male trolls did not look anything like the female ones. Whoever said that wasn't kidding. While Yallundy had been an absolute vision of beauty, Jorthan was anything but. He was tall and silver skinned like Yallundy, but that is where the similarities stopped. He had a flat sunken in face accentuated with big cracked droopy lips stuck in a permanent frown. His nose was wide at the base, with flared nostrils, but it quickly tapered down to a thin point, which dropped well past his triple chin. His prominent brow nearly completely hid his small beady eyes. The only part of the troll's face that seemed to stick out was his oversized crescent shaped ears. While Yallundy had stood tall with her height, Jorthan was hunched over, only standing a little taller than Anders. The strangest feature of the Troll was his oversized hands and forearms, they were made for a creature twice his size.

Despite the avatar's outward appearance Anders had sensed a warm and gentle spirit inside. One that was most certainly French Canadian. Anders knew enough

French Canadian to understand what was going on. Anders also knew that 'mon petit lutin' meant 'my little elf' and also sensed that Jorthan was possibly flirting with him. He did have a nice body wrapped up in his yellow monk's outfit with blue accents all things considered, even if it was hunched over.

> Anders' Text Box: The Airship was destroyed though.

> Jorthan the Male Troll Monk's Text Box: I find that out only a few cycles pass, but I am already almost here. I am hoping that I could get my provisions before thinking up of a new plan. I did not attendre to find it in such a malpropre. Or you for that matter, mon petit lutin.

> Anders' Text Box: One of Breaker's dragons had a fit and destroyed most of Onn. There are only a few NPCs left.

> Jorthan the Male Troll Monk's Text Box: Dommage, do any of them be selling the food, mon petit lutin? Me, I have not been eating in over a long semaine.

> Anders' Text Box: NPC Margarine is still alive, I am living in her Bakery Shoppe.

Anders took out ill-tasting baked goods and offered them to Jorthan. He took everything and stuffed it into his mouth, swallowing with one gulp.

> Jorthan the Male Troll Monk's Text Box: I never think pâtisserie that was not of the *Bacon* would flavour so good. Much obliged mon petit lutin. You are the resource if you have lived here long with all of those dragons in the air. It was almost the end after I found one. Thankful it wasn't as hungry as I am to be.

> Anders' Text Box: I've killed most of the dragons already, only the purple one is left. You don't need to be afraid of them anymore.

Anders was proud of himself for that. Jorthan let out a *Big Belly Laugh Animation* and hit Anders hard on the back with a giant hand, it was a tiny bit painful.

> Jorthan the Male Troll Monk's Text Box: Of course you have, mon petit lutin! That explain why there are hardly any fly around anymore here.

The statement sounded a bit sarcastic, but somehow Anders knew that the troll was genuinely impressed and believed him.

> Anders' Text Box: You said your party was trapped on the spires, did you hear something about my party before the WorldForums and Player Pagers broke? I'm really concerned that two of the spires are

missing now.

Jorthan the Male Troll Monk's Text Box: Hear a thing, mon petit lutin? I can do much more better. I heard everything! Every person in Spire A and B fine, even boss. Everyone is fine, and everyone. I mean everyone. That lad midget, the farfadet, the lutin (demi, nuit, lumière, and the squelette one, a effroi lutin he is?), the humans, the centaure, the femme chat, and even what was her again? Someone please be to helping me out here. My word is troll.

Anders' Text Box: The troll? Do you mean Yallundy?

Jorthan the Male Troll Monk's Text Box: She is the one. She was fantôme the whole time following the farfadet. Even she is being alright, alive and kicking it again.

Anders was so overcome with joy to hear that everyone was alright, even Yallundy whom he had long thought gone, that he jumped up and gave the troll a great big hug. Jorthan was too stunned to react and even changed to *Blush Shade #B*, the special troll only shade.

Jorthan the Male Troll Monk's Text Box: Wow, mon petit lutin, calming down. She is too bad that we be not with them to defeating Breaker. That Breaker has near ruined this jeu for many and split our parties up all over the monde. I like to be there when he gets what he has coming to him and gets dead.

Anders' Text Box: We can, Jorthan! I was just about to go fight a secret boss in the Coliseum to earn the *Super Amazing Hover-Motorbike*. We can use it to go meet everyone on Spire G.

Jorthan the Male Troll Monk's Text Box: I am standing impressed again mon petit lutin. You are being a wonderment. We should haste and be that before we miss what be happening.

Spiderboy's Text Box: Not going to happen! First I am going to cut that little elf bitch up into a million pieces!

Jorthan the Male Troll Monk's Text Box: Le Garçon Araignée? He did not even not bother me once the entire time I was being in Onn Forest. Why would he be showing his face now?

Yellow Quest Fairy's Text Box: Le Garçon Araignée n'est pas pertinent pour aucune des quêtes.

> Assil, the Purple Dragon of Dark's Text Box: No way Spiderbutt! You are #SoFuckedUp! I got here first and I am going to kill that elf first! I am going to kill him way better than you could. I'm Breaker's favourite, and now that I've found one of his prime targets I am going to be even more popular.

> Anders' Text Box: Oh yeah, I forgot about those two.

> Jorthan the Male Troll Monk's Text Box: What do we doing, mon petit lutin?

> Anders' Text Box: Nothing right now. They are fighting each other.

Assil had an statistical advantage over the Spiderboy, but the Spiderboy had been preparing for this moment for a long time. He had seriously hit the gym since the last time Anders encountered him, he was so much larger and more muscular than before he really should be called something besides the Spiderboy now. He had grown up into a man, so naturally Anders was going to call him the Spiderguy.

The Spiderguy was focussing on shooting out strands of web in an attempt to restrain Assil and the sixth shot connected. Assil's right paw and wing were stuck together. Assil spent the next few rounds folding the errant webbing into an origami swan to remove it. Webbing connected and fanciful origami animals were constructed, but in the end it was the webbing that won out when Assil tripped into her pile of beautiful web creations and got stuck. Anders sneakily pocketed an *Errant Web Swan* that drifted by, it would look very nice in his room for when he got it back.

Standing over Assil, the improved Spiderguy, who still probably wasn't relevant to any quests, was gloating. Jorthan casually walked up to the encounter, but the Spiderguy was too excited to care. As the Spiderboy used a move that took both of his actions, the *Widow-maker+*. He came down hard on Assil, cleaving the purple dragon into seven equal pieces.

The seven balls of light were quickly consumed by Draganders, who chirped happily as his tail changed to purple and he grew to the size of a White Wolf. Draganders was now officially a rainbow dragon, Anders was officially rainbow Armoured, and the Green Quest Fairy was now the Rainbow Quest Fairy.

> **Creature Name:** Assil, the Purple Dragon of Light
> **Class:** Breaker Dragon
> **Level:** 98
> **Special Attacks:** Breaker's Special Dark, Breaker's Special Blackout, Breaker's Special Moonburst, Auto-Fuck Pussy
> **Drops:** Nothing for you. #Nada!
> **First Player Encounter Notes:** Chirp! – Draganders

> Spiderguy's Text Box: I did it! I won! Now to taste the rewards of my
> — urk!

Jorthan had interrupted the victory pose by sticking one of his oversized monk fists into a certain tender area of the Spiderguy.

> Jorthan the Male Troll Monk's Text Box: Sorry, it has being nothing to do with amour or anything. You know I amour you most mon petit lutin amour. Time for you to be dead le Garçon Araignée.

> Yellow Quest Fairy's Text Box: Je vais peindre de beaux tableaux avec le sang de mes ennemis!

He activated a move called *Fisting Fist* and with a calm disinterest pounded the insides of the cross-eyed Spiderguy into submission. Anders had no idea what Jorthan had meant by his statement, but he was French Canadian, so what the heck. The Spiderguy collapsed into a pile of stupidly smiling limbs covered in his own dripping fluids, which gave Anders an idea.

> **Creature Name:** Spiderguy
> **Class:** Taur
> **Level:** 68 (+19)
> **Special Attacks:** Webshot+, Ensnare, Ensnare More, Widow-maker+, Spiderbite+, Drain+
> **Drops:** Tough Web+
> **First Player Encounter Notes:** The Spiderboy is not relevant to any quests. – Anders
> **Additional Comments:** Killed with easy if distracting it. - Jorthan the Male Troll Monk

> Anders' Text Box: Jorthan, do you happen to have any *Mana Potions*?

> Jorthan the Male Troll Monk's Text Box: Are you joke, mon petit lutin? I am Melee class, I do not need to use them. They are the only thing that I am having left.

> Anders' Text Box: Can I buy them from you?

> Jorthan the Male Troll Monk's Text Box: You can just have them, mon petit lutin. Onn Forest trees drop them when timber, I plusieurs centaines of them.

Anders used the *Grin Animation*.

> Anders' Text Box: Do you have a *Funnel*?

◆ Chapter 49 ◆
UNNECESSARY QUESTING G

N PC Sarge's Text Box: Okay, let's assign your positions everyone. Wait, what are you doing out of formation, NPC?

Zal Finn III's Text Box: Me? I'm not an NPC.

NPC Sarge's Text Box: Funny girl. Now get back into formation NPC.

Zal Finn III's Text Box: Why don't you believe me? I'm not a NP—

NPC Sarge's Interruption Text Box: No lip, generic NPC. Get back into formation. Which one are you anyways?

Zal Finn III's Text Box: I'm not any of them. I keep telling you, I'm not an NPC!

NPC Sarge's Text Box: A joker huh? Well, we already have the Jester, so stop trying to rank up. Just get into Guard III spot and stop complaining.

Zal Finn III's Text Box: But I'm not an NPC!

NPC Sarge's Text Box: That's it. Quest Sentries, get over here and put this errant NPC back into formation.

The Quest Sentries dragged Zal Finn away kicking and screaming, setting her amongst the other NPC guards. She disappeared into the sea of similar faces.

NPC Sarge's Text Box: Sorry about that errant NPC everyone, how embarrassing. Welcome to the Fancy Royal Gala Quest on Spire G. You only have four attempts and your total combined scores must exceed 1600/2000. If you fail four times the top of Spire G will be locked for you for 100 cycles. The goal of this quest is to make the Fancy Royal Gala successful so that NPC Princess Damselle accepts a kiss from NPC Prince Charmeng cementing their love for each other.

NPC Sarge's Text Box: Each avatar will be assigned a job and there will be no switching. Here are your randomly selected positions and how you will obtain points.

Avatar Name	Position	Obtain Points By	Lose Points By
Hippolyta	Bartender	Mixing drinks	Over shaking your drinks
Yallundy	Chef	Cooking orders	Losing control of your tools
Kray	Dancer	Hitting coloured notes	Stepping on the wrong colours
Caëlahenãilenŵhei	Fire Eater	Using dramatic fire eating techniques	Getting burned while eating fire
Mr. Max	Greeter	Greeting delegates	Getting delegates names wrong
De'vini	Juggler A	Catching batons	Standing too close to Juggler B
In'ferni	Juggler B	Catching batons	Standing to close too Juggler A
Palcath	Maid	Dusting	Missing cobwebs, higher cobwebs lose more points
samuri	Master of Ceremonies	Saying your lines	Mispronunciations

Roodg	Swinging Scribe	Swing from the Vine Puzzle Chandelier while typing	Mistypes or falls
Lissa	Server	Serving drinks	Taking too long to deliver
Gliint	Toaster	Giving your speech dramatically	Hitting your notes around #with your erection#
Fournimer	Unicyclist	Keeping your balance	Touching the ground
Trev Terra	Waiter	Confidently taking orders	Stuttering or carrying on

> Lissa's Text Box: Yeah, we are so fucked. #NoContinuesGameOver.

> E. E. Lynn's Text Box: \/\/h4t 4b0ut /\/\3?

> NPC Sarge's Text Box: We all talked it over, after what you did here last time you are banned from participating.

> E. E. Lynn's Text Box: 4\/\/3. Su><0rz. x-x

The first attempt at the Fancy Royal Gala went even worse than expected. Every single drink was over jiggled, every order stuttered over, every meal uncooked, every drink late, every line mispronounced, every unicycle toppled, and every single dance step missed. Amazingly, those were the avatars that did their jobs to the best of their ability. Every other avatar became a drooling *Spellbound* wreck after Hippolyta started to shake her first drink and began to jiggle. Kray noted with glee that his Sami-guy was unaffected, and Roodg noted that Caëlahenâilenŵhei was dizzy eyed before also joining the stupor.

The final total was 6/2000 total points. NPC Princess Damselle was so unimpressed that she slapped NPC Prince Charmeng so hard that it broke his jaw.

The second attempt used Gliint's idea, blindfolding any that Hippolyta would effect. They vastly improved their score, with a grand total of 19/2000. Only just slightly off their required total of 1600/2000. NPC Princess Damselle only gave NPC Prince Charmeng a black eye this time.

> NPC Sarge's Text Box: Is everyone ready to start your third attempt? I would also like to add that your first two attempts have been the best

thing that I have ever seen and I will treasure those memories forever.

Palcath's Text Box: I guess so NPC lad, we might as wel—

Caëlahenâilenŵhei's Box Text: No! Wait. We will be back tomorrow for our other attempts.

NPC Sarge's Text Box: Probably for the best, I think I'd vomit laughing if you guys tried again right now.

Zal Finn III's Text Box: See you NPCs tomorrow, standing here was fun.

NPC Sarge's Text Box: Where do you think you are going NPC?

Zal Finn III's Text Box: Um... to sleep?

NPC Sarge's Text Box: You will stay there in formation until tomorrow, such an insolent NPC, I should really inform an Admin.

Caëlahenâilenŵhei's Box Text: We will be back soon!

Zal Finn III's Text Box: No, don't leave me here with them!

Caëlahenâilenŵhei's Box Text: Sorry Zal, we will be back!

Zal Finn III's Text Box: Please? ... guys? So unsweet.

~ ~ ~

Caëlahenâilenŵhei's Box Text: Here is the deal, we are never going to be able to do this quest legitimately. We need a plan. Although I had already designated sleeping arrangements previously we are going to need to change them. Tonight my tent will be designated as the strategy tent and we will think up an ingenious plan to succeed. I will require the following strategists in my tent tonight. Palcath, Trev Terra, Lissa, samuri, and Yallundy. I will also require Roodg.

Palcath's Text Box: Agreed. I know that lots of people need to talk to long lost friends, but we need to get this done as fast as possible, other plot things will have to wait.

Palcath looked at Lissa while he Text Boxed this, and internally squeed that her accents were set to yellow. Fournimer had done a very good job with his task.

All the designated strategists, and Roodg, disappeared into the white *Portie Tent Ultra+*. Roodg came back out right away and ran over to Fournimer.

> Roodg's Text Box: i KNOW PLOT IS SUPPOSED TO WAIT, BUT i DON'T WANT TO FORGOT! i GOT YOU THIS. sO MUCH BETTER THAN THAT UGLY SWEATER! LoL.

Fournimer's eyes almost dropped out of his centaur head. A scarf! *A Winter Fun Scarf (s)* to be precise. It flowed in the wind even more dramatically than his old scarf had and it had multiple colours and fancy designs. Best of all, like his old scarf, it was just a scarf and showed off his muscular chest and perky centaur nipples.

> Fournimer's Text Box: wow. thank you Roodg!

> Roodg's Text Box: yOU ARE SUPPOSED TO CALL ME gUY REMEMBER? i'M GUNNA GO PLAN NOW!

Roodg jumped up and kissed Fournimer on the cheek to gain a few *Wonder Kisses* bonuses before running back into the strategy tent. Fournimer blinked dumbfounded. He was sure that Roodg had been set to a *Blush Shade*, even if it was impossible to tell under the hood.

> Gliint's Text Box: Hey! *Pout* We can be clever as well.

> E. E. Lynn's Text Box: \/\/3 sm4rt! ^-^

> Hippolyta's Text Box: Some of us are anyways.

> Mr. Max's Text Box: We could make our own plan Little Bro, there are still two tries left after all.

> Gliint's Text Box: Yeah! *Smile* We totally should.

> Fournimer's Text Box: I've never made a plan before though.

> Mr. Max's Text Box: Now is your chance then Fourni Bro.

> Fournimer's Text Box: okay, I think I already have the start of the end of a plan. I need the start to the start though. we need a way to distract the Quest Sentries.

> Gliint's Text Box: I know how to do that! *Glee* I will need Hippolyta!

> Hippolyta's Text Box: Me, help you men with your outrageous plan? I seriously doubt that.

> In'ferni and De'vini's Simultaneous Text Boxes: If we help plan it, it

wouldn't be just their outrageous plan anymore. Yeah, it would be our outrageous plan. Yeah, lighten up. Please? Come on Hippy!

Hippolyta's Text Box: Fine, but I reserve the right to veto any part of it.

Gliint's Text Box: *Frown* You probably are not going to like my idea then…

Fournimer's Text Box: I am excited now, we are going to plan! but first something is bugging me. how did Rocket do all that talking just now?

In'ferni and De'vini's Simultaneous Text Boxes: Mouthgina.

~ ~ ~

Breakfast the next morning, of power tools compliments of Roodg's cooking, started with a 42 step plan overview from the strategy tent. It was intensely intelligent and dangerously complicated. It already involved six important delegates that had a back-story of visiting from the other spires, Caela using *White Wolf Pelts* to dress up as a famous monster from Scandinavian folklore, a half used *Bear-Trap*, Palcath changing his Armour into Mr. Max's outfit to spring over a bookcase, a *Flurry of a Thousand Strikes*, Trev distracting NPC Sarge by saying hello, three *Grand FullCakes*, Roodg and Lissa doing a complicated dance routine, accessing *My Spiritual Storage Device From The Crags of Halm,* and samuri using his PVP brokenness on a frying pan. All of that and they had only covered up to step eight.

It was nearly lunch by the time they had finished going over the entirety of it. Fortunately, only avatars that had been involved in the planning of the grand idea were featured as key players, so the stunned non-strategists could say 'yes' when asked if they understood.

Caëlahenâilenŵhei's Box Text: Is everyone ready?

Palcath's Text Box: Beyond ready lass! We are going to rock this.

While it took 300 rounds to pull off, and every single part of the plan went off without a hitch, but the end result was only a 1578/2000. The score was just enough to install real confidence in the party.

Palcath's Text Box: I think we can earn at least five more points in cooking if we use a higher grade of *Fireball* lass.

Caëlahenâilenŵhei's Box Text: I was thinking the same thing. Also if we change to *Gray Wolf Pelts* the terror level would increase to orange at least.

Palcath's Text Box: Definitely lass, okay lads, lasses, and Roodgs, it is time to tr—

Fournimer's Interruption Text Box: wait! I think we might a plan as well.

Palcath's Text Box: You lot? Really, lad?

Hippolyta's Text Box: Yes us lot. Really, lad!

Gliint's Text Box: *Confused* I thought you vetoed it Hippolyta.

Hippolyta's Text Box: I did, but he just pissed me off. I am in.

Fournimer's Text Box: then we do have a plan!

Palcath's Text Box: Well, I mean we worked really hard on our plan and it—

Hippolyta's Interruption Text Box: Shut up. It's only fair. We worked smarter, not harder. Besides, we tried yours. We only need Lissa. The rest of *you lot* can just stand by and watch.

Palcath's Text Box: Yes Ma'am.

Lissa's Text Box: Me? What do i need to do?

Gliint's Text Box: Just sit on Fournimer, we'll do the rest.

Lissa was confused but complied, she was already sitting on Fournimer anyways and the party traveled back to NPC Sarge to try again.

NPC Sarge's Text Box: Ready for your fourth and final attempt? I must say that attempt three was brilliant given what you were working with.

Gliint's Text Box: Yes! *Cheer* So ready.

NPC Sarge's Text Box: Alright, then go. Time starts now.

Gliint's Text Box: Go Lissa!

Lissa's Text Box: How?

Fournimer reached up and pulled down *Lissa's Fashonista Bodice (s)*, setting her full breasts, complete with *Dragon Nipple Piercings*, bouncing free.

> Lissa's Text Box: Hey!

> Zal Finn III's Text Box: Lissa's... boobs...

> Gliint's Text Box: *Point* She's that one! Go Kray!

Kray *Double Jumped* forward and covered the eyes of the NPC guard with the shocked expression and copious amounts of drool.

> NPC Sarge's Text Box: What are you doing? That isn't allowed in the rules! Quest Sentries, stop them!

The Quest Sentries and NPC Sarge rushed forward, Gliint waited for the exact right moment.

> Gliint's Text Box: Go Hippolyta... *Lower hand* now!

Hippolyta stepped forward, opened up her peek-a-boo skin-tight shirt for maximum effect, and did the *Toe-Tapping Animation*. The Quest Sentries and NPC Sarge paused mid-step, completely *Spellbound*.

> Gliint's Text Box: Go Max! Max. Max? *Sigh*

Gliint walked over to Max who was drooling and staring at Hippolyta.

> Gliint's Text Box: Go Gliint! *I'm Gliint!*

Gliint punched Mr. Max in the stomach.

> Gliint's Text Box: Go Max! *Point*

Mr. Max threw his *Six Handed Sword* with a mighty use of *Swordarang* and PVPed the *Scenic Vine Swinging Chandelier*. It fell to the ground and trapped the Quest Sentries and NPC Sarge.

> Gliint's Text Box: Go Lesbitwins! *Point*

> Fournimer's Text Box: I totally thought that nickname up.

In'ferni and De'vini floated over to the NPC with covered eyes. Kray removed his hands. In'ferni and De'vini used their *Double Team* sex ability.

> Zal Finn III's Text Box: Oh? ... Oh! ... Ooooooh. Sweet.

The Lesbitwins worked over Zal Finn with a *Twin Fondle Dual Animation*.

> Fournimer's Text Box: it's not working yet! but we were prepared for that. we need to add more ladies!

> Hippolyta's Text Box: I'm on it.

Hippolyta rushed over to the scene and stuck Zal Finn's hands on her breasts and encouraged them to feel her up.

> Fournimer's Text Box: The Finnster is not fully charged yet, we need more bi or lesbian girls!

> Yallundy's Text Box: Caela and Roodg are both stunned!

> Gliint's Text Box: Caela? *Confused* But, she was our backup fondler.

> Kray's Text Box: Caela is bi? Roodg is a girl? Ewww, kay.

> Yallundy's Text Box: Well, not exactly.

> Mr. Max's Text Box: Hurry fellow teammates! The Quest Sentries and NPC Sarge are starting to come to.

> Lissa's Text Box: No, I totally get your plan now and we just need more girls! Not lesbian or bi ones. Just ones Zal likes! And fast!

Lissa jumped off Fournimer's back and ran over to the scene. As she ran her flower petal cast broke free and fell to the ground. She grabbed the already busy Zal Finn, pressed her still exposed breasts against the Dancing Ninja Assassin, and used the *Girls Kissing Passionately Dual Animation*.

> Zal Finn III's Text Box: Mmmm... Lissa kisses. Super sweet.

The addition of Lissa to the tangle of girls is what started the chain reaction. Zal Finn was in complete bliss, and like dominos set to fall the NPCs around her began to feel her emotional state. NPCs began to passionately make out with and feel up their NPC neighbours. NPC Guards with NPC Delegates, NPC Kitchen Staff with NPC Cleaning Staff, the NPC Jester with the NPC Horse, and most importantly NPC Princess Damselle and NPC Prince Charmeng. An orgy of NPC love had broken out.

> NPC Sarge's Text Box: This attempt is over. You have scored 0/2000 and... succeeded in making NPC Princess Damselle and NPC Prince Charmeng fall in love and kiss? What the fuck? I mean... Congratulations?

> Palcath's Text Box: That was... the absolute perfect plan. Best of all, look at all the girls kissing! I need to say lad or lass or to role-play but... whatever, I don't care! Girls are kissing!

> NPC Sarge's Text Box: Congratulations somehow G-Spotters! Here is your first reward! You may now progress to the next area!

The gate out of the area was unlocked and Sarge stopped blocking the way.

> NPC Sarge's Text Box: Here is your second reward! An Accessory for 'insert avatar name'! May whomever you choose step forward!

Palcath's Text Box: Who do we pick lads, lasses, and Roodgs? I nominate Caela, she really needs it and came up with most of our plan.

Mr. Max's Text Box: I nominate Little Bro. He really needs it and came up with most of our plan.

Palcath's Text Box: Does anyone else… besides Kray… want it?

No one else stepped forward (besides Kray).

Palcath's Text Box: Then the only fair thing to do is vote. Those that want the lass step over here and tho—

Yallundy's Interruption Text Box: Wait!

Yallundy whispered something into Gliint's ear. The gnome turned to *Blush Shade #6* and caused everyone who watched to lurch in pleasure.

Gliint's Text Box: What? Really… oh… wowzers! *Blush*

Gliint's Text Box: I nominate Caela and withdraw my entry!

Caëlahenãilenŵhei stepped forward with a look of appreciation on her face.

NPC Sarge's Text Box: #It is a *Heavy Tongue Piercing*! Enjoy your Sexcessory!#

Taking out a *Heavy Tongue Piercing* from his invisible supply NPC Sarge presented the reward to Caëlahenãilenŵhei.

The piercing flew around the avatar but was perplexed.

Caëlahenãilenŵhei's Box Text: Do this one.

The piercing disappeared under Caela's furs and the *Full Ball-Gag* was released from her face. She took a big gasp of air and wiped away the massive build up of saliva.

Caëlahenãilenŵhei's Text Box: Oh thank the Maker! I'm free and I don't need to eat my food with my crotch anymore!

Palcath's Text Box: I knew it!

Caëlahenãilenŵhei's Box Text: Even if it was really sexy!

Caëlahenãilenŵhei Text Box: Quiet you.

NPC Sarge's Text Box: Your third reward is… *pause for dramatic effect*

NPC Sarge pulled down his pants and revealed himself.

NPC Sarge's Continued Text Box: My Great G Stimulator!

> E. E. Lynn's Text Box: N0\/\/ |t's /\/\y t|/\/\3 t0 sh|n3! ^-^ kekeke!

> NPC Sarge's Text Box: No! Wait, I have a restraining order, please...

Everyone ignored the disturbing scene of E. E. Lynn and NPC Sarge, the lathe action was just too much to watch.

> Fournimer's Text Box: that was pretty noble of you Lis, taking one for the team like that.

> Lissa's Text Box: Awe shucks. It was nothing Fourn. Kissing girls was sort of hot really.

> Fournimer's Text Box: well thanks to you running to the rescue we can move on to the next area.

> Lissa's Text Box: Don't mention it.

> Fournimer's Text Box: wait... running to the rescue?

> Lissa's Text Box: No, stop thinking.

> Fournimer's Text Box: your leg! you can walk? it isn't broken anymore?

> Lissa's Text Box: Well, yeah... That is cause, well you see... um... #HolidayMiracle? Hooray!

Fournimer used the *Hoof-Tapping Animation*.

> Fournimer's Text Box: it's the middle of summer.

> Lissa's Text Box: Crap.

✦ Chapter 50 ✦
ANDERS, IN THE LAIR
OF THE MOTORCYCLE

nders descended down the secret staircase in the Coliseum to the secret boss in charge of the *Super Amazing Hover-Motorbike* for what he just knew was going to be a great battle. Illiandro had let Jorthan into the Coliseum, but since this was a special ranged class only battle, the melee class troll would have to wait upstairs. However, Draganders was allowed to come as this wasn't a normal Coliseum battle. Anders was excited to see how Draganders, the combination of the dragons he had created and then fed to his ultimate prize, would finally handle himself in a real battle.

Anders' eyes adjusted to the lack of light. It was far too dark in here, but the first thing that caught his eye was the gleam of a finely crafted fibreglass chassis. There it was, in all its glory, the *Super Amazing Hover-Motorbike*. Wow, it had different versions to select upon winning, full colour change options, including accents, and was even an officially licensed product. This was an official *McGuffin* brand bike, they made the best bikes in the industry. Why was it just right out in the open like this for anyone to take? Maybe it was for dramatic effect, so you knew what you were fighting for?

Another gleam caught Anders' eye, from the side of the room, something was near the wall. The light of his now Rainbow Quest Fairy had revealed it. It had mentioned that it did not want to become a rainbow, but it did not actually seem to have a say in the matter. Anders curiously stepped forward and saw them. A one handed sword and a bow, the two standard weapons of a Night Ranger. They were being held by the upper torso of a mannequin, and had a dark sheen to them. Anders grabbed them from the mannequin to get a better look. The weapons shifted from their blacker versions of the weapons into a *Gladiator Sword+* and a *Gladiator Bow+*. These must be additional prizes for getting this far, and Anders accepted the gifts happily, in case the next battle was to be an actual combat encounter.

It was impossible to see much of anything, but the Rainbow Quest Fairy became useful for probably the first time ever, and started to flit around and illuminate objects near Anders.

Hundreds of translucent shapes were displayed near the wall by mannequins of every sort, the shapes indicated they might be other kinds of weapons and armours that had yet to form. Anders continued down the wall and found even more mannequins. One was a near full mannequin with a complete set of jiggling Armour, the next a torso with a simple jacket.

Anders bumped into the next wall and nearly had a *Heart Attack Animation*. The next wall had a huge scenic skin of an entire Legendary 12 Headed Hydra. It was so realistic that it might as well have been breathing. Anders laughed at himself for frightening so easily, but the event has slightly unnerved him.

Uneasy, Anders headed back towards the entrance. In the middle of the room Anders ran into his old friend, a scenic pillar. Atop of the pillar, high above everything else in the room, was a set of gauntlets displayed on a completely naked male mannequin. This mannequin had four arms and two were pointing at the gauntlets adorning the others. His head had been chopped off at one point but was stuck back together with *Shrew Laces*. His eyes had been gauged out and reattached, diseased sores were covering his chest where thick black spines stuck out of it at every possible angle. Unlike many of the other mannequins that had been headless, this one's face had been frozen in a pose of agony.

> Rainbow Quest Fairy's Text Box: I am cheesing out here! What is with this mannequin? I think we should get out of here.

> Anders' Text Box: That is the flap-jacking best thing I've ever heard come out of your mouth.

Anders, Draganders, and Rainbow Quest Fairy made their way to the entrance. The Quest Fairy was too fast and Anders tripped into a table due to the lack of lighting. Potions, food, and random pieces of monster scattered every which way. A set of wide tubes fell into Anders' hand, they were hollow and wide enough to stick his hands in if he desired. The Quest Fairy flitted back.

> Rainbow Quest Fairy's Text Box: What are you doing nutbar? We need to get out of here. Right now!

> Anders' Text Box: Sorry, I tripped over this table.

Anders could now see the tubes he was holding. They were *Leather Armlets*, inside the right cuff something was written. 'To Gliint, good luck out there. - Anders'.

Anders dropped the *Leather Armlets* and ran towards the exit in terror. A floor tile clinked down and four chains on cuffs flew up from the ground and snapped across Anders' arms, legs, and torso. One of the chains had missed his left arm and gotten his torso instead.

> Anders' Text Box: Eep!

The elf was trapped. In a trap no less. A real trap. This was a trap he could get rid of, for pretty much the first time ever. He fumbled with his free hand for Xam's good luck charm and found the cord that had tied it down. Overjoyed Anders pulled out the cord and promptly fumbled the item and the *Auto-Trap Release* fell to the ground.

> Anders' Text Box: Son of a biscuit!

The *Auto-Trap Release* hit the ground and activated. Anders had forgotten that was how they worked.

> Rainbow Quest Fairy's Text Box: Quick, we need to get out of—

A thick black spike interrupted the Quest Fairy by piercing it through the chest. It fell to the ground, lifeless and lightless. The sight of the annoying, yet innocent, Quest Fairy lying dead on the floor made Anders feel level 98.99 guilt for bringing it here. Anders could see it was a her, now that the light faded. Her death was on his shoulders and he felt awful for both ignoring her this entire time, and not even knowing what her actual name was.

A panel in the floor started to shift, and it began to rise with extra dramatic slowness. Bright light from the level below started to illuminate the room, once Anders recovered from being under the *Blind Status Effect* he could see the entire room.

There were many more mannequins than he had seen, but with real light Anders could see the truth, they were not mannequins, they were dead NPCs and avatars, stitched together and posed, faces frozen in expressions of horror. Hundreds and hundreds of them. The ceiling was completely covered in dead Quest Fairies, each held in place by a single spike. The Hydra hung on the wall had been so lifelike because it was still alive. Pinned the wall with diseased black spikes, it feebly shifted in horrible pain.

Anders needed to get out of here, he turned to run but was hit by a thick black spike in the leg and was thrown across the room, getting pinned to the wall beside the Hydra. Draganders flew to his side and adopted a defensive stance.

From the pit it came, grinning with rows upon rows of sharp teeth. It's eyes brightened when it saw what it had caught. A little elf, all alone with nothing but a little tiny gay pride dragon. Holding exactly the right things to make this even more exciting. With a massive claw it ripped Anders from the wall and dragged him down into the pit, gay pride mascot dragon and all.

◆ **Chapter 51** ◆

SECRETS AND G-SPIRE SPOTS

The avatars had decided to walk through the final area of the *G Spire* in smaller groups, to make their conversations easier to follow for anyone who might be observing.

Conversation #1: Mr. Max, Gliint, Kray, and samuri

> Gliint's Text Box: Who is that, Mr. Max?

> Mr. Max's Text Box: Caela? She is the light elf Rocket Sorceress that for some reason named herself after the starting city in Gentalia. You know that Little Bro!

> samuri's Text Box: …

samuri used the *Foiled Again Animation*.

> Gliint's Text Box: How about this fine gentlemen here, who is now out of the running?

> Mr. Max's Text Box: Is that a trick question or something? That was warrier, he was Breaker's stooge but when he came here he changed his name to samuri. I suspect as a way to reinvent himself and show that he was a changed man.

samuri's Text Box: ...

samuri used the *Nod Animation*.

Gliint's Text Box: One more question. Who is Anders?

Mr. Max's Text Box: Who is who? I've never heard of that adventurette before.

Gliint's Text Box: I won! I won! I won the Mr. Max forgetfulness pool! You hear that Caela, Lissa, and Anders! samuri and Kray, you will have to pay up as well!

Kray's Text Box: Fine, if it will shut you up, kay. Man, some people don't know when to shut up.

samuri's Text Box: ...

Kray's Text Box: Where is chunky butt anyways? I have so many good put downs saved up for him, kay. I bet he is even bigger than a Bluegra Whale now!

Gliint's Text Box: Wait, where is Anders? He was supposed to be with you guys on Spire A. He posted that before the Player Pagers melted.

samuri's Text Box: ...

samuri used the *Shrug Animation*.

Kray's Text Box: We never saw him, kay. I don't think he landed in Spire A, there were a lot of big lava pools but I doubt his fat ass would have fit in any of them.

Gliint's Text Box: I need to go and see if anyone else has seen him!

Gliint was off like a shot with his impressive speed, to show up in following conversations.

Roodg's Yelling Text Box: bOOBS ARE RAD!

Kray's Text Box: Bye bye little lag gnome. Time to talk about more important things! Speaking of boobs, I noticed that the big boobed elf bimbo didn't make you all dumbfounded and drooling Sami-guy. That must mean that you really are in love with me, kay!

samuri's Text Box: !!!

samuri used the *Head Shake Animation*.

Kray's Text Box: There is no use denying it! If you don't like girls then you like boys. It is as simple as that, kay.

samuri's Text Box: !!!

samuri used the *Frantic Head Shake Animation*.

Kray's Text Box: I've always fancied a fall wedding. I just love all the shades of gray that the leaves change to in the fall! It is so romantic, kay.

samuri's Text Box: …

samuri used the *Sigh Animation*.

Kray's Text Box: I've already started the guest list, kay. I don't know who I will ask to be the best man, because well Sami-guy, you are the best man around. Maybe I'll ask Breaker since he made me so skinny and hot.

samuri's Text Box: …

Kray grabbed samuri's hand, and despite the human's continued efforts for release the elf would not let go.

Mr. Max's Text Box: Why am I still walking with you two? I have to go talk to Bro.

Conversation #2: Lissa, Fournimer, and Palcath (and Eventually Mr. Max and Gliint)

Lissa's Text Box: I am sorry, Fourn.

Fournimer's Text Box: so, how long have you been able to walk exactly? on that 'broken' leg of yours.

Lissa's Text Box: #HonestyBestPolicy. My leg started broken, but after the first time I slept, it fixed itself.

Fournimer's Text Box: you could have walked the entire time?

Roodg's Yelling Text Box: bOOBS ARE RAD!

Palcath's Text Box: Girls… boobs… kissing…

Lissa's Text Box: Yeah. See first, it started as a way to bug you. I was faking walking bad after the first cycle so you would feel sorry for me and let me ride you. It was my punishment for you calling me Chick. Then, well things built up more and more until we became friends. I couldn't just tell you that my leg had stopped being broken, or you would have gotten mad.

Fournimer's Text Box: well you are right! I am mad.

Lissa's Text Box: See, if I told you then you wouldn't have liked me anymore and we couldn't be friends.

Fournimer's Text Box: so, you pretended to not be able to walk just so we could keep being friends and you wouldn't hurt my feelings?

Lissa's Text Box: Yes, exactly! Plus we had to beat Zal Finn that one time! Couldn't have done it without a mount!

Fournimer's Text Box: I guess I can live with that. can we just be friends now? no more secrets and stuff.

Lissa's Text Box: Yes, I think we can. No wait, Mr. Slyhooves. I am not the only one here with secrets. I recall you getting out of a conversation earlier.

Fournimer's Text Box: really? I don't?

Lissa's Text Box: I do. What was it about again…

Fournimer's Text Box: nothing! nope. nothing! right Palcath? help me out here Man!

Palcath's Text Box: What? Boobs? Oh hi, Fourni. I'm glad you're here. I needed to thank you so much for spying on Lissa for me all this time. Can you believe she is Lizzy Collins? She is famous.

Fournimer used the *Facepalm Animation*.

Lissa's Text Box: What?! #SoFuckedUp! He was doing what for you dwarf? Why? How did he find out that I am Lizzy Collins? #SoFuckedUp! Did the horse spy tell you? That is #SoFuckingSoFuckedUp!

Palcath's Text Box: Oh crap! Fair Maiden was right here with us, why didn't you say anything Fourni?!

Lissa's Text Box: Well dwarf, spit it out.

Fournimer's Text Box: wait, he was just worried about you is all Lis. he was so relieved that I ended up with you to protect you, he just didn't want bad things to happen to you. I wasn't spying on you, I was... uh well I was, but not in a bad way. Man just wanted to make sure you were alright is all. besides, when I talked to him he already knew you were Lizzy, the Lesbitwins had told him.

Lissa's Text Box: How the hell did they know that?

Palcath's Text Box: I don't know, by looking at a wall! Please don't get mad at Fourni, it wasn't his fault. I asked him to watch over you. Don't ruin your friendship over it. It was my fault, I'm sorry. I just really wanted to make sure you were okay.

Lissa's Text Box: Is that true?

Fournimer's Text Box: yes, 100%.

Lissa's Text Box: Well... that is creepy, but I guess I did fake a leg injury to ride around Fourn like a horse so I am not perfect either. #ByGonesGunnaBe.

Palcath's Text Box: It doesn't matter to me anyways lass, I love that song about you.

Lissa's Text Box: Well I don't love that song! Shouldn't that be obvious? #SoFuckedUp!

Palcath's Text Box: Right, now that I think about it, the song does paint you in a bad light... I guess it is all about you being a bitch. In fact, I don't like it anymore! I think I will get rid of my *Caution Step* albums in protest.

Lissa's Text Box: Really?

Max showed up from a previous conversation.

Mr. Max's Text Box: What about *Caution Step*?

Lissa's Text Box: Nothing about them!

Gliint showed up from a previous conversation.

Gliint's Text Box: Hi, *Wave* sorry to interrupt your conversation, but I'm looking for Anders, have you seen him?

Mr. Max's Text Box: Who?

Fournimer's Text Box: no, we haven't. I'm really worried.

Lissa's Text Box: Yeah, where is Loverboy? Maybe ask Zal Finn to use her eyes?

Gliint's Text Box: Thanks, I'll try that!

Gliint was gone with his increased speed, faster than anyone could even track, to the next conversation.

Fournimer's Text Box: speaking of Anders and resolving things a bit, I need to talk to you Bro.

Mr. Max's Text Box: Sure thing Bro. What about.

Fournimer's Text Box: this is hard, but well uh, I am sort of, torn… and…

Lissa's Text Box: Gah! Feelings, dear Maker. Okay, what the centaur is trying to say is that he has feelings for both Max and for Anders (why you I will never understand) and the poor guy is confused about which way to go with his feelings.

Fournimer's Text Box: Lissa! … thanks, yes that.

Mr. Max's Text Box: Oh, wow. Um… wow. Well, I am really flattered. But, I guess I can make that easy for you. I'm really not into dudes so yeah. We can be friends though Bro. Hopefully this Anders girl, whoever that is, is a really nice dude. You deserve it Bro.

Lissa, Fournimer, and Palcath's Simultaneous Text Boxes: What?

Mr. Max's Text Box: I need to go get a sandwich. I am starved!

Lissa's Text Box: I heard his mind was clouded while trying to level up, but that is #SoFuckedUp. Being that focused in a game that you didn't even notice all the times you were having sex it was with dudes… Wow, just wow. I am out of hashtags.

Palcath's Text Box: Agreed. That lad is an entire new rank in oblivious!

Fournimer's Text Box: I guess that makes the love triangle much easier. Dude all the way! I hope we find him soon, where is he?

Lissa's Text Box: Don't worry, we will find him Fourn. Cool! So we are friends again. Well, friends still, I guess. So… um… can I ride you again then Fourn? Having my own personal avatar warhorse was pretty awesome!

Fournimer used the *Smile Animation* and helped Lissa up.

Palcath's Text Box: Speaking of being honest about thing, relationships, and riding and... uh lass...

Lissa's Text Box: Yes?

Palcath's Text Box: Nice weather up here on Spire G huh?

Conversation #3: Roodg, Caëlahenãilenŵhei, and Trev Terra (and Eventually Gliint)

Roodg's Text Box: yOU LIKE BOOBS HUH?

Caëlahenãilenŵhei's Text Box: Uh... yes I do.

Roodg's Text Box: bOOBS ARE PRETTY GOOD. sO YOU ARE A LESBIAN?

Caëlahenãilenŵhei's Text Box: No, it's not like that.

Roodg's Text Box: oH COOL! yOU ARE BI? gENDERFLUID? eVERYONE IS A LITTLE SOMETHING, THEY JUST DON'T ADMIT IT!

Caëlahenãilenŵhei's Text Box: I really am not comfortable talking about this.

Roodg's Text Box: oKAY, SO YOU SAW SOME BOOBS AND YOU LIKED THEM. dON'T BE SO EMBARRASSED! bOOBS ARE OUT THERE NOW. yOU ARE A SEXY LIGHT ELF rOCKET sORCERESS WHO IS CURIOUS ABOUT BOOBS! yOU NEED TO ROCK THAT! yOU ARE RAD.

Caëlahenãilenŵhei's Text Box: I guess I do need to! Boobs are rad!

Roodg's Yelling Text Box: bOOBS ARE RAD!

Trev Terra's Text Box: Well... uh they have their uses I guess, rather well, yeah I can admit when a girl is pretty.

Roodg's Text Box: i KNOW! eVER FEEL UP A CHICK Trev Terra?

Trev Terra's Text Box: I… uh, well what I mean is… well um… gosh, I well, actually no.

Roodg's Text Box: yOU SHOULD! tHEY ARE FUN! tHEY JIGGLY!

Trev Terra's Text Box: I don't think that my guy… well I mean J… or my boyfriend rather, gosh he wouldn't like that.

Roodg's Text Box: yOU HAVE A BOYFRIEND? nEAT! cOCKS ARE REALLY COOL TOO RIGHT?

Trev Terra's Text Box: Well, oh my, they are… well what I mean to say is, well they are… they have their uses and… so yeah, rather what I mean is… Yes. Cocks are fucking good and I like them, and asses.

Roodg's Text Box: LoL. gO Trev Terra! lOOK AT US, TALKING ABOUT COCKS AND BOOBS ON THE WAY TO THE FINAL BATTLE! cRAZY! wELL THEY ARE REALLY FUCKING GOOD RIGHT Caëlahenâilenŵhei?

Caëlahenâilenŵhei's Text Box: What? Oh um, yeah boobs are rad!

Roodg's Text Box: rEMEMBER TO OWN IT! sAY IT! bOOBS ARE RAD! cOCKS ROCK!

Caëlahenâilenŵhei's Text Box: Boobs are rad!

Gliint's Text Box: *Wave* I know, boobs are rad! Sorry to interrupt, but have any of you seen Anders? There are so many avatars up here, we forgot to take inventory of everyone.

Roodg's Text Box: hE WASN'T WITH US. wE WERE UPSET AT THE LOSS OF SCREEN TIME. hE SHOULD HAVE BEEN WITH TEAM A.

Caëlahenâilenŵhei's Text Box: Try Zal's eyes, she should be able to find him.

Gliint's Text Box: Yeah, I was going there next, thanks! *Waves*

Gliint ran off to conversation #4.

Roodg's Text Box: yOU KNOW WHAT ELSE IS RAD? mOUTHGINAS!

Caëlahenâilenŵhei turned to *Blush Shade #6*, with her only slightly ink smudged porcelain skin she turned the same red as Roodg's bright red clothing.

> Trev Terra's Text Box: Wait Gliint... I have seen Anders!

Conversation #4: Zal Finn III, Hippolyta, Yallundy, In'ferni, and De'vini (and Eventually Gliint) (Secretly Following E. E. Lynn)

> Hippolyta's Text Box: You could probably stop fondling my breasts now.

> Zal Finn III's Text Box: Not sweet, sorry!

Zal Finn dropped her hands from the fight elf's ample bosom.

> Hippolyta's Text Box: I said you could, I didn't say you should.

> Zal Finn III's Text Box: What? I could have left my hands on them? Sweet...

Zal Finn drifted away for a moment, lost in the sweet radness.

> Roodg's Yelling Text Box: bOOBS ARE RAD!

> Hippolyta's Text Box: Ye Goddess, how can you stand that?

> Zal Finn III's Text Box: What, boobs? I love boobs! Boobs are sweet!

> In'ferni and De'vini's Simultaneous Text Boxes: How great are boobs? I know I love boobs! I love your boobs. I love your boobs more! Can we agree that we both like each other's boobs? Yes of course!

> Hippolyta's Text Box: Not boobs, how can you stand having someone that talks like that in your party?

> Yallundy's Text Box: Who Roodg? Awe, Roodg is a sweetheart if you get past the caps lock thing.

> Hippolyta's Text Box: Caps I can almost handle, but not Roodg, I was talking about her. Ugh, I can't stand leet. She is also clearly insane.

> Zal Finn III's Text Box: E. E. Loon? She's not in our party.

> Yallundy's Text Box: I thought she was part of Jorthan's party.

> Zal Finn III's Text Box: Jorthan's party is here? I remember him, he's sweet.

Hippolyta's Text Box: Trev, the Lesbitwins, and Jorthan are in my party. I know the horse made that Lesbitwins nickname up but I am stealing it because I like it.

Yallundy's Text Box: She isn't one of the new avatars that ported in with the new contest?

Zal Finn III's Text Box: Is that who you guys are? Sweet! I remember you now, Jorthan's party! Wow, without wondrous boobs you looked so different Hippolyta. You two Lesbitwins look much different now that you are glued together angel demons.

Hippolyta's Text Box: So where is she from then? Didn't she tell you anything about herself?

Zal Finn III's Text Box: I don't know where she is from, she just started to follow us and we haven't been able to sneak away yet. She's crazy, that's all I know.

Hippolyta's Text Box: She isn't from either of our parties then?

Yallundy's Text Box: I haven't been able to get a read on her with my *Empathy*. She keeps on changing.

Zal Finn III's Text Box: All the NPCs and monsters are scared of her, so am I.

Yallundy's Text Box: How though? Now that I think about it, the forest exits were locked, but even all the way up here things have heard of her.

In'ferni and De'vini's Simultaneous Text Boxes: Catgirls are not even a race. I wouldn't be one if there was because demons are cool. Angels are cool! I would be a catgirl but only if you were one. Aww, thanks me too.

Zal Finn III's Text Box: So there is a girl following us, none of us know who she is, she can't be read with *Empathy*, she isn't a race that even exists, has laser guided bunny eye missiles, a vast array of other powers, carries around a magic Admin blocking hot dog, can get into areas locked to everyone else, all the monsters are deathly afraid of her, and I just noticed that I cannot track her with my eyes. That is probably something we should address with everyone.

Gliint's Text Box: There you are! *Wipes sweat from brow* I have been looking for you Zal Finn.

Zal Finn III's Text Box: Why me?

Gliint's Text Box: *Salute* I need you to use your eyes to search for someone.

Conversation #5: E. E. Lynn

E. E. Lynn's Text Box: \/\/3 h3r3! ^-^

Conversation #6: Everyone

The party merged again, they were at the entrance to the glade at the very top of *Spire G*. The music changed to *Caution Step's* upbeat *Theme of the Dragon Rider*, they were definitely here. There was no going back.

Palcath's Text Box: Does everylad remember the plan?

Zal Finn III's Text Box: Wait, we are still resolving things here in Conversation #4!

Gliint's Text Box: *Nod* It's important!

Palcath's Text Box: But I just summoned the Administrator lads and lasses!

E. E. Lynn's Text Box: Y0u d|d \/\/h4t? x-x \/\/hy \/\/0uld y0u d0 th4t stup|d?

Palcath's Text Box: It's the plan? Didn't anyone tell you the plan lass?

E. E. Lynn's Text Box: | th0ught \/\/3 \/\/4s just 4d\/3ntur|ng f0r fun! \/\/hy d0 \/\/3 n33d 4dm|ns f0r 4 b0ssfucking |d|0t?

Palcath's Text Box: Seriously lass? The epic quest to find Breaker and destroy him after what he did? We need to call the Admins to help us stop him. It's only the plot of the entire book series.

E. E. Lynn's Text Box: Br34k3r? \/\/h0 |s h3?

Lissa's Text Box: Breaker, he is the guy with the Codes? You should know who he is, you used one of his Codes to get the bunny missiles, right?

E. E. Lynn's Text Box: 0h, th4t guy \/\/|th th3 c0d3s? \/\/h4t d0 th0s3 4ssh4ts \/\/4nt \/\/|th h|/\/\?

Zal Finn III's Text Box: That's it creepy skirt! Just who are you and what are you doing here?

Hippolyta's Text Box: You better talk you little sneak.

Yallundy's Text Box: We want to know who you are and what your secret plans are!

E. E. Lynn's Text Box: /\/\3? sn34ky? s3cr3t pl4ns? n3\/3r!

Administrator Owen's Text Box: Eleanor?! What are you doing here?

E. E. Lynn's Text Box: Uh 0h. Bust3d. F0rg0t t0 put up /\/\y H0t D0g!

Administrator Ivy's Text Box: You little sneak! How did you get back in here?

Administrator Allen's Text Box: You fiend! What are your plans! What have you been preparing for? Just what have you set up?

Administrator Umple's Text Box: It wasn't enough, you just had to come back to gloat huh? Darn kids.

Administrator Ethelred's Text Box: Where is my list of commands? I'm going to need some good ones. Has anyone seen my commands? I remember I had them after I got the soda from the fridge.

Administrator Yvonne's Text Box: I also showed up!

E. E. Lynn's Text Box: | kn3\/\/ | sh0uld h4v3 p|ck3d a d|ff3r3nt n4/\/\3. x-x |'/\/\ 4 n3\/\/b!

Administrator Owen's Text Box: Is everyone ready to do this?

Administrator Ethelred's Text Box: Just found my commands. Which are we going to use?

Administrator Ivy's Text Box: L! Let's use L on her!

Administrator Umple's Text Box: Good idea, let's try out Ultra-Kill!

> E. E. Lynn's Text Box: Y34h, s0 by3 3\/3ry0n3! |t \/\/4s funz0rz! @-@ /\/\|ss /\/\3 10ts!

E. E. Lynn used the *Wave Animation* and pulled a sword out of her ass (not as in she pulled it out of nowhere, she literally pulled it out of her ass), that she couldn't technically even use as a Mystic, cut open the air and jumped through, leaving only a cardboard cut-out of a giant hotdog behind. She only just avoided the combined **Command L**, which was the horrible death lightning of the Administrators. The hotdog was not as lucky.

> Administrator Umple's Text Box: Fuck. She got away again. We should have just shot that darn kid right away instead of speaking our entire plan to her.

> Administrator Ethelred's Text Box: How many times do we have to deal with her? I had a chart, where did I put that?

> Administrator Ivy's Text Box: I wanted to see the Ultra-Kill hit. I'm all fired up now!

> Administrator Owen's Text Box: Well no matter, we will deal with the likes of her later. We have more important things to do! These avatars have finally gotten us to the top of Spire G! Let's go find Breaker!

> Palcath's Text Box: Wait Adminilads, who was that?

> Administrator Owen's Text Box: She is nobody important.

> Palcath's Text Box: The lass sounded pretty fucking important!

> Administrator Owen's Text Box: We can cover her later if you want, just pick us up and go find Breaker already. He's way more important than Eleanor.

> Palcath's Text Box: Alright, lad, but I want a full description after this. There better be charts and everything.

> Administrator Umple's Text Box: Fine, whatever. Just go.

> Yallundy's Text Box: That wasn't resolved at all. I'm just more concerned now.

> Palcath's Text Box: Everylad ready?

> Mr. Max's Text Box: Charge, fellow teammates!

The glade was impressively modelled. Tapestries hung around the room and told a meaningful story about the Dragon Rider and the history of the Island of Islana. None of the avatars had any idea what the story was or what the pictures had to do with anything as they had all skipped every quest related to the Dragon Rider. The roof and every section between the tapestries were wide open, showing clouds as far as the eye could render. A view of Islana was expected, but the clouds proved to be a more epic panorama than hundreds of island spires, forests, and big stuck on letters would have been.

A loud screech rang out, piercing the heavens themselves. It was a dragon, flying into the area. This was expected, Breaker controlled six of the beasts. What landed was not a dragon the size of one of Breaker's, but a huge and terrible black dragon.

> Lissa's Text Box: Did he combine his dragons? That is #SoFuckedUp!

> Palcath's Text Box: It's black, did the lad change himself into a huge dragon?

> Yallundy's Text Box: No, that's not him!

> The Dragon Rider's Text Box: You have come to challenge the mighty Dragon Rider? Fear my presence!

The dragon did not do the talking, someone on the back of the dragon did.

> Mr. Max's Text Box: It's not Breaker? It's supposed to be Breaker!

> Administrator Owen's Text Box: Maybe he is hiding. Come down here right now Dragon Rider!

> The Dragon Rider's Text Box: No, I'm fine up here thank you!

> Administrator Owen's Text Box: I am an Admin, I am telling you to come down here and talk to me.

> The Dragon Rider's Text Box: That's nice, but I think I'll stay up here.

> Administrator Umple's Text Box: Oh for fucks sake. **Command H**.

The Dragon Rider jumped down from the back of the dragon. No one had expected her to be both a female and completely naked.

> Administrator Owen's Text Box: What is going on here? Why in the Flaming Pit are you naked?

> The Dragon Rider's Text Box: I told you I didn't want to come down. You forced me to.

> Administrator Owen's Text Box: Why are you naked? Where is your

epic monster gear?

The Dragon Rider's Text Box: Yonks ago some crazy guy named Breaker showed up here and stole it. He didn't even fight me, just blip and I was naked!

Administrator Owen's Text Box: So he isn't even here then?

The Dragon Rider's Text Box: I haven't seen him since like the beginning of the expansion, sorry.

Administrator Umple's Text Box: Oh you idiots! What a waste of time, he isn't here! Whose stupid fucking idea was it that he would be up here anyways?

Caëlahenäilenŵhei's Text Box: Whose idea it was doesn't matter. The important thing is that he did come here at some point.

Palcath's Text Box: Where is the lad, then?

Administrator Ivy's Text Box: Crap. I just got an Admin Help Request from someone named Anders.

Gliint's Text Box: Where is Anders! We can't find him.

Administrator Allen's Text Box: Where is he? I don't see him anywhere! He is lost! Gone forever! M.I.A.!

Administrator Owen's Text Box: What? How is he hiding from us?!

Zal Finn III's Text Box: I don't see him with my eyes either. The only green avatar arrow I can even see is Hippolyta's.

Hippolyta's Text Box: Anders is in Onn With Jorthan, they are in the Coliseum. He just went into the secret battle for the *Super Amazing Hover-Motorbike* while Jorthan was forced to wait outside.

Roodg's Text Box: pOW GLUE Kray TOE BAT! i GET IT NOW! iT RHYMES WITH…

Caëlahenäilenŵhei's Text Box: Exactly! 'How do you know that?' Spit it out, how do you guys know everything that is going on?

White Quest Fairy's Text Box: Well, they could be talking through their Ques—

Trev Terra's Interruption Text Box: We are all playing in the same room… We are in Jorthan's living room. We are a local guild. I saw Anders, well Jorthan saw him rather, on his screen.

Palcath's Text Box: You lads and lasses were spread amongst our party this entire time with all communications down and could talk to each other and didn't even tell us?

Fournimer's Text Box: you knew where Anders was this whole time?

Lissa's Text Box: #SoFuckedUp.

In'ferni and De'vini's Simultaneous Text Boxes: Why is that our fault? Yeah, don't you have a chat room or each other's phone numbers? I mean seriously. I know.

Trev Terra's Text Box: Besides, Jorthan just got to Onn, he hardly has been with Anders at all… wait, he hasn't been with Anders, he hasn't seen Anders that much, well not seen as in dating, but with his eyes, which is good, because Anders is so his type.

Fournimer's Text Box: Jorthan is gay and into Anders?

Trev Terra's Text Box: Of course he is… wait, he is gay and into elves, not gay and into Anders. Well, he better not be into Anders or he's going to get a slap! I wouldn't put up with that, rather I would be upset, well hurt, I wouldn't hug or kiss him for at least a week! Maybe two.

Palcath's Text Box: I'm confused now, what's going on lads?

Hippolyta's Text Box: Men, honestly. Dumb as posts. Trev and Jorthan are dating, and so are In'ferni and De'vini. We are obviously a gaymer group, even though there are more women than boys and it should be called a lesbigame group. Do you honestly think I would allow straight male chauvinist pigs in my party?

Administrator Owen's Text Box: As fascinating as all of this is, do you think maybe we can get moving Onwards to Onn and save who is dating who for happy fun recess time?

Administrator Ivy's Text Box: We can't pop into an area we can't see. We will need to get down to Onn and break into the Coliseum.

Administrator Allen's Text Box: What is the point? It is hopeless! We are lost! We don't even know where the real entrance to the Coliseum is! That's only the first part of the puzzle.

Roodg's Text Box: i DO! i KNOW WHERE IT IS!

Administrator Owen's Text Box: That's a start. Take us there Dragon Rider! Quickly to Onn!

Dragon Rider's Text Box: No! I'm all naked.

Administrator Umple's Text Box: Oh for fucks sake. **Command H**.

Dragon Rider's Text Box: Let's go! Everyone get on Fred!

Fred's Text Box: Frrrruuuuuuuuggghh!

Chapter 52

◈ Chapter 52 ◈

ANDERS, BREAK AND ENTER

Breaker's Text Box: I can't believe it is you again, you are just the worst for being at the right place at the wrong time. I should have put that into your song.

Breaker had changed, no longer was he simply a half dragon avatar. He filled up this entire bizarre star mapped walls room. Breaker was now a hybrid cross of a dragon and a demon. He had hundreds of teeth protruding from his grinning mouth and thousands of thick black spikes covering his body. The spikes had dripping points and smelled sickly. He had two sets of wings, one dragon and one demon, and three tails, one dragon, one demon, and one thing Anders couldn't quite place.

Dressed in epic monster Armour all set to black, Breaker was ready for battle now more than ever before. Anders could tell that it was girl's Armour that had the breasts poorly hammered out, but he didn't dare tell Breaker that. Also gone was Breaker's sense of modesty, his huge dragon penis was hanging out in the open. It, like much of Breaker, was larger than Xam. Ribbed down the sides and divided into six coloured sections, red, orange, yellow, green, blue, and purple, the member made Anders think it was breathing by itself. When Breaker shifted his stance Anders realized the true nature of this dragon member. Each coloured section was its own penis, they could separate into six different members, or combine into one huge piece. Anders really hoped that Breaker was still not into rape.

Anders' Text Box: You will never get away with this Breaker! I've

> summoned the Admins, they are on their way!

Anders had six of the demon dragon's spikes in his body. One in his upper right thigh that originally had pinned him to the wall upstairs. two holding his right leg firmly to the wall in other areas, one in his left foot, one in his *#6 Hairstyle* that did not hurt at all, and a final one in his neck which was by far the most painful.

> Breaker's Text Box: Nice try, but they can't find me, I'm hidden from their eyes and so is this room. No one is coming to save you! They don't think I am in the Coliseum and your Quest Fairy is dead and can't go tell her friends.

The background music here was at least nice. It wasn't in the official song list of the game, so it was another of Breaker's custom tunes. It had great production value and certainly sounded like it could be an official song from something. There were no vocals, but the guitar solos were impeccable. If Anders didn't hate Breaker so much, he would have bought this song to add to his playlist.

> Anders' Text Box: Someone will stop you, you can count on it.

> Breaker's Text Box: I seriously doubt that. I broke the world remember? You think I didn't plan that. Besides the fact that I have six dragon slaves, thank you again for that by the way, that I can summon as many times in battle as I want, I am not considered an avatar anymore like you fools. I have modified myself to mimic my dragon's ability. I can't die, I just respawn.

> Anders' Text Box: Someone will, I don't know who it is, but someone will st—

> Breaker's Interruption Text Box: Shut up. I know what you are doing gayboy. You are trying to distract me again, but I can see you reaching for your bow. You are not going to fool me again, and you are not going to stop me. Neither you or your gay pride parade dragon can do shit against me.

> Anders' Text Box: Well, that sucks!

With a Stretching Out of His Multi-Wings and a Dramatic Movement of his Multi-Claws Animation Breaker looked at *Anders' Gladiator Bow+*. The bow rose upward and equipped itself in Anders' hand.

> Anders' Text Box: Huh?

> Breaker's Text Box: Here is your precious bow, what were you going to do with it? Charge it up perhaps and shoot me with it? Or stick it up

> your ass again to piss off Xam?

> Anders' Text Box: The first one, I was going to do the first one.

> Breaker's Text Box: By all means. Start charging it. I'll even get it all gay pride ready for you.

Anders' bow equipped six arrows and forced him to draw it back, charging itself while slowly using up Anders' Magic Point reserve.

> Breaker's Text Box: It's not your precious custom Anderses only bow anymore, now it's working for me. Speaking of which, Anders' sword, hold yourself up to his throat.

Anders' *Gladiator Sword+* complied to Breaker's wishes, and did just that. This was his stolen bow and sword, had he known that he never would have picked it up.

> Anders' Text Box: You...

> Breaker's Text Box: Ass? Genius? Bastard? Whichever, I don't really care. You already shot me once fully charged with your impossibly high magic point reserve so I am going to return the favour to you today. I have no idea how you have that many Magic Points, you sure as hell didn't use my Magic Point Code to break yourself. Or any Codes, what up with that?

Anders' Bow was fully charged. It had abandoned Anders' hand and was flying on its own accord.

> Breaker's Text Box: Where do you want it, hmmm? The face? The chest? Oh wait I know.

The elf screamed in pain as he was pulled out of the wall by an invisible force, the spikes had been pulled through his body and he was bleeding badly. The force turned him around, pulled up his *Gladiator Armour (s)'s* skirt and bent him over.

> Breaker's Text Box: You like it here don't you? That will be fun for you huh, shot up the ass by your own arrows? Or maybe right up the dick instead? I wonder what will happen when we shoot it.

> Anders' Text Box: No please don't!

> Breaker's Text Box: True, true. How astute of you to accidently call my bluff like that.

The invisible force threw Anders to the ground in a heap, a thick black spike followed and pinned Anders to the wall by his left hip. Draganders came to his side defensively.

> Anders' Text Box: Ugh… what?

> Breaker's Text Box: What indeed. I might as well tell you, I've been waiting forever for this. It wasn't supposed to be you, but no matter it will still work. It did take more time to modify your weapons to add PVP. I love it when a back-up plan works.

> Anders' Text Box: What are you talking about Breaker?

> Breaker's Text Box: You can only blame yourself really, I mean picking up your old weapons from the hands of a dead avatar that were just sitting here in my lair. You probably didn't know it was my lair, but still, you knew Xam had stolen them, and you took them off a dead avatar with his dick cut off. How stupid are you?

> Anders' Text Box: It was dark, I didn't see any of that or even know these were mine.

> Breaker's Text Box: Really? That's kinda funny then. Well, whatever. The fact of the matter is that I control them now, I've added my essence to them. They listen to me and me alone. I can control you to do whatever I want.

> Anders' Text Box: You can control me?

Anders slapped himself five times across the face hard. On the third slap Anders understood where Xam had gotten the foolish idea of controlling avatars from.

> Breaker's Text Box: Didn't I mention that? I guess I forgot. Oops! Well, who should I set you against first to kill? Not Max, I'm saving him for last so don't even suggest him. Perhaps that insufferable stuck up c word elf, or maybe that turncoat warrior? Do you have any ideas, who do you want to kill first?

> Anders' Text Box: How about you?

Breaker actually did the *Laugh Animation*, it took him several rounds to gain control of himself. Anders noted with extreme interest that during this time his bow and sword just hovered in place, not surrounded by Breaker's black fire. For the brief moment when Breaker was laughing, Anders was free and could have acted! He needed to get off the wall and struggled against the excruciating spike.

> Breaker's Text Box: You crack me up. Look at you, still haven't given up or are you just admitting defeat? Which is it?

Anders thought about that for a round. Lying to Breaker was hardly lying, he could get away with that and not feel bad about it later.

> Anders' Text Box: Admitting defeat. I don't want to die. Let me up and I'll do your dirty work, I'll kill whichever avatar you want.

> Breaker's Text Box: Hmm… I know I don't believe you, but since I will be controlling you I don't give a fuck either way. Let's go try you out, there are no avatars besides you in Onn, and I can't kill Illiandro or I can't get back outside. There are a bunch of special Coliseum monsters, a big old Coliseum crowd, and a few NPCs left outside though. We can go kill them. What fun!

Breaker wasn't as all knowing as he thought. He didn't know about Jorthan being upstairs and still thought his dragon friends were undigested.

> Anders' Text Box: Wait, you can't take me out like this. I am all bloody, they will know something is up.

> Breaker's Text Box: Nice try, you are supposed to be in a battle with my wall hanging, if you don't show up bloody they will be suspicious. Wait, they are stupid NPCs and monsters, I don't give a fuck what they think.

Anders hadn't thought of that, the NPCs and monsters probably wouldn't care what he looked like. He wasn't exactly sure why he asked that, if he looked like this Jorthan would know something was up. He had been foolish to ask that question now that he thought about it, but was happy he had.

> Breaker's Text Box: All ready little pet? Time to go try you out.

With a Stretching Out of His Multi-Wings and a Dramatic Movement of his Multi-Claws Animation Breaker flipped a switch on the wall, which started to open the hidden panel in the ceiling. He forced Anders to get up and grab his fully charged *Gladiator Bow+*, but the dragon kept the sword at Anders' throat. *With a Stretching Out of His Bow and a Dramatic Jiggle of his Butt Animation* Anders stepped outside.

Chapter 53

◈ ◈

QUICK TRAVEL WITH FRRRUUUUUGGGHHING

R oodg's Text Box: LoL. tHE SECRET ENTRANCE IS REALLY EASY TO SEE NOW.

Lissa's Text Box: This is #SoFuckedUp, what happened to Onn?

Palcath's Text Box: Nothing good lass, nothing good.

Administrator Owen's Text Box: What do we do now? Only NPC Illiandro can open this Makerdamn door! He is inside and my commands don't travel through different areas.

Administrator Umple's Text Box: I knew that was a bad idea. Why do kids never listen to my ideas? I need a beer.

Hippolyta's Text Box: It's no good, Jorthan can't open it from inside and NPC Illiandro says he will not budge until the secret battle is resolved.

Administrator Ivy's Text Box: What are we supposed to do? We are so close but can't open that stupid door!

Everyone thought long and hard for a solution. The least likely candidate piped up.

> Mr. Max's Text Box: Can we use my door?

> Palcath's Text Box: What door lad? You have a door on you? Are you serious? Since when?

> Mr. Max's Text Box: Since the Castle in the Sky, check your notes. It is a *Left Handed Door*.

> Palcath's Text Box: Wow, there it is lad. Sort of a throw-away joke though, it's barely even a paragraph. But yes, you have a door, good show!

Mr. Max took the *Left Handed Door* and placed it on the wall. Throw away joke or not, it filled the space and once opened provided entry to the inside of the Coliseum.

> Trev Terra's Text Box: Jorthan! Finally!

> Jorthan the Male Troll Monk's Text Box: Mon petit lutin amour! Missed you, I have.

Jorthan and Trev ran into each other's arms. Trev impressed many with his ability to hold Jorthan up off the ground in their embrace.

> Administrator Owen's Text Box: Open the stairs for us NPC Illiandro.

> NPC Illiandro's Text Box: I can only do that if you have completed all—

> Administrator Umple's Interruption Text Box: Who fucking programmed these dumbass things? Right, never mind. Stupid question. I know that already. **Command H**.

> NPC Illiandro's Text Box: Yes sir!

Everyone who was anyone progressed down the stairs and into the darkness. Only the copious amounts of Quest Fairy's gave off any light.

> Administrator Yvonne's Text Box: Wow, it's like wicked dark in here. Trippy.

> Administrator Owen's Text Box: But he isn't here! How? This is only a one floor area. There must be something hidden here that will let us through, everyone split up and look, quickly.

Something #1, as found by Gliint.

> Gliint's Text Box: Hey! All of the stuff I dropped to put Yallundy in

> my Backpack is on this table. Screw that, I'm going to take it back, I am all out of Potions.

Something #2, as found by Caëlahenãilenŵhei.

> Caëlahenãilenŵhei's Text Box: Wow, is this my *Initiate's Jacket*? I accidently sold it to the shopkeeper so long ago, he must have stored it here. What luck, I thought it was lost! I'm going to take it and then my collection of Attack Magic user Armour will be complete again. Why doesn't the fabric bend anymore though? It is sort of all crunchy and elfy…

Something #3, as found by Kray.

> Kray's Text Box: Kay, it's Anders' *Slime Armour* and the key to his stupid jelly-butt. I am so going to take this and make sure he never gets it back. Kray 2, Anders 0.

Somethings #4 + #5, as found by Roodg and Palcath.

> Palcath's Text Box: This thing is amazing lads and lasses. Look at all the different options this Super Amazing Hover-Motorbike has. Let's see. Okay, so if we get this we need to pick Flying Mega-Carpet style. It can seat 20, even if it is not the fastest, it would be the best one.

> Roodg's Text Box: hEY. tHIS IS THE BEST PIECE OF SCENERY EVER! i AM SO GOING TO BLOW THIS UP AND PUT IT IN MY ROOM. dIE HYDRA SCENERY!

It only took one well placed shot to finish off the Legendary Twelve Headed Hydra. It was already almost too weak to breathe. It flashed out of existence, to eventually return anew without horrible death spikes embedded in every square length unit of its body.

> Contest Announcement Text Box: Congratulations to Roodg, winner of the Coliseum Contest. Enjoy your Super Amazing Hover-Motorbike.

> Roodg's Text Box: nEAT!

> Contest Announcement Text Box: Please select a style.

> Palcath's Text Box: I know you know which one to pick Roodg.

> Roodg's Text Box: mE 2! tHAT ONE! iT IS THE FASTEST!

> Contest Announcement Text Box: You have selected the style - Magical Flying Carrot Ultra+.

> Palcath's Text Box: What?!

Something #6, as found by The Quest Fairies.

> Blue Quest Fairy's Text Box: it's Abby! she's dead.

> Orange Quest Fairy's Text Box: No! My sweet baby sister! Who could have done this?

> White Quest Fairy's Text Box: Someone... black accented. It must be that guy who killed Tyreese!

> Gray Quest Fairy's Text Box: That is it! We will avenge her, and Tyreese! No more Mr. and Mrs. Nice Quest Fairies!

Something #7, as found by Mr. Max and Zal Finn III.

> Mr. Max's Text Box: It's that *Springs Gauntlet* that I signed for that crazy fan. See, my name is signed on it! It's so high up.

> Zal Finn III's Text Box: Here, I'll grab it for you Max. I am an excellent jumper after all!

Zal Finn retrieved the right Gauntlet in the center of the room, higher than anyone who did not have *Double Jump* could reach. She handed it to Max, but he declined saying that he didn't need it which is why he gave it away and that she could keep it. The arm of the statue raised after the weight of the gauntlet had been removed and a section of the floor rose up, revealing a blinding light from within.

> Administrator Owen's Text Box: Good job random unimportant NPC finding that switch! Finally some good NPC Programming.

> Zal Finn III's Text Box: Grumble grumble.

The area was no longer in the dark, everyone could see the horrible atrocities that they had been searching through.

> Palcath's Text Box: Oh my Maker. This is... horrible lads and lasses.

> Lissa's Text Box: This is #SoFuckedUp! Like way beyond normal #SoFuckedUp. This is #SuperSoFuckedUp.

> Fournimer's Text Box: Max Bro, isn't this one Brenna Jay, cut in half?

Kray's Text Box: Wow, I knew this guy, kay.

Roodg's Text Box: tHE SHARDS Of NPC Valisha!

Caëlahenâilenŵhei's Text Box: Maker, look was I was touching, a man made of severed hands.

Mr. Max's Text Box: Pink Slime? Is that you? Speak to me!

Pink Quest Fairy's Text Box: Look at them all up there... thousands and thousands of Quest Fairies! Unsweet, we must be all that's left of our kind.

samuri's Text Box: !!!

samuri viewed the room and took stock. Every avatar that he had ever killed for Breaker was here somewhere. He had known the exact number, he knew all of their names, and it already haunted him, one hundred and nineteen. That was the number. They were all here, Brenna Jay, copyright infringement gnomes, and even Grandiger and Hellsfight, his once friends and first kills. Grandiger was even the four armed statue in the middle of the room! samuri felt very ill.

Zal Finn III's Text Box: OMM! Lissa look! Over there!

High up on the wall were five avatars in a section called *Interesting Looking Avatars I Didn't Kill.* They were all naked but displaying weaponry. The first had impossibly red hair and a ruptured stomach. The second had bright blue hair and a severed off crotch. The third had green hair and was quite bloated. The forth had yellow hair and was nothing but a skeleton from the chest down. The fifth had bubblegum pink hair and a stretched out set of privates.

Lissa's Text Box: Quoona! O'Sklorm! Nerchiner! Vendimm! and... Zal Finn I? That is my first party that all ended up dead!

Palcath's Text Box: That's it lads and lasses. This has to stop!

Lissa's Text Box: Let's go kill that twisted Makerfucker!

Chapter 54

ANDERS, DRAGON PUPPET

Fournimer's Text Box: come on everyone! let's go save Anders!

Palcath's Text Box: Wait Fourni, something is coming out. It's… Anders?

Fournimer's Text Box: Anders what happened, Dude? you look terrible! why is your sword at your throat?

Anders' was shocked, everyone was here. His friends, people he had no idea were even in the game, the Admins, The Dragon Rider and Fred, and even an eyeball covered dog and a skeletal cat were here.

Anders' Text Box: Quickly everyone hide!

The statement was met with some confused looks.

Fournimer's Text Box: b—

Anders' Interruption Text Box: Go now! Fast!

Anders frantically moved his eyes around, it was the only thing he was still in control of. The unsettling multi-directional rapid eye movement made everyone follow Anders orders. Even the Admins folded up out of concern. It was difficult to find that many hiding spots, thankfully Breaker had a great deal of mannequins. Only Zal Finn couldn't find a hiding spot in time, she was frantically running around but she remembered who she was and just stopped moving in place and turned into another generic mannequin.

Breaker had not ported in yet, but was still in control of Anders' movements. He hadn't silenced the avatar yet because he legitimately enjoyed the back and forth banter between Anders and himself.

> Anders' Text Box: We need a way to—

Breaker was in the room, more excited than ever to try out his new avatar toy.

> Breaker's Text Box: We need a way to what?

> Anders' Text Box: To try this, you are completely controlling me and I can't do anything to stop you from doing whatever you want with me, thing out.

> Breaker's Text Box: You're right! We so do! Oh I know, those Gladiator Brothers. You made so much noise with them, I bet they would love to see you again.

With a Stretching Out of His Multi-Wings and a Dramatic Movement of his Multi-Claws Animation Breaker called out.

> Breaker's Text Box: Oh NPC Illiandro! Please do fetch the Gladiator Brothers for me and bring them here.

> NPC Illiandro's Up The Stairs Text Box: Sorry, I can't do that, I used to be able to but now you are not a Ranged Class anymore so—

> Breaker's Interruption Text Box: **Command H**. After you are done that, get the Elite XIII ready as well. You know what, even go and get the other NPCs that are hiding up in Onn as well for me, I know they are up there. Then tell the crowd to come down here, I have an idea for a statue.

> NPC Illiandro's Up The Stairs Text Box: Sure thing. I'll get the monsters then go grab NPC Margarine, NPC Greeta, and that other one we were never going to mention again. Be right back.

> Breaker's Text Box: Good boy.

> Anders' Text Box: I sure hope that nothing distracts you while I do my task. I wouldn't want you to miss any of the bloody carnage.

> Breaker's Text Box: What a strange but oddly sweet thing to say.

The Gladiator Brothers entered the room at the orders from NPC Illiandro. They were excited to see their old friend again (even if some parts of them were still stone after playing with the Mandusa) and executed a *Fist Bump Dual Animation*.

Anders could see Administrator Owen unfolding behind a dead troll from here. He was quickly losing his patience with this charade, so Anders would have to act quickly.

> Anders' Text Box: I think you should take screenshots of this. It is going to be good.

> Breaker's Text Box: I am liking the new evil Anders. Perhaps I misjudged you.

> Anders' Text Box: I think you would get better lighting if you stepped back a bit. Yeah a little more, one more step…

> Breaker's Text Box: You are right, the lighting is perfect here. I definitely did misjudge you. Okay, I'm all ready now! Shoot one, you pick which.

Anders raised up his fully charged bow and aimed, not on his own accord. The Gladiator Brothers just stood there, completely oblivious, doing parts of their crowd pleaser routine. Anders had the free will to move between the targets, and to release the bowstring, hopefully that was going to be enough.

> Anders' Text Box: Now would be a good time for me to pick. Now.

> Breaker's Text Box: Yes, it would be a good time, pick one of them to shoot. I want it to be that one, I dislike his hat.

> Anders' Text Box: Seriously, I am going to pick one Now.

> Breaker's Text Box: I hope it is that one, in the dumb hat! I know I said that already, but I really want it to be him. It is such a bad hat.

> Anders' Text Box: Now! I've picked. That one! I'll just shoot right NOW and kill that one that I picked! Will it be the one in the hat, I don't kNOW! I bet it will, if only I could decide which one to pick NOW!

> Breaker's Text Box: It better be the one in the hat, after all of this build up crap.

Anders needed to signal the oblivious others. He was desperate, he needed to do something drastic. He sickened him, but he swore for real. It was the only way.

> Anders' Text Box: Holy fudging FUCK! Come on seriously! It sure is going to be that one that I picked Now! Now! Now! Now!

> Fournimer's Internal Text Box: wait a round, Anders doesn't swear! maybe he is trying to signal one of us to do something? he must be, why else would he keep saying the word 'pick'?

Fournimer had figured out Anders plan of distracting Breaker, the sly hooves. He threw his *Pick Javelin*, which just had to be part of the plan given how many times Anders had said pick, and hit exactly where he wanted to. Not Breaker, not controlled Anders, but the Zal Finn who was standing beside Breaker, sweating and pretending to be a dead statue. Fournimer was almost sure it was her in that pink leaf Armour.

> Zal Finn III's Text Box: Ouch! What the hell, Horseymer!

> Breaker's Text Box: Holy fucking shitballs! It's alive!

Breaker used the *Jump Out of Your Skin Animation*. This was perfect, Anders had just enough time to change the trajectory of his shot and let go. A super charged rainbow hurtled in the air towards Breaker.

> Breaker's Text Box: What? You little elfbitch! Dragons! Protect me! … Dragons?

The arrows hit Breaker and he fell to the ground, his huge stash of monster only Health Points fading fast.

> Breaker's Text Box: No! … Where… Dragons? Assil my love? … big Xam? … stupid Sredna? … those other ones with the horrible names?

> Anders' Text Box: I can maketh the dragons and thus I can taketh them away.

> Breaker's Text Box: It doesn't matter… *Cough* I will be back, *Sputter* I will just… respawn!

With a Stretching Out of His Multi-Wings and a Dramatic Movement of his Multi-Claws Animation Breaker fell to the ground, dead. He dissolved into a ball of black light, just like his dragons, as he had promised.

> Anders' Text Box: Now Draganders! Get him! Eat!

Draganders flew forward with a happy chirp, and with one big bite had consumed what was left of Breaker. All of his little spikes, eyes, claws and dragony ridges turned black, as did the outlines of Anders' Armour. They were both officially rainbow badasses now.

> **Creature Name:** Breaker
> **Class:** Super Awesome Dragon Demon Guy
> **Level:** 98… wait, why can't I enter 99 here?

> **Special Attacks:** #Missing entry. All attacks selected by default.#, Prismatic Dragon Cock
> **Drops:** I cannot die. I shall never drop anything. What? I need to pick something, fine Start Rat Pelt!
> **First Player Encounter Notes:** Chirp – Draganders

The avatars all rushed forward excitedly and offered their cheers and happy thoughts one at a time. Mr. Max even hoisted up Anders on his big shoulders.

> Palcath's Text Box: Huzzah, lad! You did it again, you are a true hero!

> Anders' Text Box: Thank you Palcath, lad!

> Roodg's Text Box: gO Anders! yOU ARE sAWESOME!

> Anders' Text Box: You are Sawesomer!

> Fournimer's Text Box: I'm so happy Anders! you're okay, I've been so worried! I... I... decided, and I picked you. I... am in love with you! and I am hung like a giraffe!

Anders changed to *Blush Shade #6* as Fournimer kissed him. The regular sweeping romantic music and exploding hearts were accompanied by *Slutty Kisses*, which caused a sharp breeze that exposed Anders' butt to the world and made him diamond hard. It was embarrassing, but not unpleasant. He decided that he liked giraffes.

> Lissa's Text Box: Good job Loverboy! Couldn't have done it better myself.

> Anders' Text Box: Lissa, I bet you could have.

> Mr. Max's Text Box: Great job Anders! That's right, I remembered what the Dragon Cultist's name was! I rock right? Where is your cute sister with the big boobs?

> Anders' Text Box: Really? You know who I am now?

> samuri's Text Box: Thhhank youth Anderth!

> Anders' Text Box: Wow. You can talk?

> Kray's Text Box: Kay, you just killed my best man, what is wrong with you chunky butt?

> Anders' Text Box: Oh right, you can talk too.

Zal Finn III's Text Box: Seriously Fournimer, what the hell!

Anders' Text Box: Did you hear what Fourni said? Did he say he loved me?

Gliint's Text Box: You totally rule! *Cheer!*

Anders' Text Box: I kinda do, don't I? *Smile*

Caëlahenãilenŵhei's Text Box: Way to exceed the minimal level of effort required. Beyond acceptable work!

Anders' Text Box: I appreciate your comments.

Yallundy's Text Box: Good job. I love your kid, he's so cute.

Anders' Text Box: I can't believe you are alive Lundy!

Jorthan the Male Troll Monk's Text Box: Good work, mon petit lutin.

Anders' Text Box: Thank you, mon grand troll.

Trev Terra's Text Box: Stay away from my boyfriend, you hussy!

Anders' Text Box: What?

Hippolyta's Text Box: What the hell? You are supposed to be an oppressed woman. I was going to liberate you and everything.

Anders' Text Box: Again, what?

In'ferni and De'vini used the *Kiss Passionately Dual Animation.*

Anders' Text Box: Awe look, twins!

That was almost a perfect line of happy comments. Fournimer had said that he loved him and Mr. Max knew his name, sort of. What a rush. Anders was going to gain so many levels kissing Fournimer tonight. The Administrators approached in their multi-hued glory.

Administrator Owen's Text Box: What the fuck is wrong with you?

Anders' Text Box: Pardon?

Administrator Allen's Text Box: Disaster! Calamity! Tragedy!

Administrator Umple's Text Box: Stupid punk kids! I am so mad I can't even see straight.

Administrator Ethelred's Text Box: Where did I put that sheet?

Administrator Yvonne's Text Box: A girl goes to get a sandwich and this is what you guys let happen? Seriously?

Administrator Ivy's Text Box: What have you done you fucknut?

Anders' Text Box: Um… I stopped Breaker's reign of terror on the land and defeated him once and for all, therefore returning peace and love to everyone?

Administrator Owen's Text Box: Why the fuck would you do that?

Anders' Text Box: I thought that is what you wanted us to do?

Administrator Ivy's Text Box: We asked you to find Breaker, not to kill him. We needed to talk to him you dolt.

Administrator Allen's Text Box: What are we going to do now? All hope is lost! We are doomed! Finished!

Administrator Ethelred's Text Box: I found my list.

Administrator Owen's Text Box: He was the only person who knew how to manipulate the Game Coding as well as the stupid Programmer who fucked this Game up in the first place. Breaker was the only one who we could have found to fix all of the bugs and smooth everything out! We had no other way to track him down or find out who he is! Now his avatar is dead permanently. We are all going to lose our jobs. The world will stay broken forever. The lawsuit will win for sure and Tornado Tech Games® will lose everything. The game will be shut down forever, killing everything everywhere! And it is all your fault Anders!

Anders' Text Box: I…

Administrator Umple's Text Box: I'm doing it, I don't care. I'm doing it. Are we doing it?

Administrator Owen's Text Box: Gladly, let's do this. What a moron.

All Administrator's Simultaneous Text Box: **Control L.**

Anders couldn't even attempt to dodge an Administrator attack. The Ultra-Kill Lightning hit him with the full force of all six administrators. He fell from Mr. Max's shoulders and landed on the ground. The Admins were already gone and folded before the avatar had even hit the cold bricks, already lifeless. With lightning energy flowing through him, a look of confusion in his face, and every avatar's eyes upon him, Anders turned to ash and scattered into the wind. Blip! Only his equipment remained behind, still bearing the pose of the fallen avatar.

He was gone. Anders was dead. Dead dead.

◊ END PART TWO ◊

Lissa's Text Box: What the fuck? He's dead? #ProtagonistDeath? Seriously?

Gliint's Text Box: *Gasp!* Who could possibly come back from death? Is that even possible?

Yallundy's Text Box: …